DAUGHTER
OF LIGHT

Virginia Andrews® Books

The Dollanganger Family Series
Flowers in the Attic
Petals on the Wind
If There Be Thorns
Seeds of Yesterday
Garden of Shadows

The Casteel Family Series
Heaven
Dark Angel
Fallen Hearts
Gates of Paradise
Web of Dreams

The Cutler Family Series
Dawn
Secrets of the Morning
Twilight's Child
Midnight Whispers
Darkest Hour

The Landry Family Series
Ruby
Pearl in the Mist
All That Glitters
Hidden Jewel
Tarnished Gold

The Logan Family Series
Melody
Heart Song
Unfinished Symphony
Music in the Night
Olivia

The Orphans Miniseries
Butterfly
Crystal
Brooke
Raven
Runaways (full-length novel)

The Wildflowers Miniseries
Misty
Star
Jade
Cat
Into the Garden (full-length novel)

Stand-alone Novels
My Sweet Audrina
Into the Darkness
Capturing Angels

The Hudson Family Series
Rain
Lightning Strikes
Eye of the Storm
The End of the Rainbow

The Shooting Stars Series
Cinnamon
Ice
Rose
Honey
Falling Stars

The De Beers Family Series
Willow
Wicked Forest
Twisted Roots
Into the Woods
Hidden Leaves

The Broken Wings Series
Broken Wings
Midnight Flight

The Gemini Series
Celeste
Black Cat
Child of Darkness

The Shadows Series
April Shadows
Girl in the Shadows

The Early Spring Series
Broken Flower
Scattered Leaves

The Secret Series
Secrets in the Attic
Secrets in the Shadows

The Delia Series
Delia's Crossing
Delia's Heart
Delia's Gift

The Heavenstone Series
The Heavenstone Secrets
Secret Whispers

The March Family Series
Family Storms
Cloudburst

The Kindred Series
Daughter of Darkness

Virginia ANDREWS

DAUGHTER OF LIGHT

SCHUSTER

London · New York · Sydney · Toronto · New Delhi

A CBS COMPANY

First published in the US by Gallery Books, 2012
A division of Simon & Schuster, Inc.
First published in Great Britain by Simon & Schuster UK Ltd, 2012
A CBS COMPANY

1 3 5 7 9 10 8 6 4 2

Simon & Schuster UK Ltd
1st Floor
222 Gray's Inn Road
London WC1X 8HB

www.simonandschuster.co.uk

Simon & Schuster Australia, Sydney
Simon & Schuster India, New Delhi

A CIP catalogue record for this book is available from the British Library

Paperback ISBN: 978-1-47111-482-3
Ebook ISBN: 978-1-47111-483-0

Printed and bound by CPI Group (UK) Ltd, Croydon, CR0 4YY

DAUGHTER
OF LIGHT

Prologue

❖————————————————————❖

It was as if the curtains suddenly had been closed on the bedroom window. The full moon was blacked out, as was the clear night of stars. The room was in pitch darkness, and all I could hear was the sound of my own heavy breathing. A breeze crossed my face, and then I felt a familiar warmth on my neck, the soft, moist warmth of loving lips. It was how he always kissed me good night, never on my cheeks or lips but always on my neck.

"Daddy?" I whispered, and waited. There was no response, just the heavy silence careening through my ears and down into my cringing heart. "Are you here?"

Slowly, my hand trembling, I brought my fingers to my neck and felt something hot and liquid.

Panicked, I lunged for the night-light, flicked it on, and sat up to look at myself in the mirror over the dresser across the way.

I was bleeding.

I had been bitten.

But I couldn't scream, and I couldn't breathe. I leaped out of bed.

And then . . .

I woke up.

My body was so tight that I felt as if I were wrapped in a straitjacket around my breasts and stomach. I realized it was my own arms embracing me. I was hugging myself very tightly to keep from falling apart. I was so closed up inside myself that my heavy breathing sounded as if it was coming from someone else. Outside the bedroom, the fingers of the wind scratched at the windowpane. The cloud that had covered the moon slid off like a thin slice of melting silvery ice and floated toward the horizon. When I relaxed my arms, I was still clutching my hands together so hard that I sent pain up each wrist.

"Get hold of yourself, Lorelei Patio," I whispered at the image of my stark-naked body in the mirror. Under the now radiant moonlight, my skin took on a brassy glow, and my eyes, which had flamed with fear, gradually cooled into frosted orbs, glittering and flickering out until they darkened.

I took another deep breath and then, still trembling, returned to bed. I could hear the sound of whispering in the walls, but I couldn't make out any words. Gradually, it stopped, and I closed my eyes, the lids dropping like the lids of two tiny coffins.

It wasn't the first time I had had this nightmare, and I knew it wouldn't be the last.

But this was the sort of nightmare that would shadow my days and turn every face that looked my way into a possible mask of deception.

I could trust no one, not even myself, for there was a part of me that hated what I had done and what I was about to do.

But a greater part of me refused to retreat.

1

Every time I glanced into the rearview mirror to see if we were being followed, Moses, the tractor-trailer driver who had agreed to give me a ride, grew more and more suspicious, his eyes widening, his long fingers moving nervously on the steering wheel as if he were playing a piano. I knew he was having this reaction to how I was behaving, but I couldn't help looking back to see if they were pursuing me and wondering if, with their amazing senses and insights, they could find me anywhere, no matter how far and how fast I was traveling away from them. Maybe running away was just plain stupid and futile after all.

But I had no choice.

I had learned that all of us, all of my sisters, were in our family solely to bring someone to Daddy, someone upon whom he could feed. We were his fishers of men. That was our purpose while we lived with him. As the others had done, my older sister Ava was moving on to fulfill her own destiny, and so the responsibility to help Daddy now was falling to me. I had been nurtured and trained for this purpose, a purpose I think I had always refused to recognize in myself and now was determined to reject.

Ava was always suspicious of me, even when I was much younger. Early on, she had sensed something about me that Daddy hadn't or maybe didn't want to admit, especially to her or any of my other sisters. I wondered if he had ever said anything about me to Mrs. Fennel, our nanny and housekeeper. I always felt she watched me more closely, scrutinized everything I did and said, and observed me more than she did any of my sisters with her suspicious narrowing eyes. Whatever it was about me that triggered this concern, I was sure Daddy believed I would overcome it. Never in his history had he been wrong about one of his daughters. Why should he be wrong about me, the daughter who seemed to be his favorite?

Surely there was something in me too powerful for me to deny or to overcome. I might not like who and what I was, but what difference could that make? To my father, I was like all of my sisters, all of his daughters, some meteor cast into space, unable to stop or change direction. My genetic destiny was just as inevitable. I wrestled nightly with these conflicting emotions. My moans and groans surely were overheard and raised more concern. We weren't supposed to have nightmares or bad dreams. We weren't supposed to agonize over questions like the ones that were born out of the womb of my all-too-human conscience.

Every question I asked, every note of hesitation in my voice or look of disapproval in my eyes, surely sounded more alarms. I could sense that they were all talking about me even before my defiance and flight. The echoes that were born in our house didn't die quick deaths. They lingered in the walls. They were the whispers I heard in the darkness, whispers that were like coiled wires attached to a time bomb that would soon explode.

"Lorelei will disappoint us."

"Lorelei will endanger us all."

"Lorelei is a mistake as real and as difficult to face as a deformed human baby."

Eventually, I had to be put to the test. I was commanded to make the boy with whom I had fallen in love, Buddy Gilroy, my first prey, my initial gift to Daddy to prove my loyalty and to show, once and for all, that deep down I was no different from any of them. I wasn't permitted to fall in love, anyway. None of us was. I had already gone too far, and to correct the situation, I was to deliver my love to my father, who would absorb him into his own darkness forever and ever. Daddy could wipe my mind clean of every passionate memory.

Refusal was not an option, and failure was fatal, for if I had a greater love than the love I had for my father, I was abhorrent to my sisters, my own kind, and a major disappointment to him. It could signal the end of his line, the crumbling of his crest, and the final howl of fulfillment on a moonlit night while everything around him slept in awe of his beauty and power. Silence would come crashing down like a curtain of iron and reduce us all to dust, which the envious and eager wind could scatter over the four corners of the world.

They had ordered me to bring Buddy to our house in California and serve him up on a silver platter of betrayal, but in the end, I couldn't do it. I told Buddy that my father was dangerous and was adamant about my not seeing him anymore. I tried to make him understand that there was no changing my father's mind and that if Buddy didn't leave me, I would be unable to protect him. I said everything I could to drive him away, but he loved me too much.

He was under the misapprehension that my father was probably some organized-crime boss. Little did he know how much I would rather that were so, would rather that were the reason I told him my father was too dangerous and we couldn't stay together. I thought I had rescued him, but my sister Ava went behind my back and got him to come to the house. I saved him at the last moment, but he saw Daddy, saw what he was, so in the end, I had to violate one of our precious ten commandments. I had to tell him the truth about us, about who and what we were.

Even though he had seen Daddy in his most frightening form, he had trouble believing it. Daddy once said that, as with the devil, the best thing going for us was that most people thought we were a fantasy.

"They made the rules so ludicrous that it was always easy to hide our existence. They can't see us in mirrors. We can't be in the daylight. We cower at the sight of a cross. We flee from garlic. Please," he said. "Let them keep it up. I'll bite into garlic like an apple."

At the time, I still believed I was an orphan, and Buddy insisted on coming along with me to visit the orphanage I had discovered in Oregon. I was hoping to find my real mother. By the time we arrived, my sisters and Mrs. Fennel were already there, and the reality of who and what I was came clearly home to me. Rather than accept it, I fled and once again saved Buddy from a horrible fate.

I relived most of this while I sat silently in the cab of the tractor-trailer that carried me farther and farther into what I hoped was the safer darkness. I had hitched a ride with a truck driver at the restaurant Buddy had taken me to right after our escape when he went into the bathroom.

"So what are you really running away from, Lorelei?" Moses asked me.

Moses was an African American man who looked to be about fifty or so, with graying black hair but a strikingly full, white, neatly trimmed mustache. His ebony eyes caught the glow of oncoming automobile headlights. They seemed to feed on them and grow brighter. To me right then, he resembled Charon, the mythical ferryman who transported souls to the Greek version of hell, Hades. Where else would I end up?

He turned to me. "Who's chasin' you?"

"My old self," I told him. "I'm looking to peel off the past, shed it like a snake sheds its old skin, and start somewhere new."

He laughed. "My, my, at your age? That's somethin' someone like me might say. What are you, all of sixteen?"

"Eighteen, almost nineteen," I said.

"Hmm." He hummed skeptically. He focused those ebony eyes on me like tiny searchlights and softened his lips into a small smile. "A pretty girl like you could get anyone to believe what she wants him to believe, I guess, but you better be careful out there. There are people who'll say or do anythin' to win your trust, and they won't have your welfare in mind. No, sir. That would be the last thing on their list of what's important to them. Yes, sirree, the last thing."

"I know."

He nodded. "Maybe you do. Maybe you don't. I don't know what sort of street smarts you have, girl. You look too sweet to be strollin' through any gutter, and believe me, I've seen plenty who've wallowed in them."

"I can handle myself better than you think. Looks can be deceiving," I said.

He laughed.

Once, I remember Daddy saying that if this one or that one knew the truth about us, he would shiver in his grave. Moses surely would, I thought, even after spending only ten minutes listening to him and sensing what he feared in the darkness through which he traveled.

"That's for sure about looks," he said. "Whenever I defended someone my mother thought was a good-for-nothin' and said somethin' like, 'He looks like a decent person,' she'd say, 'The devil has a pleasin' face, or how else he gonna get the doorway to your soul open enough to slip in?'"

"Your mother was a very wise woman."

"Yes, sirree, she was. Only like every other wise guy, I didn't listen enough. Where else do you get anythin' free like you get good advice from those who love and care for you? But we are all too stubborn to accept it. Gotta go find out for ourselves," he muttered, like someone angry at himself. "Gotta go make our own mess just to prove our independence."

He was probably right. *However, I certainly have to do that,* I thought. *I have no choice but to find out everything for myself now.*

A vehicle with bright headlights came up behind us quickly. Moses had to turn his rearview mirror a little.

"Damn idiot driver," he mumbled. "What's he think he's gonna do, drive right through us? I oughtta hit the brakes and have him gulp a tractor-trailer." He laughed. "That would give him one helluva case of indigestion."

I held my breath when the car pulled out to pass us. I anticipated seeing Ava's face of rage in the passenger's-side window, her eyes blazing, her teeth gleaming, and her skin as white as candle smoke, but the vehicle didn't hesitate, and there was only the driver, who didn't even turn our way. He went speeding on ahead indifferently. I relaxed, blowing air through my lips.

Moses heard it and turned to me. "Sometimes you can't just run away from stuff, Lorelei, no matter how bad it seems to be," he said.

He could see how nervous I was. *I've got to get better at hiding that,* I thought. "I know."

"Sometimes you're better off stayin' and fightin' it off."

I didn't respond. How could I even begin to describe what Buddy and I had fled from just a short while ago? When I had visited what I believed was the orphanage from which I had been taken, I had made the most shocking discovery of all. I wasn't really an orphan.

My mother was one of my father's supposed daughters, and therefore, I had inherited that part of him that I feared and hated the most. I had no choice but to hope I could overcome it. I thought that would be possible only if I put great distance between myself and them. But my older sister Ava had made it very clear to me that escaping who we were was not only impossible but dangerous. She claimed we needed one another. There was another species of us, the Renegades, who would prey upon us as quickly and as easily as they would prey upon the normal. It was all a matter of territoriality.

"You need to be with your own kind," Ava had said. "One of us alone has no chance out there."

Buddy and I had just managed to escape from the house where all of my father's daughters had gathered. It was then that Buddy finally believed what I was telling him, but he still wanted to be with me, to love me. He told me how much he believed in me and how much he believed that I would be different if I stayed with him. In his mind, we were some version of Romeo and Juliet, only we would not make any fatal mistakes and lose each other.

After we had fled, we stopped at a diner where he hoped he would convince me. I knew in my heart that if I hadn't gotten away from him by hitching a ride with Moses when Buddy had gone to the bathroom, he would probably have died a terrible death. How ironic. To keep the man I loved alive, I had to desert him and hope he would forget me. He would always be my true love, but the love I could never have.

"Exactly what are your plans, girl?" Moses asked. "I'm goin' only so far here."

"I thought I'd make my way to San Francisco," I told him. It really was an idea I had been contemplating. I thought I could get on a flight and go east. I had no specific destination in mind. The only thing I could think of was just to get away, as far away as possible.

I glanced at the rearview mirror when another vehicle drew closer.

Moses looked, too, and then he turned to me, looking more worried. "You don't think the police are after you, now, do you?"

"No."

"Whoever you're leavin' behind wouldn't want their help to get you back?"

"No, they would never go to the police," I said.

He shook his head. "That don't sound good. If you ain't eighteen, I think I could be in some trouble if we get pulled over, you know."

"I understand. I'm eighteen, but is there a bus station coming up soon?"

"Yeah, there's one at the restaurant I occasionally stop at for some dinner."

"I'll get out there and catch a bus. You've been very kind. I don't want to make any trouble for you."

"I hope you ain't makin' any for yourself," he replied.

"I'm okay."

"You goin' to family, at least?"

"Yes, I have an aunt living in San Francisco," I told

him. Spinning lies came to us as easily as spinning webs came to spiders. It was part of our DNA. "She's always been quite fond of me and has invited me many times. Finally, I can go."

"Yeah, well, San Francisco is a great town. What kind of work do you hope to do?"

"I'd like to be a grade-school teacher eventually," I said. "I'll probably go to college in San Francisco."

"That sounds good." He looked at me and nodded. "At least you don't look like some of the girls I see hitchin' rides on the highway. Most of them look like they're into somethin' bad already, drugs and stuff." He tilted his head a little, widened his eyes, and said, "And you know what I mean by stuff, dontcha? It gets so that everythin' is up for sale."

"That won't be me, ever," I said firmly.

He smiled. "You sound sure of yourself."

"I am," I told him, and thought about something my father had once told me: "We're high on life," he had said. "We don't need any drugs, and we would never lose respect for ourselves."

No, I thought now. *We don't need drugs, but we're trapped by a worse addiction.* Was I an absolute fool to think I could overcome it? Perhaps my only hope was to fear and hate my father. If I could learn to find him detestable, I could subdue all that was like him in me.

A part of me wanted this very much, perhaps that part of me that Ava had recognized. But despite all I had learned and all that had nearly happened, it wasn't easy to hate my father. For most of my life, he had been a wonderful, loving parent who wanted me to benefit from his years of wisdom and knowledge. I simply had no idea how many years there were, but despite what he was and what he could do, he rarely appeared to be anything but gentle and kind to me. I couldn't just forget all of those wonderful private moments we'd had together, our walks and our conversations, and the way he would often comfort me at night when I was small. Even now, even after all I had seen and done to enrage and disappoint him, I couldn't believe that he would hate me as much as Ava insisted he would. Of course, I understood that if I succeeded in escaping, I'd have no one but myself probably for the rest of my life, however long that would be.

"It's good you're goin' to be with family," Moses said, as if he had somehow heard my thoughts. "Family's important. People without family just drift from one empty home to another. Whatever your parents did to you, you can't forget they're your parents," he warned. "That's like a seed forgettin' the tree from which it fell."

A philosophical truck driver, I thought to myself, but I didn't laugh at him. Someone who spent so much time on the road by himself surely had to be comfortable with his own thoughts and comforted by them. How many times had he revisited his own youth, agonized over his own mistakes? With the darkness around him and the glare of passing cars carrying people to places he could only imagine were warm and friendly, he must surely have felt the pain and weight of loneliness most of the time.

Was that what awaited me, too? Would I be forever like someone traveling through a continuous night of her own making, afraid to stop here or there, eventually coming to hate her own inner voice? Did I hate myself already? Maybe I wasn't exaggerating when I first told him that wherever I belonged was somewhere out there, somewhere away from everything I had known. No, I thought, I wasn't exaggerating when I told him I was running away from myself. I really did wish I could slip off and out of my body the way a snake shed its skin. If I could only find a way to do that, I might save myself.

Moses nodded at some lights ahead of us. "That's the restaurant and the bus station."

"Okay."

He pulled into the parking lot. "How about I buy you some dinner?"

"Didn't you eat dinner back where you picked me up?"

"No, too early for me," he said. "C'mon."

He got out, and I followed him into the restaurant, one of those very homey kinds you just knew were frequented by the same people, a family outside of their family. It was fairly crowded, but a couple had just gotten up from a booth, and the hostess recognized Moses.

"Hi there, Moses. You haven't been around for some time."

"They had me deliverin' south of here for a while, Shirley. Can we get that booth?" he asked, nodding at the one becoming available.

"Sure thing," she said. She went to it and supervised a quicker cleanup. Then she smiled at me. "All set."

"Thank you kindly," Moses told her.

We sat, and the waitress brought the menus immediately.

"I bet the hostess was curious about my being with
you," I said.

"Naw. People around here mind their own business.
Besides, she knows me well enough to know nothin'
bad's going on, even though she's never seen me with a
girl young as yourself."

"Don't you have any family?" I asked after we ordered. "A wife, children? Anyone else who might ride
with you on one of your trips?"

"I have a daughter who lives in Oakland now. She's
not married, but she's seein' someone steady. I never
took her along on one of these deliveries."

"And your wife?"

"My wife and I came to a fork in the road and made
different turns, if you know what I mean. That was
nearly fifteen years ago now. She remarried and then
got another divorce. She doesn't even see our daughter
that much anymore. She never wanted to ride along
with me, and I guess I wasn't home enough to make her
happy. But some people can't ever be happy no matter
what. I hope you ain't one of them, because if you are,
you won't find the solution on the road. Take it from a
real citizen of the highway."

"I'm not sure if I am that sort of person who can't be
happy," I confessed. "But I don't want to be and will do
everything I can not to be."

"Well, that's somethin', at least," he replied. He
signaled to the waitress, who came over quickly. "Could
you get us a bus schedule, Janet?"

"Sure thing," she said.

"Might as well check to see how long you would have to wait to get to San Francisco," he told me.

When the waitress brought it, we saw there was close to two hours before the bus that would take me to San Francisco arrived. We spent nearly an hour and twenty minutes of that time eating and talking. Moses described the places he had been in his travels, where he thought was the nicest area, and where he hoped to settle when he retired. I was grateful that he didn't ask me too many more personal questions. He seemed to understand that if he did, I wouldn't be very forthcoming anyway. Before we had dessert, he went to the bathroom and to make a phone call. When he returned, he told me he had to go because he had to be somewhere sooner than he had expected.

"I've already paid the bill. You sit and enjoy your dessert," he told me.

"Thank you very much," I said. "For everything, Moses. I was lucky to have met you."

"Promise me one thing," he said before he left.

"Okay. What's that?"

"Don't let anyone convince you that you can't be what you want to be."

I smiled.

Did he come along just at the right time by coincidence, or was there someone else out there looking over me, some angel specifically assigned to helpless creatures like myself? That was how I saw myself, as a creature.

"You don't need me to promise," I said. "But I will."

"Good luck, then, Lorelei, and watch yourself. The road ain't no place for a grown man, much less a young girl," he added.

"Thanks again," I said, and watched him walk off.

I looked out the window when my dessert arrived and saw him getting into his truck. Moments later, he pulled away and disappeared on the highway, swallowed up by the same darkness that awaited me, a darkness without promise except for the promise of more danger and unhappiness.

"Excuse me," I heard just as I lifted my fork to eat some of the apple pie I had ordered.

A young man in a gray pinstripe suit and black tie poured his smile down at me like someone hoping to wash away any resistance to speaking to a stranger. He had wavy, neatly styled dark brown hair and soft hazel eyes that seemed to sparkle in the restaurant's bright lights. Clean-shaven with that well-manicured *GQ* look, he leaned against the back of the booth a little arrogantly. He was someone who knew how good-looking he was, and Daddy had once told me that those sorts of people spent most of their time posing for imaginary cameras. "Usually," he had said, "they are a lot more vulnerable than they could ever imagine."

"Yes?"

"I've been in the booth right behind you," he said, pausing as if I were to understand everything from that fact.

"Yes?" I said again, practically demanding that he come to his point and tell me what he wanted.

"Being alone and bored," he explained, "I permitted

myself to eavesdrop on your conversation with that truck driver who gave you a ride."

"I'm not sure that was something you had a right to permit yourself to do," I told him, and he laughed.

"You sound more like a lawyer than I do, and I am one. Anyway, I overheard that you were heading to San Francisco and waiting for the bus."

"So?"

"I'm heading there myself. I could give you a ride."

"I see." I shifted my eyes back to my dessert. I was dependent on the kindness of strangers at the moment, perhaps, but I still had to be careful. I couldn't just immediately agree to go with him before I knew more about him, could I? Moses the truck driver's warnings were still fresh in my ears.

The young man didn't get discouraged by my lack of enthusiasm and gratitude and walk away. I looked up at him again.

"Have you ever ridden on these buses?" he asked.

"No."

"You don't want to get on one of these buses if you can help it. The lowest element of traveler takes the bus. It's no place for an attractive young girl. All sorts of creeps will bother you, and the bus driver won't care. I know what I'm talking about, believe me."

"Really?" I asked. "How do you know? Did you used to ride buses?"

He laughed. "No, but clients told me, and I heard from other people, especially young girls who had had some horrendous experiences. In one case, I had to sue the bus company for negligence." He nodded at the seat across from me. "Mind?"

"No."

He sat. "I really am a lawyer," he said, obviously to make me comfortable.

I still looked skeptical, so he reached into his inside jacket pocket to produce a business card and handed it to me. It read: "Keith Burton, Attorney at Law, Burton, Marcus, and Lester." It had a San Francisco address.

"I was down this way because I had to do a deposition. You know what that is?" he asked, taking back his card.

"Yes. You were getting testimony for a case."

"Exactly. It fell to me to make this trip since no one else wanted to do it and I'm the youngest partner," he said with a smirk. "The deposition took longer than I anticipated, or else I'd be back by now. These things always drag on. I could have stayed overnight but decided I'd rather go home. You'd be doing me a favor if you came along. It would be great to have some company. I'm tired of my CDs, and I hate talk radio. Anyway, I just found out I have to be in court tomorrow, so I have little choice in the matter."

He signaled the waitress.

"Could you bring me another cup of coffee, please?" He smiled at me. "Please," he said, nodding at my apple pie, "don't let me interrupt your eating. I had a piece of that, too. It's great. The only advantage in coming out to these off-the-beaten-path places is usually they have food that tastes like real home cooking."

I started to eat again. He smiled, nodded, and looked around. I thought he was acting quite nervous, but I attributed that to his approaching me. Maybe, despite his good looks, he wasn't that experienced when it came to girls. And yet I didn't sense any shyness. Ava used to say we could smell it.

"So, are you from San Francisco?" he asked.

"No. I'm going to visit an elderly aunt of mine. I've been promising her I would for a long time."

"That's very nice of you. In this country, the elderly are often put on a shelf and forgotten. Until they can be declared incompetent or something and their children or grandchildren can get control of whatever wealth they still possess, that is. I just fought one of those cases recently. I kept the wolves at bay, but I had the feeling it wasn't going to be too much longer before I could do nothing more for the poor old lady."

"How long have you been an attorney?"

"Nearly fourteen years now," he said.

"You don't look that old."

"Believe me, in my profession, that is not an advantage. Everyone wants to treat you as if you're a naive kid just learning the ropes. Even the court clerks and security people treat you with less respect. I was thinking about growing a beard. What do you think? Would it help?"

"Probably not, unless it was gray," I said, and he laughed.

"You don't have school or anything right now?"

"I have a break," I said.

He nodded. The waitress brought him his coffee,

and he sipped it and then looked around. "I'm always amazed at how many people are out and about during dinnertime. Most of these people aren't travelers. I can tell. This is a night out for the local yokels, but it's not much different in San Francisco. Kitchens in homes might disappear soon."

"Are you married?"

"No. Came close, twice actually, but lost my courage at the last moment."

"Why does it take courage to get married?"

"You'll see when you get close," he replied. He smiled and leaned toward me. "When you get married, you can't be selfish anymore."

"Why do you want to be selfish?"

"We're all selfish until we have to compromise to keep someone's love," he replied. "Wow, listen to me. I sound like I know what I'm talking about. Most lawyers think that they can elaborate on any subject. Talk, talk, talk. We hammer words into people's ears like carpenters trying to build houses out of verbiage."

I laughed. Should I be so relaxed so quickly with a complete stranger? I immediately wondered. Wasn't this exactly the sort of thing Moses the truck driver had warned me about? But if I didn't trust anyone, how could I survive alone in the world? All my life, I had been overprotected. As a young girl, I believed my father had the power to keep everything evil and harmful away from us. Like most young people, I had lived in a rose-colored bubble. Everything bad happened to other people, older people, perhaps. Really terrible things didn't usually happen to us ever, unless they involved the Renegades, vampires who didn't obey the territorial rules and were dangerous to us. Of course, there were sick children, but our amazing family never experienced illness. Like my sisters, I attributed our good health to how our housekeeper and cook, Mrs. Fennel, fed us with her magic herbal potions and recipes.

The more protected you were when you were younger, the more vulnerable you were when you were older, I thought. To me, that made sense. If we lived in a world without dangerous bacteria and then traveled to places where dangerous bacteria were common, we wouldn't have the natural immunity that the people who lived there had. If that was true for germs, why wouldn't it be true for deceptive, dishonest, and violent people? We didn't have the skills and perception to recognize the signs and the clues when we were as young and as inexperienced as I was. As long as I was with Daddy, I didn't need those skills. I had no choice now that I was on my own. I had to grow up fast, very fast, almost overnight.

"So, what about you?" Keith asked. "Do you have a steady boyfriend?"

"Not anymore," I said.

"Oh, so you live in Heartbreak Hotel, huh?"

"Something like that," I said.

"Is that the real reason you're heading for San Francisco?" he asked. "I don't mean to pry," he added quickly. "If it is the reason, you're probably doing the right thing. A change of setting is refreshing. You'll meet new people, see new things. Can't hurt to be able to forget. When I broke up with my girlfriend, I took an immediate vacation and went to the Greek islands."

He finished his coffee and looked at his watch.

"I guess I have to get on the road," he said. "About three hours to go. On a bus, it will be more like four and a half. With other stops along the way, maybe even five," he warned.

I nodded in agreement with my own thoughts. How foolish it would be to pass up this good luck. Besides, I was nervous staying there, being in one place too long. I couldn't help watching the front doors, anticipating either Ava or even Daddy walking in and heading for me. I wasn't yet far enough away for them not to smell me out. Daddy might even be able to hear my voice.

"So, do you want a ride?" he asked, now sounding a little upset that I wasn't jumping enthusiastically on his offer.

"Okay. Thank you," I said. I realized that he hadn't asked me my name. However, I imagined he had heard Moses say it. He did say he was eavesdropping on us.

He smiled, put money down for his coffee, and got up. "I noticed you don't have any luggage," he said, suddenly realizing.

I wondered now why Moses hadn't asked about that and thought he had been too kind to ask me too many personal questions. No wonder I looked like someone in drastic flight. "I have everything I need at my aunt's," I said.

He shrugged. "Fine. Ready?"

"Yes."

I took my purse and followed him out. He had one of those hybrid SUVs. When we got in, I noticed the backseats were down and had a small carton on them.

He saw me looking. "That's a case of this great wine I picked up at a vineyard near here. I'm bringing it back as a gift for someone who's done me some big favors," he explained. He started the engine, and we headed out of the parking lot.

"What was your case about?" I asked.

"Case? It's Pinot Noir, a red wine."

"Not the wine case, your deposition."

"Oh," he said, laughing. "Right. It's an action involving a challenge to a will. Two brothers are at each other. When it comes to money, blood thins out," he added. "You'd be surprised at how many court actions involve family members. Families aren't the way they used to be. That's why I'm a little freaked about committing myself to a long relationship. You know how many marriages end up in divorce? I mean, that alone can support half of the legal profession in this country. I see a lot of that, and you can't help but be affected.

"And what about the children, huh?" he asked me quickly, as if I had said something to defend divorce. "That's what I mean about being selfish. They only care about their own feelings, their own egos or whatever. My parents are divorced. They got divorced when I was only six, and then they would fight over who would do what for me all the time. They both counted what they did. How would you like hearing that argument when you were only six? 'I took him to school all last week. I met with his teacher. Where were you?' 'I was there when he had a cold. I had to buy him a new pair of shoes. Where were you?'" he rattled off, changing his voice to sound like two differ-ent whining people.

He turned to me. In the vague light of cars ap-proaching, I saw his lips writhe with anger. His good looks seemed to fly off his face with the way his jaw tightened and sent currents of electric rage through his cheeks, into the bridge of his nose, and into his eyes.

"You know what I began to do?" he asked.

I shook my head. His outburst seemed to get louder and more intense with every word. I was afraid to speak.

"I began to keep track myself of what each one did for me. How's that? Pretty clever, right? I was only six, but a bright six-year-old. I wrote down what they said the way a little boy that age might, and then I made a chart with 'Daddy' on one side and 'Mommy' on the other. 'Daddy, school.' 'Mommy, wash clothes.' Stuff like that. One day, I brought it out and showed them while they were arguing, and they just stared at me and at my chart for a few moments before they turned on each other and started blaming each other for what I had done. I ripped up the chart and threw it at them.

"What do you think of that? I bet you didn't have parents like that. Did you?" he asked when I didn't reply.

"No, but I never really knew my mother," I said.

"Divorce or death?"

"She ran off when I was very young," I said.

"Selfish," he muttered. "Couldn't compromise. Never should have said 'I do.'"

He was silent a moment, but it was a deep silence, the silence of someone seized by his own dark memories.

I saw the way he gripped the steering wheel, too. His knuckles seemed to grow more pointed, the veins on the backs of his hands pressing up against his skin.

"They abuse us," he muttered finally. "They abuse us when they create us. How lucky are the sperm and the eggs that never meet."

"Who's going to win in the case?" I asked, hoping to get him onto another topic.

"What case?"

"The one you're on, the deposition you just did."

"Oh." He shook his head. "I don't care, really."

"How can you not care?"

"Hey," he snapped back at me, "do you think the doctor you go to really cares about you? He's just pumping out medicine and racking up insurance payments."

"Well, what's the argument?"

"What argument?"

"In the case you're doing? Why is one or the other contesting the will?"

"This stuff really interests you?" he asked, sounding annoyed.

"I thought you wanted to talk to pass the time rather than listen to music or the radio," I said.

"I changed my mind," he said, and turned on the radio. "No one really listens to anyone anyway," he muttered.

I was feeling more and more uncomfortable. I had made a big mistake taking a ride with him. I sat back, eager to see the lights of San Francisco, eager to get out of the darkness, for it seemed I would spend most of my life escaping from one shadow just to be overtaken by another.

And what awaited me in each was surely not pleasant.

2

The lights of a metropolitan area never seemed to be out there, no matter how far and how long we traveled. I looked at the time and realized we had been driving for well over an hour. If anything, the road looked darker, the sight of lighted house windows few and far between. I leaned forward to see if I could catch a road sign, but for miles and miles, I saw nothing.

"Are you sure this is the route to San Francisco?" I asked. A good twenty minutes had gone by without him saying a word. He had been either lost in his own thoughts or so into the music that he seemed to have forgotten I was with him.

"It's a shortcut," he said. After a moment, he added, "Look, I have to drop off this case of wine at my friend's house. It's a little off the beaten path, but I promise, it will take only ten minutes."

I didn't respond, but there was something in the air, a crackling that I could sense. I was reminded of the times when I was a little girl and Daddy would suddenly stop whatever he was doing and look as if he were listening keenly to something. I would try to hear whatever it was, too, but I wouldn't hear anything. He was always so still, his eyes so fixed on whatever he thought he could see out there. I would look out into the darkness, narrowing my eyelids the way he did and concentrating, but I never saw anything. Suddenly, he would get up.

"What's wrong, Daddy?" I would ask.

"Nothing. Just continue your reading," he would say, and he would go outside. I would go to the window and look for him. I thought I saw him moving in the shadows, and then, as if the shadows stuck to him or he wrapped them around himself, he would grow into something larger and darker. Sometimes he was out there for only a few minutes, and sometimes he wouldn't return for hours. Occasionally, I would have to go to bed before he returned, and Mrs. Fennel would always promise that she would tell him I was waiting up for him. He would come to my bedroom to be sure I was all right.

"What was out there, Daddy?" I would ask.

"Nothing you should fear," he would always say. "Never be afraid of the darkness itself. Darkness is our best friend. The shadows protect us. Don't fear them."

"I don't."

"That's my girl," he would tell me, and he would kiss me on the cheek. Then he would fix my blanket and brush my hair. I would close my eyes and feel so safe and warm that nothing I could imagine would frighten me.

I wasn't exactly frightened in the car with Keith. It was more like being cautious, prepared, triggering my personal homeland security system. All of my senses had been placed on high alert, heightened. I could feel my body tighten even more, the muscles in my arms and legs grow hard.

The road he had turned onto was bumpy and soon became more like a gravel driveway.

"Where does this friend live?"

"Not far now," he said.

I looked for some sign of life, some light, something besides the trees and the distant mountains that now looked like smudges against the horizon, as if they had all been finger-painted on a grayish-black canvas by a young god who had not yet formed his vision of the world he wanted to create.

Suddenly, Keith stopped the car.

"Why are you stopping? What's wrong?" I asked, my fingers folding tightly into fists.

"Don't like the sounds coming from the rear of the vehicle. I'll just check a moment," he said, and got out. I watched him walk to the back of the SUV and open the door. "Can you push the wine case more toward me?" he asked.

"Why?"

"Just do it," he ordered. "I think it has to do with the noise."

I hesitated, then turned and leaned over the seat and reached back to push the case. When I did so, he lunged forward and grasped both of my wrists. I was too shocked to speak for a moment. He pulled me farther forward, and then I saw a set of handcuffs, one on each side of the SUV, each clipped to a hook. He wanted to put the handcuffs around my wrists and lock them. The realization of what that would mean shot through me like an electric spasm. My body recoiled, and when it did, I turned my hands, broke his grip on me, and seized his wrists.

My strength surprised and shocked him. For a few seconds, I just looked up at him. Whatever he saw in my face terrified him. He cried out like some desperate small animal that could see its life evacuating its body, fleeing in panic. I tugged him so hard and so quickly that he came flying forward over me and the front seats, smashing his head on the dashboard. I heard him groan and fall over onto his side against the driver's door.

My heart was pounding, but I only felt stronger. I reached over him, turned the door handle, and pushed open the door. I shoved his body, and he rolled out of the SUV. I closed the door, shifted around so I could get into the driver's seat, put the vehicle into drive, and shot ahead.

I decided not to follow the road, which looked like a road to nowhere anyway. I turned around instead and started back. I saw him struggling to get to his feet and then, obviously still quite dizzy, fall over again onto his side. I didn't pause. I drove past him and made my way back to the highway. It was nearly twenty minutes later before I saw a sign that indicated the road that would take me to San Francisco. He really had taken us out of the way. I sped up and gradually felt my body soften, my pulse calm, and my breathing return to normal.

Hours later, I pulled into a gas station and fast-food shop. For a few moments, I sat there taking deep breaths, reliving what I had just experienced. Then, curious about him, I opened the glove compartment and found the SUV registration. It was registered to a Paul Bogan. He lived in Sonoma, California, and was only twenty-six years old. Those lawyer business cards were obviously either a forgery or cards he had taken from a real lawyer with that name.

Looking around the vehicle, I saw no lawyer's briefcase. I should have noticed that immediately, I thought. That was very careless of me, or maybe just a sign of my inexperience and innocence. More curious now, I opened the carton. It was filled with female clothing, hair clips, lipsticks, and makeup pads such as would be found in a young girl's purse. There was even a pair of high-heel shoes. Sick trophies of girls he had raped and maybe murdered, I thought. This was one man I would have gladly brought to Daddy.

I had started to get out to get something to drink when I saw Paul Bogan's wallet on the floor. One side had a few of those business cards. The other had his driver's license. There was more than five hundred dollars in fifties and twenties.

"There's always a silver lining," I muttered, taking the money. I got out, got my drink, and then headed for the San Francisco airport. When I got there, I left the vehicle where it was prohibited to leave one, hoping that he would get into some trouble for it. I went in to buy a ticket on the next flight out. I still had no idea where I would go. When I looked up at the schedule for one airline, I saw that I could make the next flight to Boston, Massachusetts. One place was as good as another, I decided, and bought my ticket. Less than a half hour later, I boarded the plane and took my seat by the window. I was feeling very tired and hoped that I could get some sleep.

An elderly man in a brown suit and a light brown tie took the seat beside me and smiled. "You like the red-eye?" he asked.

"Pardon?"

"You know, flights like this that fly at night. I don't sleep much anyway."

"Oh. I don't know. I haven't flown that much," I said. I wasn't really looking at him until then. He looked at least in his late seventies, if not eighties. His thinning white hair picked up the ambient light and seemed to glow like a halo. He was pale but had red blotches around his nose and over his forehead.

"Heading home?" he asked.

"No, visiting," I said.

"I bet you're going to visit your grandparents," he said.

I just smiled as if he had guessed right. Daddy taught me it was always best to let people believe what they thought if what they thought was good for you. There was no sense in wasting the truth on anyone. "Save the truth for yourself," he'd advised. His words of wisdom remained my personal Book of Proverbs.

"They're lucky. I have to go visit my grandchildren. They're all just too busy with their businesses and jobs to take the time to come see me in Boston. My name's Thaddeus, by the way. My mother named me after one of the twelve Apostles. I'm Armenian, and the Armenian church has Thaddeus and Saint Bartholomew as its patron saints. Thaddeus is the patron saint of desperate causes and lost causes. The name is interchangeable with Jude. You've probably heard of Saint Jude.

"Okay," he said after a short pause during which I just smiled. I was feeling quite tired and didn't want to get into hours of conversation. "That's all the boring stuff I'm going to say on the whole trip."

"It's not boring," I told him, and he smiled.

"Well, aren't you a sweet young lady? Maybe you're telling the truth, and maybe you're not. At my age, it doesn't matter. It's too late for me to impress anyone." He sat back and closed his eyes.

He didn't open his eyes and speak again until after we had taken off and leveled out. The flight attendant was asking if anyone wanted anything to drink. I took a soda, and he ordered a cup of tea.

"Well," he said. "As you see, I fall asleep on and off nowadays. Seems to work. But I won't keep you up," he quickly added.

The whole time, I had been thumbing through a magazine about Massachusetts and found an interesting travel article about a town called Quincy. It was close to the Atlantic, and I had always enjoyed being near a beach. From the description I read about the small city, it seemed a perfect place in which to get lost. I had come to believe in fate and coincidence and thought that whatever powers were looking over me had put this destination in front of me. It was more than just a suggestion. It was a road map to my salvation.

Thaddeus looked at the magazine and nodded. I had left it open.

"I've been to Quincy often," he told me. "It's a very nice place."

I could cling to the belief that maybe there was something out there, some great force that would want to protect me, but I had not left my paranoia behind. It sat with me in the seat. I didn't like the idea that some stranger would have an idea about where I was headed.

" 'Course," he continued, "it's been quite a while since I've been there. Now that I think about it, it's more like twenty years, so you can't take my word for it. Places change just like people, or maybe people change because the places change. I can't tell you which comes first. So much for the wisdom of old age."

"That's all right. I'm just going to Boston," I said. "I doubt I can get to anywhere else this trip."

"Sure, sure, don't rush your life along. I can tell you this," he said, sitting back and closing his eyes again, "it seems like just yesterday when I fell in love with my wife. She's been gone now close to twenty-five years, but I don't wake up any morning without hearing her tell me not to dilly-dally. If it wasn't for her, I'd have been half the man I was." A smile seemed to land softly on his dark red lips. In moments, he was asleep again.

Would I live to be his age, and if I did, would I have any loving memories to bring me comfort?

We left the plane together. He offered to give me a ride to wherever I was going, but I assured him that someone was there to pick me up.

"Well, you ever get into any trouble, you call me," he

said. He reached into his pocket and produced a light blue business card with black print. His full name was Thaddeus Bogosian. Under his name was written "Insight Books" and his address and phone number.

"I had a small bookstore, specializing in religious, philosophical material. My wife's the one who made the living in our family," he said. "She was a crackerjack real estate agent. She married me because she said she needed a dreamer. You ever have need for a dreamer, you call," he said.

I told him I would and watched him walk away. He looked as if he were holding on to an invisible woman beside him.

As soon as he was gone, I found my way to the train station. I was still undecided about where I would go or what I would do, but it felt safer to keep myself moving in almost any direction. The distance I had traveled from home gave me a sense of security. I had taken the magazine from the plane and continued to read about Quincy. It was the birthplace of John Adams, John Quincy Adams, and John Hancock. It shared a border with Boston, and its bay was actually part of Boston Harbor. It had several beaches and a community college. The train schedule showed me how to get there. I had no idea what I would do immediately once I was there, and I had no idea why I had such faith in myself, but I continued as if it had been my plan all along.

First, I went into a shop and bought a decent-size travel bag. A girl my age who arrived anywhere without a stitch of clothing or any possessions would surely attract more attention, I thought, recalling that it already had, so I then went into a department store and bought socks, undergarments, some pants and shirts, and a few simple dresses. I even bought myself a cap. After I had those things and some basic toiletries, I felt more confident about traveling alone.

I discovered that Quincy was connected to the regional subway system and was the fourth stop. At the station in the city, I found a magazine advertising hotels and apartments. One in particular caught my attention because it looked so historic and yet unpretentious. It was the Winston Rooming House. I went to a pay phone and called to see if I could make a reservation. The woman who answered sounded old, maybe as old as Thaddeus Bogosian. Mrs. Winston seemed very suspicious. I was tempted to ask her if I was the first person ever to inquire about available space.

"Where did you get my number?" she asked with a tone of suspicion.

"You have an advertisement in the *Daily Tripper*," I said.

"I do? Well, it was probably something my nephew, Ken, did without telling me. He thinks I need looking after, but I've been running this rooming house for close to thirty-five years, thank you. I always believed the right sort of people would find their way here without me doing a song and dance about how nice and clean my place is." She paused as though she wasn't going to say any more, but before I could speak, she asked, "How long do you plan on staying?"

"I'm thinking about looking for a job in Quincy," I said. "At least a few weeks, if not longer."

"Um. You sound very young. I should warn you that this is a very quiet place. I have some long-term regulars who demand it as much as I do."

"That's exactly what I'm looking for, Mrs. Winston, a very quiet place."

"Um," she said skeptically. She still hadn't told me whether she had space available. "Well, you stop in, and we'll see what we see," she said, clearly sounding like someone who wouldn't take just anyone into her rooming house.

"Okay." I nearly laughed at her obvious New England independence, but then I thought that she and her place might be exactly what I needed in order to keep a low profile. Besides, from what I could see, there were quite a few other possibilities if that one didn't work out. I headed for the subway train to Quincy. When I arrived, I looked for a taxi to take me to the Winston Rooming House. The driver not only knew it well, but he also knew Mrs. Winston, who was apparently quite a local character.

"Her family line here goes back to the mid-eighteenth century," he said, "and she'll let you know it every chance she gets. There are lots of people around here who are that way. They aren't unpleasant or anything, but they'll let you know they have a special claim on Quincy, a claim even on the air you breathe. Where you from?"

"Out west," I said. The less anyone knew about me, even a taxi driver I might never see again, the better it was, I thought.

"Yeah, well, wherever that is, it's different here," he

said. He glanced at me in the rearview mirror but then stopped talking, as if he was used to people who didn't care to talk about themselves with strangers. I could see in his face that he was full of questions for a young girl like me arriving in Quincy and heading for a rooming house, but I turned my attention to the city.

There was a calmness in the way people moved about. The late-spring sunshine seemed already to be a great contrast with the darkness I had traveled through to get here. Everything had a lazy, laid-back atmosphere. We had been living in Los Angeles long enough for me to feel at home there, but it was so much larger and so much more populated that even though I was still in a city with close to a hundred thousand people, I felt as if I had stepped into a small town. It was just large enough for me to disappear safely but small enough for me to feel I was in a friendlier, warmer community. Maybe it was all wishful thinking, but I needed wishful thinking right then. I had lived most of my life believing I was an orphan. My father had plucked me out of anonymity and given me a name, and although I didn't have a real mother living with us, I had Mrs. Fennel looking after me the way a mother might, and I had sisters. I had a family. Now I was all alone again. This time, I was truly an orphan, but this time, my chances of finding a family and acquiring a name were next to nil.

The taxi wound its way through busy city streets before turning off and following a more circuitous route to a very quiet side street with about a dozen houses. Some were relatively modern, but interspersed were much older structures. He stopped before a large, rectangular, two-story wooden building with rows of windows, chimneys at both ends, and a grand-looking portal centered in the façade. Of all of the houses on the street, it appeared to have the most land, with a richly green lawn cut in a perfect rectangle. The driveway was gravel, and except for some potted flowers in the front, the property looked quite simple and unpretentious. Just off the street, a very small wooden sign in script read "Winston House, 1748."

The taxi driver got out to open my door and get my bag out of the trunk. "You're not exactly right on top of all the action here," he said, looking down the very quiet street. No one was outside of any house. Nothing was moving. It looked more like a three-dimensional painting.

"Thank you," I said, and paid him the fare without any other comment. He looked at the front of the Winston House, shrugged, and got back into his taxi. I stood watching him drive off and then rolled my bag along the slate walkway toward the front entrance.

There was an old-fashioned door ringer that you had to turn. I did so and waited. No one came to the door, so I did it again. Twenty or thirty seconds later, the door was tugged open, and a tall, thin woman with charcoal-gray hair in a chignon stood glaring out at me as if I were an unwanted vacuum-cleaner salesperson or something. She held a dish towel and was drying her hands. There was a small sign next to the door that read, "No solicitors permitted."

"Yes?" she said.

"My name is Lorelei Patio. I called earlier about a room."

"Just a moment," she said, and closed the door.

I thought that was quite rude. For a few moments, I debated turning around and walking off to find another rooming house or hotel. The taxi driver was right about the neighborhood, however. I saw nothing remotely resembling a place to stay. It was a good three or four blocks back to the busier street.

The door opened again, and this time, a much shorter woman in a gray dress with a white lace collar looked out at me. Her dark brown hair, which looked at least shoulder-length, had been gathered into a soft knot at the top of her head. Some strands had been pulled from under her hair band and curled over her forehead.

She raked over me with her soft hazel eyes, sizing me up and then nodding. "Just as I thought. You're pretty young. I hope you're eighteen at least, otherwise you're wasting your time and mine," she said. Her voice was firm but not nasty.

"I am," I said. "Are you Mrs. Winston?"

"Well, who else do you think I'd be?" she asked, and followed that with a one-syllable laugh. She turned, and the woman who had first greeted me stepped up beside her. "What do you think, Mrs. McGruder?" Mrs. Winston asked her.

"A risk at minimum, Mrs. Winston. She has the face of an angel, however." She drew closer and looked at me harder. "I see no trouble in her eyes now, but these eyes have seen trouble," she continued.

"Exactly my thoughts," Mrs. Winston said. "Well, come into the sitting room," she said, "and we'll see about you."

Once again, I didn't know whether to be amused or angry. I wasn't at the Winston House to be interviewed for a job. I was there as a paying customer. They both stepped aside to make way for my entrance. I picked up my suitcase, hesitated, and then entered the house. Mrs. McGruder stepped forward quickly to close the door behind me.

I was pleasantly surprised by the brightness and the color scheme of the entrance hall. The walls had apple-green and white paper, divided into broad panels with white molding. The wainscoting was stained dark green. On the floor was a green-and-white-checked rug with a plain border, and against the wall were a settee and two chairs with white woodwork and green upholstery. The white console opposite was beneath a mirror. A green-and-white-lattice plant stand held purple and pale yellow irises. Ahead of us was a white stairway with box trees in green tubs at the foot of it. The air was perfumed with the scent of fresh spring flowers.

"This way," Mrs. Winston said.

I followed them to the right to enter what I thought was a small, rather cluttered sitting room. Every available space was taken up with antiques—clocks, statuary, sepia photographs in old frames, music boxes, and, of course, leather-bound books with yellowing pages. The furniture looked as if it had been there from the first day anyone had moved into the house.

There were large, comfortable-looking mahogany

chairs, a sofa, and two footstools grouped around the fire-place. To the right of that was a table with a lamp, some books and magazines neatly stacked, and two more chairs nearby. Across the way was a tall secretary with a straight chair. The woodwork, walls, and fireplace were a soft gray. The rug was a plain velvet, and the curtains were in a chintz pattern with green foliage. Despite how crowded the room was, it did look cheerful and cozy.

Mrs. Winston indicated the sofa for me, so I lowered my suitcase and sat. She took one of the chairs facing me, but Mrs. McGruder stood off to the side near the entrance.

"This rooming house has been in my family for over two hundred years. It didn't begin as a rooming house, of course. Families were a lot larger back then, but over the years, as our family thinned out, some moving away, we began to take in boarders. I've been doing it from the day I was married to Knox Winston. We raised our two children in this house while we had three boarders. They became members of our family. I'm telling you this so you will understand why it is so important to us to know all about the people who want to stay here for however long that might be.

"Now, I will say, you are the youngest person ever to wish to do so. Naturally, then, we would want to know a little more than usual about you. If this is offensive to you, please be assured that you won't be hurting our feelings by leaving right now."

She didn't look at Mrs. McGruder. I did and saw her staring at me so intently that I couldn't help but feel a little intimidated. In some ways, she reminded me of

Mrs. Fennel, who had the eyes of someone who could look through your very soul.

I shifted my legs and nodded. "What do you want to know about me?"

"Well, for starters, why are you in Quincy?"

"I wanted to start my own life, and I wanted to start as far away from my father and his current wife as I could," I began.

My story seemed to unfold as I told it, emerging from real events as much as from things I invented. My older sister Ava, when she was training me to take over her position in our family, had told me that we have a unique ability to fabricate on the spot. "We do it so well," she had said, "that we come to believe what we invent." She'd laughed. "Sometimes it's impossible to distinguish what really happened from what we claim happened. It's in our nature to be deceptive, because deception is protection. Whether you want to be a good liar or not, Lorelei," she'd said, "you are."

"My goodness, why do you want to be as far away as possible from your father?" Mrs. Winston asked, this time looking at Mrs. McGruder, who narrowed her eyes and nodded softly, as if she had always known what I was about to say or, more accurately, create.

"Where are you from?" Mrs. McGruder asked before I could respond.

"Southern California, Los Angeles," I said.

She nodded at Mrs. Winston. "Thought so," she said. "Go on."

"I'm an only child," I said. "I was very close with my mother. We were more like sisters."

Mrs. McGruder liked that. She walked over to sit beside Mrs. Winston.

"In fact, I knew she was very sick before my father knew," I continued. "During a routine physical exam, the doctor discovered that she had bone cancer. My father was never one to tolerate sickness and weakness, either in my mother or in myself. Whenever I was ill, he practically ran out of the house and always left everything for my mother to do, so you can imagine what he was like when she told him the bad news."

"And they wonder if women are stronger than men," Mrs. McGruder said.

Mrs. Winston nodded, pressing her lips together. "I should know," she said. "I had to take care of my paternal grandmother, didn't I? My husband found every excuse to avoid seeing her when she was in the hospital, too."

"Don't I remember. The burden you had," Mrs. McGruder said, shaking her head and clicking her tongue. "Any other Christian soul would have collapsed under the weight."

I could see I had begun to swim in the stream of their sympathy. I sighed and pressed my fingers against my eyes as if to stem the leaking tears.

"I was the one who took my mother to every doctor's visit," I continued. "My father was on one of his so-called business trips when I had to take her to the hospital that final time. He never said good-bye. I tried to do it for him, but my mother knew I was only trying. You can't hide the truth from someone on death's door. Lies and hypocrisy are turned away."

"Poor dear," Mrs. Winston said, nodding. She looked at Mrs. McGruder. "Some of us have no choice about when we have to grow up and put away childish things."

"Amen to that," Mrs. McGruder said, and clicked her tongue again.

I took a deep breath and looked away. I was actually forcing back real tears by now. Ava would have been proud of me if she were sitting there, I thought, but I was thankful she was not and hoped she never would be again.

"My mother died a few months ago," I said without looking at them first. Then I turned slowly, dramatically. "Later, I discovered that my father had already been seeing this woman while my mother was dying in the hospital. It was like having death stab me in the heart a second time."

Mrs. Winston pressed her lips together and shook her head.

"Mother of God," Mrs. McGruder said, and she looked up as if she could see an angel hovering on the ceiling.

"I knew it, but I said nothing to him—or to my mother, of course. Two weeks after my mother's passing, my father brought his new girlfriend home. We hadn't even put up the tombstone yet."

"Oh, the hardness cementing the hearts of self-centered men," Mrs. Winston said.

"They didn't marry. They had the decency to wait some time before they were going to do that, but she behaved as though they were married. It wasn't long before she was telling me what to do, and he was siding with her all the time. Finally, he gave me an ultimatum. Accept Veronica as my surrogate mother until they were married—that's her name; he calls her Ronnie for short—or leave."

"Your father said that? He gave his own flesh and blood such an ultimatum?" Mrs. McGruder asked.

Mrs. Winston grunted. "I don't know why that would surprise you, Mrs. McGruder. You and I have lived long enough to see it all."

"But not to abide it."

I nodded. "He gave me that ultimatum, so one night, I packed only enough to get away quickly. I had a little of my own money, and I thought I would get new things as I went along. As you can imagine, it was important to travel lightly and get as far away as I could as fast as I could. I don't intend ever to go back there except to visit my mother's grave from time to time. I know he won't."

"You poor child. Don't you have any relatives you could have gone to?" Mrs. McGruder asked.

"Both of my parents were only children, and both sets of grandparents are gone," I said. "I guess you can see how important my mother was to me and I to her. As I said, we were more like sisters."

"Yes," Mrs. Winston said. The two women were both silent a moment, and then Mrs. Winston looked up at me again. "What brought you to Quincy?"

Time to mix in some truth, I thought. *It's the recipe that always works.*

"To be honest, I read about it on the flight from

California to Boston and decided it was a good place to get a new start. I've always loved being close to the ocean, but even more, I love being close to history."

"No question about it. You'll be close to that here," Mrs. McGruder said.

"Why didn't you go to college?" Mrs. Winston asked, still holding on to some of her skepticism and suspicions. It was too much a part of her nature to let them go easily.

"I fully intended to do so, but my father told me we didn't have the funds and I should first get a job and make some money. We had the funds. I knew it, but what could I do? He made promises that I knew he would never keep. He said he would match anything I made, but once his Ronnie came to live with us, I saw the writing on the wall. There would be little or no money put away for me, no matter what I did. She was always asking him for expensive things.

"But I haven't given up on going to college some-day," I said quickly.

"Did you inquire about any job prospects here?" Mrs. McGruder asked.

"Not yet, but I'm good on a computer, and I have very good organizational skills. No matter what, I want very much to try to live here for a while," I said. "This looks like just the sort of place that's the opposite of where I was in California. I have the feeling that people are real here. I'm the sort who likes to make new friends. My mother was like that, too. She taught me that if you are honest and sincere with people, they will be the same with you. My father taught me the opposite," I added, grimacing, "but I've tossed those lessons overboard."

Now they looked as if they were the ones holding back tears.

"We have room for only six guests," Mrs. Winston said after a deep sigh. "Currently, we have three. You'll be our fourth. There are strict rules," she added with a tone of admonition.

"I'm not afraid of rules," I said.

"We'll see. We'll show you your room. You'll be sharing a bathroom with Mrs. Addison. She was recently divorced, and she is waiting for her new house to be renovated."

"And for her divorce settlement, which could go on for quite a while. The courts here are like the courts in a Dickens novel," Mrs. McGruder added. "Have you had any lunch?"

"Lunch?" I smiled.

"What's so funny?" Mrs. Winston asked.

"I was so involved in my travel, I forgot to eat breakfast, too," I said.

"I'm not surprised. Young people today don't know right from left most of the time," Mrs. McGruder said.

Mrs. Winston nodded in agreement. "Well, then, first things first," she said, rising. "You just make yourself at home here for a few minutes while we look into some lunch. I'm a little hungry now myself."

The two of them left me. I gazed around the room, which just reeked of history, of family, of heritage. I had no reason to feel at home and no expectations of finding friendship at all.

But somehow I felt as if I had.

Was it merely a wish, a need so great it would paper over reality and leave me even more vulnerable than I was before I had begun my journey?

The world was bright there, cozy and warm.

Don't fool yourself so quickly, Lorelei, I told myself. *The winds of darkness you left behind are surely blowing vigorously in every direction at this very moment, searching for you, waiting to swallow you up and take you back to the fate you were destined to have.*

Remember Ava's prophetic words.

"You can't escape from yourself."

3

I continued to elaborate on my story at lunch, building on half-truths. I held the two women in rapt attention, especially when I described the fictional Veronica, making her sound jealous of my capturing even a few seconds of my father's attention. I even suggested that she tried to make me out to be a thief by claiming that she couldn't find certain pieces of her jewelry and somehow was always missing money. Jealousy among myself and my sisters was always in the air at home. All of us competed for my father's attention, so it wasn't difficult coming up with this scenario and describing it with passion in my voice.

"Whenever Veronica brought any of this up, she fixed her attention on me in front of my father so that there would be no doubt whom she was accusing. She must have descended from Judas," I added, and their eyes widened. "It was like living with an assassin," I said. "Gradually, my father's once loving eyes turned into cold gray stones when he looked my way, and all because of her. Once my father loved me like a father should love a daughter," I added, thinking of my real father. "He loved to spend time with me, lay whatever wisdom he could upon me to guide me, but after she came on the scene, I felt like a stranger in my own home. It got so I was spending hours and hours locked up in my room, finding every way I could to avoid them. I would fall asleep with my mother's picture embraced in my arms and pressed to my heart."

I looked away as if to prevent them from seeing tears forming in my eyes. Actually, they were forming. *I'm good at this,* I thought. *I'm better than Ava ever could be, because she's too hard-hearted to create any sympathy for herself. She'd laugh in the faces of those who tied her to the stake, the most feared and ancient way to rid the world of our kind.*

"No wonder you ran off. Please, take as much time to eat as you want," Mrs. Winston said, her hand now pressed against her heart, tender with compassion. "We're in no rush here."

I hadn't realized how hungry I really was and was gobbling my food. Mrs. Fennel would say I was vacuuming it up from the plate. She'd give me a look so stern I would go into slow motion.

"Thank you. I'm sorry to go on and on like this about my father and his witch," I said. "I'm sure it's depressing you, and you don't need someone new coming here with emotional and psychological burdens. Everyone has his or her own troubles. I'd understand why you wouldn't be so eager to have someone like me as a tenant."

"Oh, no, no. We're happy to listen," Mrs. Winston said, and she looked at Mrs. McGruder, who nodded emphatically.

"I'd like to get my hands on that woman for ten minutes," Mrs. Winston said. "I just hate that type, and we've seen enough examples of them."

"Amen to that," Mrs. McGruder added, like the loyal alter ego she was.

I was confident that they wouldn't want to send me on my way. Rather than depressing them, I had the feeling I was giving them their entertainment for the day, if not for the week. Feasting on the private lives of their guests was probably what they needed to nourish their own existence in a world where the most excitement came from statues and plaques.

"This is delicious," I said, nodding at the salad.

Mrs. McGruder had made a Waldorf salad. Before she served it, she went into the history of it, telling me that it was first created in 1893 by the maitre d' of the Waldorf Astoria in New York City. I wondered if everything presented to me in that house would have a biography attached. I really was going to live in the middle of a history book, but oddly, that made me feel safer. It was as if I had gone through a door and traveled not only thousands of miles away from my father and my sisters but a few hundred years away, too.

Actually, despite the sorry face I wore, I was enjoying the first really relaxing moments I'd had since getting into the truck with Moses. The dining room was surprisingly bright and airy because of the sliding patio doors and two large windows. Mrs. Winston explained that this part of the historic house had recently been renovated. Recently, I learned, meant within the last twenty years.

"I didn't want to do it, but the business required it. Naturally, the historical society made us jump through hoops," she said.

"And then some," Mrs. McGruder added.

There was a long light oak table that could comfortably seat a dozen people, a matching armoire with shelves of very old china, and two side chairs in opposite corners. Above us was a pewter chandelier that looked as if it had once held candles instead of light bulbs. The walls there, as they were elsewhere, had pages from old newspapers in frames, drawings of Colonial government figures, and an occasional print of a watercolor depicting farms or the original streets in the city.

"We don't usually provide lunch for our guests," Mrs. Winston continued. "This is a bed-and-breakfast, but we do have what is called half-board if you want to take your dinners with us as well."

So there would be no misunderstanding, she wrote out the prices.

"The room you'll be getting is our Abigail Adams. All six of our guest rooms are named for Quincy historical figures. Abigail was, of course, the wife of John Adams, who was the second president of the United States, and the mother of John Quincy Adams, who was the sixth. I'm giving you a discount because you're just starting out here."

"Thank you," I said. "And thank you for lunch. It's delicious."

"Everything Mrs. McGruder makes is delicious. At the moment, our three other guests are half-board because they know they'll get a dinner ten times better than anything in any restaurant out there," she added.

"I'd like to do the same," I said.

"Very wise decision. Well now," she said, seeing that I had finished my lunch, "shall we show you the Abigail Adams?"

"Yes, please," I said.

We went out to the stairway and started up. It was only a short stairway, but because the windows in the upstairs hallway were small and far apart and because there were no lights on at the moment, it was much darker.

As if she knew what I was thinking, Mrs. Winston turned to say, "We don't waste electricity here. I don't put the lights on until after dusk. For years after electricity became a big thing, my family held on to candles and oil lamps. I think we might have been the last ones in this section of Quincy to install a telephone. One should not be so eager to give up one's history. Not all change is for the better, you know."

I didn't say anything, but I understood her point. None of her ancestors had given up as much as I was trying to give up and deny about my own history.

We turned right and went to the third door, where she paused as if we were in a movie and she was anticipating some entry music.

"The Abigail Adams," she announced, and opened the door.

I imagined it had been renovated, too, because it had two large windows, one on each side of the simple white enameled four-poster bed, maybe half the size of the king-size bed I had in California. It was made up with simple light blue linen. There was an old-fashioned crocheted bedspread with knotted fringe. The windows faced the street. The chintz curtains were tied back so the light fell fully on the small table beside the bed. On it was a shaded reading lamp. Although there was a mirrored dressing table with a cover of clear glass, there was also a long mirror on what I imagined was the closet door, two chairs, one of which was wicker, and a footstool. In the far right corner was a writing desk. The walls were papered with a small pattern of flowers in soft colors, and there was a large plain green woven rag rug. On the left was a bureau.

"That's Abigail Adams," Mrs. Winston said, nodding at a painting over the bureau.

Both she and Mrs. McGruder were obviously waiting for me to say something that would reveal how impressed I was.

"This is a beautiful and very comfortable-looking room," I said.

"And immaculate," Mrs. McGruder added.

"Why don't you settle in?" Mrs. Winston said. "I'm going to make a phone call for you right away."

"Phone call for me?"

"I'm calling my nephew Ken Dolan. He owns Dolan Plumbing Supply and is always looking for qualified help. I'm sure he'll grant you an interview, maybe today," she said.

"That's very kind of you, Mrs. Winston."

"Yes, well," she said, glancing at Mrs. McGruder, "you can call me Amelia."

"Thank you."

"Mrs. McGruder is not as fond of her given name and likes to remain Mrs. McGruder."

"Oh?"

"Hortense," she said disdainfully. "My brothers had a good time with that, as you can imagine." She rolled her eyes and clicked her tongue.

"Now, as to the rules," Mrs. Winston said, cutting discussion short. "Obviously, we don't tolerate any smoking in the house or on our grounds."

"I don't smoke," I said.

"Good. Hopefully, you'll keep to that. It goes without saying that drugs and alcohol are off-limits as well. We do serve wine at dinner, and we do from time to time provide after-dinner brandy and a homemade elderberry wine. I don't think it will do you any harm to partake despite your age. We do that mainly on holidays or other special occasions, but no alcohol is permitted in any of the bedrooms."

I nodded.

"We expect you will respect the furniture and the linen and towels we provide. Everything is replaced daily, but how you keep your room tells us pretty quickly how much you respect it. As to comings and goings . . . you'll be provided with your own front-door key, of course. We're not here to supervise anyone. We just ask that you take care to move about quietly after eleven. There are no overnight guests permitted," she concluded, and pressed her lips together quickly, as if to keep any other reference to such a thing from slipping out.

"You two are the only ones I know here," I said.

"For now," she instantly retorted. "Any young lady

as pretty as you will soon have a trail of young men coming to the door. We permit socializing in the living room during decent hours, of course, and you can offer anyone tea or coffee and biscuits during the visit if we know about it in advance."

She took a deep breath and looked around the room with the expectation that I would follow her gaze.

"As you see, there is no television or radio in your room," she continued, "nor is there a telephone. This is what I meant when I said we run a very quiet rooming house. There is, of course, a television set in the den downstairs. So, unless you have any questions . . ."

"No, everything is wonderful," I said.

She smiled. "Mrs. McGruder will bring your towels and washcloths shortly. As we said, you're sharing a bathroom on this side with Naomi Addison."

"She'll be surprised," Mrs. McGruder muttered. "She's had it all to herself up to now. That's a woman who is used to her own personal comfort and not used to sharing anything except her troubles and unhappiness."

"Yes, well, I'm sure you will not monopolize the bathroom, nor will she," Mrs. Winston said firmly. "As in any good rooming house, we are all dependent upon everyone else, respecting everyone else, Mrs. Addison included."

Mrs. McGruder grunted with some skepticism. Mrs. Winston glanced at her, thought for a moment, and then turned back to me.

"Mrs. McGruder is of the opinion that Mrs. Addison . . ."

"Soon to be ex–Mrs. Addison," Mrs. McGruder corrected.

"That ex–Mrs. Addison has her sights set on my nephew, Ken Dolan, and that this was her true intention when she came here to stay until her matters are settled. Ken's wife left him soon after she gave birth to their son, Liam. Ken had a daughter with her, too, four years earlier, Julia. Liam is twenty-one, and Julia is twenty-five. Neither of them is at all fond of Mrs. Addison—I mean, the soon-to-be-ex–Mrs. Addison—but men are blind when it comes to the wiles of coquettes."

I couldn't help smiling. The wiles of coquettes?

"Amen to that," Mrs. McGruder said. "My husband made an absolute fool of himself whenever he was confronted by a bubbling bosom or a seductive wisp of a smile to accompany a wiggling hip."

Mrs. Winston cleared her throat and gave Mrs. McGruder a chastising look. "Yes, well, I wasn't going to turn her away. How would that look? A woman in the midst of a bitter divorce left out in the cold. But I'm not worried. Ken won't fall for a woman who resembles his first wife. Fool me once, shame on you. Fool me twice, shame on me."

"Amen to that, too," Mrs. McGruder said.

"One of our current two other guests is Mr. Jim Lamb, a twenty-four-year-old man who teaches English in the Adams School for Girls," Mrs. Winston said. "It's a private secular school for grades six to twelve. He mostly teaches the high school students. He's a very serious young man. And our other guest is Mr. Martin Brady, a man in his fifties who is a dental supply salesman. You'll meet everyone at dinner, if not before. Do you have any questions, dear?"

"No. I'll just settle in, as you say," I said.

She nodded. "I'll let you know what my nephew says."

They both left and closed the door behind them, their looks and voices fading quickly, like breath in very cold air. The resulting silence felt heavy.

Everything that had happened to me and everything I had done had gone by so quickly that I hadn't paused long enough to think about it all and fully contemplate the possibilities that loomed on the horizon. Now that Mrs. Winston and Mrs. McGruder had left me alone, it all came flooding back at me. The reality was that this was the first time I was really on my own, the first time I was away from whatever family I had known, and the first time I was totally responsible for myself.

As it would for any older teenage girl, that prospect filled me with mixed emotions tugging against one another, especially excitement and concern. For a few moments, I thought only of my freedom to do whatever I wanted. The rules Mrs. Winston had described were restraints that applied only in the house. Out there, I could dress, say, and do whatever I wanted whenever I wanted. I didn't have to worry about what my father would think or say, what Mrs. Fennel would think or say, or what Ava would think or say. The only one I had to please was myself. If I wanted to get drunk and make a fool of myself, I could. I didn't have to be careful about whom I spoke to and what I said, as long as what I said had nothing to do with the life I was fleeing.

I wasn't afraid of my freedom, either. I had always had great self-confidence, even though there were times when I doubted or questioned it. In my heart of hearts, I knew that I could compete with any other girl my age or older in any way on any field. None of them was as well equipped for life's normal challenges as I was.

Now, on my own, I was even more grateful for my extraordinary intelligence, the speed with which I could master any new subject, the breadth and depth of my memory, and the perception I possessed, a perception that for other girls came only after years and years of experiences and acquired wisdom and that wasn't guaranteed. Mine was inherited. There was no ordinary human being I couldn't handle, master, and defeat if I had to. Look at what I had just been through with that fiend who had pretended to be an attorney. I smiled to myself, imagining how Mrs. Winston and Mrs. Mc-Gruder would have reacted at lunch if I had described those events in any detail.

How silly and insignificant their concerns for me were. My biggest problem should be sharing a bathroom with a divorcée who was full of herself.

All of this filled me with optimism, but when I gazed out of my bedroom windows and looked down at the bright, Norman Rockwell streets reeking of peace and contentment, imagining the happy families that occupied the other houses, with their manicured front lawns, their sparkling driveways and walks, their potted flowers and sprawling old trees that had quietly witnessed the birth of a nation, I could imagine the creeping, crawling, dark shadows seeping in and over it all, finding the cracks in the perfection, slipping through any tiny opening, oozing over the immaculate streets and sidewalks, embracing the houses and darkening the hearts of parents who would suddenly fear for their teenagers as much as for themselves.

Was Daddy ever far away? Had I been deluding myself?

I opened the window and listened to the breeze tiptoeing over the tops of houses and trees until it circled the house to dance a ballet in the sunlight. On the right side of a house across the street, a tree of metal butterflies jingled. Down toward the west end of the street, a car door slammed. Someone called out to someone. There was a trickle of laughter. High in the sky above, a twinkling star metamorphosed into a commercial jet. I suddenly could hear Mrs. Winston and Mrs. McGruder below discussing the dinner menu and then dropping their voices into whispers, surely to talk about me. How quickly they had begun to care and worry about me.

What a wonderful choice I had made. Life here was surely a breath of fresh air. I told myself that Ava, Daddy, and the others most likely expected that I would flee to some darker sanctuary, a place where my inherent nature would feel more at home. They'd search for me in urban alleyways, large, busy cities where someone like me, and like them, would have an easier time disappearing. For a frightening moment, I wondered if they weren't right to assume that and if I wasn't wrong to ignore it. Would my true nature be too obvious in a place like this? Would these people take second looks at me, see the veil of darkness that was always beside me, step away, and then choose to avoid and ignore me? Would they, in short, become afraid of me?

It didn't matter that they could not identify what it was exactly that turned them off to me. Whatever it was, they would instinctively feel that it was something born out of a netherworld, some grotesque swamp crawling with repulsive creatures, some so loathsome that they weren't even imagined in nightmares. My terrible fear was that they would sense all of this, and I would soon be on my way again, fleeing, searching for that impossible place that would enable me to deny my second self and let me become ordinary.

I couldn't help wondering, maybe wishing it, if such a hopeful dream existed for my sisters, too, if during some free moment when they were alone, they permitted themselves to admit to the same longing. For them, however, the moment they opened that door, the terror and guilt came rushing in behind their fantasy, ripping and tearing it apart, growling and roaring until they cowered and chastised themselves for having even a moment like mine. It occurred to me that they might be pursuing me not out of anger but out of jealousy. I had gone farther away than any of them had. They couldn't tolerate the fact that there was one of us who could escape, because that reinforced and drove home their own failure. And for me, at least right now, their own doom.

I would not succumb.

I would not surrender.

I would not turn back.

Daddy would turn back. In the end, he would

reluctantly decide to let me go. He would be touched by mercy and also by the love he once held so strongly for me. Maybe it was the last trace of humanity at work in him, some part of his early existence that had lingered. At least, that was my prayer.

I turned to my small suitcase and unpacked my things. The very act of settling into another room in another house felt like another big step in my emancipation. I decided to take a shower and change into fresh clothes. While I was dressing, there was a knock on my door.

"Yes?"

"When you are ready to come down, let me know," Mrs. Winston said through the closed door. "My nephew just called back. He would like to interview you this afternoon. He'll send a car around for you."

"Really?" I opened the door, even though I was still in my bra and panties. I saw that wasn't something Mrs. Winston easily accepted. Her eyes widened, and she looked away.

"You have to be more discreet, dear. Anyone could have been in the hallway," she said, still not looking directly at me.

"Oh, I'm sorry. I was just so excited with the news." I grabbed a towel and wrapped it around myself quickly.

"Yes, well, all young people today have trouble harnessing their horses," she said.

"It's the first time I've been outside of my own home. It does take some getting used to, I imagine."

"Yes, it does," she said, with a little more understanding and forgiveness in her tone. "Put on something nice but not something that's . . . that's . . . what's the word they use today, obvious? I'm sure you know what I mean. Shall I call him and tell him you'll be ready in ten minutes?"

"Yes, thank you so much, Mrs. Winston."

"Amelia," she said.

"Amelia." I smiled and closed the door.

Could all of this happen for me so quickly? Was there some good angel looking out for me after all?

I went into a small panic. This was no time to make any mistakes, but I had only two outfits from which to choose. One was a skirt and blouse, and the other was a pair of designer jeans and a blouse. Which was more conservative? The skirt's hem was about two inches below my knees. Was that too "obvious"?

I decided not to risk it and settled on the pants outfit. I pinned up my hair quickly. I rarely needed more makeup than a little brush of lipstick. Any more than that might ring some alarm bells. After one more look at myself, I hurried out and down the stairs, to where both Mrs. Winston and Mrs. McGruder waited to inspect me.

"I don't have very much with me," I said, nearly moaning when I didn't hear either offer some approval.

"With her looks and figure, you can't do much more to be subtle, anyway," Mrs. McGruder said.

Mrs. Winston nodded. "That's fine. For now," she added. "If you should get the job, you'll need to buy some appropriate dresses, however. Ken has a number of young men working for him." She made them sound like a disease.

"Of course," I said. "Thank you."

We heard a car horn. Actually, it was a pickup truck that had pulled into the driveway. Mrs. Winston opened the door so quickly and roughly I thought she might rip it off its hinges.

"There's no need to wake the dead!" she cried at the slightly balding man in a khaki shirt sitting behind the steering wheel.

"Sorry, Mrs. Winston," he called back.

"That's Michael Thomas. He's been with Ken a long time," Mrs. Winston said. "Married to a woman nearly fifteen years younger," she added, with disapproval leaking out of the sides of her mouth. "They have four children now. She's a practicing Catholic."

How small was this city? I wondered. How long would it be before they knew some of the real details of my life? I smiled at the women and headed for the truck.

"Good luck," Mrs. McGruder called after me.

I turned, smiled, and waved.

Before I got into the truck, I glanced down the street. Something had made me turn to look, even though it was very quiet and there was no other traffic.

Maybe it was my imagination, but I thought I saw Thaddeus Bogosian, the elderly man on the plane, standing on the corner and looking my way.

I blinked, and he was gone.

But the image remained on my eyes like the blinding light of a flashbulb in the dark.

4

"Hello there," Michael Thomas said when I got into the truck. "I'm Michael, Michael Thomas."

"Lorelei Patio," I said.

We didn't shake hands as much as just graze palms. His were quite rough with calluses.

He looked out at Mrs. Winston and Mrs. McGruder, who were still watching us with hawk eyes. "Those two can be real pissers," he said, nodding at them before he began to back out of the driveway.

They didn't go back into the house until we pulled away. I glanced into the rearview mirror and saw that the street was still empty. My imagination was playing games with me, I guessed. Actually, I hoped.

"How long have you been in Quincy?" Michael asked. He appeared to be well into his fifties, the hair along his temples more white than gray, but he also looked hard and muscular, like someone who had worked with his hands most of his life. His face was narrow, the skin on his cheeks as tight as the skin on a drum. I thought his best feature was his eyes, the color of rich, healthy grass.

"Only a few hours," I said.

He nearly lost control of the truck. "A few hours?"

"Yes."

"Are you a friend of the family or something?"

"No. I just met Mrs. Winston. I found her rooming house listed in a travel publication, called, and just settled in."

He shook his head. "And she recommended you to be her nephew's private secretary? The quickest decision I understand that woman's made was deciding to marry her husband after a five-year engagement. What'd ya do to win her over, recite the Articles of Confederation word for word?"

I laughed. "I didn't even know it was for the position of Mr. Dolan's private secretary. Besides, I'm just going in for an interview," I said.

"Yeah, but you don't know the influence that woman has with my boss. She had more to do with his bringing up than his own mother, her sister."

"Well, despite that, I'm sure he'll decide for himself about something as serious as his private secretary. I think she was just being kind."

"Just being kind?" He laughed and looked at me. "What are you, all of eighteen?"

"Every day of it and some more," I said.

He nodded and smiled. When he smiled, his tight face softened and brought out the bright green of his eyes even more. It helped him look younger. "Well, I'll say this much. You hit town at the right time. Ken's looking for a replacement for Michele. She's like ten months pregnant. The joke is she's in the right place to break her water, a plumbing supply company."

"What exactly is a plumbing supply company?" I asked.

He laughed. "Sometimes I have to wonder myself. We sell mostly to builders and plumbers. There is a division for design, too, so we can contract to do the plumbing and plumbing fixtures in a newly built home, bathrooms, kitchens, and commercial buildings. Ordinary do-it-yourself guys come around for parts, tools, and supplies like filters. We're the biggest plumbing supply outfit in Quincy, which brings in customers from Boston proper, too. It's a multimillion-dollar enterprise with more than fifty employees."

"Sounds like Mr. Dolan's secretary has a lot to do."

He nodded. "A lot, but there are five additional secretaries, bookkeepers, and receptionists. What's your experience as a secretary? Not that someone as young as you would have much, I'm sure."

His question brought home how utterly ridiculous it would look to anyone else for me to be rushing to an interview for such an important position. And yet, although it would be impossible to explain to anyone outside of our special family, I wasn't inordinately nervous, nor did I feel foolish.

"I'll save my answers for my actual interview," I replied.

Instead of being offended by the tone of my reply, Michael nodded, impressed. "Okay. Let me give you a little advice, though, if I might."

"That's fine. Thank you."

"Ken Dolan's picture is next to 'workaholic' in the dictionary. As Mrs. Winston might have told you, he suffers no fools. He can be abrupt and very impatient. He expects everyone who works for him to be fully prepared whenever he or she speaks to him. He built his father's little business into what it is today. You'll find him very competitive and"—he paused to lean toward me—"very anal about what he wants done. Michele Levy has been with him for nearly three years, which is a little more than two years longer than the last secretary he had. The one before that lasted a little less than two months." He stared at me a moment to see the effect his description had on me.

I shrugged. "If I don't get this job, I'll get another," I said, so matter-of-factly that he dropped his jaw for a moment and then roared.

"That's just the sort of attitude Ken admires. Anyway, thar she blows," he added, nodding at the very large fenced-in warehouse and office building just ahead of us. It had taken only a few minutes to get there. I realized it was walking distance from the Winston House.

There were a half-dozen delivery trucks parked outside the warehouse, and on the opposite side was a parking lot for employees' vehicles. Two spots had signs posted to reserve them, one for Ken Dolan and the other for Liam Dolan. That parking space was empty. Michael nodded at it when we parked.

"Liam is Ken's son. Ken would be the first to say in name only," Michael said.

"What does that mean?"

"Here's a hint. The parking spot has been empty all day. He's not exactly a chip off the old block. Ken gives him responsibilities, but more often than not, he comes up with some excuse for why he hasn't done the job. I don't know how much Mrs. Winston's told you about her nephew's family. Anyway," he quickly added, as if he'd just realized how much he was saying, "it's not my place to talk about it. I'll show you to Ken's office." He got out of the truck.

I glanced again at the empty parking spot reserved for Liam Dolan and then followed Michael into the building. We went directly into a showroom filled with all sorts of plumbing fixtures. There was a second showroom just to the right of it. Glancing through the door, I saw sinks and tubs, whirlpools and shower stalls. We continued down a hallway, passing an office where two women were working furiously on computers.

"Accounting," Michael said.

We almost paused at the door of another office that had "Liam Dolan, Assistant Manager" printed on it. Michael just smirked, and we continued to a very nicely appointed outer office. There was no question that the woman standing behind the desk and filing something in the cabinet was Michele Levy. When she turned, I saw that she did indeed look like a woman hours away from the delivery room. She instinctively put her hands at the bottom of her stomach, as if to keep her baby from being born right in front of us, and gazed from Michael to me, her hazel eyes widening with surprise. I thought she had a pretty face, but because of some bloating, I didn't think her very short haircut worked. She wore a plain light blue maternity dress.

"This is Lorelei Patio," Michael told her. I couldn't see his face when he spoke, but I imagined he was telegraphing his surprise, too.

Michele looked at me with disappointment. I had the sense that a few candidates, maybe more than a few, had come and gone, and she was hoping for a replacement as soon as possible.

"Hello," she said. "I'll tell Mr. Dolan you've arrived," she added before I could respond. She didn't want to waste much of her time and energy on the likes of me, I thought.

Oddly, none of this discouraged me. If anything, I felt up to the challenge. It was in our nature to be competitive. Daddy had always told me that. I recalled how pleased he was when I brought home very high grades or won a contest in school.

"There are so many things about us that are false or exaggerated," he had told me recently. "We don't live forever and ever, but we don't feel that we have to. We don't have to feel and want most things they have to feel and want. What we must never do is feed any self-doubt. Our confidence is our special armor, Lorelei. Don't be afraid of being accused of arrogance. Most of the time, it will be the envious who will accuse you, anyway."

I had fled from Daddy. I was afraid of him now, yes, but I would never forget his wisdom.

"Good luck," Michael said. "They'll call me when it's time to run you back."

"Don't go too far," Michele told him before she buzzed Mr. Dolan on his intercom.

"I won't need you to run me back, Michael," I said. "Thank you, but I would like to walk and see some of Quincy."

"If you change your mind, I'll be nearby," he said. He glanced at Michele and left.

"Mr. Dolan, Lorelei Patio is here to see you. Okay," she said, and cradled the receiver before putting her hand against her lower back and coming around her desk to escort me to the inner office door.

"It's better if you walk more than sit and stand in one place," I told her.

She smiled quizzically and tilted her head to the right.

"How would you know? Don't tell me you've had a baby."

"I won't. I just know," I said.

She raised her eyebrows and started to reach for the doorknob.

"I have it from here, thank you," I said, and opened the door, stepping in front of her and entering Ken Dolan's office.

He looked up from his desk, not so much with surprise as with confusion.

"I guess I'll be right outside as usual," Michele said from behind me, and closed the door.

Ken Dolan rose slowly. He was easily six feet two or three, with a compact, athletic build. He wore a light blue sports jacket, a white shirt with an opened collar, no tie, and dark blue slacks. His dark complexion highlighted his clear sea-blue eyes. There were strands of light gray in his stylishly cut light brown hair.

Some men simply radiated authority, I thought. They look as if they should run companies or be U.S. senators. Maybe because I could see and feel it so easily in Daddy, I could recognize it when I saw it in ordinary men. Ken Dolan was one of those men, and yet there was nothing hard or unpleasant in the face he was showing me at the moment. If anything, he now looked somewhat amused.

He came around his desk and, still smiling, offered me his hand. "Come, sit," he said, indicating the dark brown leather settee on his right. "I hate sitting behind that desk when I interview someone for any position here. Makes me feel like a school principal or something."

I sat, and he sat beside me but leaned back.

"Tell me about yourself," he began. "My aunt filled me in on your unfortunate family situation."

"She's very kind," I said.

"She's got good instincts when it comes to people, especially strangers. What is it she saw so quickly in you?"

"Determination to succeed," I said without hesitation. His eyes told me he liked that reply. "Except for getting my father to realize he's making a mistake, I've never failed at anything I've attempted to do."

"Does that include computer skills?"

"It's in our DNA these days," I replied. "We had an excellent program at school."

"My current secretary, who you see is desperate to get relief, has developed an amazing sixth sense when it comes to what I want and need done. I'm looking for someone with initiative, someone I don't have to tell when something has to be done and, after a short period, what else has to be done. She's got her work, and I have mine."

I looked around his office. There were plaques on the walls from the Quincy Chamber of Commerce and plaques congratulating the Dolan Plumbing Supply Company for years of service and exceptional sales. I also saw plaques from organizations showing appreciation for charitable contributions. A variety of framed pictures with Ken Dolan and who I imagined to be state and maybe federal dignitaries were there, along with a picture of who I assumed to be his son, Liam, and his daughter, Julia. There was a separate framed photograph of Julia in a graduation robe and another of her in what looked like a nurse's uniform.

"I don't judge people on how young or old they are per se, but I do find that young people your age generally don't know how to answer the phone properly," Ken Dolan said. "Nor take a message correctly, when it comes to that. All of this texting and electronic media are damaging the basic but important communication we need, especially in a business that depends on customers feeling properly addressed."

"I suppose it's how you're brought up, too," I said. "My mother set a good example for me when it came to people-to-people relations. I'm probably as frustrated by some of the careless and sloppy talk we get on the phone these days as you are. I'm not Miss Perfect, but I think I know when to put my own interest on hold and service the priorities of other people. It's a matter of self-survival, anyway, isn't it?"

He stared at me a moment and then smiled. "Self-survival?"

"I've had to fend for myself more than most lately, Mr. Dolan. You tend to grow up faster when that happens. My age and my appearance are somewhat deceptive, but then again, there will be women who come in here looking for this position who will be older and might even appear to be responsible and mature but who will be just as deceptive."

His mouth opened a little, and then he laughed, holding his smile. "I'm beginning to understand what my aunt saw."

I shrugged. "I won't make any claims about myself. Your aunt would surely say the proof is in the pudding, anyway."

He nodded. "You read her right. I like it when I meet someone, young or old, who has some good perception."

"Survival," I emphasized. "When you don't have much of a safety net, you had better be right about people you meet the first time."

"You're a very pretty girl, Lorelei. Do you see that as an advantage or a disadvantage?"

"Depends. With men, it's usually an advantage. Most women see me as a threat," I said, and his eyes brightened.

"You don't sound conceited, but you don't back away from a compliment, either."

I shrugged. "What is true is true, Mr. Dolan. Why put on false humility? Besides, I don't want to tell you that you're wrong the first time I've met you."

He laughed so hard I thought he would have a pain in his stomach. "Where do you come from again?"

"I'm from California, but we lived in other places."

"And you have no family here or in Boston?"

"I'm on my own, Mr. Dolan. I'm responsible for myself."

"What brought you here, I mean, this place in particular?"

"It looked like a good place to start anew. I was tired of big-city commotion. I suppose I'm a little too old-fashioned for most of my contemporaries, but I want to have a solid beginning and be somewhere where people are more substantial. I know I can succeed here."

He nodded, his eyes warming with his appreciation of me. "I like your determination and confidence, Lorelei. Unlike most of the young people your age I have met, you seem quite centered, but what do you know about plumbing supplies? I like all of my employees, even those who do nothing but drive trucks, to know something about what we do and have for our customers. Questions and complaints come rushing in here daily."

"All I can tell you, Mr. Dolan, is that I am a quick learner, and I know that when I don't know something, I should turn to someone who does and not try to fool anyone, especially a customer of yours."

"Hmm . . . well, I'll see about your getting the full tour and tutoring. In the meantime . . ."

He got up and went to his desk to pick up his phone and buzz Michele Levy. "Michele, I want you to try something for me. I want you to give Lorelei Patio all of the paperwork you have left to do today. That's right. Just point it out on the computer and describe it quickly. Show her how to use the phone system. Then go take a break. Go to the lounge, and return in two hours. She'll be right out." He hung up and looked at me. "That okay with you, some pudding?"

"I hope there will be proof in it," I replied.

He laughed.

I stood up. "Is that your daughter in the nurse's uniform?"

"Julia, yes. She works ER at the hospital here. I couldn't get her into the business. She told me she preferred human plumbing to steel and copper. Don't know where she gets it. I get woozy at the sight of blood."

"Most people do," I said. "We have to appreciate those who don't."

He liked that; he liked it very much.

I thought that was something ironic that Daddy would have said with a smile hidden in his lips. I imagined I would spend the rest of my life thinking of things that he would have said. The longer I was away, the deeper was my understanding of what Ava meant when she told me I could never escape who and what we were.

Maybe she couldn't, I thought, but I could.

I hoped.

I stepped out of the office. Michele Levy looked up at me with an even bigger smile of surprise than when I had first arrived with Michael Thomas.

"What did you do?" she asked in a near whisper, gazing at the inner office door.

"Told the truth," I said.

She shook her head. That answer made no sense to her. "Bring that chair over," she said, indicating a chair on the right, "and we'll begin."

I know she was pleasantly surprised at how quickly I picked up on the software they used. It wasn't brain surgery. Actually, I held myself back a little, maybe a lot, because I was afraid she might be spooked by my intelligence and instinctive abilities.

While she was away, I completed all of the work she had set aside and answered five phone calls, two of which Mr. Dolan was waiting for. He asked me to get back to each of the other three and was on the final call when Michele returned. She looked over what I had done and then looked up at the clock.

"I don't understand how you got all that inventory done this quickly and wrote those letters, too."

"Computers aren't such a mystery," I said.

"I don't mean the computer." She seemed suspicious and even a little resentful, jealous.

No one likes to be easily replaced, I thought. I should be more humble, go slower. "Well, you left very good instructions," I told her, which seemed to help.

Mr. Dolan suddenly opened his door and stepped into the outer office. "So?" he asked Michele. "Do I have her go to the business office and give them her social security number, or what?"

"She's done it all, Mr. Dolan, and quite well."

He nodded. "Why don't you go home, then, Michele? Lorelei can finish the day here. Come back in the morning for a few hours to be sure she has a handle on it all, " he added, turning to me, "although I have no doubt she will." Mr. Dolan winked at me and returned to his office.

"I don't know who you are, Lorelei Patio, but you've gotten off to the best start of any employee since I've been here. Don't do anything to ruin it," Michele said.

She had started to gather her things when a young man I recognized from his photo as Mr. Dolan's son entered. To me, he looked as if he had just gotten out of bed. He paused, looked at the two of us, and smiled.

Wiping his long pecan-brown hair away from his eyes, he asked, "Who is this, Michele?"

"A possible replacement for me, Liam," she replied.

"My father hired you to replace Michele?" he asked me, his smile widening.

Liam had his father's eyes and was even more handsome—and not simply because he was younger. His features were perfect, like the face of a Greek statue where so much care was taken to keep everything in proportion. He had that unshaved look and was at least an inch taller than his father. Although not as athletically built, he was tight and slim. At the moment, his khaki shirt was opened low enough to show his chest hair and a gold Cuban-link necklace that looked at least fourteen-karat. I couldn't help but be drawn to the sexual energy in his eyes. There was a sweet but strong masculine aura radiating from him. I could deny many things about myself, perhaps, but not the underlying lusts that shaped who and what we were. If we were to succeed for Daddy, we had to generate raw sexual energy as well as, if not better and stronger than, any other young woman. Liam looked like a young man who could comfortably satisfy my desire. His smile was awash in his self-confidence, and yet there was something boyish and innocent about him that kept him from appearing too arrogant. I could imagine him crying with grateful joy at the pleasure he would find in my kiss, my embrace, my ultimate act of love.

"He's trying me out, yes," I said.

"I wouldn't have to try you out. I'd hire you immediately," he said with a softness that helped me easily imagine his lips brushing my neck and following the line of my collarbone to the small of my throat until I gasped and he pressed his mouth to mine. I could feel a stirring under my breast when I imagined this. It was as if a sleeping serpent had slowly lifted its head and flicked its tongue to taste the raging desire that had come so close.

Neither of us shifted our gaze away from the other until we heard Mr. Dolan's office door open. He stood there glaring out at his son. If anger could take the form of tears, he'd be drowning in them, I thought.

"Hey, Dad. Congratulations on your choice of secretary. Didn't know you had such good taste anymore."

"Never mind your stupid remarks, Liam. Why didn't you tend to the Sheinman account? I had to send Michael over there this morning, and he had other things to do today that were equally important."

"Oh, I had a bad night, Dad. Matter of fact, I just managed to get out of bed."

"What for?" his father asked, backed up, and slammed the door.

Michele looked at me and continued to gather her things a little faster.

"You'd think he'd be in a better mood after meeting you," Liam told me. He didn't look even slightly shaken by his father's rage. "I know I am."

I returned to the paperwork. I wasn't looking to get into the middle of this, especially so soon. Fortunately, before he could say another word, the phone rang.

"Dolan Plumbing Supply, Mr. Dolan's office," I said. "One moment, please."

I buzzed Ken Dolan.

"A Mr. Marcus on the line, Mr. Dolan. Okay." I returned to the phone call. "Mr. Marcus, Mr. Dolan is in a meeting. Could he call you back in an hour or so? Yes, sir. I'll make a note of it. Thank you."

Michele smiled at me. Liam just stood there gaping as if I had accomplished some major feat. How bad were the other applicants? I wondered.

"You need anyone to show you around, you drop into my office," Liam told me. "I'd better go see if Pam is still awake," he told Michele. "My father deliberately assigned her to me. She's a week away from social security, so he thought she would be safe." He worked up a charming smile mainly for my benefit.

He waited for some reaction, but neither Michele nor I responded. We watched him go, and then she turned to me. "I hope you have a steady boyfriend, Lorelei, or he'll hit on you until you see him in nightmares."

"He's not my type," I said, even though the feelings I was sensing at the base of my stomach were telling me he was, as Ava would say, prime prey.

"What's your type?" she asked with a skeptical smile. I knew she was thinking that I would be interested in the boss's son for obvious reasons.

"Healthier."

"Healthier?"

"In mind and body," I said, and she laughed before looking at the door to be sure he was gone.

She turned back to me, looking more serious. "I'm sure you'll get an earful from Mrs. Winston, but as you can see, Liam and his father are usually at the tip of double-edged swords. Liam dropped out of college last year before they threw him out. You might know already that Mr. Dolan's wife ran off and left him with the children years ago."

"Yes, Mrs. Winston did tell me that much."

"Well, you can see the result of that when it comes to Liam. He's nothing like his father. He doesn't have any sense of responsibility. You don't even have to be an amateur psychiatrist to see that he's acting out because of all his pent-up anger. Julia's completely different. You will have trouble believing they had the same mother."

"Children are most often different in the same families," I said. She didn't realize it, of course, but I was saying it more like a prayer than a fact. If there was anything I wanted to be true right then, that was it.

She looked at me oddly, obviously not expecting me to be so calm and sound so wise. "You haven't been to college?"

"Not yet," I said. "I might start in a year or so."

"You seem a lot older than you claim to be. At some

point, that's true for every woman, but it looks true for you already."

"It's not time that matters; it's what experiences you have within that time. My father always said that," I added, smiling to myself.

"Well, he's obviously a very wise man."

"Men are men," I said, quickly remembering the story I was giving about my family.

"What's that mean?"

"They might come up with some wisdom from time to time, but they don't always think first and then act. They're led about on a leash of testosterone most of the time, especially my father."

She laughed. "Well, Liam won't disappoint you there. He has quite the reputation." She looked at Mr. Dolan's closed door and leaned toward me. "The inside joke here is that he would go home with the right pipe fitting if he couldn't get a date."

"If he's depending on a date with me, he'll empty out the warehouse," I said.

She laughed so hard she had to hold her stomach. "You'll have me give birth right here."

"Oh, don't do that. Go home."

"I almost wish I could be a fly on the wall these next few weeks."

"It's not worth your curiosity, Michele. Believe me," I said.

She nodded, obviously impressed with me but still a little skeptical. "We'll see. I'll see you in the morning and spend more time with you. I've lived here most of my life, so if you have any questions about anything in Quincy . . .'"

"Thank you. Have you and your husband chosen a name for your soon-to-be-born son?"

She started to speak and then stopped. "I didn't tell you I was having a boy. I haven't told anyone here that, not even Mr. Dolan. We didn't want anyone to know we had broken down and given in to find out. We haven't even told our family. My mother would carry on about ruining the surprise. I know my grandmother would. She says all this technology takes the romance out of our lives."

I shrugged. "I thought you did say boy. Sorry."

"No. I mean, we are having a boy, but how . . ."

"Not much of a magic trick on my part," I said. "There were only two choices, Michele. I just hit the right one. Maybe I'll go find a roulette wheel."

She laughed, but I held a steady serious look. I didn't want her even to suspect that I had any special powers. I couldn't explain the sharp insight that all my sisters and I possessed. Daddy had told me it was part of what helped us survive the ages. He had told me there were all sorts of vision, and many times, it was wiser to see through your feelings rather than through your eyes. At least, that was true for us.

"We're thinking of naming him Nathaniel," Michele said after a moment of deciding whether to share something so personal with someone she had just met. "That was my paternal grandfather's name."

"That's nice. I prefer older names and not the flavor of the month."

"Now you're sounding more like my grandmother. How old are you, really?"

"Ages and ages," I said. "I drank from the Fountain of Youth."

She nodded. "I bet you did. See you in the morning."

I watched her leave, and then the phone rang again. I could see it was an internal call. I didn't have to wait to hear his voice to know who it was. "Mr. Dolan's office," I said dryly.

"I heard you've only been in Quincy one day and you're staying at my great-aunt's place," Liam said. "How about I show you the town tonight? It looks like you're practically a member of the family already."

"Excuse me. Who is this?" I asked, knowing well who it was.

"Liam. Liam Dolan. We just met," he said, sounding amazed and a little insulted.

"Oh. Sorry. You were in and out so quickly, I forgot your name. Thank you for the invitation, but I'm otherwise occupied."

"Huh? What's that mean?"

"Translated, that means I have things to do tonight that make my accepting your invitation impossible."

"All night?"

"No. I think I'll spend some time sleeping. But thank you," I said, and hung up.

I waited to see if he would call back. A part of me wished he would, and I sat there chastising that part of me. He didn't call back, but I had no doubt that he would not give up so easily.

Maybe it wouldn't be long before he wished he had.

5

At the end of the day, Michael Thomas stopped in to see me. I could see from his expression that news about me had spread with electric speed through the company. I had stopped in the business office and met the head accountant, Mrs. Lovejoy, a woman in her late fifties who looked as if she had absorbed decimal points into her eyes. They were spotted black and gray. She gave me a form to fill out and mechanically explained the company's pension plan. I sensed that despite Mr. Dolan's eagerness to hire me, she didn't believe I would be with the company long enough for anything she said to matter all that much.

Afterward, I returned to the office. Mr. Dolan was having a meeting with an attorney named Stan English. From the way Stan had looked at me when he arrived, I had the feeling Mr. Dolan had already told him about me, filling his description with compliments.

"If for some reason Ken doesn't want to keep you on, you call me," he said, winking.

"Control yourself, Stan," Mr. Dolan told him. "You've got three grandchildren."

"And a fourth on the way." He smiled at me. "I was eighteen once. Don't rush your life."

"Sorry," Mr. Dolan told me, continuing with the lightness, "but Stan, like most lawyers, is always eager to give someone else advice. Get in here, you idiot."

"Come see me," Mr. English mouthed as he went into Mr. Dolan's office. Mr. Dolan had already told me that his meeting would go past the end of the day and I should just let him know when I was leaving.

I was glad to see Michael Thomas because I anticipated Liam Dolan returning to pursue me despite my having turned him down on the phone, and I was afraid that I would weaken and go with him. I told myself it was far too soon to experiment with another romance. Buddy's face was still vividly in my mind and in my dreams, not that I had any hope of ever seeing him again.

"Congratulations," Michael said. He was obviously very surprised that I had been hired. "I just stopped by to see if you had changed your mind about a ride home, since from what I've heard, you've done a day's work in a matter of hours."

I imagined I had been a big topic of discussion. "I'm not exhausted, Michael. Thank you, but you know what I would like, if you have a few minutes?"

"Sure, what?"

"A quick tour of the showrooms. I've been mostly shut up in here and haven't had the opportunity to look at an actual saddle tee fixture, and since I wrote the letter informing the wholesaler who won the bid for that and other things with us, I thought I should know how to tell it from a chocolate ice cream cone."

Michael laughed. "Absolutely. Glad to do it."

"I'll just let Mr. Dolan know I'm leaving," I said. I buzzed him and told him. I added that Michael Thomas was giving me a little tour of the company on my way out.

"Good idea. See you in the morning," he said.

As Michael and I started out, Liam Dolan appeared in the hallway, just as I had anticipated. He looked from Michael to me. "I'd be happy to give her a ride home," he told Michael.

"She's not going home," Michael said. Neither he nor I added anything.

We continued down the hallway to the showrooms, both of us smiling at the way Liam just stood there looking after us, confused.

"Just give me a quick brush of it all, Michael," I said as we entered the first showroom. "I'll work myself deeper into it as I go along."

"No problem. Let's start with fixtures," he said.

I had not realized how much there was, and after a good half hour, we had just scratched the surface, even of only a superficial view of it.

"I don't want to take up any more of your time," I told him. "And besides, I don't think I should be late for my first dinner at the Winston House."

"No, I wouldn't do that," he said. He looked at his watch. "You'd better let me drive you there. It's on my way home anyway," he said. I had a feeling it wasn't, but I agreed, and we left together. Liam's car was already gone. "He obviously didn't make any effort to make up for the time lost today," Michael said, nodding at the parking space. "I don't know why that kid even bothers to show up at any time."

"His father told him the same thing, practically."

Michael grunted.

I thought about Liam. It seemed that everyone was down on him—not that he didn't deserve it, but if no one was in your corner, you began to believe all the negative things people were saying about you. It reminded me of what Daddy called self-fulfilling prophecies. If enough people told you that you were a failure, you could start believing it, and if you did that, you would cause yourself to fail more and more, fulfilling the prophecy.

"Does Liam live with his father?"

"I suppose you could say that. Yes, of course. The Dolans have one of the biggest houses in Quincy. It's really a mansion. Three or four families could live in it without getting in each other's way. I'm sure Ken avoids him, or vice versa. Julia is still living there, too. I hear she's in a romance with an X-ray technician at the hospital." He smiled and leaned toward me. "Quincy's small enough for gossip, but even if it wasn't, people would still be interested in the Dolans. They're like that family on that television show. Ken's a very powerful guy in this city. Politicians are always knocking on his door."

He stopped talking, shook his head, and looked at me.

"I don't know what it is about you, Lorelei, but you get me blabbin' like no one I know. Some days you can count on your fingers how many words I've spoken. I'm supposed to be the closed-mouthed, tight-lipped New England guy who's suspicious of gossips. Look what you're doing to me."

"Don't worry about it, Michael. I'm not much of a gossip. My father always told me to be a good listener first and a speaker later, much later."

Michael laughed. "Good advice. Maybe he's from New England?"

"No, Michael. He isn't from anyplace you'd know."

"Huh?"

I smiled. "We're here," I said, and he hit his brakes.

"Almost forgot. See how much of a creature of habit I am?"

"Thank you, Michael. See you tomorrow."

"I can pick you up in the morning," he said as I got out.

"I'm determined to get that walk in," I said. "Don't stop if you see me. I won't want to hurt your feelings."

He laughed. "Have a good night, Lorelei, and welcome to Quincy. And Dolan Plumbing Supply," he called as he drove away.

I watched him go. Another vehicle pulled into a driveway a few houses down on my left, but other than that, the street was as quiet as it had been when I first arrived. I stood there, however, and concentrated on the place where I had thought I had seen the elderly man who had sat with me on the plane. Daddy had once told me that he was capable of envisioning more than imagining. When I asked him what that meant, he said it was like being a visual prophet. Sometimes he saw what would be before it would be.

"It doesn't always happen, and it's not a hundred percent accurate," he had told me, "but I don't ever belittle or disregard my visions."

Thinking about that now gave me the feeling that he was nearby, warning me. Perhaps greater than my fear of Ava catching up with me was my fear of the Renegades, those of our kind who were outlaws, who followed their own rules and had no respect for territoriality. They moved about at will and endangered us all with their kills. Pursuing one of us was something they did with relish, as if destroying one of us strengthened them.

Despite the strength of the late-afternoon sunlight, the shadows it cast seemed to grow thicker and darker right before my eyes as I stood outside the Winston House studying the street. The shadows' chill sent me hurrying into the house, where the sound of applause greeted me. Mrs. Winston and Mrs. McGruder stood in the living-room doorway, smiling.

"My nephew called earlier to thank me for sending you over," Mrs. Winston said. "Seems I haven't lost my touch when it comes to judging people, and that's pretty important these days."

"Amen to that," Mrs. McGruder said.

"Come in, dear, and enjoy a glass of my special elderberry wine in celebration and meet Mr. Lamb."

They stepped back, and I entered. Mr. Lamb rose from the sofa. He wore a light brown jacket, a dark brown tie, and dark brown slacks with laced walnut-colored shoes. His reddish-brown hair was cut short, with just a small wave at the front. His smile began in his hazel eyes and drifted through his soft, full cheeks to his pale red lips. He had a cleft chin and was just under six feet tall. He didn't look chubby so much as slightly overweight, with an almost feminine gentleness to his demeanor. Perhaps, I thought, I was having this reaction to him because I had been confronted by so many muscular, hard-looking men at the plumbing supply company all day.

"Hi," he said. "Welcome to the Winston House and to Quincy."

"Thank you, Mr. Lamb."

"Please call me Jim. Glad you got here. They wouldn't let me sip the wine until you had yours, and Mrs. Winston knows how much I love her homemade elderberry."

He nodded at the bottle and glasses on the silver tray Mrs. McGruder hovered over beside the end table. She looked to Mrs. Winston, who nodded, and then she began to pour us each a glass. She handed them first to Mrs. Winston, who then handed one to Jim and one to me.

"This is my great-grandmother's recipe," Mrs. Winston explained. "If taken in moderation, elderberry wine has many health benefits. The ancient Egyptians used the plant and its flowers to heal burns, and the British used it as a cure for the common cold and heartburn. Anyway, to our newest Quincy citizen, Lorelei Patio," she said, raising her glass.

We all sipped.

"Thank you," I told her. "I don't think my own grandmother could have done as much for me in one day or been as considerate."

Her eyes glittered, but she quickly recovered her New England proper posture and demeanor. "Well, since this is a special evening, we're having one of Mrs. McGruder's best dinners, roast leg of lamb. We'll have to get to it," she said, nodding at Mrs. McGruder. She made sure to pick up the bottle of elderberry wine as they started out. She paused in the doorway. "I'm sorry the other two guests weren't here early enough to toast with us, but at least you and Mr. Lamb have time to get to know each other," she said, and nodded, as if she were giving us her blessing and permission.

I looked at Jim Lamb. He smiled and glanced at the chair I was near, urging me to sit.

"I should really go up and shower and change for dinner," I said.

"Yes. I will change, too, but they don't serve until seven sharp, so we have some time."

I sat, and he sat on the sofa quickly.

"I don't know much more about you than that you just were hired at Dolan Plumbing Supply and arrived here in Quincy today. Neither Mrs. Winston nor Mrs. McGruder volunteers much information about any of their guests."

"Oh?"

I laughed to myself, thinking about how much they had told me about Naomi Addison, but I did consider that they told me those things because she and I were to share a bathroom, or because they weren't all that fond of her.

"I teach English literature and composition at the Adams School for Girls. I'm in my third year there.

I was born and brought up in Boston. Attended Boston University. My family used to come to Quincy for weekends often, and I fell in love with it when I was only twelve, I think. Always knew I wanted to live here someday."

"What age do you teach?"

"Tenth to twelfth grades. The age of wild hormones," he added, but he blushed before I could, not that I would have. "I was told that if I could survive them, I could teach anyone anywhere."

"You were told right."

"And you're from?"

"The West Coast," I said. "We traveled about a bit."

"What brought you here?"

I thought about being silly and saying "a jet plane," but I smiled instead and told him I had discovered it in a travel magazine.

"Well, it takes a lot of courage to just pick up and start someplace new, especially someplace like Quincy, which I imagine is quite different from where you've been."

"Sometimes we don't have much choice but to be courageous." I glanced at my watch. "I don't mean to be abrupt, but after the day I've had, I think I need a little rest. I want to be up for the other guests and Mrs. Winston's special dinner celebration."

"Oh, sure." He smiled. "I guess we have plenty of time to get to know each other anyway."

"Have no fear. It won't take much time to get to know me. I haven't done all that much yet," I said.

My reply took him by surprise. He tried to hold on

to his smile, but I could see he was a little speechless. I wasn't all that used to shy men. Ava used to say they made her stomach churn. She didn't have the patience for them. Whether I wanted to admit it to myself or not, I shared some of that with her.

I finished my wine, put the glass down, and stood. He rose immediately.

"See you at dinner, then," I said.

"Yes, yes," he replied as I started out.

I was going to lie down for a while. Everything had happened so quickly, I did feel as if my thoughts were jumbled and floating like snowflakes in a Christmas snow globe. In less than a day, I had found a new place to live, a job, and a possible pool of new friends, including two young men who were obviously eager to get to know more about me. I had a great deal yet to do, of course. I needed to complete my meager wardrobe and get familiar with the city. Always lingering at the edges of my thoughts would be the question of how long I would stay there. Would something soon happen to drive me on? Would I find it impossible to be anything other than a fugitive? Was this idea of starting a new life in a new place so impossible that only someone as desperate and foolish as I was would even attempt it? How long could I keep all of my secrets, anyway?

This was the first time since I had arrived in Quincy that I could stop to think. Without the clatter, the activity and chatter about me, my mind sank softly into the pool of darker memories, still quite vivid. On top of that, I couldn't help but imagine poor Buddy returning from the bathroom and seeing that I was gone. He probably first thought I was in the bathroom and waited hope-fully, but when I didn't emerge, he might have asked someone who was going in or who had just come out if I was in there. When they said no, he would have charged out of the restaurant and looked frantically toward the car and then all around the parking lot. If there was ever anything like cruel kindness, this was it; this was what I had done to him.

I could picture him trembling, believing that my sis-ters and my father had caught up with me and scooped me away. How frantic and frustrated he must have felt. What was he going to do, run to the police to tell them a tale that competed with a television horror movie? He probably wouldn't be able to get a patrol car up to the house. He might not remember where it was himself, anyway. Even if he had found the courage and gone up there himself, he would find nothing. I was confident of that. All he could hope for was that I would call him, if not soon, someday, but that was something I would never do.

Now that I was seemingly safe for a while, I had to remain vigilant and paranoid. Had I seen a vision? Was the old man a Renegade? If I confronted one during my normal daily activity, would I have the power developed in me to sense him? A part of me didn't want these powers. I couldn't pick and choose from the list of skills and insights that made Daddy and my sisters so extraor-dinary and powerful. I had to accept it all, give myself up to the genes raging angrily within me, demanding that I permit them to mature and be who I was meant to be. How dare I challenge the fates?

But challenge them was what I was determined to do. Somehow, some way, I would be different. Surely there was some avenue of escape, some secret antidote that Mrs. Fennel, Daddy, and my sisters knew but had kept from me. I had only one goal in life now, and that was to find it.

I was so lost in these thoughts that I didn't hear the first few raps on my bedroom door. They grew louder, almost like pounding.

"Yes?" I called. I rose quickly from my bed and opened the door. The woman standing there had to be Naomi Addison.

Daddy used to tell us that a divorced woman, especially a recently divorced woman, had a certain desperation in her face. I so enjoyed those evenings when we sat at his feet and listened to him describe the people who populated the world outside. He never came right out and referred to them as our cattle, our livestock, our garden of vegetables, but there was little doubt that he saw them that way most of the time.

"No matter how justified she is in placing blame for the failed relationship on her ex-husband, she can't help but feel not only a sense of failure in herself but also renewed deep insecurity. How did she miss them, all those failings in her man? Will she miss them again in another? There are women out there who have been married two, three, even four times. Is it always the man's fault? Can that be? They have to wonder, even though they would never admit such a thought to their friends.

"And what about those friends? Can they trust them

now? Do they see accusation in their faces? Can they hear the insincerity in their words of support? Are they talking about her behind her back? It's endless when you fail, because even if you can support and justify blaming it all on him, you can't escape the fact that you missed it, chose him, and put yourself in this world of failure.

"So, there is this look of desperation in their eyes. I mean to say this is true for the men, too. They're just as insecure about themselves, despite the bravado. You want to recognize the desperation and the insecurity in the people you meet, my lovelies," Daddy had told us. "It will make you superior and far more confident, which is what you should be, what you are."

Naomi Addison wore too much makeup, I thought. She was one of those women who thought that if they put a stronger bulb in their socket, they would seize the attention of eligible men and wash out the competition. Her torturous, painful hunger to satisfy her need to be loved again was not unlike Daddy's thirst, I thought. Maybe that was what revolted me about her more than anything.

"God, get a life," I wanted to say. "Don't grovel and plead with your sexy clothing, lustful eyes, and voluptuous body to get yourself a new companion, who most likely will bring you back to the altar of divorce you now flee."

If she would wash most of the heavy makeup off her face, take the brassy gold color out of her natural light brown hair, wear less ostentatious jewelry and bras and dresses that didn't exaggerate her nice five-foot-seven, nearly hourglass-perfect figure, she just might find someone substantial. But that thought left me the moment she opened her mouth. Her voice was thin, whiny, and nasal with condescension.

"I'm Naomi Addison. I understand we're sharing the bathroom," she began. "I understand you've been here at least twenty minutes. Does that mean it's mine now? I need a good half hour before dinner."

"Oh, I'm sorry," I said. "I just lay down for a moment after returning from work and lost track of time. I need about five minutes."

"Five minutes," she said disdainfully. "What can you possibly do in five minutes?"

"Get cleaned and refreshed," I said.

She twisted her mouth. Her lips looked artificially boosted into fullness and ballooned a little when she curled them. There was something about the color of her eyes that suggested tinted contacts, maybe designed to make them seem bluer.

"Where do you work?" she asked, solely out of curiosity and not friendly interest.

"I just started as Ken Dolan's secretary at the Dolan Plumbing Supply Company, mainly—"

"Ken Dolan's secretary? You mean, his private secretary?"

"Yes."

"Oh." Her expression softened instantly. Then she smiled. "I would have applied for that if I knew the difference between a computer and a commuter."

Figuring that was her best effort at a joke, I smiled.

"Well, I really don't need as much time as I said. You take ten, fifteen minutes. I'll be fine," she said.

"I won't be that long."

"Don't worry about it. Nice to meet you. I look forward to getting to know more about you."

"Likewise," I said, and closed the door so she wouldn't see me giggling. Could anyone be more obvious? Surely she was hoping to get me to say something complimentary about her to Mr. Dolan. I'd have to remind her that the one with the most influence on him was Mrs. Winston, but more important, after knowing Ken Dolan for only a few hours, I could easily predict that he would never involve himself seriously with a woman like her. I wouldn't be the one to tell her, but something told me I wouldn't have to.

I hurried into the bathroom to shower. I would take only five minutes. She could take all day if she liked.

It wouldn't make any difference if winning Ken Dolan's affection through his aunt's recommendation was her sole purpose this night or any night.

At least for a little while, it was a relief to think about the sorry state of someone else's life instead of my own.

But I knew that wasn't something I could do for long. Every crawling shadow outside my bedroom window was ready to remind me.

And they would.

6

I could see that Mrs. Winston and Mrs. McGruder were surprised that Naomi Addison was not the last guest to arrive at the dinner table. Apparently, that was her modus operandi. She thought it was important to make a grand entrance, but that night she obviously wanted to have the seat next to me. Mrs. Winston sat at the head of the table, and she had placed me to her right, across from Jim Lamb on her left. He had just gotten up to pull out my chair for me when Naomi arrived.

"Good evening, everyone," Naomi sang, and she waited for Jim Lamb to pull out her chair, too.

"Thank you, Jim," she said. "And where's our Mr. Brady? On another road trip?"

"Right here," we heard.

Martin Brady sauntered in, wearing the sort of wide, deep smile on his round, plump face that Daddy used to call synthetic. "For some people," Daddy had said during one of his lectures at dinner, "a smile is almost a part of their uniform, especially salesmen. The secret is to look into their eyes. Do they look like they are lit by sunshine or neon bulbs? Is it the smile of a mannequin or a man?"

I supposed that for the rest of my life, however long that would be now, I would rely on the fruits of Daddy's wisdom, which he handed out to us so freely and eagerly. I would never forget how happy it made him to see us listening so attentively and absorbing everything he said so eagerly. We had the hunger because we instinctively understood that there were all kinds of starvation. We would always have a thirst for knowledge, especially the knowledge that Daddy eagerly imparted to us about people.

When you thought about it, understanding people was probably the most challenging of all things to understand. You could read and study science and math. There were rules applying to them that were true today, yesterday, and tomorrow, but people were often too unpredictable. Whom had I met other than us who could quickly adjust to someone's mood, taste, and inclinations? We were blessed with insights and perceptions. We could see through false faces, feel quickened heartbeats, and seize upon the fears people possessed. These were powers I wanted to keep, but could I do that and give up that which was our true essence?

"Don't fret, Mrs. Addison. I'm here for you," Mr. Brady continued, somewhat boisterously. I glanced at Mrs. Winston and saw her displeasure. You didn't have to be one of us to read the way Mrs. Winston felt and thought about something. The way she would twist her lips, raise her eyebrows, tweak her earlobes, or narrow her eyes spoke volumes to me. She was one of those people Daddy had said were born with a layer of medieval armor. They were impervious to criticism and couldn't care less what other people thought of their opinions or reactions.

"I love their arrogance," Daddy had said. "They have the blood of royalty—rich, thick with history, and sprinkled with what makes something eternal and true."

I think Martin Brady was making his entrance the same boisterous way he usually did because he didn't know I was there. The moment his eyes fell on me, his smile softened, now with more curiosity than his artificial salutation.

"Well, now, who have we here?" he asked.

Mrs. Winston was the first to reply. I had the feeling no one would have dared step on her doing the introductions anyway. "Our newest tenant," she began. "Lorelei Patio. She began work today at Dolan's Plumbing Supply. Ken Dolan's personal secretary," she added, sounding proud.

"Oh. Welcome, Lorelei. I'm Martin Brady," he said, and offered his hand. I started to rise. "No, don't get up. If anyone should rise, it should be me."

"You're standing, Mr. Brady," Mrs. Winston said dryly. "Unless you mean to lift off the floor."

Martin Brady roared with laughter, but it sounded like an old-fashioned laugh track. "So I am, so I am. Naomi," he said, nodding at her. From the way he looked from me to her, I could sense that he was wondering how she took to having me next door to her, sharing the bathroom.

"Hello, Martin. I've already welcomed Lorelei. She's a breath of fresh air, don't you think?"

"Sure is," he said, sitting next to Jim and across from her.

"Don't hog the television, then," Naomi told him. "The younger guests don't want to fall asleep watching the business network."

"Heaven forbid," Martin said, winking at me. "How you doing, Jim?" he asked, unfolding his napkin to place it on his lap. "Catch any of those girls smoking or anything lately?"

"We don't have those problems at the Adams School, Mr. Brady. I told you so," he added, looking to me as if he were afraid I would think he worked in some slum school full of troubled teenage girls whose faces, stomachs, and ears were dotted with piercings and whose necks and arms boasted tattoos.

Martin Brady laughed robustly, this time with a little more authenticity. He was a good twenty pounds overweight at five feet eight or nine, with a dark brown receding hairline. The crow's-feet at the corners of his eyes seemed etched into his skin with a package-cutting tool, deep, thin, and dark. There was a real scar just under the left side of his jaw.

"Looks like a really special dinner tonight, Mrs. Winston," he told her.

"In honor of our new tenant," she replied, and Mrs. McGruder began to serve.

"I don't recall a special dinner when I moved in," he said, pretending to be upset.

"With what you're used to eating on the road, I doubt you would have noticed the difference," Mrs. Winston replied, and Martin Brady laughed again.

"As you can see, I'll need an ally here, Lorelei. I hope I can count on you."

"If there's one thing Lorelei doesn't need right now, it's another burden," Mrs. Winston said.

"Burden? Do I look like anyone's burden?" he asked with that synthetic smile.

Mrs. McGruder began to serve the main dish. Food had often been a problem for me when I began to attend school. Until then, I, like my sisters, had been brought up on Mrs. Fennel's special recipes. Even afterward, our dinners at home were different from the food we ate in restaurants because of the herbs she employed in everything. Ironically, perhaps, sweets and what my classmates called junk food never appealed to me, and when I ate them, I was always disappointed. All of us thought there was something magical in what Mrs. Fennel served the family. Even though I felt confident that there was not, I was nervous about being away from her food. On the other hand, I knew that once my sisters left our home to be on their own, they no longer needed anything "magical" to eat. I hoped I had reached that point, too, despite my leaving prematurely.

I convinced myself as I ate that it was only a matter of getting used to it, reeducating my taste buds, so to speak. For the moment, hoping that no one would notice, I reacted to everything only after the others did. I tried to sound enthusiastic.

"I'm sure you have no friends yet," Naomi said as the dinner progressed. "I have more time to myself these days than I care to have. I'd be happy to show you around, help you shop for your needs. I know where the best shops are, and I'm very up on the latest styles."

"Well," Martin Brady said with a teasing smile, "it's not often I hear Mrs. Addison being so charitable with her time. Better jump on the offer."

"You're not in the least bit funny," Naomi told him.

He covered his face with his hands and moaned. "Oh, the whips and lashes I must bear at the hands of women."

"Idiot," she muttered.

"Thank you, Naomi," I said. "I appreciate your offer." I looked at Mrs. Winston, who didn't seem happy about it.

"So," Martin said, lowering his hands, "where are you from, Lorelei?"

"Recently, California, Mr. Brady."

"Oh, you can call me Martin. Please. Where in California?"

"Los Angeles."

"I worked that market for a year about five years ago. Cutthroat," he added. "Fierce competition. I sell dental supplies. I'm proud to say I'm my company's number one salesman in this market. I have a new sample power toothbrush. If you need one, it's yours."

"Thank you. I'm fine," I said.

"Well, one of the first things I notice about a woman is her teeth, and yours look perfect."

"Thank you."

"I strongly doubt that's the first thing you notice about a woman, Martin," Naomi said.

Mrs. Winston liked that. Martin Brady feigned hurt feelings. "My goodness. You'll give the young lady the wrong idea about me. My father, it happens, was a Presbyterian minister, and, as Mrs. Winston knows, other Presbyterians of note were Presidents Andrew Jackson, James Knox Polk, James Buchanan, Grover Cleveland, Benjamin Harrison, Woodrow Wilson, and Dwight Eisenhower. My father made me recite that at every Sunday dinner when I was a little boy," he said, looking to Mrs. Winston for some credit.

"So was Aaron Burr," Mrs. McGruder muttered as she replenished the jug of water. "Who killed Alexander Hamilton in a duel."

"Now, it was a fair fight, Mrs. McGruder."

"Nevertheless, the better man was killed," she insisted.

"See what I mean, Lorelei, how they pick on me? So, what brought you to Quincy?"

"Why don't we give the girl some time to settle in before we interrogate her?" Mrs. Winston said sharply.

"Exactly," Naomi Addison followed.

"I was just making conversation," Martin Brady said, now losing his sense of humor. He looked at me and then at Mrs. Winston, who could burn through a steel vault with her eyes when she wanted to, I thought. The conversation moved quickly to the food, the weather, and some historical events on the calendar. Before dessert, Naomi leaned over to whisper in my ear.

"I'd be glad to take a walk with you after dinner. I know what it's like being a young, unattached woman in a place like Quincy, especially one with no family or close friends yet. I'm sure there are some things you need and haven't had a chance to get. I could drive you, of course, but it's not that far to the small strip mall, where you'll find a nice drugstore."

"Thank you," I said. "But it will have to be a short walk. I want to get to bed early tonight. With my traveling, starting a new job, and a new place to live and all, I'm a little tired."

"Oh, of course. Would you rather I drove you?"

"No. A little walking will help me sleep better."

She sat back and smiled at Mrs. Winston. "This was a wonderful dinner, Mrs. McGruder," she told her the moment she returned from the kitchen. Everyone agreed. "I will certainly miss your fine cooking when I leave."

"And have we gotten any closer to knowing when that would be?" Mrs. Winston asked.

"Oh, I'm not in any big rush," Naomi said. "I want everything just right before I leave your wonderful, hospitable rooming house."

I thought I heard Mrs. Winston grunt. Mrs. McGruder looked at her and then started to clear the table. All the while, I watched Jim Lamb out of the corner of my eye. He didn't say much, but he looked at me as much as he could without being too obvious about it.

When we all rose, Jim also offered to take a walk with me.

"Oh, I'm going with her, Mr. Lamb," Naomi told him. "I'm sure you have papers to grade."

He looked at me with disappointment. Mr. Brady left for the den to watch television.

"You'll both need a little jacket or wrap tonight," Mrs. Winston told us. "We have a cold front starting."

I realized all I had was my light jacket. I would have

to do some serious shopping soon. When I stepped out of my room wearing it, Naomi, who was wearing a fur-lined black leather jacket, suggested I wear something warmer.

"It's all I have right now," I said.

"Oh. Just a moment. I have something for you," she told me. "Come in, come in."

Her room was similar to mine, a little narrower but with similar furnishings. She had a large trunk on the floor to the right. The closet was so full her clothes were crushed together. She plucked out a very nice white leather jacket with a black mink collar.

"That's so nice," I said.

She held it out, and I took off my light cotton jacket and slipped it on.

"It's beautiful."

"Why don't you hold on to it until you get a proper jacket?" she said.

"Oh, I'll go shopping this weekend and—"

"You don't have to wait for the weekend. The stores I'll take you to are open until eight at night. I'll pick you up at the end of your workday tomorrow, and we'll go directly to the mall."

"That's very kind of you, Naomi."

"Not at all. Let's take our walk."

Mrs. Winston was in the living-room doorway when we descended. I had the feeling she had been waiting to see what I would be wearing, and she nodded to herself when she saw that I was wearing one of Naomi Addison's jackets.

"Is there anything we can get for you, Mrs. Winston?" Naomi asked.

"My youth," she replied.

Naomi laughed, and we walked out before anyone else could appear and make a comment or offer to join us. She was obviously in a rush to get me away from the others.

"That woman," she said when the door was closed behind us and we were starting down the walkway, "must have been breast-fed on sour milk."

"Why did you come stay here during your divorce?" I asked.

"Well, they do run the cleanest temporary housing, and I won't deny that Mrs. McGruder is an excellent cook. I certainly wasn't going to stay in some depressing hotel and have the staff gossiping about me daily. It is so unfair the way a divorced woman is discriminated against, don't you think? For a man, it's almost a mark of accomplishment to have married and divorced. People always look at a divorced woman as though it was somehow all her fault. She failed the marriage by being too cold or self-centered or stubborn. I didn't cheat on my husband; he cheated on me, but again, in this male-oriented society, he gets a pat on the back and licentious smiles in some men's club or the men's lavatory at work, and I get the pitiful looks of other women.

"I'm sorry," she said. "I shouldn't go off on all this the first time we have a chance to be together alone. Besides, you're too young yet to appreciate the unfairness, I imagine."

"No, no, I understand. And I don't see you at all as someone to pity. You seem very strong."

"Well, thank you, darling. That's so sweet to hear, especially from someone who has just met me and has no built-in prejudices against me. Actually, I am strong, and I hope I'm still attractive enough to win the heart of someone new."

"You're very attractive, Naomi."

"You sound sincere."

"I am. I don't need to tell people what they want to hear in order to win their friendship. That's not a real friendship anyway," I said.

"How wise."

"My father taught me that many years ago."

"Not too many. You're too young," she said, smiling. Then she lost her smile and paused so we'd stop walking. "Let me tell you the problem for someone like me, because I can see you're a very, very bright young woman who will quickly understand. I'm not one of those divorced women who swear off all men or something stupid. I'm not even down on marriage just because I was in a bad one.

"But," she continued, "eligible men around my age are not so common, because the ones who haven't been married are, as I said, somewhat prejudiced against divorcées. Used goods and that sort of thing, as well as the stigma of having failed a man. Few have the sympathy to appreciate that I might be the one who was failed. No, my best hope for a new relationship is with someone who, like me, was disappointed in a relationship. We have something in common, understand?"

I nodded. I knew where she was going, but I didn't show it. I knew that wouldn't discourage her from pushing on.

"Now, someone like your boss is absolutely perfect for

someone like me, and I'd be perfect for him. And it's not because of his wealth. I'm very comfortable financially. Frankly, I thought Mrs. Winston would see the obvious advantages for her nephew to involve himself with a stable and attractive woman eager to succeed in a relationship, but she has done little, if anything, to encourage it. Sometimes I think she might even discourage it. She can be very cagey when she wants to be, so be careful with her. Anyway, as time goes by and you become closer and a more trusted personal secretary for Mr. Dolan, perhaps you could, from time to time, drop a hint about me, maybe mention how serious a woman I am and how sympathetic I am to his own dreadful relationship. Frankly, I wish I had started my divorce years ago so I could help Ken with his son, perhaps. His daughter is fine, but I know that all his boy needs is someone to show that she sincerely cares about him. Those floozies I hear he sees from time to time wouldn't care one iota about his children. I regret so much that I didn't have any."

I nodded and started walking again.

"You understand what I'm saying, don't you?"

"Oh, yes, but I don't think I could have much influence on him when it comes to his personal relationships, Naomi."

"You never know. You're there. Opportunities often just pop up."

"Maybe. Oh, is that the strip mall over to the right?"

"Yes, yes."

"I do need some things at the drugstore."

"You were wise not to take Martin up on his offer of that toothbrush. Once you accept something from someone like that, you're indebted forever to him. He'll annoy the hell out of you, and he's not above trying to offer you more than his dental surgical instruments. I speak from experience," she added.

"No worries there," I told her.

"Now, Jim Lamb is obviously already smitten with you," she continued. "He's a nice boy, but what are his prospects? Someday he might become the headmaster? Wow, what an achievement. You're too beautiful to settle for anything less than a really successful business-man or politician. Besides," she said, nudging me with her shoulder, "I think you are so much more sophisti-cated than Jim, you wouldn't be able to think of him as anything but a simple young man. Am I right?"

"Only time will tell," I said.

She laughed, but I could see from the way her eyes caught the streetlight illumination that she was very unsure of me. She even looked a little afraid, I thought.

On the way back, she talked more about the city, shopping, and restaurants. She thought it might be fun for the two of us, despite the differences in our ages, to hang out a little, go to the finer restaurants where we could meet "the proper people." I made it clear to her that I wanted to get myself established first, get a firm footing on my new life, before venturing out too much.

"How sensible you sound," she said. "I know I'm right about you. There's something very mature about you, something that suggests you know a lot more than most girls your age about . . . everything."

Was I that transparent?

If so, what could I hide about myself?

The cold front Mrs. Winston had predicted was coming in quickly. I could feel a chill in the breeze, and the partly clear night sky had turned quite overcast. Dark purple clouds were puffing like flexed muscles, thickening the shadows that seemed to seep out of the darkness beyond the reach of streetlights, darkness that leaped to the right or left of car headlights. I could hear my quickened heartbeat, like distant drums. Something ominous was watching us. Of course, all Naomi Addison felt was the chill.

"It could rain tonight," she said. "If it's raining in the morning, I'd be happy to run you over to Dolan Plumbing Supply."

"You're up that early?" I asked, a little surprised.

She laughed. "Not usually, no. That's why you won't have trouble getting into the bathroom in the morning." Then she stopped abruptly. She turned slowly and looked toward a line of hedges.

"What? Did you forget something?" I asked when she didn't speak. "Naomi?"

"Nothing. I thought . . . I saw . . ."

"What?"

"A pair of eyes . . . illuminated in the darkness."

She pressed her right hand against her breast just over her heart.

"Stupid of me," she said. "There's obviously nothing there. After all, what could it have been, a werewolf or something?" She laughed and started walking again.

I looked back.

Or something, I thought, *yes.*

But I walked on with her. Maybe, without her realizing it, to save her life.

7

I stood by my bedroom window, looking down at the street, for nearly twenty minutes before deciding to go to sleep. The night sky didn't clear at all. Where we lived in Los Angeles, there were no streetlights, but I recalled that it was no different no matter where we had lived. Daddy always preferred the darkness, emphasizing whenever he could that the darkness was our friend.

"We exist because of the darkness," he told me once. "All of you are daughters of darkness."

I wasn't sure what he meant by that back then, but I was sure now. Darkness, secrets, and anonymity were tools that helped keep us alive and safe. More than any other living thing on this earth, we fled intense scrutiny. When questions started, our skillfully orchestrated ballet of avoidance and equivocation immediately began.

Maybe that was why Ava thought I was different, why she thought I might be afraid of myself or for myself. She knew that I was never completely comfortable in the dark, or at least not as comfortable as she and Daddy were. I didn't want to admit to being afraid of anything, ever, but I was, and "fear" wasn't a word we used in our family. As far as I could see, there was nothing either Daddy or Mrs. Fennel feared, and Ava was capable of facing down a stampede of elephants.

The darkness I gazed down at outside seemed to follow me to bed when I turned away from the window. The lights were not shut off yet. There was just a sliver of illumination sliding under the door. For a while, I lay there concentrating on it the way a moth was drawn to a candle. It was as if as long as it was there, I was safe, protected. Then it went off, and I was dropped into a swirling ball of darkness.

The visions I saw spinning inside it weren't nightmares. They were irrevocable memories permanently printed inside my mind. I saw some of the men my sisters had brought home being swallowed up in Daddy's overwhelming embrace. I saw Ava's eyes brighten lustfully at the prospect of a new, healthy young man. I saw my boyfriend Buddy sinking deeper and deeper into the trap my love was designed to create, and I felt my ever-growing inadequacy when it came to protecting him.

Closing my eyes and pressing my face to the pillow didn't stop the visions and the memories. They twisted and turned, slithered and slipped in under my eyelids. I thought I might burst out with screams of frustration. Would this ever end? Did this mean that Ava was absolutely right, that I couldn't escape because all that I had been and all that I was part of were attached to my soul like some horrid umbilical cord no one could cut or tear? Gathering up all of my resolve, I fought back as hard as I could, and eventually, I fell asleep.

The lateness didn't matter. I didn't need as much sleep as they did. I envisioned all of them down the hallway: Mr. Brady on his back sinking into a grave of repose, snoring; Jim Lamb curled comfortably in a fetal position under his blanket, dreaming about me; and Naomi across the way fantasizing a romance with Ken Dolan. It was as if I had the power to pull their heads apart and peer into their dreams like some voyeur of other people's imaginings, other people's deepest secrets. That at least distracted me and became my temporary form of escape from all that haunted me.

I woke early and hurried into the bathroom to shower, as if I thought I could wash away the bleak and morbid flashbacks that had attached themselves to my subconscious. It was as if I believed I could scrub them off me as easily as I could wipe away cobwebs I had gone through during my fevered tossing and turning in the darkness of my bedroom. I tried not to make much noise, as it was early, and contrary to what Naomi had told me, she wasn't rising. I didn't hear a sound coming from her room, and when I gazed at her door, I could sense her still in a deep sleep embraced by her dreams.

I dressed in the clothes I had arrived in, because I hadn't had time to shop for anything new yet. The overcast night sky hung on and hovered over the Quincy morning. The clouds were lighter but still tenaciously dulling the morning sun. After I brushed my hair and put on a little lipstick, I went down to breakfast. Jim Lamb was the only other guest dressed and eating. He rose as soon as I entered the room.

"Oh, sit, please," I said, pulling out my own chair.

Mrs. McGruder popped in from the kitchen with a platter of thin blueberry pancakes. There was sliced mixed fruit on the table, along with a jug of maple syrup, a small pitcher of milk, and a pot of coffee on a ceramic base.

"Orange juice, dear?" she asked.

"Thank you, yes," I said. She placed the platter of pancakes at the center of the table. "They look delicious."

"We get the blueberries locally," she said, and went for my juice.

Jim handed me the platter of pancakes. "How did you sleep?" he asked.

"Very well, thank you."

"These bed frames are old, but the mattresses are very comfortable. I mean, at least mine is," he corrected quickly. "I haven't slept in any other."

He must have been referring to any implication that he had slept with Naomi Addison. Of course, there might have been another woman there before she had come, I realized. The crowns of his cheeks turned a little crimson with the unintended allusion. Who could be shyer than someone who was embarrassed not only by what he had said but by what he imagined someone else might think of him?

"Yes, my bed is very comfortable," I said.

Mrs. McGruder brought me a glass of orange juice. "Would you like tea instead of coffee, dear?"

"No, this is fine. Thank you. Is Mrs. Winston still asleep?" I asked, doubting the possibility.

"Oh, no," Mrs. McGruder replied, smiling. "She

was up more than an hour ago and out to the fisherman's market. She likes to be one of the first to get the freshest and the best."

I poured some maple syrup over the pancakes I had taken. Jim moved quickly to pour me a cup of coffee.

"Thank you."

"I wanted to offer to drive you to work this morning," he said. "But we'd have had to get started a little earlier if we had planned on my doing that. I have a homeroom, so I have to be at school on time and—"

"Oh, don't even think of it," I said. "I'm really looking forward to the walk."

"Yes, well, I know Mrs. Addison volunteered to take you shopping later, but if she's not available for some reason, I'd be more than happy to drive you to the mall and any other shop you might want to try."

"Thank you. I'll keep that in mind."

He looked nervously at his watch. "I'm so sorry to have to desert you," he said. "But the headmistress, Mrs. Damian, stands in that hallway with a stopwatch. I like to be a few minutes early so there's no doubt." He leaned over to lower his voice, even though there was no one else in the dining room. "I swear, I think she transferred from some position in a women's penitentiary."

"I know the type," I said, smiling.

"Do you?"

He looked at me a little more intently. Was he wondering if I had been in some girls' detention facility? His concern brought a smile to my face.

"I meant I've met women like that in the school I attended."

"Yes, I'm sure. I really have to find the opportunity to get to know you. When you settle in, that is. I know you're pretty occupied right now."

"We'll find the time," I said.

He brightened with the promise and then folded his napkin perfectly and neatly before he rose. "Well, off to the chain gang," he said, and he ran his right forefinger across his throat.

"Don't you like your work?"

"I love my subject, but remember, I teach—or try to teach—adolescent females, that mysterious species who laugh for almost no reason and cry for definitely no reason. Sometimes I feel as if I'm teaching extraterrestrials on a different planet."

I smiled, recalling some of the similar complaints my junior and senior high school teachers had about the girls in their classes. Because I was so different from my classmates when it came to those hormone-driven giggles and flirtations during lectures, my teachers favored me. It wasn't that I didn't begin to have crushes on certain good-looking boys. I did, but funnily enough, boys, and girls, too, assumed that I came from a fanatically religious family, a family of Puritans. They thought this was why I wore no makeup and no earrings or bracelets. In their minds, it explained why I didn't participate in clubs and games or go to dances. Surely they thought that trying to be friends with me would be a total waste of time. I could see it in their faces. To them, my whole life was a waste of time.

Not long before I had met Buddy, however, I'd become very self-conscious about my maturing figure and my growing sexual interest in the boys I thought were good-looking. When I had admitted to Ava that this was happening to me, she had warned me about falling in love, even if it was only a teenage love.

"What's wrong with falling in love?" I had asked her.

"Love is poison for us," she'd told me, but she wouldn't explain what that meant—not then, not until later, when my relationship with Buddy had developed.

"Well, have a great day," Jim said, and he started out. He kept his eyes on me and bumped into the chair at the end of the table. Flashing an embarrassed look, he hurried along.

Mrs. McGruder, who had been watching from the kitchen doorway, laughed. "He's a sweet boy," she said.

"Boy" is the key word, I thought, but smiled and nodded.

"This was wonderful, Mrs. McGruder. Thank you," I said, taking my last sip of coffee.

"Have a successful second day," she told me. "There's an umbrella by the door. Maybe you should take it. It looks like we might see some of God's tears." She smiled. "That's what my mother called the rain."

"How sweet," I said, and thought, *My father called it white blood.*

I scooped up the umbrella and left the rooming house. I didn't feel the first drops until I was a good block and a half away. Just as I paused to open the umbrella, I heard a car pull up to the curb right alongside me. I anticipated seeing Michael Thomas when I turned, but it was Liam Dolan. He inched up closer and lowered the passenger's-side window.

"Morning. Hop in before it really starts."

"Oh, I was going to walk."

" 'Was' is the key word in that sentence," he told me. "C'mon. I promise I won't bite."

The rain was intensifying. I decided that I looked foolish even thinking of resisting. I opened the door, closed the umbrella, and slipped in quickly.

"Thank you," I said. "How fortuitous it was that you happened along just at the right time," I added as the raindrops thickened and began to patter on the windshield. Even the wind strengthened, and looking toward the far corner, I could see it toying with the downpour, sweeping small waves of water over the street and sidewalk, as if some invisible large hand were waving in the rain.

"Fortuitous?" he asked, not starting to drive forward. He held his charming smile. Now that I took a good look at him, I saw that he was blessed with a cinematic face, the sort of face never caught unawares by a camera or a glance. His features weren't capable of becoming awkward, even for a second. They clung to their symmetry, and the light in his blue eyes didn't diminish in the grayness thrown over us in the downpour. If anything, they brightened.

"Yes, fortuitous. You're not intimidated by multisyllabic words, are you?" I asked.

"If I were, the word 'intimidated' would get me," he replied.

I laughed.

"Good," he said immediately. "I was afraid you were

one of those women hatched in one of my aunt's favorite historical museums."

"What's that mean?" I asked.

"You know the type, terrified of smiling or laughing
for fear they won't be considered seriously or something. Ask my aunt to let you look at one of her family
albums. You'll see that in not one picture is there a
female smiling in front of a camera. They were taught
that was too frivolous."

"A lot about our lives now is too frivolous."

He glanced at me. "Uh-oh. I suspected that you
might have been sent by one of my aunt's archaic
friends to stay at the Winston House. Some of them
swear they have conversations with John Quincy
himself. Is that how you came to stay at the Winston
House?"

"No," I said. "No one directed me specifically to
your aunt's rooming house."

"Just fate?"

"If you want to call it that. I saw the advertisement
and called to see if there was any vacancy."

"Then it's all meant to be," he declared.

"What's all meant to be?"

"This," he said, and turned at the corner. It was
raining much harder now. I would never have been
able to walk the whole distance without getting soaked.
There was just too much wind.

"Even the rain?"

"Especially the rain," he replied. "If it hadn't started
when you left my aunt's place, I bet you wouldn't have

gotten into my car. You've been told to stay away from me. Oh, don't deny it," he quickly added. "If I were any of them, I would probably have given you the same warnings."

"So, you know you have a bad reputation and you don't do anything to improve it?"

"I'm here, aren't I?"

"Meaning?"

"I haven't gotten up to go to work this early for weeks, maybe months. I can't remember. You're already a good influence on me."

"Me? I hardly spoke to you."

"Exactly, and as I said, I know why, so I woke up this morning and thought I'd win your approval as quickly as I could by turning over a new leaf. I intend to work harder today than my father or anyone else at the place."

"One day doth not a life make," I recited.

He laughed. "I know, I know. Anyone who uses multisyllabic words is no one who can be convinced of anything simply."

"Why do it to please me? Why not do it to please your father? Or, more important, yourself?"

The soft smile withered on his face. "I'd rather do it to please you."

"A stranger?"

"Anyone as beautiful as you are can't be a stranger, at least to me," he said.

"You're right," I said.

"What?"

"I can't be convinced of anything simply, especially when prefaced with flattery."

He laughed, like someone who understood that he

was laughing at himself. "All right, all right, but I'm not using my well-tested pickup lines on you. I'm speaking from the heart. True blue," he said, and pulled into the parking lot and into his parking space.

The rain slowed to a steady pour as the wind diminished. He shut off the engine and turned to me.

"So, Lorelei Patio, where are you from? What was the stroke of luck that dropped you into Quincy and then into my world?"

"I wasn't driven here by luck," I said. If he had tried to find out anything about me from his aunt, she had obviously resisted telling him any part of the story I had told her and Mrs. McGruder. At least, until now.

"Oh? What, then?"

"I've got to go in and get to work," I said. "Thanks for the ride."

"Hey!" he cried when I opened the door and stuck out the umbrella to open it for the walk to the front entrance. "I didn't bring an umbrella. At least let me share yours."

I looked back at him. For a moment, my mind went into rewind, and I recalled the first time I had met Buddy. Ava had taken me to a bar to practice flirtation while following our own special rules concerning what to do and what not to do with men. She had assured me that I would have no trouble being served alcohol there. Someone old enough would surely buy us drinks. It was a bar frequented by college men, and when we had approached the bar, Buddy had stepped forward, bowed like some medieval knight would bow to royalty, and presented us with the bar stools. Ava hadn't given him more than a glance, but I'd thought immediately that he was different from the other young men around us. He had a sweeter, gentler face. Right from the moment of meeting him, I had trouble not being honest with him. There was something about him that cried out for sincerity.

Liam looked like that. Despite the bad-boy image he obviously had earned, I saw past it and saw that same vulnerability, that boyish innocence that every man wanted to keep safely and snugly tucked away in his heart to revisit when he felt it was safe to do so. Perhaps men were far less tolerant than women of any of that naiveté. It smelled and tasted too much of virginity and timidity. It threatened their manhood.

How complicated this was, especially for women, I thought. There was a part of us that was drawn to the gentleness and simplicity in a man. Maybe that was the mother in us that wanted to cuddle and soothe them and longed to feel that need in them, a need we also possessed. But there was also that raw lust in us that drew us to the aggressive, domineering, and demanding force in them. We wanted to be ravished and taken. For almost every woman, this was the conflict, the complication that made navigating in the sea of romance difficult and dangerous.

Suddenly, hesitating in Liam's car and looking at him while all of this came rushing over me, I realized just what made my sisters so grateful for who and what they were. For us, the daughters of darkness, this conflict did not exist. That was why we weren't supposed to fall in love. We were never to have the need to cuddle and soothe any man, and we were certainly never to surrender to any lust, only to use it as we would any other tool.

But this wasn't true for me. I had fallen in love with

Buddy, and what was drawing me to Liam right now were feelings and instincts supposedly deadened in my father's daughters. But they weren't deadened in me. If I didn't belong with them, where did I belong? For I didn't yet feel comfortable in this world to which I had fled.

Seeing the puzzled look on Liam Dolan's face while I hesitated and pondered this, I realized also how difficult, if not impossible, it would be to start a relationship with him, with Jim Lamb, or with any man I would meet while I was there. This was a difficulty that none of them would understand. I was confident that they would all lose patience with me quickly, and the problem for me would dissipate like smoke.

"Of course I'll share my umbrella," I finally said.

I stepped out, closed the door, and hurried around the car with the umbrella opened. He got out and joined me by putting his arm around my waist and stepping under the umbrella, so close to me that our legs touched as we walked and the aroma of his aftershave floated around my face. Laughing at how awkward we were while trying to stay dry, we stepped into the lobby and shook off like two puppies. I glanced around for a place to put the wet umbrella. He took it from me.

"Here," he said, and put it behind a counter.

Those who had already arrived for work all stopped whatever they were doing and looked at us. Some of the women nodded or shook their heads slightly. I was sure they were thinking, *Didn't take him long.* Some of the men smiled licentiously, already way ahead in their fantasies, imagining Liam and I groping each other in some motel or his bedroom.

This is why it's so easy for the daughters of darkness, I thought. *Look at them all assuming, imagining, lavishing in the erotic, all immediately caught on the sexual hook.*

Once they were past puberty, nothing was innocent anymore, not a look, not a touch, not a whisper. And so we baited them with a suggestive smile, a shifting of our eyes, or an innuendo, and they were all ours, practically gift-wrapped for Daddy. Ironically, I had chosen to be like them, the vulnerable ones. I had left the security and the power inherent in Daddy's world, but at the moment, I detested their weakness. I was still in that love-hate relationship and could feel the struggle for dominance going on inside me.

"Maybe I can see you for lunch," Liam said. "You do get an hour," he added, seeing my hesitation. "Dad's phone goes on automatic voice mail. Didn't Michele show you that?"

"No. She had so much to tell me that she probably forgot, but I'm sure she will this morning."

"Great. I'll stop by. There's a nice café just down the street."

"Let me see how things go," I told him. I wanted him to understand clearly and immediately that I would not be rushed into anything.

"Sure," he said. He was too proud to show his disappointment, but I could feel it.

"Thanks for the ride," I said, loudly enough for the woman behind the reception desk to hear. "So fortuitous that you happened along," I added, and I started quickly for Ken Dolan's office.

Michael Thomas stepped out of a door to the warehouse.

"Hey," he called. "I looked for you on my way to work, but I guess you got yourself a ride. You look dry."

"Yes, thank you, Michael. I tried to walk to work. Liam came along just as it really began to pour."

"Liam?" He looked down the hallway and saw him talking to the receptionist. "He just happened to come along?"

"I guess," I said.

He looked at me skeptically, even, I thought, a little critically, as if he believed I was trying to deceive him. "So, you're telling me it wasn't something planned?"

"No."

The lines in his face creased and twisted to form a mask of skepticism.

"That's what happened. Why do you look so doubtful?"

"The Dolans' house is on the other side of town. He wouldn't be just coming along when the downpour started. Not that it's any of my business," he added.

"Oh," I said, realizing that Liam must have planted himself on the street waiting for me to start out.

Michael shrugged, seeing the sincere surprise in my face. "Look at it this way. You got him here to work on time for a change. That's something his father couldn't do."

He paused. I could almost hear his thoughts. *Maybe that's why Ken Dolan hired you so quickly.*

Maybe, I thought, but I hoped not.

It would be like some other man using me for bait.

I simply couldn't escape my destiny.

8

No one wants to feel used, manipulated. I decided that if I concluded that this was the sole reason Ken Dolan had hired me, I would quit and maybe move on to another town or city along the East Coast. Maybe I would even go to Europe, London, anywhere but Quincy. That morning, when he had greeted me, Ken Dolan did look as if he knew his son had driven me to work. One of his employees might have told him, or maybe Liam had told him. Although he didn't say anything about it, he did look happy that I was behind the desk a few minutes early, perhaps because of Liam. I could almost hear Ava's laughter.

Michele Levy was there early, too, so she could finish up what she wanted to show me with the office filing system and some other minor issues. I was impressed with her dedication and loyalty to Mr. Dolan. I knew she still had doubts that I could fill her shoes, despite the abilities I had demonstrated and the speed with which I had grasped the tasks. Maybe in her mind, it diminished her importance and achievements to have someone as young as I was fill her position so easily.

Periodically, other young men stopped by, ostensibly to welcome me to the company. From the smiles on their faces and the way they lingered, it was clear they were there to look me over. One of them was Terrence Stone, who managed the showrooms. I knew he was just thirty, but he looked older because he was prematurely balding. I knew he was a smoker, too. I could, as could any of my sisters, smell the scent even before the smoker arrived. All of our senses were sharper and keener. I wondered if mine would diminish with time. Anyway, Daddy didn't want his daughters to bring him men who were heavy smokers. He didn't like the taste of their blood.

"I didn't know who you were when Michael Thomas ran you through the showrooms yesterday," Terrence said in an apologetic tone. "I thought you might be one of these recently wed women looking to set up a new home. Welcome," he added, offering his hand and holding on to mine a little too long. He had a soft voice with a British accent that Daddy used to call the king's English.

"No problem. I saw you were busy," I said.

He offered to give me a better tour of it all. "I've been here longer than most of the employees," he bragged. "And I grew up in this town, so don't hesitate to ask me anything. If you have a free weekend, I'd be happy to show you around, take you to lunch, whatever."

"Thank you. I have it all under control for now," I said as sweetly but as firmly as I could. He looked surprised more than disappointed as he left.

"You dented his ego," Michele said. She had overheard

it all. "Second to Liam, he's the Don Juan of the company. Don't let that accent fool you. He's nowhere near as bright as he pretends to be." Unable to disguise her jealousy, perhaps her longing for her own youthful, carefree time, she added, "They're all going to hit on you. The word's out, apparently."

"What word?"

"That you're young, beautiful, and available."

"I'm not so available," I said sharply.

"Oh. Are you seeing someone here already?"

"No."

"Someone in Boston?"

I shook my head but offered no other explanation.

She shrugged. "Whatever." She checked her watch. "I hope we don't have any other interruptions. I've got to go to a doctor's appointment. Let me just run through this list of important names, people Mr. Dolan considers his A-list. There are some politicians on it, so not everything here involves plumbing supplies, if you get my drift."

"I do," I said. "Thank you."

I was too busy the rest of the morning to give Liam or the other young men who had stopped by much thought, even if I had wanted to, and when the women from accounting invited me to join them for lunch, I agreed, actually jumping at the invitation. They told me they sent out for sandwiches, and we would all have lunch in an area reserved for employees to have lunch or take snack breaks. There was a refrigerator and a microwave for our use. I checked what sandwich I wanted on the takeout menu and returned to the letters and phone calls. Just before noon, Liam stopped by to see if I was going to join him for lunch.

"You'll really love the food at this place."

"I'm just too busy," I said. "I agreed to join the other employees ordering in sandwiches. It's probably a good idea for me to get to know them all, anyway, don't you think?"

Of course, he didn't. "It's better to get to know me," he half kidded. "But whatever . . . I'll go with Michael to this new job site to help formulate a bid, then. You're forcing me to be a good employee, too."

"It's not castor oil," I said. "And I repeat, you should want to be that without my influencing you."

He laughed. "You sound like one of my high school teachers trying to motivate me."

"Did you ever wonder why you needed motivation?"

He lost his smile. "Despite what you've been told and what you see, my life isn't, nor has it been, a bowl of cherries," he countered.

"Neither has mine, but wallowing in self-pity doesn't help."

"Oh, brother." He looked up at the ceiling. "Mercy," he pleaded with his hands up. I laughed at his histrionics. That brought a smile back to his face. "How about I give you a ride home, at least?"

"Oh, I'm shopping first. Mrs. Addison is taking me."

"Naomi Addison?" He smirked. "She's twice your age. What is she going to know about the things a young woman like you needs?"

"Don't you respect the wisdom of older people?" I asked.

He shook his head. "You're different, all right." He didn't make it seem like a compliment. It rang like a complaint.

"Why do you say that?" I asked. Was there something now so immediately obvious about me?

"Let's just say you seem older than you are and leave it at that."

"Whatever."

"Well, how about dinner one night this week?"

"I signed up for your aunt's bed, breakfast, and dinner package."

"Well, you don't have to eat there every night, do you?" he asked, his frustration building.

I sat back, looking at him and then at his father's closed office door. "Does your father approve of your taking out employees?"

"What? I don't think he has much to say about it," he replied.

"I just thought there might be a company rule."

"Well, there's not."

Just at that moment, Ken Dolan opened his office door and paused on his way out to look at me and then at Liam, his eyes accusing him of wasting time. "You doing that bid research today with Michael or not?" he asked him.

"Yeah, I'm going. I was hoping for something more exciting, but that didn't pan out," he said, looking at me.

"I'm sorry that keeping this company solvent and successful isn't exciting enough for you."

"What's more thrilling than a new toilet?" Liam said dryly.

"If the business is so uninteresting for you, you could have remained in college. I got you into the best school."

"Right. It's all my fault. It's always been all my fault."

Ken shook his head softly and paused at my desk. "I'm meeting John Langerfield at his office and will be at lunch with him, too. I don't anticipate being back before the end of the day. You have my cell-phone number if you need something quickly."

"Yes, Mr. Dolan."

"Oh," Liam said as his father turned to leave. "Lorelei was concerned that you might have a company rule against either of us asking an employee on a date."

"What? Either of us? Why would I ask—"

"I mean me," Liam said. "Or the executive branch of the company."

Ken looked at me. "I think she's old enough and smart enough to know whom and whom not to go out with," he said, and left.

"So?" Liam said. "Are you smart enough?"

"You mean if I said no, I wouldn't be?"

"Oh, jeez," he cried, raising his hands toward the ceiling again. "Do I have to beg?"

"Let's just say that for now, at least, I'm not looking for a relationship, Liam."

"That's not the signal I'm getting," he retorted.

"Maybe you're seeing what you want to see. I'd like to settle in, get the lay of the land, so to speak."

"You mean shop around a little," he said, with sarcasm dripping from the corners of his mouth. "I heard about the parade that went through here this morning. My aunt calls it kicking the tires first before buying."

"I'm not kicking any tires. I don't know the kinds of girls you're used to, but I'm not shopping for a new boyfriend, and I did nothing to encourage anyone here."

"Yeah, sure," he muttered. "Then I guess my father just reinforced my reputation as a loser, and that's turned you off to me."

"That's not it."

"Right."

"Look, Liam, I was with someone before I came here. I thought he was a responsible, considerate, and stable young man, but he finally clearly demonstrated that he was more interested in a good time for the moment than in any planning for the future. There is nothing a girl with half a brain should resent more than feeling like someone's good time. Too many men I've met think we're some sort of video game they can click on and off whenever they have a mind to do so. Those who don't mind get what they deserve. I'm not one of them, and my disappointment in love set me back. I need time to catch my breath."

My imaginary revelation caught him completely off guard. The sadness and sincerity in my voice quickly wiped away his disdain and self-pity. He shook his head, impressed. "I don't know any girl your age or even ten years older who thinks like you do. Most of the girls I know are just the opposite."

"They'll regret it when they wake up one day alone and realize life is a lot shorter than they thought."

"How old did you say you were?"

"I didn't say. Besides, it's not the years you put in; it's what you put into those years."

"What's that, something you heard my great-aunt Amelia say? Don't get her started on Ben Franklin quotes."

"No, it was something my father once said," I told him, "but like most people, he didn't follow his own advice."

"Okay, okay." He put up his hands like someone surrendering and started to back away. "I know when to go into a strategic retreat. Lately, that's all I've been doing."

"I hope your attempting that new leaf is not going to stop now," I said. "I meant what I said. You should do what's right and important to do for yourself and not as part of some illusion you design to seduce the new girl."

He just stood there staring at me so hard that I thought he could see something really different in me, something that made me clearly a daughter of darkness.

"What?" I asked.

"I don't know what to make of you. You look like a stick of dynamite but act like a ballpoint pen. Discovering the real you is going to be a challenge."

"Maybe the effort to find out will do you some good. Things that come too easy usually lose their value quicker," I said, and turned back to the work I had on the computer. I knew he was still looking at me, but when I looked, he was gone. Romantically, maybe for good.

My lunch with the other women at Dolan's Plumbing Supply was as I had anticipated. They were friendly but mostly full of curiosity, women Ava liked to call "pokey" because they poked their noses into everything.

One woman, Helen Carter, voiced what they were all thinking, maybe after talking about me with Michele. "I was very surprised Mr. Dolan would hire someone as young as you for the position. I don't know any businessman as serious as he is when it comes to running a company. He puts a great value on experience. You must have done or said something very impressive. What experience have you had as a personal secretary? Were you just recommended by Mr. Dolan's aunt, Amelia Winston?"

They all paused to hear my answer. "My father always said that quality is far more important than quantity."

They waited to see if I would add anything, but I just bit into my sandwich, and they started talking about something else. Inevitably, the conversation turned back to me, however. They wanted to know more about my personal life. Instinctively, I knew that they would be more inclined to be on my side if they felt sorry for me, especially if they knew the story I had concocted for Mrs. Winston and Mrs. McGruder, so I told it in an abbreviated form. Nevertheless, I had their rapt attention.

"So, you're really a young lady on your own," Clara Weintraub said, and all their heads were nodding, or I should say bobbing, in agreement and sympathy.

"I'm afraid so. I was lucky to find Mrs. Winston's place, and one thing led to another, which is how I came to be here. Sometimes you can be just lucky. It's not my usual history, as you can now understand, but when good fortune shines on you, you should turn your face right into it. My father used to . . . it was something he once said."

"Of course, dear. You just call on any of us if you need anything, anything at all, including advice," Helen Carter said.

"Men," Clara Weintraub followed, practically spitting the word. "You take your time with that," she warned, even waving her right forefinger at me. "Don't let anyone, especially here, take advantage of you. Most of the young men here live from paycheck to paycheck and think saving for a rainy day simply means buying an umbrella."

Heads bobbed.

"Oh, don't worry about me," I said, smiling at them. "For now, I'm wearing a No Trespassing sign around my neck."

That got them all laughing. They followed me out, chuckling and hugging me with warm welcomes. When I paused in the hallway, I saw that Liam had returned and was looking our way. Although he smiled, he shook his head with disappointment and went quickly into his office.

Exactly at the end of my workday, Naomi Addison arrived, as she had promised. She looked dressed to go to a fancy restaurant and not for shopping in a mall. I could see that she had gone to her stylist and had her roots highlighted and her hair done in a new style that made her more attractive. It also looked as if she'd had her makeup done by a professional.

Naomi was a full-figured woman who babied her

complexion and, from what I understood, had a personal trainer. What she was wearing accentuated her attractive features. Her dark blue jacket was semifitted, lined, and below the hip in length. The shoulders were slightly extended, and it had long sleeves. Her matching skirt, also semifitted, was straight, lined, and below mid-knee. She wore a silver beaded necklace with matching earrings. In short, she was a perfectly put-together package.

Ava would call her "dressed to hook."

"Am I early?" she asked.

"No, I was just finishing up," I said. "You look very nice, Naomi."

"Thank you." Her eyes went to Mr. Dolan's closed door. "Is he in? I'd like to say hello. We've known each other a long time."

"No," I said. "He had a lunch meeting in Boston today and hasn't yet returned."

"Oh," she said, deflating like a punctured balloon mannequin of herself. She even seemed to turn a little pale with the disappointment. "What time did he say he would return?"

"He didn't say a time, but he didn't think he would be back before the end of the day."

"Oh. Well, don't rush. We have plenty of time," she said. "I know Chet McKinney. He's still in sales, right?"

"Yes, I met him today," I said. "Among others," I muttered, too low for her to hear.

"I'll just go say hello."

"He might be gone. They close about now."

"I'll check," she insisted, and left.

I knew she was just looking to kill time in the hope that Ken Dolan would return before we left. A moment later, one of the younger salesmen in the appliances section stopped in. He had introduced himself earlier, during the parade. I sensed that they had all taken bets on whom I would favor the most. His name was Bobby Potter, and I thought he was in his mid-twenties at most, because he still had that just-out-of-high-school look, sweet, still innocent and optimistic.

"Hey, how was your second day?" he asked.

"Very good, thanks."

"A few of us are getting together for happy hour at a place called Cappy's, and I thought you might want to come along. It's pretty laid-back, not fancy. It's a great way to get to know everyone," he added.

"Thank you, but I'm technically not of drinking age."

"Oh, that's no problem at Cappy's. I'll buy the drinks for the gang. No one cares."

"Thank you, but I have other plans tonight."

"Oh. Well," he continued without skipping a beat, "we're there just about every night. Great way to relax after work, let your hair down. What about tomorrow night?"

"I'm really not ready to start socializing yet," I said. "But thank you."

"Not ready? None of the girls does anything special for Cappy's. You don't have to put on airs with us. What do you have to do to get ready to start socializing?" he asked, now making my reply sound stupid.

I gave him a hard, cold glare. Maybe it was the Ava

in me, but I didn't have the patience. "Brush my teeth," I said.

"Huh?"

Naomi walked in, glanced at Bobby, and said, "You were right. They already left. Are you ready?"

"Yes." I rose, gathering my things.

Bobby looked at Naomi, glanced at me, and then, blowing air through his lips, left in a huff.

"What was that all about?"

"Turning on faucets."

"What?"

"This is a plumbing supply company, isn't it?" I asked. "You have to speak the language."

She stared a moment and then laughed. Her attention returned to Ken Dolan's door. "He hasn't returned, has he?"

"No. He did say he might be going to dinner with someone," I added, even though he had said nothing of the kind.

"Oh. Is he seeing someone socially?"

"I really haven't been here long enough to know his private business."

She twisted her mouth with displeasure. "Not long enough. It doesn't take much time, especially these days. Gossip is probably the most exciting thing you'll discover in a business like this, anyway. What else would you talk about, washers and bolts?"

"To tell you the truth, Naomi, I've been too busy to talk about anything or listen to anything other than what I need in order to do my work for Mr. Dolan."

"I see you need some good female advice," she

said. "I don't want you to make the mistakes I made."

I flashed a smile and came around the desk to leave.

As we headed out, I felt the eyes of some of the young men still loitering around looking our way. Liam's car was already gone. If Michael's insinuation was right and I was hired to revive Liam's interest in the family business, I could be terminated by the end of the week, I thought.

Whatever.

My life was taking turns for itself these days. I felt as if I was just along for the ride. I would go with the flow and not resist the tide, even if it washed me out to sea and set me sailing in another direction.

"I used to see Ken at some of the better restaurants, but most of the time, he was alone," Naomi said as she drove. "When a man has been burned by a woman the way he was, he's understandably gun-shy. That's why I'm so curious about whom he might be seeing. Maybe it's someone from Boston," she added, looking to see if I had any information after all.

"I don't know. He said nothing about anyone but this attorney he was meeting."

She drove on, her frustration and disappointment reviving her own misery. I wanted to feel sorry for her, but I suspected that a woman as pushy as she seemed to be was probably more than half responsible for a failed relationship. I really knew so little about male-female relationships. What else did I have to go on but my time with Buddy? Daddy had had girlfriends from time to time, but there was no one who even superficially resembled a wife. I observed other people; I read books and saw movies and went to the theater, but in the end, or at least right now, I had to rely on my own instincts, even when it came to what clothing I would buy for myself.

I didn't think Naomi's taste was going to be mine, especially when it came to my office wardrobe. I knew she was surprised at how conservative I was with my choices, but it was precisely the impression of my being older, wiser, and more responsible that was winning me the respect I wanted. As Daddy would say when he quoted the Bible, which he often did out of amusement as much as anything, " 'When I was a child, I spoke as a child. I understood as a child. I thought as a child. But when I became a man, I put away childish things.' You must take heed of those words, my darlings," he would say. "As soon as you feel it, put away childish things."

"I'm very up on what young women your age are wearing these days, Lorelei," she insisted when I didn't take to some of her suggestions.

"For work, this is just fine," I told her, looking at alternative skirts, blouses, and dresses.

"Nothing should be 'just fine.' A woman never stops trying to be as attractive as she can, whether it's at work or on a date," she said. "I'm afraid you've been a little too cloistered to handle yourself in this competitive world. Every woman, especially every woman your age, is competing all the time."

"For what?" I asked.

"For men's attention. What else?"

I laughed. "You should have been with me today. You'd see I don't have that problem, Naomi."

"Well, don't be too arrogant, Lorelei. I can tell you from experience that it's not an attractive feature when it comes to holding a man's interest. That's why I think Ken Dolan would appreciate me more. I'm sure the women he's seeing are snobs. I want you to tell me who they are when you find out. I'm sure there's more than one."

I didn't respond. I continued to shop for what I thought I needed. She trailed along, limply now and clearly with little interest.

"If we're going to eat at the Winston House, we'll have to move along," she said after a while. "I feel a little foolish dressed like this. The place is filling up with mall rats."

"Mall rats?"

"Teenagers and preteens who think of it as a hangout. Don't tell me you never did that."

"I never did," I said.

"What sort of a childhood did you have?" she asked, sounding even more annoyed.

"Unusual," I said. "I'm thinking of getting some new shoes, Naomi. Why don't you head back? I'll grab a taxi. If I'm going to be late or not going back for dinner, I'll call Mrs. Winston," I said. "No worries."

She looked at me suspiciously. "Are you sure you haven't made some sort of secret date with one of those plumbers?"

"First, they're not all plumbers, and second, no."

Her eyes narrowed with all kinds of new suspicions. I could practically hear her thoughts. She was oblivious to the noise around us. "How did you get Ken Dolan to hire you so quickly? I'm sure he had many applicants for that job. I can't believe he did it based solely on Mrs. Winston's recommendation."

"She didn't actually recommend me, Naomi. She arranged for my interview. It was really up to me."

"Well, how did you do it? What did you promise?"

"Efficiency, dedication, and loyalty," I said, emphasizing loyalty.

"You're a fool if you bought into any promises a man makes, even a man like Ken Dolan," she said. She looked around and then turned back to me. "I just decided. I'm not returning to the Winston House for dinner with those boring people. I'm going to the Quincy Seaport Club. I still have a membership. If you were dressed properly, I'd bring you along."

"Thank you for bringing me here," I said. "I know you did it out of pure kindness."

She pressed her lips together, pulled back her shoulders, and mumbled "See you later" before marching away, her high heels sounding like small hammers driving hateful nails into the mall's tile floor.

Maybe I was too hard on her, I thought as she rounded a corner and disappeared. My experiences with other women aside from Mrs. Fennel and my sisters was very limited. Other girls my age relied on those experiences, whereas I kept reminding myself that I had to rely solely on my instincts and my perceptions, which were sharper and keener and went deeper than those of ordinary young women but still left me at some disadvantage.

And then I thought perhaps I was wrong about that. Truthfully, I had no disadvantages when it came to comparing myself with other girls. Perhaps in my determination to flee from who and what I was and was meant to be, I had blinded myself to a greater reality and ignored an insistent realization that I was more capable, stronger, and less vulnerable than any other girl my age or even older. I vowed to stop belittling myself. I was behaving no better than Liam, soaking in self-pity. *Get over it, Lorelei. You're on your own,* I told myself.

I did look for new shoes and also made sure to get myself a warm jacket so I could return Naomi's to her. It was clear that I would be beholden to her for anything. I concentrated so much on what I was doing that I lost track of time and had to rush out to find a taxi. It was too late to cancel dinner at the Winston House. I thought I would just go right to the dining room after I put my packages in my room.

But as it turned out, that wasn't going to be as easy as I thought.

9

My arms were full of bags when I stepped out of the mall to look for a taxi. The sky was partly cloudy, but I could sense oncoming showers blowing in from the east. A chill hung in the air, but that made it sharp and clean. All lights were brighter, all sounds clearer. I felt a healthy surge of energy building in my body. It reminded me of how tight and firm I had been when I had been attacked by the fake lawyer in the back of the SUV. Like some primeval creature always depending on her instincts and that magical sixth sense, I felt something threatening nearby and slowly began to look around myself.

There were three teenage boys on the corner to my right, smoking cigarettes and talking. They all paused to look my way. They didn't know I could hear them despite the distance.

"I wonder what she has in her bags," one said.

"If you have to wonder what she has in her bags, you need help," another teased, and they all laughed. I could see they were just about to start in my direction.

I looked for a taxi but saw none. For a moment, I debated going back into the mall. I didn't want to have any physical confrontations on my second night there. Just before I turned to find some way to retreat, I heard my name called out and saw Jim Lamb hurrying down the sidewalk toward me.

"Jim?"

I looked back at the boys. They hesitated and just watched us.

For a moment, I thought he was either unable or unwilling to explain his presence. The fact that he was actually standing in front of me seemed to overwhelm him.

"I'm surprised to see you," I said, hoping to help him along. He smiled.

"Yes. I happened to be here and saw Naomi leave by herself a while ago. Of course, I remembered you were supposed to be shopping with her. I looked for you inside but didn't see you, so I thought you might not have come here with her after all. I was just getting into my car when I saw you come out. I imagine you want to return to the Winston House."

"Yes."

"Do you have a car picking you up?"

"No. I was looking for a taxi."

"Look no more," he said. "Here, let me help you with some of those bags. Did some shopping, I see."

"Yes." I looked back at the boys. They headed for their corner, looking like cowardly coyotes searching for easier, unprotected prey. "Cutting it close for dinner, aren't you?" I asked Jim.

He nodded, embarrassed that he had looked so hard and long for me. "Don't worry. We should still be there in enough time. Not much traffic in that direction. Why did Naomi leave you here?"

"I think she was bored. She was going to some seaport club."

"Oh, right. The Quincy Seaport Club. Pretty high-end. This is my car," he said when we reached the parking lot. He had a late-model Toyota Prius. "I'm green-conscious," he added. Under the parking lot lights, I could see him blushing. "Not that I could afford anything much more luxurious anyway."

"This is fine."

He opened the back and began putting my bags in. "Did you get everything you wanted?"

"Let's just say that it's a start."

"I bet."

"How fortuitous that you were here," I said, recalling how Liam had reacted to my use of the word.

"Well, to be honest, I was worried about you," he said as we got into his car. He paused and looked straight down at the steering wheel. "I mean, I know how Naomi is, and I thought you might get frustrated with her. So I thought that if I happened by, I could sort of take her place, and you'd have the time you needed to shop. I stayed late at the school correcting papers. I like it when everyone's gone. Anyway, I thought about the mall and you and . . . just stopped."

"That's very thoughtful and, as it turns out, prescient."

He smiled. "I've known Naomi a little longer than you have. Sometimes it's not all that difficult to predict how some things will turn out."

We drove out of the parking lot. I asked Jim about his teaching day, and he described some of the problems he was having, not with the students, surprisingly, but with their parents.

"They think because they're paying for their children to go to the school, they deserve some special treatment. Most of them rationalize every problem I have with their daughters. They turn it around to somehow being my fault or the school's fault or another student's fault. You would think I was teaching a classroom of angels."

"Why did you take a job in a private girls' school?" I asked. "You must have had some idea what it would be like."

"I thought it would be worse in the public school system, but I think I made a mistake," he said.

He had started to ask me about my work when, all of a sudden, just after we had made a turn and he was accelerating, he cried out and swung the car so abruptly to the right that we went onto the sidewalk and slammed head-on into a mailbox. Our airbags exploded in our faces. I had better and faster reflexes than he did and had pulled back quickly enough for the bag not to smack me in the face, but his hit his face so hard it nearly snapped his head off. He groaned and pushed the airbag away. I had already done so with mine.

"Are you all right?" he asked. I saw how banged-up his nose, forehead, and cheeks were. There was a thin line of blood cutting just over his right eyebrow.

"Yes, I'm okay. What happened?"

"Didn't you see him?"

"See whom?"

"That old man. He was suddenly just there, directly in front of us. I thought for sure I was going to hit him. I can't imagine how I didn't."

I looked back and across the street but saw no old man. Another vehicle pulled up right behind us against the curb, and a man and a woman got out quickly.

"Are you two all right?" the man asked after opening the driver's-side door. I stepped out of the car. The woman came around quickly.

"You okay? We were right behind you and saw you turn abruptly."

"I'm okay, but he's pretty hurt," I said. "The airbag."

I kept looking up and down the street, searching for any sign of a pedestrian. "Did you see anyone step in front of us?"

"No," she said. "I mean, there could have been someone, but I didn't see anyone. I wasn't paying that much attention until my husband cried out, 'Look at that!'"

Her husband was on his cell phone. Another vehicle going in the opposite direction pulled to the side, and then another car pulled behind the one at the curb.

"What happened?" the driver of the second car asked the woman.

"He says someone stepped in front of them and he had to turn abruptly to avoid hitting him and lost control. Airbag kept him from getting too badly hurt, but he seems a bit banged up," she said.

"Yes, don't move," her husband said, returning to us. He looked at Jim and saw how much more badly hurt he was. "We're getting you an ambulance. You probably should have an X-ray of your neck to be sure."

Jim protested. I knew he was more embarrassed than seriously hurt, but it was better to be certain.

"They're right," I told him. "Just sit quietly, Jim."

Moments later, a Quincy police patrol car pulled up, and two officers got out. The younger one approached me after they both had heard Jim's explanation.

"Was he drinking?"

"No, he just came to the mall to pick me up and take me back to the Winston House."

"Amelia Winston's rooming house?"

"Yes. We need to call her. We're both expected for dinner."

I reached into the car to find my purse and dig out my cell phone. While I was talking to her, the ambulance arrived. Jim tried to resist, but by now, a small crowd had gathered, and the police were insisting that he get checked out.

"You okay?" the younger policeman asked me. He looked at the exploded airbag on the passenger's side and then at me. "You don't have a scratch on you," he remarked, amazed.

"Just lucky," I said.

"Did you see the old guy in the street, too?"

"I was looking off to the right. It all happened too fast," I said, not wanting Jim to get into trouble.

"Um. We'll take you over to the hospital for a quick examination anyway."

"I have things in the car," I said.

"I'll get them," he offered. He looked like he was in his late twenties and gave me a flirtatious smile. While he gathered my things, the paramedics put Jim into the ambulance. Moments later, a tow truck arrived.

"They listen on a scanner," the young patrolman told me. "This guy is always one of the first to arrive on an accident scene, but you can't leave the car here, and that front is bashed in pretty good."

"It's not my car, but I'm sure Mr. Lamb wouldn't object."

"Couldn't leave it on the street here, either," the patrolman said. "I might have to turn you both over to the FBI," he joked as he led me to the patrol car.

"Oh, and why is that?"

"Destruction of federal property, a mailbox."

"Looks to me like you just have to stand it up again."

He laughed and opened the door. "I'm Tom Westly," he said, and pointed to his name tag.

"Lorelei Patio," I said.

"Just relax for a moment, Lorelei. We'll get you taken care of," he said, loading my bags into the backseat with me. I watched him talking with his partner for a few moments. They watched the tow-truck driver get Jim's car pulled away from the mailbox and lifted to be taken off. The ambulance left, and the two officers returned to the patrol car. All the while, I searched the street, the houses, and every shadowy area I could see, looking for signs of an elderly man.

In my heart, I feared who it might have been. He was too old to be active, obviously, but he could easily be the patriarch of a Renegade clan. "Nothing that happens to us," Daddy once said, "happens by accident."

"So, tell us again how this happened," the older patrolman said when we were driving to the hospital.

"We were talking. I turned to the right, and the next thing I knew, we were crashing into a mailbox. Jim told me an elderly man stepped in front of the car."

"If you were looking to the right, he would have had to come from the left. It's a busy street. That's no place to cross it."

"Which is why Mr. Lamb had to turn so suddenly," I said.

Tom turned back and smiled at me, as if he appreciated how I was defending Jim Lamb.

"Whenever you lose control, you know you're going too fast," the older patrolman insisted.

"He wasn't," I countered firmly. "He's a very conservative person. He teaches at the Adams School for Girls."

"I know some teachers who aren't so conservative," the older patrolman said.

Tom laughed. "He's referring to his brother-in-law."

"Among others."

"Is he your boyfriend?" Tom asked me.

"Hardly. I've been here only two days."

"Two days! And you're in an accident already? That's bad luck," the older patrolman said. "But you look fine."

"She looks more than fine," Tom said. He smiled at me again.

Twenty minutes later, I found myself sitting in the

ER waiting room. I had given my personal information to the receptionist, who didn't look all that surprised to learn that I had no health insurance.

"Everyone your age thinks he or she doesn't need it, and then you're here in the ER suddenly, and everyone else has to pay for it."

"I can pay for it myself," I told her. "I don't even need to be here. I'm fine. The policemen insisted."

She shrugged. "Take a seat," she said.

When another quarter of an hour had passed, I debated gathering my bags and calling for a taxi, but before I could, a nurse came heading my way. She was smiling so brightly that for a moment, I thought she had mistaken me for someone else, someone she knew. I thought she was very pretty, with a bob-inspired, one-length cut to her light brown hair. It had an off-center parting and razor-softened ends. When she drew closer, I recognized those blue eyes. This was Ken Dolan's daughter. She was about five feet eight, with a buxom but trim figure. Now that I studied her a little more, I realized that she had Liam's smile.

"As soon as I saw your name, I thought, That's my father's new secretary. Am I right?" she asked.

"Yes."

"Are you okay? What happened?" she asked, and quickly sat beside me. "Oh, I'm Julia Dolan," she added.

I summed up the accident for her.

"And he was nowhere around afterward? Freaky," she said. She looked around. "C'mon with me," she said. "I'll help you with those," she added, reaching for a few of my bags.

She led me to an examination room and looked me over closely before taking my blood pressure.

"Any pains, aches?"

"No, nothing."

"You don't even look a little shaken up, and there's not a mark on your face."

"It all happened too fast. I was lucky I was leaning back."

"Yes, lucky. Dr. Knotts is on duty, but he's a bit overwhelmed. It's his third week here. I don't think he'll get to you for at least an hour, if not longer. There are four ahead of you."

"How's Mr. Lamb doing?"

"They took him to X-ray. He's quite banged up. That airbag hit him like a pie in the face. He'll be here for a good few hours, if not more, even though he's a priority," she added in a little over a whisper.

"I'm fine. I really don't have to stay. The police insisted on bringing me here, otherwise I would have just continued on to the Winston House. The younger officer was quite concerned. His name was Tom."

"Tom Westly," she said, nodding. "I'm sure he was quite concerned. I'm half surprised he didn't try to stay and hold your hand." She laughed.

"He was a bit of a flirt," I said.

"A bit? He thinks he's the Blue Streak, every girl's fantasy policeman, ready to put her in handcuffs and do an investigation."

I thought that was very funny. She was so much more outgoing and relaxed than Liam, and yet they had suffered the same family disaster.

"How did you know I was your father's new secretary?"

"Dad's been bragging about you. Normally, he feels uncomfortable around any woman who's less than twenty-five, thirty. We make him too nervous with our explosive, unpredictable energy, but you apparently have the demeanor of someone older, calmer, and what he calls man-sensible. He said you've restored his faith in the female species."

"I hope he continues to feel that way."

"I'm sure he will. I'm glad you're okay. I'll call a taxi for you."

"Thank you."

"Were you working on a relationship with Mr. Lamb?"

"No," I said. "He was just being . . ."

"Hopeful?"

"Something like that," I said, smiling. "He's very sweet, but I'm not looking for a romance just yet."

She nodded thoughtfully, started out, and then paused. "Maybe after you're settled in a bit, we can go out together, have a little dinner, and get to know each other better. I'm sort of seeing someone—actually, the radiologist on duty right now who'll handle Mr. Lamb—but with his schedule and mine, we're often like two ships passing in the night, if you know what I mean, and I hate to stay at home on my nights off."

"Yes. I'd love to go out with you when you're free."

"Maybe this weekend," she said. "Clifford, Dr. Longfellow, is on Saturday night. I'll call you." She flashed a smile and left.

She returned about ten minutes later to tell me a taxi would be pulling up outside the ER entrance any minute. She said Jim Lamb had been concerned about me, but she had managed to get a message up to him telling him that I was fine and heading home.

"Thanks," I said.

She helped me with my bags again.

"I have to build a whole new wardrobe," I explained as we walked out.

"Sounds like you left home in a hurry."

"That's an understatement," I told her. I smiled. "You mean you don't know?"

"Well, something," she admitted. "I look forward to hearing all about it. If you have any aches or pains during the night, just call the ER and ask for me. I'm here until six in the morning."

"Thanks. I'm fine."

The taxi pulled up, and the driver got out to help with my things.

"I'll call you," Julia said as I got into the taxi. She waved, and I sat back.

All the way to the Winston House, I looked out the windows, searching for signs of Thaddeus Bogosian, the elderly man I had met on the plane and the man I thought I had seen on the street in Quincy yesterday. If he was the same man Jim thought had stepped in front of his car, he had done so knowing that he would cause an accident. Why? Was he testing to see what would happen to me? Was he trying to hurt me? Or was this all just in my paranoid mind now? That could have been any old man I had seen or imagined, and it could easily have been another gentleman who wasn't watching where he was crossing and then had fled because he had caused an accident and didn't want to be blamed. If I permitted myself to be frightened away, how could I ever find any safe haven? Something similar would happen to me no matter how far away I went.

The taxi driver helped carry my bags to the front door of the Winston House, but before I could open it, Amelia and Mrs. McGruder were there, with Mr. Brady standing behind them. They had obviously been watching out the front window.

"How did this happen? Where is Naomi Addison? I thought she was taking you shopping. How did poor Jim Lamb get into this mess?" Mrs. Winston rattled off her questions in shotgun fashion.

"Let the girl get up to her room," Mrs. McGruder said, reaching for some of the bags. "I'll bring you something hot to eat," she told me.

"I'm fine," I said.

"She looks okay," Martin Brady said from behind. Both women turned and glared at him so sharply that he shrugged and retreated.

"You are probably in a little shock," Mrs. Winston insisted. "Just listen to Mrs. McGruder."

I nodded and followed them to the stairway.

"How is Mr. Lamb?" Mrs. McGruder asked me as we went up.

"He's still in radiology. He had some bad facial trauma from the airbag deploying."

"Didn't yours work, too?"

"Yes, but I was lucky," I said. "I was leaning away at the time and took the brunt of it lower down."

"Well, didn't that hurt?" Mrs. Winston asked.

"I'm fine," I said.

"You should probably take a warm bath and get into bed," she said.

"I'll bring you some tea and toast and jam," Mrs. McGruder told me as we reached my room and they carried my bags in.

"Let me help you put your things away," Mrs. Winston offered.

"I'm fine," I told her. "Really. No need to worry."

"Um," she said, pressing her lips together. "What happened with Mrs. Addison? How did you come to have Mr. Lamb taking you home?"

"Maybe you're being a little too nosy, Amelia," Mrs. McGruder told her. They looked at each other.

"Maybe, but something doesn't smell right to me," Mrs. Winston suggested.

"Let the girl settle herself. I'll bring up your tea and toast," she told me, and left.

Mrs. Winston hesitated, then said, "Mr. Lamb doesn't strike me as being a careless young man. Was he driving too fast?"

"No." I gave her an abbreviated version of the story.

She didn't look satisfied, but she nodded, offered to put away my new things again, and then, after I insisted I was fine, finally left, mumbling to herself.

I laughed, thinking about how she would attack

Naomi Addison the moment she stepped into the Winston House. I had all of my new things put away by the time Mrs. McGruder arrived with my tea and toast.

"How are you doing?" she asked.

"I'm fine. Really. This is very kind of you. Thank you," I said.

"Well, don't hesitate to call on either of us if you need something. Sometimes you don't realize how hurt you are until much later. That happened to me one winter when I slipped and fell on some ice. I thought I was more embarrassed than anything, but it turned out I had a fractured hip bone."

I started to sip the tea and eat some of the toast and jam. Mrs. McGruder smiled and left, and then I did decide to soak in a hot bath and go to sleep. A little after midnight, I awoke to the sound of loud voices and realized that Mrs. Winston had been waiting to greet Naomi Addison.

"When you offer to do something for someone, you don't just up and leave her like that. If you had done what you promised, she wouldn't have been in any accident, and Mr. Lamb wouldn't still be in the hospital. They have him under observation because he suffered a slight concussion," I heard Mrs. Winston say.

"They're both adults. You can't blame me for that. How is Lorelei?"

"She's fine. Luckily. I can tell you this," Mrs. Winston added. "If you're hoping to get to my nephew through her somehow, you can bury that plan in the cemetery of bad ideas."

"I don't need anyone to help me get to any man," Naomi retorted. "I'm giving you notice. I don't have to tolerate this."

"Your notice is welcomed," Mrs. Winston said.

The moment Naomi reached the top of the stairway, the lights went out. I heard her cursing under her breath as she made her way to her room. Either deliberately or because she had limited illumination, she made a lot of noise going into the bathroom and back to her room.

All of it brought a smile to my face. Mrs. Winston and Mrs. McGruder had no special abilities or powers, but there couldn't be two more protective people when it came to me. Despite what had happened, I closed my eyes and felt snugly safe in their rooming house. The shadows could surround it, and the dark figures could loiter in them, but it was as though I had luckily found an island upon which nothing that wished to harm me could set foot.

For a little while, at least, that pleased me, even though I knew that it was the world outside, the world I had to be in, where I was now as vulnerable to the horrors of the darkest places in my imagination as ordinary human beings were.

10

The two of them were just as concerned about me at breakfast as they were when I had returned from the hospital the night before. They hovered over me like two private-duty nurses, making sure I ate well. Of course, I wasn't used to such mothering. Mrs. Fennel had always been intolerant of any weakness or pain in any of us. As an infant, I was forbidden to cry too much or too long, and I quickly realized that crying didn't get me anything anyway. Mrs. Fennel had never been physically rough with me. She had never struck me or spanked me; she didn't have to do that. Her stern looks, with those gold-tinted black eyes that were like laser beams cutting through me, were far more than enough to get me to swallow back a wail or a sob.

Tall and thin, with a hardness in her arms and body that had me believing she was made of iron until I saw her naked once, Mrs. Fennel had radiated a firmness and confidence that gave me, my younger sister Marla, Ava, and I'm sure our older sister Brianna a sense of security. As long as she was there, nothing could harm us. Even germs feared her. No one ever got sick or injured.

None of us ever needed a Band-Aid. The first time I saw a bruise on another girl at school, I wondered what it was. Did she have a disease?

Since I had left my father, my sisters, and Mrs. Fennel, however, I wondered if I had already lost my invulnerability. This car accident and how I had come out of it without even an irritation on my body convinced me that I still had most, if not all, of whatever special gifts I once possessed. Would they stay, or would they slowly diminish? As nutty as it might sound, I wanted to be like everyone else even more now and was willing to give that up.

Naomi didn't show up for breakfast while I was still there. I was happy for that. Mrs. Winston, unbeknownst to me, had called Mr. Dolan early in the morning, and he had arranged for Michael Thomas to swing by to take me to work. Mr. Dolan was just learning about what had happened from his daughter, Julia, when she returned from her night shift. Of course, I protested over all this concern, but no one would hear of it. Whether I liked it or not, I was being adopted into the lives of these people. Did I dare think it? It was almost like having a family again.

Michael wanted to hear all about the accident when I got into his truck. After I told him, he went into his own experiences with auto accidents.

"I had an airbag explode on me once, too," he said. "Some idiot backed out of his driveway without looking. It was little more than a fender-bender, but I had bruises on my face for weeks. You were really lucky. All of us were. We wouldn't want to lose that pretty face."

I thanked him.

It was funny about compliments. I knew it was wrong not to be modest and show your appreciation when you received them, but I had grown up in a house where it was assumed we would always stand out when we were with normal girls. The difficulty for me, more than it obviously was for Ava, was how not to seem conceited or arrogant. The truth was, I was grateful for every kind word now, every sincere show of appreciation and concern.

Mr. Dolan also showed his concern about me as soon as I arrived. He told me to take whatever time off I needed if I had any aches or pains. I assured him that I was fine and went right to work to prove it.

"You're a real trouper," he said before going back into his office.

Liam was standing in front of me only moments later. "Julia told me what happened," he began. "I thought you were going shopping with Naomi Addison. I would have been glad to take you shopping last night."

"I did go shopping with her. She decided she didn't want to stay in the mall with me any longer. Mr. Lamb just happened by when I was leaving."

"I should have given you my cell-phone number just in case. Maybe this wouldn't have happened."

"It wasn't Mr. Lamb's fault," I said.

"Oh, right. I'm sure he just happened by. He didn't wait too long to pounce," Liam said disdainfully.

"Neither did you," I retorted. The aggressive manner in which I came back at him took him by surprise.

"What, you like this guy?"

"I don't dislike him, but I told you, I'm not looking to like anyone just now."

He nodded but stood there, obviously debating whether to say something.

"What?" I asked.

"Some of the guys here are thinking you might be gay."

"Really?" I sat back, remembering how Ava could dispose of any young man she wasn't interested in. They were always bitter when they were rejected and usually found a way to blame her.

"How typical," I said, recalling what I called her "male lessons." "The last thing a man will think is that if he's rejected, it was something about him, some way his fault. It always has to be something else, like the girl is gay."

Liam laughed. "Okay, okay. Got it. I'm around if you need anything or have to go anywhere."

"You're supposed to be doing that Bronson bid today, aren't you?" I asked. "That should keep you busy most of the day."

"Jeez, you're more of a nag than my father," he muttered, but I saw him smile to himself as he sauntered off. I knew he was thinking that I knew about his responsibilities because I was, despite how I appeared, interested in him. Maybe I was, but I wasn't about to admit it yet. Maybe I never would.

What I did realize about myself and other girls was that unraveling our true inner feelings was like navigating a maze planted somewhere between our hearts and our minds. People wandered about confused for years, maybe most of their lives, before they discovered who they really were and what they really wanted. That would be fine for them, but perhaps for me, it might inevitably be too late. A lost true love, with kisses drifting on the wind and embraces left only to imagine, was as dark a fate as any from which I had fled.

Everyone was extra nice to me all day. I had lunch again with the other women who worked at the company. Naturally, they were interested in the details of the accident. Afterward, I called the hospital and spoke briefly with Jim. He kept apologizing, but I pointed out that he was the one in the hospital, not I. He said they would release him the next day, but only if he promised to take off the remainder of the week. I did feel sorry for him. If a Renegade was out there and had caused him to lose control of his car, I was indirectly responsible.

It also occurred to me that I could be the one considered a Renegade.

I recalled what Daddy and Mrs. Fennel had explained when I was first told about them. Mark Daniels, a boy at school, had been pursuing me romantically, and I was attracted to him. When he came to our house one night with lethal intentions, my father destroyed him. Of course, I had been full of questions, the main one being who was Mark Daniels?

"He was a member of a Renegade family," Daddy had told me. "That's a family like us who do not follow the rules. Every family has its own territory. These things are decided in advance. There's good planning here, careful planning, so nothing is left to chance. No other family must settle in territory claimed by another. For two families to be there, to operate there, would do much to bring more and possibly fatal attention to us. There are other rules. No daughter is ever to be chosen to be a victim. Once something like that occurs, there are power struggles. We end up destroying ourselves. The Renegades don't care."

"That's not the only difference. There's something wrong with them," Mrs. Fennel had said, her teeth clenched to show just how much she despised them. "They have a ruthless bloodlust. One feeding a month is never enough."

Now I realized another possibility and understood the full meaning of what Ava had been telling me when she had said running away was dangerous. What if I had entered another family's territory? There was always that chance when someone like me ventured out alone, denying her own family and trying to break ties. Did they think I was establishing myself there and that my family would follow? In their minds, I would fit the definition of a Renegade, and they might be out to destroy me.

Would I be able to recognize them? I hadn't been able to recognize what Mark Daniels was. Had I matured enough to strengthen that perception, or was I still vulnerable when it came to others of our kind? I had been sensing some danger, something pursuing me, but I was still unsure, even after this accident, that it wasn't just a figment of my active imagination, made more active because of the fears generated by fleeing my father and sisters.

Mr. Dolan checked on me twice in the morning and was finally satisfied that I was doing okay. Later that afternoon, Liam came by to meet with his father and make a report on his bidding work. They were in his office for nearly an hour. When Liam came out, he smiled at me, but to my surprise, he hurried off without another word. Mr. Dolan emerged moments afterward. I could see the satisfaction in his face. The tension I had immediately observed whenever he was with his son was gone.

"I don't know whether I should be thanking you or what, but he's suddenly showing interest in his work and approaching something called responsibility."

"Sometimes all it takes is convincing someone you have faith in him," I said.

He looked at me strangely for a moment. "One of these days soon, I'd like to spend some downtime with you, Lorelei, and learn how you came to be so wise at so young an age."

I smiled, remembering what my father had told me concerning wisdom. I think I was just twelve at the time. Now it seemed like ages ago, and as with all my good memories, when I recalled them, I wasn't sure whether they were just dreams and wishes or real events.

"My father once told me we're not so unlike sponges when it comes to wisdom. Just like some sponges can hold more, absorb more, different people have different capabilities when it comes to taking in what we might call common sense. Mrs. Winston has plaques with quotes all over the house. One of them is 'There is nothing more uncommon than common sense.'"

"Maybe I should send Liam over to read his great-aunt's walls," he said. He started to turn to go back into his office but stopped, smiling at me. "Something tells me he'll be around there more often, and it won't be because I tell him to visit."

I took a deep breath when he closed his door. Mr. Dolan's terrible marriage experience not only made him cautious and skeptical when it came to other women he might date, but it also gave him grave concern for Liam's relationships. What I had learned already was that Liam was in and out of so many so quickly that he appeared incapable of having any substantial involvement.

How difficult it must have been growing up under the circumstances Liam experienced. Surely, at a young age, he had witnessed his father's great sorrow and disappointment. I realized that it would be harder for a son than for a daughter, because he would have his father's disastrous relationship as a prime example of how it could be with women. I didn't have to be an amateur psychiatrist to realize how his home life and his mother's desertion had affected the way he conducted himself with women and reacted to his own feelings.

Probably the thing I had anticipated the least after I fled from my father and sisters was my feeling sorry for someone else in this world. Right now, I was feeling sorry for poor Jim Lamb, Mr. Dolan, and Liam. They added to the heavy bag of sorrow I was carrying because of how I'd had to leave Buddy. It was impossible not to envision him standing there in that restaurant, stunned, his heart sinking when he discovered I was gone. What I kept thinking about now was the possibility that he thought my father and my sisters had found me while he was in the bathroom and taken me off. I hoped he had asked someone about me and that someone had seen me walk out freely. Perhaps they had seen me getting into Moses's truck. Eventually, he would understand my reason, but that wouldn't diminish his pain. I had deserted someone who loved me, too, but I'd had very good reasons to do so.

Even though I wanted to walk home after work and could certainly do it easily, Mr. Dolan insisted that I let him drive me. I was surprised at his offer at first, but then I realized that he was looking for any opportunity where he could be more personal. I saw Liam standing in the front window of one of the showrooms, watching enviously when his father and I left together. Mr. Dolan had explained that Liam, on his own, had decided to work overtime to catch up on things he had let slide.

Whom was he trying to impress more, I wondered, his father or me?

"My aunt told me your story, of course," Mr. Dolan began as we left the parking lot, "but only in a brief outline in her special Aunt Amelia way. To be honest, I was positive she had exaggerated about you and agreed to the interview more to please her than anything. What a wonderful surprise to find that she was more than right."

"Thank you, Mr. Dolan."

"If it doesn't disturb you to talk about it, tell me how you came to decide to up and leave your father."

"It's painful to remember all of the details. The

situation simply became impossible for me. My father was no longer capable of seeing anything from my point of view or, more accurately, of tolerating it. It was better for all of us."

"He'll come to regret it someday," Mr. Dolan said. I knew that deep in his heart, he was hoping that was also true for his ex-wife. "Whatever spell he's under now, he can't be sorry he had enjoyed you for so long. He must have been very proud of you very often."

"I like to think so," I said.

"Well, I hope you can be happy here and enjoy working for us. I have some big ideas for expansion but have held back on them until I was certain that Liam would be a real part of my efforts. I'm not totally convinced yet. Let's just say I'm a little more hopeful."

"He'll come through for you," I said.

He was silent for a few moments. "I know he's very fond of you already. To be honest, I think what's impressed him the most is your reluctance to ask how high when he said to jump."

"Yes, well, I'm not quite ready to start a relationship, and I told him so. However, I'd be a liar if I told you he wasn't very good-looking and personable. But don't tell him I said so," I added quickly, and he laughed.

Just before we pulled into the driveway at the Winston House, I told Mr. Dolan about Naomi Addison hoping to get to him through me. He listened but didn't say anything until we stopped and he turned off the engine.

"I don't mean to influence you to be against her, but

I don't like being thought of as anyone's little spy. She strikes me as someone who's capable of saying something like that in the end. People who are disappointed can be cruel," I said.

"Very, very true. Don't worry about it. I know about Naomi. My aunt doesn't let anything get past her. I've never given Naomi Addison any indication that I would be interested in a relationship with her. Don't you give it a second thought."

He followed me into the house so he could say hello to his aunt. She and Mrs. McGruder were just setting the dinner table. I saw that there was one place setting missing and felt sorry again for Jim Lamb.

"Hello, Auntie," Ken said. They hugged. He hugged Mrs. McGruder, too.

"What a nice surprise. You're welcome to have dinner with us," Mrs. Winston said immediately.

"Oh, thank you, but I have a dinner meeting all set."

"You have to relax a little once in a while, Kenneth Sullivan Dolan. Your mother was always worried about you burning out. Even as a young boy, he was ambitious and a determined worker," she told me.

"I will, Auntie Amelia. Promise. Well, our new girl seems fine. But keep your eye on her. I don't want to lose her this soon," he added, winking at me.

He visited for a while longer and then left. Before I went up to change for dinner, Mrs. Winston told me that Naomi Addison had checked out.

"I'd hate to think it was my fault. I didn't mean to bring you any problems," I said.

"Nonsense. I regretted taking her in almost the day

she moved in. I knew what she had on her mind. If I even hinted that my nephew might stop by, she would plant herself in that living room like a piece of furniture."

I told her I had spoken to Jim Lamb and that he was planning to return the next day. She already knew about it. Mrs. McGruder and she were thinking about how they would accommodate his recovery. They were obviously very fond of him.

Most of my young life, either Mrs. Fennel, Daddy, or one of my older sisters would warn me about people. From the way they spoke, we were immune to the seven deadly sins that at one time or another took over their lives. They had spoken about it as if we were more in danger of becoming their victims than they were in of becoming ours.

But so far in this, my first experience of living among them, I had found much to recommend them. The kindness and loving concern in Mrs. Winston and Mrs. McGruder especially made me question the harsh sketches and depictions of people that my family had imposed on me. Perhaps, I thought, they lived with these thoughts to rationalize what they were destined to be and to do. It was always easier to kill a poisonous snake or spider than to kill a graceful bird whose only fault was being too trusting. Jim Lamb reminded me of a fragile, gentle bird.

I didn't see him until I returned from work the following day. At my determined insistence, I refused all offers for a ride home and finally took the walk I had wanted to take from the first day. The late-spring sun held the eager darkness back a little longer every day now. Despite always being told that darkness was our friend, I walked at a pace that would get me to the Winston House before the shadows began their snaillike crawl toward one another.

All along the street, men and women were returning from work. At some houses, children who had been waiting at windows anticipating the arrival of their fathers or mothers came running out to greet them as soon as they were out of their cars. I couldn't help but remember the times I had been there to greet my father after he had been gone for days. When I was very young, I couldn't wait to hear him call for me the moment he came through the front door.

"Where's my Lorelei? Where's my little angel?" he would cry, and I would come around the corner, shyly at first, and then, bursting with happiness, rush into his powerful arms. I had thought he had the strength to toss me into a cloud. His laughter had resonated throughout the house. Ava would appear behind me, her eyes two pools of green envy.

"And you, my darling?" he would ask her. "How have you been? Didn't you miss me just as much?"

More timidly, more reserved and ladylike, she would approach to hug him. More often than not, he would have some sort of gift for us, such as new necklaces or rings or bracelets. Even if he had been gone for only two days, he would want to hear about every moment that had passed and how we had filled it. I had always felt as if he were memorizing the sound of my voice, the music of my laughter, and the love for him in my eyes. His attention had been so strong and so intense that I had felt absorbed into him.

Right now, I paused to listen to some children laughing. I heard people greeting each other, asking how they were, how their day had been. No one watching me and seeing me seize on every syllable, every smile and hug, would understand how much it all meant to me. I was like a visitor from another planet, amused and delighted in the joy these inhabitants had in their world. I yearned to be a part of it. If Daddy were there and saw the smile on my face, he would know that there was no longer any reason to pursue me. I would never return.

Of course, if he was pursuing me or sending Ava after me, bringing me back might not be his purpose.

Out of nowhere, a cold chill slipped under the sunshine and down my back. I shivered and then walked faster toward the Winston House. When I drew closer, my attention was drawn to the windows of my room. I was sure that I saw a curtain parting and Thaddeus Bogosian looking down at me.

He was gone as quickly as he had appeared.

Please, I thought, *let that be my overworked imagination.*

11

"Well, thank goodness you're home," Mrs. Winston said as soon as I entered.

I barely heard her. My first thoughts went to what I thought I had seen up in my room. Was he waiting for me there? I doubted that Mrs. Winston would permit any guest to wait in a tenant's room without the tenant present.

"Lorelei?"

"What? Oh. I'm okay, Amelia," I said, thinking that she had heard that I was walking back and had been worried about me. "I had no problem."

"Yes, I can see that, and I'm glad, but you have a stubborn young man in the living room who won't go up to his room and rest as the doctor ordered until he sees you to confirm that you are indeed all right."

She stepped back from the living-room entrance so I could enter.

"Jim?"

"Who else? Please tell him he has to follow the doctor's orders, or he'll only make things worse for himself.

Apparently, he needs to hear it from you," she added firmly when I didn't move.

"Yes, of course," I said, and hurried in.

Jim was sitting back on the sofa. He wore a light blue robe and black fur-lined slippers and looked as if he had been in a brutal prizefight in which his opponent didn't wear gloves. Days later, the bruises from the airbag were larger, darker, and deeper. He was also in a neck brace.

"Why aren't you upstairs in bed?" I demanded, looking as cross as I could.

"I'm not as bad as I look," he said, leaning forward. He was staring up at me, almost as if he didn't know who I was. He looked as if he had fallen under a spell. He smiled. "I'm truly amazed at you, Lorelei."

"Why?" Had he seen something, realized something, and learned something that I'd rather no one there knew?

"You really didn't get a scratch. I'm so happy."

"Oh," I said, relieved. "I told you I was fine. Now, you had better listen to Mrs. Winston and your doctors and go back to your room."

"He knows we're bringing his dinner up to him," Mrs. Winston said. She was standing right behind me. "And he knows he's not to be walking around the first day home, for sure."

"I feel terrible having everyone wait on me. I can walk up and down the stairs and sit at the dinner table. The doctor didn't say I was confined to my room. Exactly."

"Maybe we don't want to look at you," Mrs. Winston said, half kidding. "It could ruin our appetites."

"Oh. Well, I'm sorry. I didn't mean—"

"Look at him," she told me. "He's ready to burst into tears."

"Jim, she's only kidding. You should follow the doctor's orders and give yourself a chance to heal. I'll stop by to see you after dinner."

That put a smile back on his face. "I never properly apologized for all of this," he said, rising. "I know I must have looked like a fool driving into that mailbox, but I would swear on my mother's grave that there was an elderly man standing right in front of us."

"Sure, put it all on your mother, even now," Mrs. Winston said. "Just like all you young people these days," she added, as if she had actually lived during the time of John Adams.

"I was just trying to impress Lorelei that I had no choice but to turn quickly and—"

"I'm not blaming you, Jim. I told you that. C'mon. Go up to your room and relax. I'll walk up with you," I said.

He nodded and headed out. Mrs. Winston gave me a nod of approval for how I was handling him. She followed us to the foot of the stairs. I looked up. Had I imagined it, or was he there in my room waiting for me? It was on the tip of my tongue to say something, to ask Mrs. Winston about it, but I held back.

I followed Jim to his room. Mrs. Winston or Mrs. McGruder had brought him additional pillows, and there was a tray at the foot of his bed. His room was very neat and organized. There was an antique maple hutch with a drop-down secretary desk on the right. A small pile of books and some papers were on the desk.

He nodded at it. "My substitute teacher sent along the essays I had assigned last week. The problem is, I get a little headache every time I start reading."

"They'll just have to wait," I said. "Go on. Get into bed. I'll stop by later."

"So, you're really not mad at me?" he asked.

"Of course not, Jim. You did what you thought you had to do."

"But the police claim there was no one at the scene of the accident fitting the description I gave them."

"Once he saw what he had caused, he ran off. Case closed," I said.

He nodded. "You really look great," he said. "I'm very relieved."

"Thank you. Now, get yourself better or I will get mad."

"Right," he said, and headed for his bed.

I waited a moment and then left, closing his door quietly behind me. For a long moment, I just stood there looking down the hallway at my door. As I stepped toward it gingerly, I could feel my heart begin to pound, the beat reverberating through my body and making my bones tremble. I had witnessed Daddy's attack on Mark Daniels. It was as if his body had turned into a tornado of darkness. Was that what awaited me on the other side of my door?

I could feel a defensive hardness coming into my body. I braced myself, listened for a moment, and then, gathering all of the courage I could, I turned the door-knob and entered.

There was no one standing there, but the air in the room felt like the cold air that strikes you when you open a freezer. I froze, waiting for the deep chill to pass. After a few more moments, it did, and I closed the door. I looked around carefully. There was no physical evidence of anyone having been in my room. Nothing looked touched or disturbed. I felt myself soften and relax.

However, I had no doubt that if Thaddeus was one of us, he would have no difficulty slipping in and out of practically anywhere unnoticed. That was why I believed he or someone like him had stepped in front of Jim's car, causing the accident.

I sat on my bed to think. Should I remain there, or should I pack up and leave quietly, perhaps during the night? Could I find a safer place? Was there anywhere in the world where I could disappear? I had no doubt that wherever Ava was, she was feeling confident about her predictions for me. Maybe she was expecting me simply to return after coming to the realization that she was right, that there was no escape.

This deepening sense of fear was a feeling I was unused to having. I had grown up believing that I would always be safe because Daddy would always be there to look after me. Even after the Renegade had come for me, I did not live in fear. There was no one stronger or smarter than my father.

But I had betrayed him and angered him. If he came after me now, it wouldn't be to protect me. No one here had the power or the ability to protect me, either. In fact, I had already endangered one of them by coming here. Who would be next? What was the use? I had to leave Buddy in order for him to survive. Why wouldn't that be true for anyone I liked or anyone who liked me? I had only two simple choices to make, I thought. I could return and see if I would be accepted into my family again, or I could flee and be a fugitive forever until somehow, somewhere, one of the dark forces caught up with me. All I was capable of doing was prolonging the inevitable.

Depression hung around me as I started to freshen up and change my clothes. The sun had lost its grip on the day, and shadows came charging through the windows to dull every bright and happy color. Even the sound of car horns turned mournful. It made me think of Shakespeare's line about graves that yawned. Troubled souls were released until morning to dance in the darkness. My gloom was nurtured and strengthened. Whatever joy had lit up my face dwindled until the bright candlelight in my eyes was reduced to weakened embers.

I didn't want anyone to see me like this. They might think I was being haunted by my past. Whatever sympathy they had felt for me would look pathetic. They'd want to show more and comfort me more. Until now, I had escaped too many personal questions. No one really had interrogated me on the details of my flight, nor did anyone challenge my story. I hoped that I could keep it that way for as long as I needed to, but not if I greeted them with these eyes. I had to find the strength to push back on the doleful memories that wanted to overwhelm me.

I hardened my heart, pinched my cheeks to bring back good color, and charged out of my room, closing the door on the gathering shadows that wanted to carry me off. I was confident that I could keep up my cheerful appearance.

Down at dinner, Martin Brady was full of questions, however. Like everyone else, he wanted to hear about the accident. Mrs. Winston pounced on him like a protective grandmother swatting away annoying flies from her granddaughter's face and hair, telling him that he was causing me to relive a nasty event just to satisfy his curiosity.

"Leave her be. She's just settling down after a horrendous experience. What she doesn't need at the moment is someone like you barking questions at her."

He apologized and tried to change the topic to Naomi Addison to find out what had happened there, but Mrs. Winston was determined not to be a gossip.

"I don't need to spread any more stories about that woman. She does a very good job of denigrating herself, thank you."

"Amen to that," Mrs. McGruder said, overhearing the conversation when she brought in a bowl of freshly made mashed potatoes.

Finally, having one door after another shut in his face, Mr. Brady started to talk about himself and his work. He rattled on about the difficulties in the business world today. Mrs. Winston gave me a smile of amusement after she asked some questions that would keep him talking about himself, which was obviously the topic he favored the most, anyway. Even I threw in a few questions about his travels and clients, which brought more smiles to Mrs. Winston. I felt as if she and I were conspirators.

To carry the conversation even further away from me, she began to describe how difficult it would have been for a traveling salesman to make any sort of living in Colonial times. Mr. Brady looked as if he would fall asleep at the table when she went into all that.

Just after dinner, Mrs. McGruder came in to tell me that I had a phone call. I could see the assumption on Mrs. Winston's face. She was expecting her great-nephew Liam Dolan to call me, I knew, but it turned out to be his sister, Julia.

"I was so happy to hear how well you're doing," she began.

"Thank you. Jim Lamb was sent home today."

"I know. How is he?"

"He looks terrible, but I didn't tell him that."

She laughed. "He'll be fine. Especially if you show him any attention."

"I like him, but I don't want him to get the wrong idea."

"Somehow I think you know how to handle that," she said. "Anyway, I'm calling to see if you're free Saturday, as we had discussed. Don't get trapped into babysitting Jim Lamb," she added quickly.

"No, I won't do that."

I thought about her invitation. Was I going to leave, or wasn't I? I'd like to get to know her more. What would it be like to have a real girlfriend? How much could I confide in her? I was always jealous of the girls at school who hung out together. They seemed to move in their own world, speak their own language, and have experiences I could only imagine. I had wanted to be part of all that back then, and I certainly wanted something like it now. The only time I had ever been out where people my age were enjoying themselves was when I was on a training session with Ava. The truth was, none of us had anything remotely resembling a social life. Could I? Would it be unfair, even dangerous, for Julia to be my friend?

"Well?" she asked when a long moment of silence had passed. "Do you have intentions of getting someone to ask you out? Is that why you're hesitating?"

"No, no. Yes," I said impulsively. "I'd love to go out with you."

"Great. I'll pick you up at seven. You'll love this place. Great food, great music. It's a happening place."

"You know I'm technically not of drinking age."

"Don't worry about it. We'll hang in the restaurant section. No one checks much there. I'll buy the drinks."

"Okay, thanks."

Mrs. Winston looked at me when I returned. She would never think of herself as a busybody. I knew she was simply concerned about me.

"That was your great-niece, Julia. I met her at the hospital."

"Oh, yes. She's a delightful young lady."

"She and I are going out this Saturday night."

"That's wonderful," she said. I couldn't tell if she

was disappointed or relieved that it wasn't Liam who had called for a date.

"I wish I had the energy to go out and party on weekends," Mr. Brady said. "Too often, I have to work on Saturdays."

"And too often, you imbibe with your prospective customers," Mrs. Winston said.

He started to protest and then stopped and admitted that she had a point. I left them talking about the benefits and dangers of alcohol. Mrs. Winston was already well into the most popular beverages in the John Quincy Adams White House. It brought a smile to my face as I left to do what I had promised and stopped in to see Jim after dinner.

"I guess I didn't give you such a great introduction to Quincy, Massachusetts," he said, still feeling sorry for himself and still trying to get me to say kind things.

"I never asked for that. You were very kind to worry about me and offer to take me home, Jim. Let's leave it at that. Get back on your feet, and go back to work."

He nodded, looked down for a moment, and then raised his head slowly. "Can I make a confession?" he asked.

"It's not necessary," I told him.

"But I'd like to be honest. Somehow, when I'm in your presence, I feel a greater need to be so. Not that I'm a dishonest person ordinarily," he quickly added.

"Okay, what is it?"

"I pretended to be leaving the mall and just happen to see you. I was there much earlier, watching you and Naomi. I saw her leave you, and that was when I planned how I would supposedly luckily spot you."

I nodded softly. "I'm flattered," I said. He started to smile. "But it's only fair to tell you that I'm not looking for a romantic involvement right now. I've just come off a very hard disappointment. I need time and space. I'm not even sure I'm going to stay here."

His face, even his bruises, lost color instantly. "Why not?" he practically whined. "You have a great new job, and I heard from Mrs. Winston how much Mr. Dolan likes you already. Why would you consider leaving?"

"It's complicated," I said. "For now, I appreciate your friendship, but let's not think of it as much more."

He swallowed his disappointment so hard that it made his Adam's apple bounce, but I thought I had to say what I had said. I didn't want to hurt or disappoint someone as vulnerable as he was. Looking at him, all banged up and already head over heels about me, I couldn't help thinking what an easy target he would be for Ava or even for me if I were doing what Daddy expected of me. Now that I was thinking about that in relation to him, I also thought about the young men who had introduced themselves to me at Dolan Plumbing Supply. All of them were prime prey. They looked as if they would be willing to fall into any trap I had set. Why was it so easy?

I had always thought Ava was joking when she told me that we had a special aroma that excited the lust in men.

"We almost don't have to be sexy and attractive," she had said. "Not that we aren't."

"I don't smell anything different about you, nor did I smell anything different about Brianna," I had told her.

"You can't. Only a man can, but we have to direct it at the one we target when we're ready, when we have chosen him."

"How?"

"Just concentrating on him," she had told me, and then she'd laughed.

I had never asked Daddy or Mrs. Fennel about it. I'd thought she was just teasing me. Anyway, if she had been telling the truth, I didn't think I had concentrated on any young man long enough or with any sort of desire yet. I did the best I could to avoid that with Liam, and I certainly didn't feel any sexual attraction to Jim Lamb.

"When will you make up your mind about whether you will stay here or not?" Jim asked mournfully.

"I don't know. Soon, perhaps," I said. "I don't want to get too involved if I think I'm not right for this place. Anyway, don't you worry about that now, Jim. Concentrate on yourself."

"Who else have I had to concentrate on?" he asked, angry enough to bring some heat into his face.

I couldn't help it. Whenever any of us saw someone soaking in self-pity, we were literally nauseated. "There's no one at school?"

"School? Oh, no. All of the women there are old enough to be my mother."

"Maybe Quincy isn't right for you, then," I said, a little more harshly than I had intended, but Julia's words still rang in my ears about how I would deal with

Jim's interest in me: "Somehow, I think you know how to handle that."

I was doing so right now, but I couldn't escape knowing that it was cruel to do it while he was so weak, just beginning his recuperation. I hadn't thought I had this hard impatience and indifference in me. I guessed I was learning more about myself during this escape than I had thought I would, and I had to accept the possibility that I might not like everything I learned.

"I'm a little tired myself," I continued. "I think I'll do a little reading and go to sleep. You have a good night. I'll see you tomorrow."

"Right," he said. "Thanks for stopping by."

I smiled at him and turned to leave.

"Oh, there was one other thing," he said before I reached the door.

"What's that?"

"At the risk of your thinking I'm crazy or still very shaken up from the accident . . ."

"What is it, Jim?"

He looked down again.

"Just say it," I told him, now impatient with his shyness.

"I feel like such a silly teenager, having spied on you like that at the mall."

"Yes? I'll live. So?"

"Last night, when I was going over the accident for the hundredth time, I remembered that I had seen that elderly man before."

I turned completely back to him. "Where?"

"In the mall. He seemed to be spying on you, too."

I stared at him. I had felt nothing in the mall, no threat, no sense of being watched. That was unusual. "Are you sure of that?"

He shook his head. "So much of it is a blur now. It's an image I see, but . . . maybe that is part of my nutty imagination. I mean, I see him in the mall, and then he just appears in front of the car, and then no one can find him or claims to have seen him rushing off? Sounds nuts. I know what I'm doing. No one has to tell me."

"What are you doing?"

"Searching for a way to blame someone else for my own stupidity."

I wanted to reassure him, but I didn't. There was no way to do that without opening a portal to a world that would surely make a man like him afraid to take one step out of his room, much less out of the Winston House.

"Forget it," I said. "Just get better."

I left quickly.

Naturally, what Jim had just told me made me even more concerned. So much of what Daddy had done when he was gone and whom he knew, not only in America but in other countries, was left mysterious. No matter how close to him I had felt, there was always a line I couldn't cross, a question I shouldn't ask. Why wasn't it possible that Thaddeus knew him, reported to him, and even carried out his orders? Daddy knew that I couldn't be hurt in such a minor car accident, but he also knew that Jim Lamb could be. Anyone I knew could be. Was this a way of telling me so?

What if I had just introduced the possibility of Julia being hurt by agreeing to our date together?

I felt like someone who was afraid to turn left or right, to step forward or backward. But as I sat there worrying, I suddenly felt a surge of defiance and anger swell under my breasts. I was, after all, one of Daddy's daughters of darkness. Looking at myself in the mirror, I saw the fire and strength in my eyes, like two tiny tunnels through which I could see banners of confidence and pride flown by my ancestors throughout the ages. I would not sit in my room trembling like some terrified child. I would not run off with my tail between my legs, limping and whining through the darkness, chased by hounds of the night gnashing their teeth. Anything worthwhile, Mrs. Fennel had once told me, was worth fighting to keep or to get. Well, I thought, living in Quincy could very well be worthwhile to me.

I went to sleep that night defiant and eager for the following morning to get up and go to work. I rose much earlier than I had the day before. Mrs. McGruder was just rising herself and was surprised to see me enter the kitchen.

"I don't need much for breakfast today, just a little toast and jam," I told her.

She hurried to put up the coffee. "That's not much of a breakfast for a workin' girl," she told me. "My father used to say a good breakfast puts wind in your sails."

"I'll be fine," I said, and drank some orange juice, more to satisfy her than myself. I still had my problems eating food that didn't contain Mrs. Fennel's miraculous herbs, which she had grown in her own garden.

Mrs. Winston was surprised to find me finishing up

my toast and coffee when she stepped into the dining room. "Couldn't you sleep?" she asked.

"I had a very good night's sleep, thank you. I want to walk to work before someone volunteers to pick me up," I added pointedly.

She nodded. "Well, we'll look after Mr. Lamb."

"I'm sure you will," I said. "He's lucky to have you two. Doesn't he have any family near?"

"In Boston, his mother, a widow. He's an only child, but anyone could see that."

"Why?"

She paused to smile at me. "People who have siblings are more competitive. It's been that way since Cain and Abel."

But as far as she knew, I realized, I was an only child. Why didn't she think the same of me? Or did she?

She looked at me as though she could hear my thoughts. "That's what puzzles me about you, dear," she said. "You have strong independence." She shrugged. "Maybe that came from the competition you had for your father's affections."

If you only knew, I thought.

But if you did, you'd not only chase me out of your home. You'd chase me out of your memory.

12

The rest of the week was so uneventful and ordinary that every passing day was indistinguishable from the one before or the one after. The big news at the Winston House was that Jim's doctor gave him the green light to return to work on Monday. I didn't visit him in his room anymore, and I tried to spend as much time talking to Mr. Brady, Mrs. Winston, and Mrs. McGruder as I did talking to him, but it was obvious to the others that he wasn't discouraged. I avoided saying anything harsh to him, since he was still on the mend.

Meanwhile, I barely saw or spoke to Liam Dolan. He was there every day, but he was at his work with a vigor and intensity that seemed to lift a weight of worry off his father's shoulders. When I did see him, he flashed his charming smile, gave me a "How are you doing?" or sometimes just nodded in passing through. From the paperwork I filed, I could see that he was really taking on his responsibilities.

Mr. Dolan's only comment to me about him had all sorts of double meanings for me. "When it comes to my son, we've seen night, and now we see some day."

I just smiled.

I looked forward to the walk to and from the company. Some of the people on Mrs. Winston's street who were getting used to seeing me waved; some stopped whatever they were doing to say hello or ask how I was doing, as if they had known me for years. I began to feel a coziness about it all, as if I could wrap the community around myself snugly and feel myself settling into the welcoming smiles. We had never lived long enough anywhere or close enough to any people to feel a sense of neighborhood. Daddy had always said it was better to be inconspicuous except with those of our own kind. We were an island unto ourselves, no matter where we were.

Both Mrs. Winston and Mrs. McGruder seemed to blossom under the glow I was feeling. The windows were opened wider, curtains drawn back. At dinner, they talked about changing drapes, maybe a rug here and there to bring in more color, and even possibly modernizing some of the kitchen. They were constantly asking my opinion. There was much in the house that Mrs. Winston would never replace, of course. For her, historical artifacts were as sacred as religious icons and relics.

She had an armoire filled with old clay pipes from the seventeenth and early eighteenth centuries and could explain all of the details about them and other things such as buckles, coins, cutlery and spoons, locks, and wig curlers. There was a colonial rocking chair in the living room that was out-of-bounds for anyone. No one could sit in it. Whether he was kidding me or not, Mr. Brady told me he had stepped into the living room and seen the chair rocking to a standstill many times.

"Would you know it if you sat on a ghost's lap? Ask about any one of these old things," Mr. Brady warned me, "and prepare yourself for a lecture not only about the item but who used it and why whatever it is is better than the modern-day replacement."

I took his advice, but I didn't mind whenever Mrs. Winston went on about one of her prize antiques. It brought the big house to life by giving the furniture and the artifacts their own histories, even their own personalities. This was the grouchy chair, because Sir Isaac Caldwell, from whom it could be traced, suffered gout and took out his unhappiness on his wife and children, for example. Mrs. Winston had the letters or diaries to prove it, as she could prove that the Windsor chair in the den once belonged to William Smith, Abigail Adams's father. Like pedigreed dogs, practically everything in the old house had papers to authenticate it.

Maybe I was living in a museum, but there was a warmth to it. I appreciated what Mrs. Winston said about modern homes being way stations, "as temporary for the families living in them as were mass-produced modular houses." That was, after all, how I had lived and how I would have continued to live. Putting down roots anywhere for too long was not something we could do.

Was I being a silly Pollyanna, dreaming of having a life in that small city and eventually meeting someone I could love and with whom I could even have children? I could almost hear Ava laughing at the very thought and see Daddy shaking his head in pity. Would I ever forget Mrs. Fennel's look of rage on that horrible final day? Sometimes, even now, I would stop whatever I was doing and stare at my wall of memories and think again about just packing up quietly and sneaking off in the night.

But I didn't, and I woke on Saturday morning full of both anticipation and anxiety about my date with Julia. This would be my first night out with anyone besides Ava and Buddy.

Jim had to go get his car from the auto-body repair shop that morning. He asked me to go with him and have lunch with him, but I told him I was just going to do a little shopping nearby and wash clothes. I made sure he knew that I was going out in the evening with Julia Dolan, too.

"I don't blame you for not wanting to ride in a car with me again," he said bitterly. "Or even wanting to be seen with me."

He was referring to his lingering bruises, which were healing well but remained like large spots of measles on his cheeks, chin, and forehead. I could just imagine how the girls in his classes would react when he returned on Monday. No one had to tell me how cruel teenage girls could be. They'd giggle behind his back and come up with derogatory names for him.

"That has nothing to do with it," I told him.

The Ava in me made my face flush with impatience and annoyance. Jim was the first man I'd known who was so whiny and meek. If Ava or Brianna had brought him home to Daddy, I was sure he'd have turned him out. Lust and virility were two ingredients in the blood he sought. Ava, in one of her moods of sick humor, had told me, "You don't bring meat loaf home to Daddy; you bring filet mignon, or you don't bring anything."

"Nothing happened to me, Jim. It was a freak accident. I'm not afraid to ride in your car again, and I'm not worried about being seen with someone who's recovering from injuries. Don't be ridiculous," I said more forcefully.

"I'm sorry. I just thought . . . okay. Maybe I'll see you before you go out tonight," he followed, and then hurried off to get his car. I'm sure my indignant look put fire in my eyes such as he had never seen.

I actually did what I had told Jim I was going to do, shopping at the small mall nearby and then washing clothes. Later, I spent a lot of time on my hair and makeup for the first time since I had arrived. I remembered how much attention Ava would give to her appearance, no matter what she was doing or where she was going. It was as if there were cameras turned on her the moment she would step out of our house. I had been just a little girl then. Sometimes I would sit in her room and watch her work on her hair and makeup. She had taught me a great deal about how to enhance my appearance, passing along her special beauty tips as if they were ancestral secrets that had been handed down for generations, if not centuries.

"Are you looking to attract someone special?" I had asked her. Her eyes had flamed as if I had criticized her for spending so much time on her appearance.

"I don't make myself beautiful for someone else,"

she'd snapped. "Women like us need to look good for ourselves. It pleases us, gives us confidence, and makes us feel worthy of our name and our heritage. You will do exactly what I do when your time comes. It will become second nature, part of who and what you are."

She had calmed and continued to brush her hair, looking at herself in the mirror as she spoke to me.

"For us, being beautiful is being alive. We treat it the way the ordinary treat their health or are supposed to treat their health. Our beauty makes us healthy."

"Will I be as beautiful as you, Ava?"

She had stopped and looked at me with as much love and affection for me as she was capable of showing. "In your way, you will be. None of us is more beautiful than the other. We're each special in some way. Your way will come."

I had no doubt that mine had. I couldn't describe it exactly, but there was something exotic about me, something that would make me both exciting and attractive. I wasn't as obviously sexy as Ava, but I was very sexy. What would I do with this power now that I was no longer one of Daddy's daughters of darkness? At least, I hoped I was not. Only time would tell if it was something I could turn off.

I had made it clear to everyone in my new home that I wasn't looking for any romance, not even for a good-time onetime date, and yet, just as Ava had predicted, it was important to me, to my well-being, that I look as beautiful as possible. Obviously, Ava had been right about this. I just hoped she hadn't been right about everything else. I pushed it all out of my mind before I left my room and descended to wait for Julia Dolan.

Jim and Mr. Brady were in the living room. They heard Mrs. Winston and Mrs. McGruder complimenting me on my hair, and both came hurrying out to see.

"You look great," Jim said.

"Very beautiful, my dear," Mr. Brady said. "I've taken note of how perfect your teeth are, by the way. Are you using anything special to keep them that white, because I have a new product . . ."

"No, nothing special. I've always had good teeth."

"No cavities?"

"No," I said, smiling.

"I have about a dozen," Jim said. "Ate too much candy when I was a teenager."

"You know, we have this new mechanical toothbrush I mentioned," Mr. Brady told him. "I can give it to you wholesale."

Jim nodded but kept his eyes on me. His obvious longing made me uncomfortable. I was happy when Julia Dolan opened the front door. She was right on time. I thought she looked very pretty, too.

She spent a few minutes talking with her great-aunt Amelia and Mrs. McGruder, and then we left. I could feel Jim Lamb's love-sick eyes on the back of my neck.

"How long did you plan on staying there?" Julia asked, nodding at the Winston House as soon as we got into her car. She had seen the way Jim was looking at me, too.

"I don't know. I haven't thought about it."

"My great-aunt's very nice, but the two of them

daily would make me a little nuts. Jim Lamb was practically busting out of his skin gaping at you," she added.

"Tell me about it. Maybe I will start looking for a small apartment."

"Good idea. I'll help you look when I have time," she said. "Clifford found a very nice apartment in a complex called the Forefathers' Gardens. Maybe there's an opening for another. I'll have him check."

"Thank you."

"So, tell me about yourself and about California. I haven't been there yet. Is it as great as everyone claims?"

"I don't know what they claim. We lived in a few places other than California."

"Where?"

"Well, I lived in upstate New York and then Nashville before we moved to Los Angeles. The best thing about Los Angeles was that we weren't far from the ocean. You can be swimming one day and drive up to Big Bear and go skiing the next. The traffic's depressing, though."

"It's not bad right here, but it's no walk in the park to drive to Boston and back during rush hour, either. And besides," she said, "even in a smaller city with less traffic, what's the first thing that happens to you? A car accident."

I was silent.

"I'm sorry," she said. "Let's not bring up one sad thing tonight. I'm not going to ask you one other thing about your past. I know you had a painful time with your father and his new girlfriend—who I understand is now his wife?"

"Yes. But I agree, let's not dwell on the past. You have your burden, too."

She beamed a smile with her eyes wide with excitement, the sort of smile that can be contagious. "Exactly. Let's just let loose a bit and enjoy ourselves. Moving into a new town must be like getting into a hot bath. You've got to do it very slowly."

I laughed. "It is, especially for me," I said, and left it at that, even though I could see that she was dying to know why.

The Underground, the dance club and restaurant Julia took me to, was larger than any I had ever seen, not that I had seen many. It had a huge horseshoe-shaped bar composed of some translucent material. Multicolored lights thumped and rotated beneath it. In fact, the entire place seemed to move in sync with the rhythm of the disco music. Against one side of the club were tables and booths for those who wanted to eat farther away from the frenzied activity at the bar, and on the other side of it was a floor made of the same material as the bar and with its same rainbow of colors thumping and rotating beneath the feet of those dancing, if you could call it dancing. Some of them looked as if they were in some sort of convulsion, trying to toss their arms and hands off their torsos. Waitresses in abbreviated rainbow-colored uniforms glided somehow gracefully through the crowd and around the tables, carrying trays of drinks and plates of food. We stood inside the entrance, taking it all in.

"What do you think?" Julia asked, shouting to be heard over the music. I could see that after a few drinks, most people didn't notice or care about the volume.

"I could make a fortune selling cough drops at the exit," I shouted back, holding my hand over my throat, and she laughed. "It's fine."

"I have a table booked."

"Great," I said.

We were led to a booth at the far end just before the bar started to curve. Julia opened the drink menu first.

"This is pretty good and potent," she said, pointing at a drink called the Volcano. "I'll order it, and you can taste it. If you like it, I'll order another. No problem, as long as we order something to eat, too."

"Fine with me," I said. Alcohol never bothered any of us, not that I was much of a drinker anyway. "I think I'm just going to have an appetizer. I'm not that hungry."

"Really? They have great burgers and sweet potato fries. It comes with a small dinner salad."

"I'll get the shrimp cocktail."

"Okay," she said, and ordered for us.

I looked around. It was hard to tell who were couples and who were not. Everyone at the bar and mingling around it looked more like groups of friends. It occurred to me that maybe this was the sort of place where you would hope to meet someone and start a relationship, rather than a place that established couples might frequent. I wondered if that made any sense, but I was afraid to ask Julia, because she might realize just how inexperienced I was when it came to the dating scene.

"Are you very serious with your boyfriend?" I asked instead.

"Clifford? It's getting there," she admitted. "I've been

seeing him longer than I've seen anyone else. He came to Quincy about a year and a half ago, and we started dating about six months later. What about you? Any long romances before you left home?"

"One," I said. "It became impossible, however."

"Impossible? Why?"

"It was complicated. We were from two different worlds."

She just looked at me with her soft smile. *Some people can't subdue their personalities,* I thought. *No matter what they wear, what they hear, where they are, their inner self shows itself.* Julia was what Daddy would call "a sweetheart, someone who almost always saw the glass half full and never half empty." She didn't look at the world through rose-colored glasses so much as she avoided looking at anything or hearing anything that would diminish her optimism. How she could do that and work in a hospital ER was a puzzle to me.

"Care to explain? I mean, was he very wealthy or something?"

"Something like that. He comes from one of those families who think they are tied to royalty. I didn't fit the picture for his parents. Of course, he assured me that it wouldn't matter, but it always matters. In the end, no matter what they say, blood is too strong to ignore."

I thought that was a good mix of what was true and what was not.

She pursed her lips and nodded, impressed. "Daddy keeps telling me you seem like a woman twice, if not three times, your age. He keeps looking at your application form to see if that one in front of the eight isn't really a three."

"Events have a way of aging you prematurely," I said.

"Yes. Oh, damn."

"What?"

"I said nothing sad, and here I went and made you talk about a sad love affair."

Our waiter brought her the Volcano. She seized it and gulped half of it in defiance. "Here, try it," she said. I laughed and emptied the remainder. She immediately signaled the waiter and ordered another. "Tell you what," she told him. "Save yourself a trip. Bring me two."

He looked at her with a smirk, looked at me, and went off to get the drinks.

"I hope you don't get yourself in trouble or anything. I know this is a small town and—"

"Don't worry about it. If you don't flaunt it, no one makes a big deal, and don't worry about my drinking too much. This place provides a taxi if needed," she told me. "Something tells me we're going to need it."

The waiter brought us the two drinks. This time, she sipped hers and started moving with the rhythm of the music.

I drank from my glass and looked out at the crowd on the dance floor, who acted as if we were at the last ten seconds of a New Year's Eve celebration. We could hear their cheers and cries as they delighted in abandon and bathed in the passion and lust that seemed to settle over the whole dancing mix of young men and women like an invisible cloud of pure sex. They danced as if each was on his or her own private stage, but every chance they got, they rubbed bodies, caressed, and even kissed.

Suddenly, I thought that a young woman who had her back to us resembled Ava. My heart stopped and started. I sat up straighter and shifted so I could get a better view. The young woman moved behind two other couples, one quite plump.

"Something wrong?" Julia said.

"I thought I saw someone I knew," I said, and continued to shift in my seat to get a better view. The young woman seemed to have literally disappeared. I looked everywhere I could.

"You want to go out there?" Julia asked, mistaking my interest in the dancers as envy.

"To dance?"

"It's what people do here."

"Yes," I said, realizing that I might be able to see the young woman more easily from the dance floor.

We stepped away from the booth, me more slowly than her, and then she laughed, took my hand, and tugged me onto a clear spot on the dance floor. The music seemed to come up from the floor, through my legs and torso, driving me to move faster whether I wanted to or not. She was a good dancer. In moments, we seemed to be challenging each other with dramatic steps and moves. I was so into it that I forgot to look for the young woman, but soon I did.

There were a few who could have been the woman who had caught my attention. They were about Ava's size, with similar hair. That had to be it, I thought. Relieved, I let myself go even more. We were attracting the attention of young men nearby, who tried to insert themselves between us. For a few minutes, we let two of them do so, but then Julia looked at me, laughed, and nodded toward the bar, where our food was waiting on us.

To the disappointment of the young men, we hurried off. They kept beckoning for our return, but we went back to our booth. Julia finished her drink, and I finished mine. She ordered two more and began to eat. I was really only nibbling on my shrimp cocktail.

"Did you eat some of my great-aunt's food before coming out?"

"No. I think I'm just a little nervous," I said.

She nodded with understanding and held up her burger. "Delicious. You can always order one later."

I smiled and looked around. The place continued to fill up.

"I guess this is the big hot spot here," I said.

"I don't come here that much. Clifford isn't that fond of it. He likes it to be mellow when he eats, and he's not into the club scene. Talk about your upper-crust people, he's from one of those aristocratic Boston families, but he can let his hair down, too. When I inspire him," she added with a wide smile. "And I do."

"I'll bet you do."

"Forget me. You were inspiring quite a few young men out there."

"So were you."

"Not as much," she said.

Was she right? Was that something obvious?

"It was like flies to honey," I said, and she laughed.

"Look," she said, leaning toward me. "I'm not trying to push you on anyone. I'm no one qualified to give anyone advice about romance. I had two or three disappointments in college, and until I met Clifford, I wasn't what you would call the belle of the ball. In fact, I think I was beginning to worry my father."

"Why?"

"He's never come right out and said anything, but I know he's afraid that our growing up under the circumstances of his failed marriage, my mother running off, that sort of thing, would pollute any relationships we had. I know he's been disappointed in Liam. They had a few bouts over Liam's behavior, as you probably know by now."

I nodded.

"Speak of the devil," she said, and nodded in the direction of the entrance.

I turned and saw Liam Dolan enter alone.

"I didn't tell him we were coming here," Julia swore.

"It's all right," I said.

She finished eating. Liam moved to the other side of the bar. He did look a little lost and unsure of himself and not as if he knew we were there. He wasn't looking around for us. Some women spoke to him, but he didn't give them any encouragement. I saw him order a drink and gaze at the dancers for a few moments before turning and looking down as he cradled his glass in his hands. If anything, he looked sad and lost. Finally, he spotted Julia and me across the way in our booth. I saw his face brighten. I wanted to look away, pretend I hadn't noticed him, but I couldn't do it. Despite myself, I smiled back at him, and he immediately started in our direction.

"What's this?" he asked his sister.

"What's it look like, genius?"

"Two young women out on the town," he said, smiling at me. He turned to Julia. "You never said you were going out with our newest employee."

"Sorry, Dad."

He smirked. "You know, my sister can be a pain in the rear, and not only when she gives someone a shot there, either," he added.

Julia laughed. "No hot date tonight?" she teased.

"No. I've cooled down."

"The feminine world breathes a sigh of relief," she said.

I was truly enjoying the banter between them. It was loving, I thought. That was something I had never had with Ava. I could remember only tension, challenge, and a sense of competition.

"You guys dance?" he asked me.

"We went at it for a while," I said, looking at Julia.

"She's being modest. I had to swipe them away," she told him.

"I believe it. Any interest in going back out there?" he asked me.

I looked at Julia.

"I'm fine just watching. Have to digest my food," she said.

Was this a little brother-sister conspiracy? Did I care?

When you were with someone, there was that moment when you knew that if you said yes to something, a whole series of events would follow, cascading down through you to take a hold on your future.

You could certainly regret it.

Would I?

"Okay," I said, and got up to dance with Liam Dolan.

13

Being so close to him, our bodies moving slowly in synchronization, I felt whatever resistance I had mounted since the first time we had met begin to defrost and melt away. He was a very good dancer, and unlike most of the other young men around us, who seemed so incapable of controlling their female partners that they looked as if they were dancing alone, Liam slipped his arm around my waist and kept us close, turning me and then moving around me, holding my eyes on his and keeping us so tightly connected that I felt we had instantly become two halves of the same newly created dancing body.

Whenever he could, he brought his face to mine, brushing his lips against my hair, my cheeks, and my forehead. My imagination exploded. I saw us naked together in a shower, embracing, drinking the water from each other's face, caressing and kissing until it became impossible to keep standing. Soaked, we retreated to a bed and began making the most passionate love, lovemaking that resembled our dancing, slow at first and then building and building until we buried each other's scream of deep sexual satisfaction in a long kiss that threatened to draw the breath from our bodies.

When I looked back at Julia in our booth, I saw her gazing at us with a smile of delight. She looked more like an older sister taking pride in her younger brother. It was as if he was finally doing something right. *I'm only dancing,* I told myself. *It doesn't mean anything.* But one look at Liam's face, a face that was reflecting the way I was looking at him, told me I was lying to myself.

Finally, we both had enough and, holding hands, fled the music and the lights. Julia clapped for us when we joined her.

"If they were giving prizes tonight, you'd be the winning couple. You must have done quite a bit of dancing in California," she told me.

"Some," I said. "Mostly in my bedroom," I added, and they both laughed.

"Another drink?" Liam asked.

"I already had another while you two were out there, but maybe one more."

He ordered one for me, too, pretending that it was for himself. "Don't tell my father I'm corrupting a minor," he quipped.

"Minor," Julia said. "She's more mature than every legal drinker here. Anyway, why this Lone Ranger act tonight?" She looked as if her first three Volcanoes were already overflowing in her blood and her brain. Her smile was a little twisted, and her eyes were glassy.

Liam shrugged. "I want to take my time." He glanced at me. "Too many impulsive, wrong decisions."

Julia laughed. "Take your time?"

"I'm serious," he said.

The new drinks arrived.

"And to what do we owe this new sense of responsibility and caution?" she asked, throwing me a conspiratorial grin.

"See that?" Liam said. "They complain and complain about me at home, and as soon as I turn a new leaf, they ridicule it. How can I win with my family?"

How can I win with mine? I thought.

"You can't blame anyone but yourself. You're like some of the smokers we get in the ER. The doctors tell them they have to quit, and they say sure, they've done it many times." She laughed and drank more of her Volcano.

Liam looked a little annoyed. He turned away for a moment, probably to calm himself, and then turned back, concentrating only on me. "So, how are you getting along living in my great-aunt's rooming house?"

"It's very comfortable," I said, and sipped my drink.

"Aren't there dozens and dozens of things in it that you're not permitted to touch? When I was a little boy, she practically had me in a straitjacket whenever I was there."

"Some items are off-limits, like her old rocking chair," I said, smiling. "Mr. Brady thinks there's a ghost in the house, maybe the ghost of John Adams."

"If there was such a thing as ghosts, I think they would find my great-aunt most accommodating," Liam said. "Julia?"

"As kooky as she is sometimes," Julia said, "you can't

help but love her. No matter how close she is with Mrs.
McGruder and her tenants, she's really a very lonely
woman."

"Great-aunt Amelia? Lonely? She's surrounded by
our forefathers," Liam joked.

Julia only smiled and then turned to look at the
dancers. I wondered if the alcohol was now making her
more melancholy.

"Is Clifford working all night?" I asked her.

"He gets off about ten, but he won't meet me here,"
she reminded me.

"Maybe you should go out there on the dance floor
and find someone you know who would," Liam told
her.

"I'm all right. I like Clifford. There are no surprises," she added, a little sadly, I thought. "Nothing to
worry about."

"Boring," Liam teased, and looked at me. "Back out
there?"

I looked at Julia.

"Go for it," she said, and turned around to cup her
drink the way I had seen Liam first doing it. I hesitated,
and she looked up at me. "I'm fine. Go on. I like to
watch you dance."

"Me, too," Liam added, and tugged my hand.

This time, when we danced, we talked, too.

"You going out with my sister to play it safe or
what?" he asked.

"To have a good time," I replied. "I like her. She's
refreshing."

"Why?"

"There's nothing dishonest about her," I replied.

"And you can tell that how?"

"I have powers," I said.

We drew close.

"I knew that from the first time I set eyes on you."

"Oh, how?"

"I have the power to recognize power," he joked.

We both laughed and got into our dancing again, this time so intently that I forgot to look back at Julia. When I did, I saw that she was talking to a tall, dark-haired man whose complexion under the club's lights looked like a luminous olive. There was something about him that made me uneasy. He was talking to her, but he looked our way periodically. I saw him sit at the booth and then talk Julia into another Volcano.

"Who's that with your sister?" I asked Liam when we drew close.

He glanced her way and shrugged. He continued to dance as if we were the only ones out there, but I couldn't concentrate. I kept looking back at the booth. Finally, I paused.

"What?" he asked. "Don't tell me you're tired already."

"No. I'm just concerned about your sister. That man bought her another drink. That's too much. She's had enough."

"Yes, Mom," he joked.

"I'm serious, Liam. She already had too much."

He changed expression and looked at her again. "Okay," he said, pausing. "Let's see what's what."

The moment we started off the dance floor, the man Julia was talking to rose and walked away.

"Who was that?" Liam asked, looking after him.

"I don't know," Julia said. "He claimed I was the nurse for his mother when she was brought to the ER a few months ago. He told me I was very nice. He said if anything happens to him, he wants to be sure I'm on duty at the ER."

"He didn't tell you his name?" I asked. I saw him disappear into the crowd, almost evaporate.

"I don't know if I heard much of what he said. He has beautiful eyes. He bought me this drink," she continued.

"You know you've had too much already," I said.

She nodded. "I guess I'm not out enough. I should know when I overdo it. If anyone should know, a nurse should."

I picked up her drink before she could sip any more and drank it all in one long sip. "Sorry, I was a little thirsty," I said.

Both she and Liam were smiling.

"You almost had as many as I had, but you don't look any different from when we got here," Julia said. She swayed a little too much when she talked, and I put my hand on her shoulder to steady her in the seat. Then I looked at Liam.

"Maybe you should go home, Julia. Are you on tomorrow?" he asked.

"Not until the afternoon. I'll be fine. Just don't expect me at breakfast," she added, laughing.

"I'll drive you home," he told her. "And I'll take you home," he added, turning to me. "Unless you want to wait here."

"No, I've had enough," I said.

"Oh, I don't want to spoil your good time," Julia moaned.

"You haven't. It's because of you that I had a good time. C'mon," I said, taking her hand.

Liam paid our bill and followed as we started out, Julia a little unsteady but quite happy.

When we reached the entrance, she paused and looked back, wobbling a little. "Where is he?"

"Who?"

"That guy who stopped by to tell me what a great nurse I am. I thought I'd say good night."

I looked, and so did Liam. "I don't see him, Julia."

She shrugged and leaned over to whisper, "He was more interested in you than me, anyway."

"Me?"

I looked again for him, and then we headed out to Liam's car. I looked around in the parking lot, too, but saw no one who resembled him.

"Can you follow us in Julia's car?" Liam asked. "I'll go slowly," he promised when I hesitated. "Give her the keys, Julia."

She started to protest and then realized how she was and nodded.

We stood there while she fumbled through her purse. I continued to look toward the club entrance and around the parking lot.

"You all right to drive?" Liam asked me. "I didn't even consider that."

"I'm fine."

"Okay."

He took the keys from Julia and handed them to me. Then he opened his car door and helped her in.

"Wait," Julia cried. "What about Lorelei?"

"Julia, you just gave me your keys for her to follow us. I said I'd take her home afterward."

"Oh. Right," she said, laughing.

Liam shook his head and smiled at me. "Let's get her home," he said, "and to bed."

I nodded and went to Julia's car. After I got in and started the engine, I looked to the side, where I thought I saw someone standing in the shadows. Liam sounded his horn, and I had to back out to follow them. When I glanced in the rearview mirror, I was sure I saw the man who had stopped at the bar to talk to Julia. I was looking at him so hard that I nearly hit the rear of Liam's car when he stopped at the driveway entrance. He looked out of his window at me. I indicated that I was fine, but he didn't look confident about it. I was fine. The alcohol had no effect, as usual, but I was definitely spooked by the man in the shadows. He gave off a familiar vibe. My mind raced. *He's one of us,* I thought. *He must think I'm a Renegade.*

I drove on, following them and fleeing him at the same time. About fifteen minutes later, we turned up what I thought was a new street but actually was the long driveway to the Dolans' New England mansion.

I realized that because of the height, there was a clear view of the ocean. The large house had been built with that view in mind. It had what looked to be at least a forty-foot tower that reminded me of a lighthouse, a peaked turret and projecting bays wrapped in glass to accommodate the ocean views. As I followed Liam around the front of the house to a garage with five doors for five cars, I looked up at the second story of the house and estimated that there were more than a half-dozen bedrooms. Liam pulled close to what I could see was a side entrance to the house and waved at me to drive up beside him.

"Just leave it in front of the third garage door," he said, and went around to help Julia out. She looked as if she had fallen asleep. I parked and stepped out as he was guiding Julia toward the entrance. He waved for me to catch up. Julia leaned against Liam's shoulder, her eyes closed. He nodded at the door, and I rushed forward to open it.

"We'll get her upstairs," he told me.

I followed him as he continued through a small entryway and then into a wide hallway, dimly lit by small chandeliers all the way to the main entrance of the house and its winding marble stairway with a rich, dark mahogany balustrade. Above that was a very large chandelier, also dimly lit. The house was dead quiet. I had been wondering if Mr. Dolan would hear us and come out. He wouldn't be happy about Julia, I thought. He might even blame it on me.

Julia groaned and then tried to walk completely on her own. When she stumbled, she laughed. Liam smiled at me and shot forward to get a good grip on her as she started up the stairs.

"Where's your dad?" I whispered.

"He's away for the weekend," he replied. At the top, we turned right and followed a similarly dimly lit hallway to the first bedroom on the right. Liam opened the door.

It was much larger than any bedroom I had ever had, even larger than my father's bedrooms in New York, Nashville, and California. Despite its size, it looked cozy and warm, with walls of gentle pink, a soft darker pink rug, and light maple furnishings, including a four-poster canopy bed. The windows were large and with drapes of white with swirls of pink. On one wall, I saw shelves of all sorts of dolls—dolls from other countries, antique dolls, and rag dolls. There looked to be a few hundred.

"Whenever Dad went anywhere, he brought home a doll or two for her," Liam explained, seeing where I was looking.

There was even a doll on her bed, between her oversized pillows.

Julia smiled and stepped forward to embrace her doll. "Someone I can depend on," she said.

"Why don't you help her to bed?" Liam whispered. "I'll wait for you downstairs."

"Okay."

He left, and Julia sat on her bed, looking a little stunned.

"How did we get here?" she asked, and laughed. Then she closed her eyes and wobbled.

"How about you get to sleep?" I said, and knelt down to take off her shoes. She laughed and then moaned and fell back onto the bed.

"Look at me. The one who should have known better," she muttered to her doll.

I helped her undress and searched a dresser drawer for a nightgown. She was practically in a dead sleep before I was able to get her to put it on. I don't think she realized what was happening, but moments after I had folded her things and placed them on the dresser, she was dead away, still clinging to her doll.

"I wish I could tell you that you'll feel better in the morning, Julia," I whispered. I really liked her. If I had a sister in the normal world, she would be whom I'd choose, I thought, and leaned down to kiss her cheek, brush back her hair, and fix her blanket. Then I turned off the light and closed her bedroom door softly as I backed out.

The enormity of the mansion struck me as I stood there and contemplated the wide hallway and how far it went to the right and then to the left. Looking down from the top of the stairway, I could appreciate the size of the entryway. There were beautiful paintings on the walls, scenes of the sea, sailboats, and some rural settings. As I descended, Liam stepped out of a doorway and looked up at me.

"That stairway fits you," he said.

"How can a stairway fit you?"

"You just look like you belong in a house like this, like you're used to it. Most people who come here for the first time are a little intimidated."

I nodded and looked around after I reached the bottom. "I've been to many mansions and castles, but I haven't lived in one. I'm sure there are maids, house-keepers?"

"The maids come and go, but our house manager, as Dad likes to call her now, is and always has been Mrs. Wakefield. She oversees all of the housework. She served as our nanny after my mother left. She's a widow with no children of her own. Tonight happens to be her night off. She's probably here but asleep. Otherwise, she would be out here, X-raying you," he joked. "Can I give you some coffee, something cold, anything?"

"I'm fine."

"You look like you can hold a drink. My sister isn't really the partygoer. You want to see the rest of the place?"

"Sure," I said.

He led me into the living room. I thought it had one of the most beautifully designed fireplaces I had ever seen. The stones continued to the ceiling but arched out in both directions. All of the furniture was oversized, but considering the vastness of the room, I thought it had to be. Liam showed me the den, where they had a very large-screen television, a pool table, and dark brown leather furniture. After that came the dining room, with a table that could seat twenty.

"You eat here every night?"

"Not really. We have a kitchenette we use most of the time. With Julia's crazy schedule and my comings and goings, we rarely eat together these days anyway."

The kitchen looked as if it could service a small hotel.

Just off of that was the kitchenette he had mentioned. All of the rooms in the house, even the kitchen, had enough windows to make them bright.

"You can't see it well now because it's dark, but we have a pool out back and a tennis court we rarely use. We own about eighty acres around the house. Sure you don't want anything to drink?" He opened the refrigerator. "We have all sorts of juice, sodas, and mineral waters."

"Okay, I'll have a mineral water, thanks," I said.

He took out a bottle, opened it, and poured us each a glass. We sat on stools at the kitchen island.

"I don't know how much Julia's told you about us," he said, looking down at his glass. "She was ten and I was four when our mother took off. Neither of us suspected that was about to happen. I'm pretty sure Dad did. I can't say how much he tried to prevent it. He was devastated for a long time."

It occurred to me that both he and I had been brought up by women other than our mothers. He had his for at least four years, although by the sound of it, she wasn't there for him much.

"Why did your mother leave?"

"Despite what you see, how much we have, I don't think she was comfortable and happy here. I get bits and pieces. At first, we were told she had some kind of a nervous breakdown, and then it went to her just being a self-centered woman who really didn't want to be bothered with children and a husband. She was seeing someone on the side, someone who I guess promised her more excitement." He paused. It was painful for him to talk about it, but it obviously helped him.

"Did you . . . were you and your sister . . ."

"Sent to therapy? Yeah, some. I hated it, and although Julia claims it helped her, I know she hated it, too. It never really helped me understand. I mean, I think it's just natural to ask why she married my father in the first place. She must have known what she was in for, right? Then I think, maybe he promised her a different sort of life. Dad's always been anal about his work. I'm sure she was left here many times while he was out carving new territories, bringing in more lucrative business projects. She had plenty of household help. We had a nanny for years. She didn't have to do any of the things ordinary housewives do. She had her own sports car, a limousine driver whenever she wanted to go to Boston, but . . . it wasn't enough."

"The house didn't fit her," I said. "What I mean is, the life she was leading. I imagine she had a lot of high-society events?"

"Yes, but I don't remember my father talking about her having any close friends. Julia says all she had was her gang of phonies."

"She didn't feel she belonged, I suppose. It happens. You ever see the movie *Citizen Kane*?"

"I don't think so."

"You'd remember if you did. A very wealthy and powerful man brings his new wife to a mansion ten times as large as this, surrounds her with guests, gives her any material thing she wants, but she ends up very lonely and leaves him and all that."

"She had a prenup agreement. But for a mother to desert her own children?"

"It sounds like she pawned you off as much as she could anyway. I know that's not pleasant to hear."

He nodded. "Dad withdrew from us, too, during those first years. I'm not trying to blame anyone else for my own failures, but . . ."

"But you couldn't help feeling that if your mother could leave you, there had to be something wrong with you."

"Right. The therapist tried to help me deal with that, but the feeling never goes away. You grow up going to ball games at school, being on teams, and seeing parents dote on their children, and you look at the stands and see no one there for you. Dad was always working, and Mom was gone with the wind. I did see that movie."

"And Julia?"

"Much the same but better at being stable. She stuck it out through nursing school. She's probably told you about Clifford, and maybe that will work out. She hasn't been able to hold on to any relationship yet, however. She has the same self-doubts. She just isn't as bitter about it as I am. I only worry that she'll stay with Clifford not because she wants to but because she's afraid to lose him. Understand?"

"Yes, I do. I think it's too early to say."

"I love talking to you. I have trouble talking to girls. The ones I've been with, that is. They seem to have brains made of jelly beans."

I smiled. "Don't shop for a girl in a candy store, then," I said.

He sat back with a frozen smile on his face. "Where are you really from, Lorelei Patio?"

"Planet Earth."

He laughed, twirled his glass in his hands, and took a sip. "I know you've had your own family problems. You don't need to hear about mine."

"I don't mind. Really."

He nodded and smiled. "I believe you. Maybe I got off on the wrong foot with you," he said.

"I think, if I could give you some advice, you should stop blaming yourself for things."

He actually blushed. "Wow. Thank you, Dr. Patio," he said.

"I don't mean to sound condescending, Liam. It's just something I see clearly, that's all."

"You know what I see?"

I felt my body tighten in anticipation. Was he going to attack me for being too arrogant?

"I see one of the most beautiful girls who ever set foot in Quincy. And from what I can tell, one of the nicest and brightest, too."

I felt myself relax again. "Lots of times we see what we want to see, Liam."

"Then what's the difference?" he said, smiling. He thought for a moment. "If it's not too late, you want to take a short walk outside? I have a favorite spot I'd love to show you."

"Okay," I said.

At so many moments during the night, I could have stopped this from becoming something, but every time I thought of it, I backed down. There was something stronger than my caution, stronger than my fears. Was that good? Daddy always said, "We don't fear, but if you should feel like you do fear something, don't be afraid of that. Most of the time, it's a warning."

He led me through some glass sliding doors that opened onto a large patio with a fireplace at the center. Reaching to his right, he flipped a switch and lit up the rear of the mansion with lighted paths, landscape lights, and lights in the pool and the whirlpool.

"My father designed every inch of this place," he said. "After my mother left us, he spent most of his free time working on the estate, as if he wanted to reassure himself that having it, being here, was right."

"How can something so beautiful be wrong?" I said.

He widened his smile. The outside light made his eyes glitter, but most of the brightness came from inside him, I thought. He took my hand and without speaking led me down the lighted pathways and then off to the right, where there were large maple and oak trees. On one was a ladder that led to a pretty sophisticated-looking tree house. It had four walls and a large window looking toward the ocean.

"It looks good enough to live in," I said.

"My father provided all of the materials for me, but he didn't come out here and build it with me. He gave me instructions and occasionally checked out my work, but nothing more."

"He wanted you to have something solely yours," I said.

"That's what Julia says."

"Listen to the women in your life," I playfully advised.

"Are you in my life?" he quickly countered.

"I am at this moment," I said.

He nodded and looked at the tree house. "Want to?"

"Well, it isn't exactly where I expected to end up tonight, but . . . okay."

We shot forward like two preteens. He helped me onto the ladder and followed me closely, protectively, as I made my way up to the tree-house floor. I was surprised to find some soft cushions, but the most delightful and surprising thing of all was the view. We here high enough to look out over the trees on the east end of the property.

He scooted in beside me, and we both lay back against the cushions, gazing out at the ocean and the boats lit up against the inky blue.

"Sometimes they look like stars that have fallen out of the sky," he said. "See that one off to the right, how it twinkles?"

"Yes."

"Okay. I know you won't believe me, but you're the first girl I've brought up here."

"What made you think I would do it?"

"I don't know. Yes, I do. You don't seem afraid of anything or anyone. I mean, it had to take a lot of courage to just leave home and start out on your own."

"Sometimes we do things because we have no choice," I said.

He was quiet, and then he leaned over and kissed me softly. He held himself over me, gazing down into my eyes. "That was one of those things I had to do. No choice," he said.

I couldn't help but smile, and he kissed me again. This time, I kissed him back, and it lasted longer. I could feel my body tightening with passion. It rushed through my veins. He kissed my neck, my chin, and my cheeks before finding my lips again. He started to caress me, moving his hands to my breasts. I stopped him by seizing his wrists.

"I have to go slowly, Liam. This is already more than I had intended."

"Okay," he said. "I'm cool. But can I have my wrists back?"

I released him and sat up.

He rubbed his wrists. "Wow. You are sure full of surprises. What a grip. How did you get so strong? Gymnastics or something?"

"Something. I think I had better go," I said. "It's late."

"Right. Be careful going down."

He backed out and started down the ladder, waiting for me. Together we descended. For a moment, we just stood there looking at each other.

"I don't know too many girls who would have gone up there," he said.

"Now, don't tell me I'm the first girl you kissed in your tree house," I said.

He laughed. "You are. I said I never brought any up there."

We started into the house. He flipped off the lights.

"You have to come back here in the daylight to really appreciate it."

"Okay."

He was silent until we got into his car and started away.

"I don't blame you for wanting to be cautious with someone like me."

"There's no one like you," I said. "Besides, it's not you per se. My father once told me that tasting love is like tasting good wine. You sip. You don't gulp."

"Wow. I love that." He laughed and shook his head as we shot forward into the night. "Thank you, Julia," he cried, "for drinking too much!"

I smiled to myself.

And then I thought that if there was anyone Ava would target for Daddy, it would be Liam Dolan. He was virile, strong, and sexy, with blood so rich she could taste it yards away from him.

Was that still inside me, still something that drove me to do what I was doing? This need to please my father?

Was I still thinking more of Daddy than of myself?

As we continued on into the darkness, I knew that the answer was lying out there, like some predatory animal waiting to pounce.

14

"I know it probably sounds silly," Liam said when we pulled in front of the Winston House, "but I had a really good time tonight."

"Why silly?"

"We didn't do that much, and you didn't start out with me. It wasn't my date."

"I think it's safe to say that you made it your date," I said.

He smiled. "Hope you weren't disappointed."

"Are you fishing for a compliment?" I teased.

"Absolutely."

"I enjoyed myself. Thank you," I said.

He leaned over to kiss me good night.

"How about I do it right and pick you up tomorrow late in the morning and we go for a ride on our boat? We'll stop along the coast to have lunch and then just cruise for a while afterward. Pack a change of clothes, and we'll go back to my house and freshen up, and then I'll take you out to dinner. Very casual. We'll make it an early night. Promise," he quickly added. "I've got to go to Boston early in the morning for a job Dad's won the bid on anyway."

I could feel the struggle inside myself. The arguments against a yes were so clear and so strong. I really wanted to get settled before starting a relationship. That wasn't just a quickly thought-up excuse I had used to avoid relationships. I should be more worried. And what about the fact that I had been seriously considering sneaking off into the night and fleeing this place just a short time ago? There was much to worry me. This could end up as badly as it had with Buddy, and I could leave another young man brokenhearted just to save his life. I might leave a string of them as I continued my flight from one place to another. Was there any point?

But the other side of me, a side that had come to life with Buddy, was coming alive again, and if I ever hoped to escape what and who I was, I had to nurture it. I had to see if there was a way to escape from one world into another. I did like Liam. I was very attracted to him. I liked his sister and his father. I loved the idea of the neighborhood, the community. I wanted all of it desperately. I was sure none of my sisters ever wanted anything similar. I was different, and if I didn't nourish the difference, I would not have an inkling of hope.

"Okay," I said. "What time?"

"Ten-thirty okay?"

"Yes."

Elated, he practically leaped out of his car to go around and open my door. He gave me an exaggerated stage bow. "Madam Patio."

"Thank you, good Sir Dolan," I said.

Laughing, we walked to the door. He started to speak loudly, and I put my fingers on his lips.

"Got to be quiet. You don't want to wake up one of your great-aunt's ghosts."

"Right," he whispered. He kissed me again. I expected it to be a second short good-night kiss, but his lips were so demanding and mine were so responsive that our kiss lasted as long as it had in his tree house.

" 'Night, Lorelei," he said so softly it was almost mouthed.

I opened the door and entered. He stood there looking in at me as if he couldn't turn away until I closed it. I smiled at him, but when my eyes lifted just a little, I was sure I saw someone standing across the street in the shadow cast by a large maple tree. The silhouette was darker, maybe formed out of the shadows themselves. It looked like the man in the Underground dance club. I was tempted to step out again and approach him, confront him and show him defiance. As if he sensed it, he pulled back into the darkness and was gone.

Liam looked a little confused at the way I had been staring past him. He turned to look. When he turned back, I shook my head and closed the door. I certainly wouldn't say anything to him about it, but I didn't go to the stairway. I went to one of the front windows instead and watched until he got into his car, backed up, and drove safely away.

I shouldn't have agreed to the date, I thought almost immediately. It was too soon. I wasn't sure. I walked up, thinking that I might call him first thing in the morning and come up with an excuse to cancel. However, when I got into my room, calmed down, and prepared for bed, I had second thoughts about my second thoughts. Was that man really out there? Was I imagining it? Perhaps it was just the shape of branches that suggested someone, but no one was there. Maybe the man who approached Julia at the bar was really someone whose mother Julia had helped in the ER. Was my paranoia running rampant? I had to control it. How could I hope to have any sort of life if I didn't try?

Naturally, I didn't get much sleep. So many visions from my youth recurred and interchanged with what I had seen or imagined now. Twice I woke up because I thought someone was standing in the shadows looking down at me. I could feel my body harden, my muscles tense up. In moments, like a ghostly shadow, it disappeared. I fell into a deep sleep just before morning and slept much later than I had until then. I was sleeping so late, in fact, that Jim took it upon himself to knock gently on my door to ask if I was all right. He woke me. When I looked at the clock, I sat up quickly.

"What?" I called.

"Are you okay? Everyone was just wondering. We all had breakfast and—"

"I'm fine. I'm not hungry. Tell them not to worry about me," I called. I could feel him continuing to stand there, probably trying to think of something else to say. A wave of impatience and intolerance washed over me. I rose, threw the coverlet around myself, and jerked open the door. "What?" I asked. He stepped back, surprised.

"Nothing, I . . . just . . . worried."

"I'm fine, Jim. Thank you for your concern. I'll be down soon."

He nodded, looked shyly at me again, and then hurried away. I showered, dressed, and went downstairs. Mrs. Winston and Mrs. McGruder were still in the dining room. Both looked up when I stepped in.

"Everything all right, dear?" Mrs. Winston asked.

"Yes, thank you."

"We kept some hot oatmeal on the stove for you," Mrs. McGruder said.

"I just need some coffee, if that's still available."

"Oh, of course it is, but you should put something in your stomach," she said, and went into the kitchen.

Mrs. Winston looked at me askance when I sat at the table. "I happened to be up late last night and glanced out my window when I heard a car pull into my driveway. I couldn't help but notice that it wasn't my great-niece, Julia, who brought you home. Wasn't that Liam?"

"Yes," I said.

She nodded, grimacing as though she had figured out the entire plan. "Did Julia take you out in order to . . . what do you young people say . . . set you up with Liam?"

"No," I said, smiling. "We happened to meet him where we were."

"Happened?" she said, still skeptical.

"Julia assured me that wasn't her intention."

She said "um" with closed lips and skeptical eyes. Mrs. McGruder brought in my coffee and a small bowl of oatmeal.

"Just in case," she said.

"It's true, Amelia. We just happened to meet, and he offered to take me home," I said. I thought it was best not to mention Julia's drinking too much.

The two women looked at each other.

"I don't mean to be discouraging, dear," Mrs. Winston said, "and I hate talking down my own flesh and blood, but my great-nephew doesn't have an admirable track record with young women."

"Yes, I know about all that."

"You do?" Mrs. McGruder said, her eyebrows looking as if they had just woken up on her face.

"What is that old-fashioned expression, 'His reputation preceded him'?"

"Exactly," Mrs. Winston said.

"Don't worry. The minute he steps out of line, I'll drop him like a hot potato."

Both laughed.

"Well, he would be a real fool to drive someone as sweet as you away," Mrs. Winston said.

They looked up, and I turned to see Jim Lamb in the doorway.

"Ah, you're up and okay. I got my car back. It looks like new," he said.

"I'm glad, Jim. You're feeling better, too?"

"Oh, yes." He looked at Mrs. McGruder and Mrs. Winston. "Thanks to all the tender loving care I received."

"Good."

I tasted the oatmeal just to make Mrs. McGruder happy. It was very good, not like some of the gruel Mrs. Fennel used to make us eat, so I ate a little. Jim didn't move from the doorway. Everyone's eyes went to him.

"I was wondering if you were free this afternoon. I could show you around the area a bit. You might like to see the John F. Kennedy National Historic Site, his birthplace. I'm sure you would enjoy the House of the Seven Gables. And if there's time—"

"I'm sorry, Jim. I've already made previous arrangements for today."

"Oh. Sure," he said, his whole face sinking in disappointment. "Well, maybe some other time," he added, and was gone.

I looked at the two women to see their reactions. I was sure that in the back of her mind, at least, Mrs. Winston was thinking that Jim would be a safer beau. I said nothing and ate a little more oatmeal during the silence.

"We're getting a new tenant later today," Mrs. Winston said when I looked up.

"Oh?"

"Another young man. He'll be here for a few weeks. He's from Boston University and has very good references. He's doing some historical research for a doctorate in history and just happens to be specializing in John Adams. He was very excited to learn about the Winston House. Perhaps he'll be good company for Mr. Lamb."

I knew she meant to take his attention away from me.

I nodded. "Thank you for this," I told Mrs. Mc-Gruder.

"So, you are going somewhere today?" Mrs. Winston inquired. "With my great-nephew?"

"Yes."

"Forewarned is forearmed," she said with a small smile.

I nodded and left them. *Poor Liam,* I thought. *Or maybe poor me.* I wondered if I should feel sorry for him or be wary for myself.

He arrived a little early. Diplomatically, he brought his great-aunt a gift, a bouquet of fresh lilacs.

"Thank you," Mrs. Winston said, standing beside me. She was eyeing my larger bag, which contained my clothes to change into for dinner. "I'm lucky Lorelei came to stay with us, or I might not have seen you for another four months, Liam," she added, her face as chiding as that of a grade-school teacher bawling out an errant little boy.

Liam blushed, surely because it was happening in front of me. "Now, Great-auntie Amelia," he said. "You know I'm always thinking about you."

"Mind reading is hard enough when the person is in the same room, but across town? Not easy," she said. Nevertheless, she gave him a kiss on the cheek and nodded at me. "You had better treat this young lady with respect, or you'll hear more from me than you ever have," she warned.

"No need to worry," he said.

"We'll see," she countered. "Have a good time," she told me, and went off to put her flowers in a vase.

Liam hurried me out. "She's a tiger," he said, opening his car door for me.

"I think she's very fond of you and just wants the best for you," I told him.

He looked surprised, and when he got in, he just sat there for a moment. "Do you really think that about her?" he asked, still looking forward.

"Yes, why?"

"She's never given me that feeling. Sometimes I felt it was because she saw more of my mother in me than my father, and I know how she felt about my mother. She rarely misses an opportunity to tell me."

"Sometimes people want to feel differently and look for ways to do just that if you give them the chance," I said.

He turned quickly and smiled. "You know, if you keep this up, I'm going to believe I'm with a sixty-year-old wise old lady in a beautiful eighteen-year-old's body."

"And?"

"Nothing. I'll take you any way I can," he said, and started his engine.

Would you? I wondered. *I doubt it.*

"How is Julia this morning?"

"She didn't come down to breakfast. Mrs. Wakefield brought it up to her, and you can be sure she wasn't happy about that."

"Who? Julia or Mrs. Wakefield?"

"Both," he said. "Mrs. Wakefield is a tough old bird, but she has a genuine fondness for us, as close to the love a mother would have for her children as possible, I suppose. My father was lucky to have found her at the right time. Her husband had been killed in a boating accident when she was in her late thirties. She never remarried, and they didn't have any children of their own.

We were a good fit, I guess, but she's what you might call overprotective. Any woman my father might bring into that house is scanned better than by the scanners they have at the airports."

I laughed. "I guess that will be true for me, too," I thought aloud.

"Don't worry. I'll protect you."

"Will you?" I asked, but it was meant to be almost rhetorical, a question that would be carried off like a leaf in a breeze.

"Damn right. Every chance I get," he said. To punctuate his determination, he took my hand and squeezed it gently. "Let's have a helluva good time and not dwell on the past," he added, just as Julia had said. We drove on.

I really had nothing to compare to this day I spent with Liam. My times with Buddy were always in secret and confined. By necessity, my sisters and I had been closed in, our lives cloistered. Even on the brightest days, I had felt as if I were moving in shadows. We had worn them like second skins. The instructions were clear. Unless my sisters and I were involved in a hunt, we were to avoid spotlights and not draw too much attention to ourselves. How different this day was. It was as if I had been reborn in the sunshine. Automobile tops down, hair blowing in the wind, voices excited and loud, no hiding of faces, no smothering of smiles and laughter—all of it was part of a world I had dreamed of being in but never thought I would.

We went directly to the dock where the Dolans' boat was kept.

"My father is always threatening to sell it," Liam told me as we parked near the boat, a Stingray sport boat. "Boats need a lot of attention, and he doesn't think I give it enough. Supposedly, he bought it for me. We went out together a few times, but I can't tell you when the last time was. It was that long ago. Julia never uses it, of course. I gave it a total overhaul this past week," he continued as we got out and walked to the dock. "I guess I was dreaming of taking you out. Did you do any boating in California?"

"No. I've never been on a private boat."

"Really? I thought you California girls did it all."

He helped me onto the boat.

"I'm not really a California girl, not in the sense you mean," I said. "I wasn't born there, and we lived in other places."

"Right."

He got the boat untied and started the engine.

"I thought we'd go to Salem for lunch," he said. "The town's about a fifteen-minute walk from the dock. I know a great pub restaurant, the Witches' Brew. Get it? Salem, witches?"

"Yes, I get it," I said.

"Get comfortable," he said, nodding to the seat beside him.

I sat, and then he smiled, and we shot forward into the water so fast and hard I screamed. He slowed down, and we began to cruise to Salem.

Salem, I thought. I recalled Daddy talking about witches when Ava was reading *The Crucible* by Arthur Miller for her college class. I knew the play well. Of course, Daddy did, too. He knew more about books, theater, and film than anyone I had ever met.

"They feed on their own fear," Daddy had said. "What they don't understand they condemn or denounce so they can keep their power and wealth. Remember this, my darlings, you can use fear as a tool to protect you. They can only use it as poison to weaken and defeat them. You are the beautiful, the perfect, as long as you are one of us."

"Hey," Liam said. "Don't you love the scenery, the ride? You look so damn serious."

"Of course," I said. "I was just thinking of where I was not so long ago, how unhappy I was, and how amazing life can be."

He smiled. "Come over here and steer, get the feel of it," he said. "C'mon. Don't be afraid."

"I'm hardly that," I said, and slipped in front of him to take the wheel. It was exhilarating. I was so into it that I didn't realize he was still behind me, his hands on my arms, his face close to my cheek and my neck, his lips finding my ears and moving along my neck to the curve into my shoulders. "You're distracting me," I complained, but not forcefully.

"I love this spot on your body. It's so soft."

With his right hand, he pulled the lever that slowed us down, but the waves, as calm as the ocean was, lifted and bounced us. He turned me around to kiss me.

"I thought you might never have been kissed on the Atlantic Ocean," he said. "Wanted to be sure it happened."

"You did all this just for me? Thank you," I said, laughing.

"What a wise-ass."

He accelerated again, and we went bouncing hard over the waves, the spray finding its way to my hair and my face. None of it was unpleasant.

Ava would never enjoy this as much as I am, I thought. She might pretend she did in order to draw in her prey, but to go out simply for the joy of it wasn't something she ever did or mentioned. *Everything I'm doing reassures me that I'm different,* I concluded, buoying up my courage and determination.

We docked in Salem and, holding hands, walked up the street to the restaurant he had described. It was a replica of what an old colonial pub might be, with the waitresses and waiters in costume, the menu describing foods the way they would have been described in the seventeenth and eighteenth centuries. While we were eating, a town crier entered to announce the daily news, describing an upcoming wedding and the arrivals of ships.

"Sometimes the news is real," Liam said.

Afterward, we stopped at a shop, and he bought me an old-fashioned rag doll.

"I don't think Julia has this one," he said, and then he did something that I thought was very nice. Despite all of the dolls Julia had, he bought her one, too. On the way back to the boat, we stopped for some homemade ice cream cones. As I licked mine, I recalled how forbidden sweets had been to us, how adamant Mrs. Fennel had been about our not eating candy and ice cream. I used to think of it as poison, and if I did stray, I'd wait to be thrown into some dire condition and hear all of the "I told you so's," but that had never happened, and it wasn't going to happen now.

What I realized was that Mrs. Fennel would forbid things that would make us crave a different existence. Taste the world beyond, and we might start to wish we were in it, she surely thought. She had been the keeper of our souls until we made the ultimate sacrifices for Daddy and then determined that any change, any diversion, any escape, was not only forbidden but impossible. Full of defiance and new joy, I wanted to embrace this life fully and make it impossible to return to my prior existence.

We took a beautiful ride back, slowing down and stopping occasionally when we were in calmer waters. Liam sat with his arm around me, and we watched all the other water activity going on. He talked about boats, some of the other places he had been that were very beautiful, but mostly, I sensed how much he really loved where he lived, loved where we were.

"My great-aunt's kooky sometimes," he said, "but she's not all wrong about heritage. I feel like I'm part of this, part of the history. Don't tell her I said that. She'll pile books in my arms and send me to museums galore."

We kissed. We held each other, and I felt strengthened, hopeful, and ready to deal with any darkness that awaited. But anyone could easily say, "That's because you haven't done it yet."

After we tied up the boat, we drove back to the

Dolan mansion. Now that I was seeing it in daylight, I could really appreciate its size, the beauty of the grounds, and the acreage it included. Liam pulled up to the front rather than bring his car to the garage.

"You can use one of the guest suites to shower and change," he said. "Remember, we're staying casual."

"That's all I have, casual clothes."

I saw about a half-dozen grounds people working on the bushes, flowers, and lawns.

"I used to do some of that," Liam said, seeing where I was looking. "We had a great head gardener in those days, Pepe Rosario. I thought of him as my Latino grandfather. He retired and returned to Venezuela."

"What about your real grandparents?"

"My mother's family disappeared along with her, and my father's mother died when I was fifteen. My grandfather is in an adult residence in Boston. They had my father late in their marriage. No other children. So I really only have my great-aunt Amelia, my grandmother's sister. I'm about as poor when it comes to family as you are," he said.

Family poor, I'm not, I thought, but I couldn't imagine ever telling him why.

The instant we entered the house, Mrs. Wakefield appeared, as if she had been beamed down from someplace upstairs. I didn't see her standing there near the bottom of the stairs until Liam said, "Hi, Mrs. Wakefield."

She stepped forward.

Unlike Mrs. Fennel, Mrs. Wakefield looked plump,

with a soft face nearly absorbing her two hazel-brown eyes. She wore a light brown one-piece dress with a dark brown belt. I saw no jewelry except for her modest wedding ring. Her gray hair was nicely styled, neatly trimmed at her jawline. I had no idea what her age was, but she had very little in the way of wrinkles or even crow's-feet. There was something almost alabaster about her complexion. It reminded me of smooth soapstone, her features gently chiseled so that her nose was well proportioned to her thick, rosy lips and plump cheeks. Not pretty and not unpleasant-looking, she struck me as someone who guarded her plainness, avoiding too much makeup or any cosmetic emphasis that would attempt to make her more striking by emphasizing her best qualities. There were no best qualities. "Comely" was the adjective that came to mind, for someone with a good appearance, not homely or plain and yet not outstanding, and probably never the cause for a man to have a second look.

When she stepped forward, however, it was as if those eyes widened and rose to the surface of their eye sockets almost like a telescope expanding, the lenses focusing. Her lips tightened, as did the muscles in her neck. I saw her shoulders rise like the shoulders of a hawk preparing to pounce. She was studying me very hard, her look full of suspicion and distrust. I imagined that this was the sort of reaction she first gave any young woman Liam brought to the house.

"This is Lorelei Patio, Mrs. Wakefield. The young lady you heard my father rave about," he added in an attempt to ensure that she had a good impression of me. However, I could see that she wasn't easily influenced. Her face didn't change; it was almost a mask.

"Yes, I have heard a great deal about you. So much, in fact, that one wonders if it could possibly be true."

"Time will tell, Mrs. Wakefield."

"It always does." She turned to Liam. "Will you be joining your father for dinner tonight? He has a guest. Your sister is going somewhere after work."

"Oh. No, we have reservations," Liam said. "Who's my father's guest?"

"He's in his office," she said as a response, and started away.

"Mrs. Wakefield?"

She paused. Although she looked at Liam, I could feel that she was really looking at me. She held a tight smile on her face, the sort of smile that bore no warmth but designed itself more to hide a minor annoyance. At least, I hoped that whatever it was, it was minor.

"Yes, Liam?"

"Lorelei will be using the brown guest room to pre-pare for our dinner engagement."

"It's not brown, Liam. It's beige. How many times have I told you that?"

"Whatever, it looks brown to me," he said, smiling.

She raised her eyes toward the ceiling and continued down the hallway.

"It takes a little time for her to warm up to someone new," Liam said. "But once she does, she's about as faithful as a golden retriever."

"Golden or beige retriever?" I asked.

He laughed, took my hand, and led me up the stairs to the guest room. "If you need anything, just pick up the phone, press intercom, and hit three. That's me. Everything else you need is in the bathroom. Take a rest. Before we leave, we'll have a cocktail in the den. I'd better go down and see my father. He hasn't had a guest for dinner in some time."

"I hope it's not Naomi Addison," I said.

He laughed. And then he thought a moment, looked worried, and hurried out. As soon as he did, I dropped myself onto the bed and looked up at the ceiling. The circles embossed over the faux finish seemed to turn first clockwise and then counterclockwise. I closed my eyes. I wasn't tired, exactly. It had just been a day filled with new sensations, new images and feelings. They had come at me so quickly and were so abundant that I was feeling like someone who had overeaten. I wondered if my capacity to be more sensitive, to hear and see and taste everything to its fullest, could ever be overloaded. Maybe that was why Mrs. Fennel and my father had wanted me to spend less time experiencing the world outside our world. The darkness I had lived within drove me to seek colors, brightness, warmth, and softness. Perhaps they had feared that I would hunger and thirst for so much of it that I would explode. It was the way I felt right now.

Liam's kisses, his gentle embrace, the sound of his laughter, and the light of his smile danced on the insides of my eyelids. I thought I could replay every second, every moment of our time together, from the first time his fingers touched mine to the moment he just let my hand go. At this very second, I was happier than I had been, maybe ever. I felt guilty being happier with Liam than I had been with Buddy, but my time with Buddy had been too clandestine. Along with our joy had ridden the fear of being discovered, of me being exposed as a traitor. Whether or not I was deluding myself, I felt free here, free to be who I believed I really was.

I almost fell asleep thinking about all of this, but I gathered myself and took a long, delightful shower under a large rain head that splattered my body with a torrent of warm, soft water. The towels were soft and large. I wrapped myself in one and sat at the vanity mirror, drying and then brushing out my hair before pinning it back and up. I wore just a little lipstick. There was nothing much to do about my face, which at the moment looked as if it was stuck in a constant blush.

Liam had emphasized "casual," so I slipped on a pair of sateen skinny ankle pants with a pair of backdrop kindle buckle boots and a long-sleeved lamb's-wool antique-cream sweater. I thought it would be perfect for the cooler evening air. When I had gone shopping with Naomi, I had bought myself a pair of deco disc rusty torch earrings. I thought they looked good with my hair up. I wore no other jewelry. I had nothing else, actually. Just as I finished, I heard a knock on the bedroom door.

"Perfect timing," I called, expecting it to be Liam. To my surprise, when I opened the door, I was facing Mr. Dolan.

15

"I don't mean to disturb," he began. I thought he looked stunningly handsome in a black velvet sports jacket, a black shirt, and a red tie. *Daddy had a sports jacket like his,* I thought.

"No, no. It's fine. I'm really ready," I said, stepping back.

He nodded and entered. For a moment, he simply stood there looking at me with a soft smile on his face. "You're a really beautiful young woman, Lorelei," he said. "A natural beauty. Most of the women I'm introduced to these days look like they would come apart in a hot shower."

"Thank you, Mr. Dolan."

He laughed.

"What?"

"I love how you don't blush and yet you don't come off being conceited or arrogant. It's so matter-of-fact with you, your beauty."

It wasn't in my nature to blush. How could I explain that? Daddy had filled me with too much confidence, but, like a skilled sculptor, he had managed to keep us all from appearing smug or vain.

"Nevertheless, I appreciate the compliment, Mr. Dolan."

He nodded.

"I didn't get a chance to tell you yet," I continued, "but speaking of beauty, you have a beautiful home."

"Thank you. A lot of thought went into it. You can be confident that we have the best plumbing," he added, smiling. He glanced around and then sat in the side chair and nodded at the one beside it. I sat.

"Is something wrong, Mr. Dolan?"

His eyes shadowed and grew deep and dark for a moment. I thought that Mrs. Wakefield might have seen something in me that she didn't like and had already said something to him.

"No, nothing's wrong. My daughter, Julia, is very taken with you. She's a perceptive young lady. I respect her opinion."

"I like her, too."

Where's the second shoe here? I wondered. *What's going to be dropped on me?*

"The reason I snuck up here once I learned you were here was to have a brief chat. I want to be sure that seeing Liam is something you really want to do. What I mean to say is, don't do anything you think might be necessary to hold on to your job."

I sat back sharply. "I don't know what sort of girl you're used to seeing with your son, Mr. Dolan, but I assure you, I wouldn't spend a moment with him outside of the company if I didn't want to do so. And if my job depended on my pleasing the boss's son, I'd be out of there in what I've heard people call a New York minute."

Instead of being annoyed at my sharp comeback, he smiled. "You reassure me that my initial instincts about people, especially young women, are not as dull as I feared. I don't doubt that the difficulties of your own family situation have hardened you. What's that quote, 'If it doesn't kill me, it makes me stronger'?"

"Nietzsche. It's 'What does not destroy me makes me stronger.'"

"Yes, well, I wish that were true for Liam."

"Give him a chance. Maybe it will be," I said. "Sometimes we're too close to see."

His smile widened, and his eyes lost any trace of darkness.

The truth was, I wasn't thinking of Liam. I was thinking of myself and my father and sisters.

"I won't deny that for the time being, he seems to have developed a sense of responsibility. Look at how he dresses for work now and how he goes at it. I have a sneaking suspicion, however, that he's really trying to please you more than me."

"I hope that doesn't upset you."

"Upset me? Hardly. I just wanted to be sure you were fine with it." He leaned toward me to whisper. "I was secretly watching and laughing to myself at how hard a time you were giving him, and also the other young men."

"A girl alone my age has to be careful."

"Absolutely, but don't ever think of yourself as alone

as long as you're working for Ken Dolan," he said. He slapped his palms on his knees and stood. "Okay. I feel better. So, I understand you went out on our boat. Did you have a good time?"

"It was a beautiful day, Mr. Dolan. Salem was fun, too."

"You know," he said as he walked toward the door and turned after he opened it, "I think that out of the office, you can call me Ken."

"I'll try," I said. "No promises."

He laughed. "I just have to get something in my room. I'll meet you downstairs for a cocktail before you two go off."

I wondered how Liam would react if he knew his father had come in to cross-examine me. I hoped he didn't know. I hurried out and down the stairs. Mrs. Wakefield was standing there, as if she had been assigned to wait for me.

"Liam is in the den," she said. "Right this way."

"That's all right. I know where it is," I told her.

She turned, surprised.

"I was here last night."

"Oh?"

"It was late."

She looked more thoughtful than upset about it. "Yes, well, when you're young, you can burn the candle at both ends, but when you're older, you realize you use up the candle twice as quickly that way."

Even though she didn't have to show me where the den was, she continued to walk alongside me, step for step. In some ways, she reminded me of a protective guard dog, keeping one careful eye on anyone who approached her master.

"I understand you've been here for quite a long time," I said as we walked down the wide, grayish-black slate corridor.

She paused. "Yes. In a world where there is such little permanence and commitment, I imagine I'm a bit of a relic."

I paused and smiled. "That can't be true for a city like Quincy that has held on to its history so dearly. I haven't been anywhere that has such a sense of the permanent."

She almost smiled, too, but settled for a short nod to illustrate that she liked my answer. When we arrived at the den, she nodded and continued on. Liam was standing in front of the bar. He turned quickly when I entered.

"Wow, you make casual look like elegant," he said, rushing over to kiss me on the cheek.

"Thank you."

"A glass of wine, maybe?"

"Yes, white. Do you have a Chardonnay?"

"Do we have a Chardonnay?" He opened the glass door of the wall wine cooler to show me what looked like more than a hundred different bottles. "And one from California, too. Maybe you've heard of it."

He put it on the bar. I had heard of it.

"It's good."

He began to open the bottle, keeping his eyes on me.

"What?" I said.

"I can't help staring at you. I hope you don't mind. Trying to get me to stop is hopeless, anyway."

"As long as you don't do it while you're driving," I said.

"Yes." He popped the cork. "I'm glad you're all right. Is that what he was doing at the time?"

"No. Something else distracted him."

"The imaginary old man?" he asked as he poured my glass.

"How do you know about that?"

"It's a small town. No. I was interested in everything about you from the first moment I saw you."

I sipped the wine and walked around the den, looking at the paintings and at the case of DVDs and CDs. Again, it looked like hundreds. I browsed the bookcases, too. I could feel Liam's eyes on me constantly. There was a white faux-fur area rug between the two settees that faced each other. I knelt down to run the palm of my hand over it.

"How cozy. It's so white that it's intimidating. I'm afraid to walk on it."

He laughed. "Mrs. Wakefield used to make me take off my shoes first whenever I entered the house. When I complained, she would tell me I was lucky she didn't make me take off all my clothes, too."

"Oh?"

"Just her way of making me grateful that it was all she demanded," he said, shaking his head. "No dirty thoughts, please."

"*Moi?* Never."

He laughed, and I came around and sat on a bar stool.

"You saved my life, you know," he said, leaning over to get closer to me.

"What? How?"

"If you hadn't said yes to my invitation to spend the day with me, I would have drowned myself."

I laughed, but I couldn't help wondering if there would be a time, and soon, when I would have to think about saving his life.

"Don't tell me you haven't left a line of broken hearts back in California, where the preferred method of suicide is surfing."

"You're very funny, but no, I have not left a line of broken hearts trailing."

"Must be at least one."

"Let's talk about something else," I said. "Where are we going?"

"This great little Italian place, DiBona's. It's a true family-owned restaurant. Alberto DiBona cooks everything. His wife, Francesca, helps, but she's more like the hostess, and they have two daughters and a son who work as the waitstaff. I think there's a nephew in there, too. For some people, family is still a very big thing," he said, and bit down on his lip. "Sorry. I keep forgetting about your own situation."

"Yours doesn't exactly fit on Christmas cards, either," I said.

He nodded.

We heard some voices in the hallway.

"My father, unbeknownst to either Julia or myself,

had started dating again. He's seeing Kelly Burnett, the administrator at the hospital. I promised we would stay long enough to have one drink with them and meet her. She's been divorced for a few years and is only seven years younger," he finished in a whisper as they entered the den.

Kelly Burnett was as tall as Ken Dolan. She was svelte in a stylish black three-quarter-sleeve dress with an elegantly paneled bodice. She wore her dark brown hair parted in the middle and shoulder-length. Dark-complexioned, with intelligent ebony eyes and firm, feminine lips, she reminded me of my older sister Brianna, especially the way she fixed her gaze on someone. I could almost hear her thoughts rolling through quick impressions.

"Liam, Lorelei, I'd like you to meet Kelly Burnett."

"Hi," she said, holding her hand out for Liam first. He took it and smiled. Then she turned to me and said, *"Enchanté,"* as if she expected that I spoke French. It was almost a challenge.

"Oui, je suis heureuse de vous rencontrer," I said.

Her eyes widened, Ken's smile exploded, and Liam looked at me as if he had just first set eyes on me.

"I really don't speak French," Kelly said, laughing. "I just like the way they greet each other. What did you say?"

"Yes, pleased to meet you," I told her, and shrugged. "What else would I say?"

"You speak French?" Liam asked.

"I've had some lessons," I said.

"Well, I'm impressed," Kelly said. "I understand you were in my hospital recently, unfortunately."

"Yes, a car accident. Julia took good care of me," I said.

"So, you're all right?"

"Fine, thank you."

"Chardonnay?" Liam offered her.

"Thank you, yes," she said.

Mr. Dolan sat beside her at the bar and looked at both Liam and me with pleasure. Liam knew his drink, a Scotch and water, and prepared it.

"I'm sorry you're not having dinner with us," Kelly said.

"It's a date we made in advance," Liam explained, and winked. "We're just getting to know each other ourselves. I'm sure you understand."

"Yes, of course," Kelly said. "Perhaps another time."

"We'll know after tonight," Liam joked.

"Where are you going?" Mr. Dolan asked, and Liam told him.

"Good choice. I'll have to take you there one night," he told Kelly.

"You're staying at the Winston House?" she asked me.

"For now, yes."

"Thanks to my great-auntie Amelia, I discovered her," Liam said.

"Sounds like something meant to happen," Kelly Burnett said, and raised her glass. "To destiny. Hopefully good for us all."

We clinked glasses and drank.

"How long have you been at the hospital?" I asked her.

"Two years this coming December. I'm sure you'll find Quincy a very nice place to start a new life," she added. I glanced at Mr. Dolan. How much had he told her about me? I wondered.

"I agree," I said. I could sense how much she wanted to ask me questions about my background, but I also sensed that Mr. Dolan had told her to hold off on that.

"I think we have to get started," Liam said, finishing his drink. I finished mine, too. "It's a small restaurant, and they might not hold the table if we're very late. Besides, I promised Lorelei we'd have an early night. You guys have a great time."

He came around the bar quickly, took my glass, and put it on the bar before taking my hand.

"Just be careful out there," his father said. "You're carrying a precious company asset."

We laughed.

"As long as you don't think of me as an elbow joint," I said, and everyone laughed again.

We started out.

"I feel guilty not staying for dinner," I told Liam.

He leaned over as we entered the hallway to whisper, "I'm not sharing you with anyone just yet."

He kissed me on the cheek and hurried me out to his car, as if we were making some sort of escape. I looked back at the house. We hadn't closed the front door properly, I guessed. Mrs. Wakefield was there looking out at us. She closed the door, shaking her head as she did so, like someone who believed we would come to no good.

I was able to put all dark thoughts out of my mind once we were in the small restaurant, cozily seated in a red imitation-leather booth with Italian sopranos singing through the wall speakers and the warm, friendly family atmosphere hovering around us. All around us were pictures of small Italian villages, some on the sea and some in areas like Tuscany. On one wall were shelves of wines on display, and on another wall were what I assumed to be actual old photographs of family, some obviously taken in Italy. The owners were very happy to see Liam. Apparently, he had not been there for some time.

"I thought this was your favorite restaurant," I said when Francesca left us. "You made it sound like you're here very often."

He looked guilty for a moment and then smiled and said, "The kind of girls I was with recently wouldn't have appreciated this."

"How did you know I would?"

"We both have a longing for family," he replied. "This feels like someone's home dining room and kitchen. Smell the garlic?"

I smiled. Daddy used to enjoy making fun of the idea that garlic would be dangerous.

"Think I'm funny?"

"No, you're right," I said, looking around. "I was just thinking about something someone once said about garlic."

"I've got a lot to learn about you, Lorelei Patio, but I don't mind how long it will take if you don't mind."

"Let's—"

"Take it a step at a time. I know," he said. "For now, that means ordering a bottle of Chianti and something to eat."

It was a great dinner, one I was sure Mrs. Fennel would disapprove of, especially when we were served homemade tiramisu. The owners treated us to a glass of limoncello. The other customers were naturally curious about us because of all the attention we were getting.

During the meal, Liam was more forthcoming about his youth, growing up without his mother, and how distant he felt from his father.

"It was almost as if he was blaming my mother's desertion on us, or me," he said. "Like if I hadn't been born, she wouldn't have had the right to leave or something."

"That makes no sense, and you know it," I said. "More likely the things you heard, what you saw, and how it all made you feel fed your own anger and poor self-image."

"Me? Poor self-image? From what my father and Mrs. Wakefield say, you'd think I was a walking egotist."

"That's all show," I said.

The way he looked at me made me wonder for a moment if he was growing angry. Was his male ego damaged? Did he think I was putting him down? Was I too truthful about what I saw?

"Do you care to explain that, please?"

I shrugged, trying to make it seem simple. "You didn't do poorly in school and college because you're not up to the challenges, Liam. Sometimes we feel the need to live up to the impressions people have of us, to shove it back into their faces . . . defiance born of an inner rage that seems far beyond our control."

"Our? What about you?"

"In my way, I wasn't much different. I suppose we're both trying to escape ourselves or what we think we are."

He crinkled his eyebrows and shook his head. "You're right in front of me," he said. "I can reach out and touch you. I've kissed you, held you, but most of the time, it's almost as if you're not really there. You're an image or like a virtual you."

"It takes time," I said, hoping I was right. "Sometimes the time it takes is too much and it's easier to give up."

"Oh, no," he said, shaking his head emphatically. "Don't even think it. I'm in for the long haul."

He finished his limoncello as a toast, and I smiled. Liam came with his own personal baggage, I thought. Any relationship I would dream of having with any man was going to be hard enough. Was I foolish for even thinking of starting one with him? Maybe not, I thought. Maybe my spending more time on building him up would help me worry less about myself.

Francesca came over to give me a hug good night and then hugged Liam, shaking her finger at him for staying away so long. He promised he wouldn't do it again, and we left holding hands.

"They're delightful," I said. "You were right. It is like eating with family. Thank you for thinking of it for me."

We got into the car.

"Do I have to keep my promise?" he asked.

"Early night?"

He nodded.

"I'm afraid so," I said.

"Okay, okay."

"But there'll be times when we won't worry about the clock so much, I hope."

He looked as if he would explode with happiness. "Can I pick you up in the morning?"

"It's out of your way."

"There is no way," he said, punctuating each word hard, "that you will ever, ever be out of my way."

"Okay," I said, laughing. "But people will talk."

"You mean Great-auntie Amelia?"

"And Mrs. McGruder."

"I'm sure they've been talking about us all night," he said.

When we arrived at the Winston House, we sat and talked a little more about his family. I saw how much he loved Julia. At times, he spoke about her as if she had been his mother, always looking after him, always more disappointed than anyone for his failures and mistakes.

"You're lucky to have her," I said.

"You didn't have any brothers or sisters?"

"No," I said. I wondered, if we did see each other steadily, whether he would begin to know when I wasn't telling the truth. My sisters had always been confident in their ability to handle any man, twist and turn him whatever way they wanted, and get him to believe whatever they wanted. When I was very young, I had witnessed

Brianna bringing home her catch. I had even overheard some of the lies she told, and I had seen how easily the man had accepted them as the truth.

"They want to believe what we tell them," Ava once said. "They don't want to do anything to endanger their fantasy and their ultimate success. No one fools himself more than a man does when it comes to the woman he wants."

The implication had been clear: I, too, would have all of this power.

But did I want it?

Liam and I kissed good night, softly, lovingly. He touched my hair and looked into my eyes as he stroked my cheek.

"Okay," he said. "I have you memorized. I'll fall asleep with your face on the inside of my eyelids."

"Good night," I whispered.

"I'll be right here at seven forty-five."

I stood watching him drive off. When he was gone, I turned to walk to the front door.

I was halfway there when she stepped out of the shadows.

16

"What the hell do you think you are doing?" Ava asked.

When I was a little girl, Ava could frighten me with her angry words, said so sternly that I would feel my spine shake. She could send a chill through my chest and into my heart, as if I had gulped a glass of ice water. I remember that even my lips felt numb.

It was as if I were a little girl again. I stood there frozen, unable to speak. She was wearing a black velvet hooded jacket and tight black jeans. Her face caught in the lighted door lamps had a yellowish glow, with her eyes like two burning coals. I glanced around nervously, anticipating Daddy, but there was no one but her. She had started to take a step toward me when Jim Lamb pulled up to the curb in front of the Winston House. Seeing me just outside the door, he tapped his horn and leaped out of his car.

Ava stepped back into the shadows when I turned to him.

"Hi," he called. "Great coincidence. Come here and take a look at the good job they did on my car."

When I looked back at Ava, I saw she was gone. She

had slipped farther into the shadows and glided through the pockets of darkness. Jim stood in front of his car, his hands on his hips, looking at the repair job and waiting for me. Still trembling, I walked toward him.

"I was at a movie with one of the guys who teaches at my school. Terrific little film. Won't make any money, though. So?" he said, nodding toward the car. "What do you think?"

"You'd never know anything had happened to it," I said, looking back nervously for Ava. She wasn't there.

"Exactly. Something wrong?" he asked, noticing how I was searching the darkness.

"No. No. Everything's fine."

"Good. So, how was your day?"

I turned again toward the house but perused the lawn and the houses nearby, searching for Ava's dark silhouette. I didn't see her, and for a moment, I questioned whether I actually had seen her. Could I have imagined it, imagined the conversation? What made me question it was my belief that Ava was not one to retreat, especially from a young man like Jim Lamb. Why wouldn't she have put me in an embarrassing position by trying to explain who she was? Why wouldn't she have used the occasion to ruin my stay here? Why else would she have followed me?

"What? Oh. Very nice," I said, realizing that Jim was waiting for an answer. I started for the front door again, walking gingerly, my eyes panning every possible nook and cranny in the darkness where Ava might be hovering. Jim walked alongside me.

"Did you hear that there's a new tenant coming tomorrow?"

"Yes," I said.

"Sounds like an interesting fellow. Our dinner table could use some new conversation."

He lunged forward to open the door for me.

"Thank you," I said, and entered.

The house was quiet, but I couldn't believe Mrs. Winston would have gone to sleep without first seeing what my day with her great-nephew was like. Sure enough, she stepped out of the living room with a book in her hand.

"Well, now," she said, surprised that we were entering together. "Where did you two meet?"

"Right outside. Just a coincidence," Jim said, a little sadly.

Mrs. Winston held her tight smile and looked at me. "Would you like something before you go to bed, Lorelei? A cup of tea, hot cocoa?"

"I don't think so, thank you."

She looked at Jim, who realized he was standing there awkwardly, especially since she had not asked him if he wanted something.

"Well, I'd better get to bed. Early to rise, of course. Always have to get myself fully awake before those girls hit the school. They take no prisoners," he added, fidgeting with the buttons on his jacket. " 'Night."

"Good night, Jim," Mrs. Winston said.

" 'Night. Your car looks great," I added.

He flashed a smile and went to the stairway.

"Before you ask," I said to Mrs. Winston, "I had a wonderful time."

"Well, I'm happy to hear that."

"Your nephew has a beautiful home."

"Mansion, you mean. That land once belonged to John Hancock. He bought it on speculation but didn't do much with it. It had an interesting history before it became a Dolan property. One family in the mid-nineteenth century buried a child there, but the coffin was dug up and planted in the Hancock Cemetery. Now, that's an interesting bit of ground. The Puritans didn't always have grave markers, and cattle roamed freely over it, so there are many more people buried there than indicated. I actually took Liam there once when I was trying to build his appreciation of our history. He didn't find anything impressive about it. I don't think I was very successful at building his appreciation of Quincy."

"Oh, no. Liam has a real feeling for this place. You'd be surprised."

"I would. Sometimes it takes a virgin set of eyes to see what we've been looking at for decades. Maybe you're right. While I'm happy that it was a good experience, I know you're probably ready for bed. I won't keep you," she said. "Good night."

She returned to the living room, and I hurried up the stairs. I wanted to get into my room, first to see if Ava would surprise me by somehow being there and second to look out the window to see if I could spot her on the street. The room was empty. I gazed up and down the street from every angle but saw no one. A few cars went by, their headlights scraping away some darkness for me.

Finally, I sat on my bed. I felt stunned, confused.

Did I really see and hear Ava? Would she appear again? How long had she been there? Was that her I had seen at the dance club after all?

I prepared for bed slowly, keenly listening to every sound, every creak in the house. The footsteps I eventually heard on the stairway and in the hallway were Mrs. Winston's, but when I got into bed, I just lay there with my eyes open, anticipating. A stronger breeze kicked up, and the branches of a close maple tree scratched the siding of the house with an almost perfectly constant rhythm. I closed my eyes. I was tired and wanted to sleep, and the best way to do so was to convince myself that I had imagined Ava. Otherwise, it made no sense. She would never cut and run. Comfortable with my theory, I drifted off, and when the first rays of sunshine penetrated the curtains, I was elated. Nothing had happened. She hadn't appeared.

Forget it. It was your overworked imagination, I told myself, and got up to get ready for work.

Liam was there early, but he didn't come into the house. He sat in his car, waiting. I had a feeling he would be there already, so when I had finished breakfast and my last preparations for leaving, I stepped out of the house.

"'Morning," Liam said. "You look like you had a good night's sleep."

"Looks deceive," I said after getting into the car.

"I'm easily deceived, then," he said. "But happily deceived as well."

I asked him about the work he had to do in Boston. He talked more about the business and his father's efforts to get him to be part of it.

"I know I was a brat," he said. "When a father builds something as big as Dolan Plumbing Supply and has a son, he hopes he'll have the same interest and enthusiasm and carry it on. That's especially true here, where there are so many family businesses, houses people have lived in for generations, and proud family trees. Just ask my great-auntie Amelia."

"I don't have to ask. She doesn't miss a chance to tell me," I said, and he laughed.

"Lorelei Patio," he said, and repeated my name like a prayer. "I don't know where you really came from or why you are here, but some angel is looking out for me."

"Maybe it's a fallen angel," I said. He shook his head.

"No way, José."

When we reached the company, he went in to get last-minute instructions from his father. On the way out, he stopped at my desk.

"I know you have my aunt's half-board plan or whatever she calls it, but if I get back early enough . . ."

The vivid memory of Ava in the shadows returned as he spoke. If she really was there, this budding romance was already on a fatal trajectory. But the look on his face, the desperate hope that I would show at least as much enthusiasm as he was showing, warmed my fearful heart.

"Just call from the road," I said. "I should let Mrs.

McGruder know. That's a house filled with little courte-
sies to be observed."

"Exactly."

He kissed me quickly and hurried away.

To keep myself from thinking of anything dark and
treacherous, I went at my work with a furious passion.
I nearly worked through lunch and would have if it
weren't for Carol Charles, one of the women in accounting, stopping by to get my sandwich order. After
lunch, I took a call from Kelly Burnett for Mr. Dolan.
She knew I was his personal secretary, of course, and
asked me how my evening had been. She said she
looked forward to seeing me again. She suggested that
Mr. Dolan might be planning something for the four of
us, "maybe even six of us if Julia and Clifford can manage it."

I couldn't help but like the way I was being included, accepted, so quickly. But why? Was it because
I was doing good work or that Liam was undergoing
some sort of change for the better? No one really had
yet pursued my family story. Everyone had accepted
my rendition of it, and I had apparently left them with
the sense that talking about it would be painful for me.
How long would that work? When would the detailed
questions be asked? How could I survive dishonesty
long enough to be truly accepted?

I had the feeling that this broken family needed me
almost as much as I needed them and that in their way
of thinking, nothing could change their minds about
me. *Just let it go,* I told myself. *Just let it run its course.
You'll know when to pull back, when to leave, but for now,*

enjoy what you've always wanted to enjoy, a normal way of life.

Liam called at three. He wasn't on the road back, but he was determined to be home early enough.

"I'll hire a helicopter if I have to," he joked. At least, I thought he joked.

"I'll call Mrs. McGruder," I said. "How is the job?"

"It's going great. It helps when you give a damn," he added, and laughed.

Yes, I thought. *It does.*

He called me from the highway later. He had already asked Michael Thomas to drive me home so I could get ready to go out. I saw the half-surprised, half-suspicious look on his face when he came to get me.

"Now, I'm not judging you," he said, smiling, when we got into his truck, "but talk about your fast workers. It's like a tornado ripped through this place, but not a destructive one," he quickly added. "What have you done to Liam Dolan? The man looks and acts like he cares. I know Ken is walking straighter."

"My father used to say you can be told a hundred times to pick up after yourself, but until you tell yourself to do it, you won't change, not really. Maybe something sleeping inside him finally woke up."

"Yeah, right. Maybe you woke it up," he said.

I smiled like a conspirator, and he laughed.

"I hope my daughters have a little of what you have," he said.

Whenever I received any compliment in Quincy, my first reaction was guilt, because I felt like a phony and a liar. I was deceiving them all. Could I tell Michael that he would never want his daughters to have any of what I had? Of course not, but something inside me wouldn't permit me to accept such strong compliments gracefully. The best I could do was smile and maybe say thank you, but I was afraid I was going to appear arrogant, conceited, or too indifferent.

"From what I see, I hope they have a lot of what you have, Michael."

He brightened like Christmas lights. "If only I was eighteen again," he sang, and we rode on, laughing.

When I entered the house, Mrs. Winston came out of the kitchen, wiping her hands on a small dish towel, to greet me before I started up the stairs.

"Now, your canceling your dinner can't be to have another date with my great-nephew, can it?" she asked with a teasing smile.

"Very likely," I said.

"Well, I trust you have good judgment. Oh," she added after she had started to turn away, "the new gentleman has arrived and has taken Naomi Addison's old room. He's aware that he's sharing the bathroom with you. I would have put him on the other side, but that bathroom has two already sharing it, and—"

"I'm fine with it, Amelia. Don't worry."

"If there's even the slightest problem, don't hesitate to tell me," she said.

I smiled and headed up.

As soon as I turned to go down the hallway, the new tenant stepped out of his room.

I stopped as he lifted his head slowly and looked at me. He wore a dark green long-sleeved shirt with jeans and a pair of white running shoes. Although he had long licorice-black hair, he kept it smoothly brushed and with trim bangs. When he looked at me, his silvery-gray eyes brightened the way someone's eyes would when they had run into someone they had known years ago. There was nothing immediately familiar about him, and if he was truly who he was supposed to be, there was no way we could have ever met. He had a light, almost pale complexion and was not ugly but not terribly good-looking, either. His nose looked too thin, his lips a little too thick, and his oval face emphasized his round, weak chin. He was stout, with a soft-looking belly, and about Jim's height.

"Hi," he said, moving forward with his hand extended. "I'm Collin Nickels. And yes, I get kidded a lot. You know, like can I put more than two cents in, or are there five in my family. Stupid stuff like that. You're Lorelei. I was told we're to share the bathroom. You'll have no problem with me," he continued, as if once he started to talk, there was no way to stop him. He seemed not to need a breath. "I'm up so early in the morning, almost always before the sun rises. Most of the time, you won't even know I'm here. I keep my stuff in my room, too, so there'll be no clutter, and don't worry about any noise. I'm up late reading and working on my laptop and out most of the day doing my research. I'm working on a doctoral thesis. My parents call me the constant student because I've been in school since age five and never had a real job."

I realized he was still holding my hand.

"Pleased to meet you," I said, taking my hand back.

Was he babbling out of nervousness? I thought he

was amusing, but I was afraid to let down my guard. Paranoia was the sister who would never leave my side. Would I ever meet a stranger or be introduced to anyone without going into some defensive mode, always anticipating trouble? This young man seemed to come from some casting director looking to fill the part of a college male nerd in a B-movie. If he was a Renegade or even someone in my father's clan, I would have to give up any hope of being prepared for trouble. I'd never recognize him.

"Yes. If you ever have any free time, I'd like to tell you about it. I like to tell anyone about it. I'm sort of proud of what I'm doing, even though my parents are waiting for me to tell them I have some sort of job out of all this money they're spending on me. Parents. Are your parents proud of you?"

Obviously, no one had told him much about me, and I wasn't in the mood to go into my fictional background.

"If they are, they haven't said so yet," I replied.

"Well, that surprises me. Don't give up hope," he said. "See you at dinner?"

"No, I'm going out."

"Oh, you have a date. That doesn't surprise me," he said. He smiled and continued down the hallway. I watched him walk away to see if he would turn to look back at me, but he didn't.

Harmless, I told myself. I hoped I wouldn't regret it.

Liam was back from Boston by seven, and we went to another one of his favorite restaurants. This time, when friends of his approached, I had the sense that he didn't want us to spend any time with them, and it wasn't only his burning desire not to share his time with me with anyone. I picked up the vibes and asked him about it.

"You were pretty curt with those guys," I said.

"Somehow, I can't lie to you, Lorelei," he said. "I don't want to have anything to do with those guys anymore. They were part of my history that I'm not proud of."

I understood. It got so that if he saw any of these old rotten buddies, as he liked to call them, he would turn us around and go someplace else. We didn't go out every night of the week. Sometimes the work he had really did keep him away. One project kept him out of town for three days, but he was always on the phone with me as much as he could be.

"I bet you think I'm like some teenager with a terrible crush," he said.

"No," I told him. How could I tell him that I really wouldn't know? I had never been a real teenager. I'd had no teenage boyfriends calling me on the phone. "I hope it's more than a crush."

"Do you? I was hoping you would. Dad wants to take us all out to dinner this weekend, Julia and Clifford included. I told him I'd let him know. I don't want you to feel like I'm pushing you into anything."

"I really like your father and your sister, Liam. No worries."

"No worries? What are you, Australian now? You forgot to say 'mate.'"

I paused. That really was a funny thing to say. Daddy used to come up with expressions from everywhere because of how much he had traveled. Whether I liked it or not,

I was a Patio in more ways than anyone could imagine. Daddy's influences on me were impossible to cast away.

"I'm a good mimic. What can I say? Soon my vowels will sound like yours."

"Good. I'll see you in the morning," he said. "I'll be back later tonight."

"Be careful, Liam."

"Sure." He paused. "Any special reason why?"

What would I tell him? That there was the possibility that some elderly man would suddenly appear in front of him, causing him to veer too quickly and crash, or that I thought my sister Ava was there and might pursue him and have him destroyed?

"No reason except that I care," I said.

I had the feeling that if he could have crawled through the phone line to kiss me, he would have after I said that.

That night, I went to sleep happier and more optimistic than any other night. This was really working. I could become someone's wife and someone's mother. I could live a normal life. Couldn't I? Days were passing into weeks without any more serious threats or looming dark shadows.

I saw little of Mr. Nickels. He was, as he said, practically nonexistent. When I did have dinner at the Winston House, he was always late and confused, but most of his discussions were with Jim, who, as Mrs. Winston had predicted, enjoyed the topics and the whole education scene. Jim had finally given up on me. He was polite but kept his distance more and more. Liam and I were becoming too much of an item.

Not once during any of our dates, however, did we get

so close to the point of making love that I couldn't pull back. I kept control like some preadolescent who was terrified of what would happen. Truthfully, I was afraid of the sex, but for far different reasons. What changes had occurred in me? How different would it be from when I had made love with Buddy? Would my body tighten and harden even more? Would Liam notice what was unusual, and would that create some new tension? More important, would that frighten him away from me? Would I have to leave Quincy almost immediately afterward? Was this part of what Ava had warned me about?

One night, after we'd had dinner and had driven to one of his favorite spots where we could look out over the ocean, he said a surprising thing. All the while, I was afraid that he was getting impatient and annoyed with me, with my teenager-like resistance and reluctance.

"I like the fact that you're different from most girls I've been with, Lorelei. In fact, every girl I've been with," he added. "Those idiot friends of mine I've been avoiding have this rating system for girls they take out. They use stars to disguise it."

"Oh? What is it?"

"It's how many dates they have to go out on before they can score. More girls than you might imagine are one-star girls. The unwritten law is that if they reach five stars with a girl, they bail.

"Maybe I'm becoming old-fashioned or something. Maybe my great-auntie Amelia and her way of refusing to look at the world today and not see the world she would rather be in is rubbing off on me after all. My father used to make me spend a lot of time with her. I didn't want my friends to know, because I knew they would tease me, but at least she was family. I like Mrs. Wakefield, don't misunderstand me—and I know that once she really gets to know you, she'll warm up to you, and you'll like her more, too—but I always liked being with Great-auntie Amelia more."

"She'd like to hear that."

"Yeah, well, I'm afraid she'll run me through the entire eighteenth century or something if I do tell her."

I laughed. There were more ships coming and going that night than usual, I thought. I had been toying with taking a cruise as the way to leave if and when I had to. Out there, I could feel safer, I thought. Daddy had told me about cruises he had been on, the times he crossed on the *Queen Mary,* taking one of my sisters, but they did nothing unusual until after they had docked and walked in some European city.

"You're quiet," Liam said. "I hope you don't mind what I just said about you."

"Oh, no. Of course not."

"Good, but I think you still need something to put a glow into that beautiful face, not that it doesn't glow all the time."

"Now, what do you have in mind, Liam Dolan?" I asked, turning to him.

He already had it out and in his open right palm. I looked at the small velvet box and felt an overwhelming chill at first, and then, as if some invisible large hand was around me, I felt the chill driven off and replaced with a warm excitement.

"Liam?"

"Go on. Open it," he urged.

I plucked it timidly from his palm and opened it to see a very large diamond engagement ring.

"I thought it should be a good size, because my great-auntie Amelia once told me the larger the diamond, the shorter the period of the engagement. And I agree."

I shook my head.

"Don't say no, if that's rolling around in your head. Take it and think about it. You don't have to wear it. Just think about it. Please," he begged.

"Liam, you know so little about me, really."

"I know enough. What I want to do, Lorelei, is start your life from the day we set eyes on each other. Nothing else matters."

How I wish that were true, I thought, but didn't say. I just stared at the ring.

"I know I'm not making a mistake, Lorelei."

"But it's so quick. How can you be so sure?"

"I spend all my spare time thinking about you. I go to sleep with your face in my eyes, the scent of your hair in my nose, the softness of your lips on mine. How much surer can I be?"

I could feel my arm moving forward as if it had a mind of its own, pushing the ring back at him, but I took a deep breath and fought back.

"I'll think about it," I said.

"Good. I'm confident you'll make the right decision."

He leaned forward, and we kissed.

Then, without either of us speaking, he started the engine, and floating and drifting on our own sea of thoughts and feelings, we were silent all the way back.

17

I'm sure Liam was afraid that if he rushed me, I would turn him down. For days, it was as if he had never given me the ring. At night, I put it on my bed and sat with my legs folded beneath me, staring down at it, letting the diamond seize on the starlight to twinkle in my eyes.

Do I dare? Can I dare?

From the night I had fled until now, I was truly in a whirlwind. I read romantic novels and articles about love and relationships like any other young girl. I knew what it meant to have a rebound affair after a lost love, and I knew how easily anyone could warn me that I didn't have the experience to fall in love so quickly a second time. Does having many past romances really equip you better to find your true love? Is it like trying on pairs of shoes until you find the most comfortable? And therefore, is it not true after all that there was someone special out there for you, whether you called him your soul mate or not?

Did I love Liam enough to want to spend my life with him? How much was enough? Except for when I was busy at work and the times I worried about being pursued, he was always on my mind. Recalling his smile comforted me whenever I was anxious about anything, and he had been so truthful and forthcoming about his own failures and weaknesses that I felt the sincerity two people had to feel in order to trust each other. Of course, there was a limit to what I could tell him now. Buddy didn't believe me at first, and when he had found out that I was telling the truth, he said it didn't matter, but I couldn't help wondering if that would have been true the following day, the following month, even the following year. Would the tension and the fear eventually beat down whatever love and affection he had for me? Wasn't it better to keep the truth from Liam somehow?

Could I?

Was I absolutely mad even to consider the possibility?

Why had I run away at all otherwise? If I couldn't make this happen, what was the point? Most likely, my father and my sisters expected me to turn back. I was sure they were confident about it. I could almost hear Daddy telling them to let me go. "She'll be back once she realizes how impossible it is for her out there alone." Whether I had imagined her or not, Ava was frighteningly positive that I was going to realize this. What more could I do to show my defiance?

What more?

The ring, I thought, and lifted it out of the box. I turned it slowly in my fingers. The diamond glittered like a precious stone with more than simply monetary value. It was a magic stone for me, a stone from which I could draw power and strength. Once my sisters saw it on my finger, they surely would fall back. It was one thing to have a boyfriend like Buddy but another to be actually moving forward toward marriage. Surely they'd see that. They'd see that it was too late to change my mind or interfere.

Slowly, fighting back my natural resistance, I slipped the ring onto my finger. As soon as I had done so, I felt a sharp chill of fear so deep inside me that it made my heart writhe as if it were recoiling in my chest and, in doing so, pull my outer body inward toward my spine. I had to take deep breaths, but after a moment, I felt the resistance retreat and become replaced with a warm feeling, a feeling that traveled on the surface of my blood, coursing through my veins and lifting my spirits. I felt so good that I stood up and laughed, turning my ringed hand this way and that, as if I were displaying the diamond for a crowd of onlookers, perhaps my ancient ancestral spirits. I could imagine them cringing, shocked, and then shrinking until they were gone completely. It was a feeling of being free, untied. I had thrown off the chains of my heritage and, in this symbolic move, defied a thousand years of destiny.

To drive home my determination and prove to myself that I was not doing this just for the moment, I called Liam.

"I need to see you right away," I said.

"Is something wrong?"

"I need to see you," I said. "Can you come?"

"I'm on my way," he said.

It was nearly nine. The house was quiet. Jim Lamb was in his room correcting student essays, I was sure.

The new tenant, Collin Nickels, had so far lived up to his predictions for himself. I rarely saw him in the hall-way. He was never in the bathroom when I went to use it, and if it weren't for seeing him at dinner occasionally, I would not know whether or not he was still there. I was sure that both Mrs. Winston and Mrs. McGruder were downstairs in the living room. Perhaps Mr. Brady was with them or watching television in the den.

I waited and watched from my bedroom window until I saw Liam arrive. Then I went down slowly. He had already entered the house and was chatting with his great-aunt and Mrs. McGruder. They all turned my way when I appeared. I kept my hand in the pocket of my jeans. For a moment, no one spoke.

"Everything all right?" Mrs. Winston asked.

"I think so. Liam?" I headed for the front door. He nodded at his great-aunt and followed me out.

"What's up?" he asked as soon as he had closed the door behind him.

I walked to his car without replying. He hurried to open the door and got in quickly.

"Are we going somewhere?" he asked.

"I'm not sure," I said. "I hope so."

He tilted his head and smiled with confusion.

"What . . ."

I took my hand out of my pocket and showed him that the ring was on my finger.

Like July Fourth fireworks, his face burst into a smile full of electric sparks. He gazed at me with his heart in his eyes, so full of happiness that he brought tears of joy to mine. *Yes, this is right,* I thought immediately. *Yes, this is good.* Without speaking, he embraced me and kissed me.

"I swear," he said, whispering into my ear, "you'll never be sorry."

I didn't say it, but I thought, *Yes, but will you be?*

We kissed again.

"You know," he said, nodding toward the house, "you have those two on pins and needles."

I nodded. I knew what he wanted. "Okay," I said.

We got out and reentered the house. Mrs. Winston and Mrs. McGruder rose from the sofa in the living room and hurried to the doorway the moment they heard us returning. Their faces were full of concern. Had Liam done something terrible? Were Mrs. Winston's warnings justified?

"Great-auntie Amelia," Liam said. "We decided you should be the first in the family to know."

He held up my hand so they could see the engagement ring.

Neither woman looked as if she could find the words. They both looked from the ring to Liam and then to me. Finally, Mrs. Winston stepped forward to hug me.

"Welcome to the family," she said, and kissed my cheek.

"Congratulations, Liam," Mrs. McGruder said, hugging him. "Finally, you made a wise decision."

Everyone laughed.

"When's the wedding going to be?" Mrs. Winston asked. She wasn't one to beat around any bush and never one to fear telling you what she really thought.

"The wedding?" Liam said as if the concept had just occurred to him. "Yes, the wedding. Well . . ." He looked at me. "Sooner rather than later, I'd say."

"That's no date. You can't leave something like that hanging in the air, Liam, and don't think you two can just elope. This is a historic family. We have roots. Your father has important friends," she lectured. I could see she would go on and on.

"We haven't quite gotten to that yet, but we will immediately," I said.

That seemed to relieve and calm her. She nodded and then smiled again. "I guess we are the first to know," Mrs. Winston said. "I'm glad it's not going to be one of those disturbingly long engagements. Summers are wonderful for weddings in Quincy," she added pointedly. "John Hancock was married in August."

"Well, we'll check with you once we find a date," Liam said. "And make sure we're not stepping on some important holiday. Right now, I think we'd better inform my father and my sister."

"Of course you should."

I nodded, and we started out. Mrs. Winston followed us to the door. She hugged me again. I saw the question in her face, but I didn't want to answer it. Was I going to tell my father? Even if I didn't, I thought, he was bound to know. I looked out at the street and the now-familiar shadows. *If he doesn't know already,* I thought.

We hurried off. *Keep your eyes on the road,* I thought. If ever there was a moment when they would want to interfere, it was now. Liam was talking almost as fast as he was driving, describing what were obviously well-thought-out plans for us. He thought we'd live in his father's mansion to start while he built us our own home, probably on the family land.

"Dad will put up an argument, trying to persuade us just to live in the mansion, but I think you'll want your own home, don't you?"

Before I could answer, he continued.

"I have all sorts of suggestions for our honeymoon. Have you ever been to Europe? I don't know if you mentioned it or if I asked. Anyway, depending on when we do actually get married, I think you'd absolutely fall in love with the island of Capri. I was there as a teen-ager and didn't appreciate any of it, but for some reason, it has never gone out of my mind. I mean, I'm sure it's one of the most romantic places to honeymoon."

"It sounds wonderful, Liam, but your great-aunt Amelia is right. We should talk about a wedding date."

"Oh, absolutely. Does sooner rather than later suit you?"

I paused before answering. I was thinking of Naomi Addison, who would be the cheerleader calling me a gold digger for sure. *Takes one to know one.*

"After we take a breath, we'll talk about it, okay?"

He looked at me askance.

"What?" I asked.

"Why are you hesitating? You think people will accuse you of something?"

"Has that happened with other girls you've known?"

He shrugged. "If it did, they deserved it," he said.

"The only thing authentic about them was how in-authentic they were."

"How come you never fell for it?"

"I've never been in love before," he said. "Honest," he added, holding up his hand. "And I have a built-in sincerity scanner."

"Right."

"Not me," he said, smiling.

"Mrs. Wakefield?"

"Herself," he said.

"And she's passed judgment on me already?"

"Not a negative word," he said.

"But she doesn't know about this," I said, holding up my ringed finger.

He was silent.

"Does she?"

"I have no mother, Lorelei. I checked out the ring with Mrs. Wakefield first. To be sure it was good enough."

I was silent.

How much of an influence would Mrs. Wakefield be after we were married? Should I be concerned? He seemed to hear my thoughts.

"But you'll be the number one woman in my life forever. Sooner rather than later," he emphasized.

We drove on.

Mr. Dolan and Julia, who was off that evening, were watching television together in the den. Mrs. Wakefield saw us first. I looked at her for a reaction. She didn't smile. She just nodded. Obviously, she had kept it secret. Maybe she had suspected that I might not accept Liam's proposal. I had taken my time, and that could have made her think so. Any other girl Liam knew would surely have clutched the ring instantly, behaving like someone lost in a desert who was being offered a glass of water.

When we entered the den, both of them looked up quickly.

"What's going on?" Mr. Dolan asked. He rose, reaching for the remote control to put the television sound on mute. Julia looked at us suspiciously but with a soft, sweet smile.

"I've asked Lorelei to marry me. I've given her an engagement ring," Liam blurted.

Mr. Dolan's eyes smiled first, and then his lips softened and he stepped forward, extending his hand to Liam before hugging me and kissing my cheek. Julia stood up and held her arms open for me to embrace her.

"Well, I am surprised," Mr. Dolan said, looking serious again. "Not because you proposed to her but because she accepted so soon. She's a perceptive young lady, so I'm confident she's seen you as a good bet, son. You don't know how good that makes me feel."

"I have some idea," Liam said dryly. "I don't blame you, blame anyone, for having those thoughts."

"Well, let's not talk about the past. Let's talk about the future," Mr. Dolan said, and he turned the television off completely. "Do you have any dates in mind?"

"Tomorrow," Liam joked.

When I glanced at the doorway, I saw Mrs. Wakefield standing there.

"Come in, please, Mrs. Wakefield," Mr. Dolan said. "You're as much a part of this family as any of us. And I have a sneaking suspicion that you knew about this," he added, pretending to chide her.

"I won't play poker with you," she told him, and everyone laughed.

Was she really warming up to me? Somehow, I thought that if I had her blessing, I would be safe. That would be good. I had rarely met anyone besides Daddy and Mrs. Fennel with as scrutinizing a gaze as hers. She was better than an airport full-body scanner, because she seemed to be able to see your thoughts and your personality along with your bones.

"My son seems to want to get married as soon as possible." Mr. Dolan paused and looked at Julia. I saw her shake her head slightly. He looked at me and then at Liam.

"We're getting married because we're in love with each other, Dad. There's no other reason," he said.

I saw Mr. Dolan look at Mrs. Wakefield. She closed and opened her eyelids to confirm what Liam had said. Mr. Dolan nodded, relieved.

"Okay, so we're back to the date. What's your wish, Lorelei? Don't think about anything but the date. This is one event that I had fears I'd never live to see."

"I don't know. In six weeks?" I asked.

"That would take us to August, John Hancock's wedding month," Liam said.

"What?" Julia asked, laughing. Her eyes widened. "You told Great-auntie Amelia already, didn't you? You told her before you told us."

"That's all right," Mr. Dolan said. "She's the matriarch of this family. That was a nice thing to do, Liam." He turned to Mrs. Wakefield. "Mrs. Wakefield? August? The second week, perhaps?"

She considered. I fully understood that she did more than just run the house and the kitchen and supervise the maids. She was more like an estate manager. With Mr. Dolan so occupied by his business, he probably had turned over more and more responsibilities to her.

"We can manage it all," she said.

"The entire affair will be here, is what she means," Mr. Dolan explained. "We'll build a temporary altar. We'll have tents, a dance floor, caterers, the works. Julia will help you with the invitations," he told me, "and with a wedding dress, too. Won't you, Julia?"

"Of course. I'm owed two weeks' vacation. I'll put in for it tomorrow." She shot forward to take my hand. "C'mon up to my room," she said. "We have a lot to discuss. You'll sleep here tonight."

"But my work clothes," I said.

"You can go in late tomorrow. Okay, Dad?"

"Let me ask. I have a certain influence with the boss," Liam said. "Dad?"

"It's fine. I have other things to do in the morning," Mr. Dolan said, laughing. "I'll ask Carol to cover for you."

I could feel the joy returning to the house, seeping in through every window and under every door. It was in the warmth of their smiles and the excitement in their eyes. Even Mrs. Wakefield seemed to soften some.

As I ran out with Julia, who was still holding my hand as if she were a little girl afraid that her new friend would change her mind, I thought about what the atmosphere in the house must have been like after Liam's mother left them. For Mr. Dolan and Julia, it was probably the same as it would have been had she died. Liam hadn't known her enough yet, but I was sure that every baby, every child, could sense the loss when his or her mother was gone. There had to be an invisible umbilical cord through which a mother's love continually flowed. It was simply natural, but then, how could Liam's mother have deserted him, deserted Julia? Was whatever bothered her about her life so strong that it could cut that cord? How many times, how many days and nights, did she pause to think about it and maybe regret it? Was there a deep empty place in her heart now, forever and ever?

Thinking about her desertion of her family caused me to think about my own. How alike were we? Did we both realize that we were too different from our own families to remain with them? How could a mother be so different from her children? But wasn't I different from mine?

As if she could feel me being too serious, Julia shook my hand so I would snap out of it and return to the new world of excitement that had entered the house along with me.

"Stop worrying!" she cried as we bounded up the stairs. "Mrs. Wakefield will work wonders with the preparations, and my father will call in every favor ever owed him to make things smooth and wonderful."

She paused for a breath at the top of the stairway.

"It will truly be one of the best weddings in Quincy in modern times. Great-auntie Amelia will rank it along with the wedding of whatever governor or president ever married in New England."

"I don't want to be up on any stage," I said softly. "We just want to get married."

"Don't be silly. I'm not going to just want to get married, and neither should you. You're going to be a Dolan, and if you believe Great-auntie Amelia, you are a member of American royalty."

I thought about what she was saying. My picture would be in newspaper social columns, maybe even in magazines. I never had any doubt that Daddy and my sisters eventually would find me. Perhaps this would discourage them from trying to get me back or caring about me any longer.

Who gets married holding her breath?

Lorelei Patio, that's who, I thought.

Julia tugged me forward into her room and to her computer.

"We'll search the Internet for wedding dresses until we find the one you want," she said, and put a chair next to hers. Then she just hugged me and began the search.

She was right. There was no time to be too philosophical or too serious. Bells were ringing, rice was raining down, and cans were clinking behind our car. Those were the images I should be seeing and nothing else.

18

The whirlwind I thought I was caught in before was a slow boat to China compared with what went on now. Even if I had wanted to dwell on my past and my concerns about myself, I rarely had time for it. Between my work and the many small decisions to make about the wedding and ordering that had to be done on a priority basis, there was hardly time to do much else. Liam and I had many discussions with Mrs. Wakefield about the way the ceremony and the reception were to be set up on the estate grounds, down to the color of the tents. I found her to be a very efficient person who was not as controlling as Mrs. Fennel but equally confident in her ideas and decisions. Liam was respectful but always watching to see if I was in any way annoyed. Little did he know how used I was to someone like her. I did, however, begin to believe that she sincerely approved of me.

My most enjoyable times were with Julia, right from that first night when we hurried up to her room to huddle together and look at possible wedding gowns on the Internet. At times, I thought she was more excited about it all than I was, and I had the feeling that she might have often felt wistful, fearing that her wedding might never happen. Right from the start, I had sensed an underlying current of gloom running beneath the seemingly stable and secure, wealthy Dolan family. All of that, I was sure, flowed from Liam and Julia's mother's desertion.

"I've always wanted a younger sister," she told me that night. "You can't imagine what it's been like living in a house with two men and Mrs. Wakefield. Don't misunderstand me. I love her, and she loves us, but sometimes, most of the time," she said, leaning toward me to lower her voice as if someone was listening right outside her door, "I can't imagine her as a young woman in love. Her parents brought her up very strictly, and it wasn't because they were overly religious people, either. Her older brother was killed in a car accident. He was the driver, and he was miles over the blood alcohol limit. Two other young people were killed, too, one being the girl he was with. They hit another vehicle head-on. The couple in it survived, but their ten-year-old boy died. I don't know how many times she's told Liam that story over the years, making it sound more and more gruesome as he grew older. I guess I can't blame her, but it hasn't exactly made for bubbles and lights whenever either of us had a social affair to attend."

She paused like someone stuck in a memory for a moment and then shuddered and forced a smile.

"Anyway, forget all that. We should talk only about happy, exciting things."

She turned back to the computer and started to

pull up wedding gowns on the Internet, but then she stopped again and turned back to me.

"How did you do it? How did you get Liam to fall in love with you so fast?" She blushed and lowered her eyes. "I'll confide in you the way I would confide in a sister. I'm trying to get Clifford to fall head over heels in love with me. I know I love him."

"Did you tell him that?"

"Oh, no."

"I don't know that there is any secret way to get someone to fall in love with you," I said. "I know it doesn't sound very scientific, but there has to be something mysterious and at the same time obvious to both. I think it takes a great deal of trust to tell someone you love him. It's the most revealing thing of all. You've totally exposed yourself, and I imagine being rejected after that is devastating."

She stared at me and then tilted her head a little when she smiled. "Why do I feel that you're way older than I am?"

Her question reminded me of my discussion with Michele Levy, Mr. Dolan's pregnant secretary, the first time I had met her. I gave Julia a similar answer. "It's not time that ages you; it's the experiences you have."

She nodded. "Yes, I keep forgetting what a miserable family life you've had. That's because you don't wear it on your sleeve like I do, I'm sure. At least, you don't when you're with me and obviously when you're at work and with Liam. My great-auntie Amelia says you're never a sourpuss, either.

"I don't know how you do it," she continued. "Every

time I see a mother with her child at the hospital, see how devoted and concerned she is, I feel a pang of envy and then a surge of bitterness. Of course, Liam can't remember her as well. He was only four, but I remember my mother, vaguely. It's still enough to invade my dreams and thoughts with visions of her face, memories of her voice, flashing pictures, if you know what I mean. Mrs. Wakefield has been wonderful and devoted, but no one replaces a mother, not really. Oh, I'm sorry," she cried, shaking herself as if to get some insects off her back and shoulders. "I keep pulling us back into the dark."

"It's all right. I'm flattered that you don't mind confiding your feelings in me."

"Well, you're going to be my sister-in-law, actually more like my sister. Right?"

"Yes."

"And you've never had a sister, either, so you've probably felt most of the same things I've felt growing up."

"Probably," I said. My eyes shifted. Images of Ava, Brianna, and my little sister Marla came rushing back at me.

Julia sensed something, sensed that I was holding back. "There's so much about you that I have to learn, but I have to win your trust and confidence first. I will," she vowed. "I'll be your best friend in the world, so that you won't hesitate to tell me intimate things about yourself and your past. And don't think just because I'm Liam's sister that I would always take his side in any argument," she added emphatically.

"Okay," I said, smiling. *Get her off me as a topic,* I told myself. "As far as you and Clifford go, I don't know him well enough, of course, but maybe he's hesitant to show his feelings because you are. If you care that much for him, take a chance, trust him, and tell him," I said. "Or at least hint at it strongly enough so that he won't feel foolish or afraid to tell you his honest feelings for you."

She nodded. "I will. You ought to be writing an advice column for lovers in need or something." She started to turn back to the computer and paused again. "I really don't care," she said. "I mean, I wouldn't condemn you or Liam ever for it, but did he tell my father the truth? You're getting married this quickly because you both want to and not because you're pregnant?"

I knew how to convince her beyond any doubt and at the same time make her feel as if she was my sister already. "We haven't even had intercourse yet, Julia."

Her eyes widened. "My brother . . . showed that kind of restraint?"

"Maybe it's an old-fashioned idea, but I thought it was important, especially with someone like Liam, who, shall we say, suffers from a reputation."

She laughed. "I understand exactly. Back to this dress," she declared, and we drew closer to look at the choices.

That night, we shared her king-size canopy bed, giggling and talking late into the wee hours, as Daddy might say. There had never been any of this sisterly feeling between myself and Ava or Marla. Brianna was too old even to get to know. Marla was too young. Most of

the time, Ava was so into herself. I was sure she saw me
as a distraction when I was younger and tried to talk girl
talk with her. When I was older, I could feel the sense
of competition, a competition that went far beyond
normal sibling rivalry. It was too intense and at times
almost violent. I didn't know who was more critical and
demanding of me, Ava or Mrs. Fennel. If Ava gave me
any sort of compliment, it was that I was doing something she had taught me well and only because she had
taught me. Everything that I did well, even what I did
for Daddy back then, was always because of her influence, her advice and instruction.

"Daddy expects me to help shape you," she would
say, as if I were a lump of clay.

However, I never lost the feeling that she was worried that I was moving too quickly into her shoes. I supposed any sister would resent how much attention her
younger sister enjoyed from her father, but there had
been no higher goal than pleasing Daddy. I learned that
it wasn't simply to win his love, of course. It was the
way for us all to survive. That was something abhorrent
to me eventually. I hadn't changed my mind. It still was
today, and I hoped it would be forever.

There were moments during the night when I came
close to telling Julia more than I thought I should. She
was so forthcoming about her earlier romances, her sex
life, her needs and dreams, that I felt guilty lying beside her on my bed of falsehoods and deceptions. I was
bound to make mistakes, to cause confusions and raise
doubts as time went by. Most important of all was my

insecurity about what I was physically capable of. Could Liam and I have a child together? Would it be wise for me to have Julia arrange some sort of physical exam?

Put it off until it's a must, I told myself. *Don't rush the future, or you'll end it.*

Julia fell asleep before I did. She kept apologizing for keeping me up with what she called nonsense teeny-bopper talk about music and fashions, colors and foods, and the different quirks about men that annoyed her. How could I tell her that for me it was like turning to a television channel I had never seen or even known existed? I encouraged her to keep talking until she finally confessed that she was exhausted, leaned over to kiss me good night, and fell asleep almost immediately while I lay there looking up into the darkness, listening for something, anything, that would warn me that what I was trying to do was impossible and would bring harm to these people whom I wanted to be my new family.

I put away those fears and carried on. It was the busiest few weeks since I had come to Quincy. I didn't make a single dinner at the Winston House, but I could feel the excitement building in Mrs. Winston and Mrs. McGruder. Whenever I was home, they wanted a detailed report on what we had done that day concerning the wedding and our future plans.

Liam was serious about our honeymoon in Capri and made arrangements for us to stay at the Casa Morgano immediately. He brought me brochures and pictures of the island. We even watched a short video about it. I couldn't help but agree with him and be excited.

Aside from my flight, I had never taken a trip with any-one but Daddy. Suddenly, I did feel as if the world was opening to me.

Three weeks after we had told his family we were engaged, Mr. Dolan had it in the Quincy society pages. My biography was kept generic and vague. I was sim-ply one of his newer employees who had come from California. No mention was made of my family. He had influence with the paper and the writer, so nothing was questioned further. He was always looking out for me, protecting me, as if I were already a part of his family. I knew that didn't mean that questions wouldn't come up. I had to prepare how I would respond.

And then that problem ended, but not the way I would have wanted.

One day at work, Mr. Dolan called for me to come into his office.

"Close the door," he said as soon as I had entered.

My heart began to race. The look on his face was more serious than ever. Once in a while during the past weeks, I would pause to wonder if Mr. Dolan, per-haps at Mrs. Wakefield's request, had decided to hire a private detective to track my past. Maybe some of his friends at the golf club or other business associates had warned him about so-called gold diggers. I was sure he would testify that I was too wonderful to fall into that category, and he might even go into how much I had changed Liam for the better. I could imagine him say-ing something like "Even if she is, she's worth it."

But then again, he might have concluded that it was his responsibility to protect his son. How could I blame him for it? I was sure that Liam would get very upset about it if he found out his father was spying on me. That might have been the only reason Mr. Dolan hadn't done anything of the sort, as far as I knew. He wouldn't want to ruin his renewed wonderful relationship with his son.

Until now, my personality, my work ethic, and my relationship with Mrs. Winston and Mrs. McGruder had surely pushed back any unpleasant suspicions, but how long could I carry on? Maybe no longer. Perhaps that was why he called me into his office, I thought as I took the seat in front of Mr. Dolan's desk. I was prepared to learn that this was the beginning of the end.

He sat forward, his hands folded. I thought he looked even more nervous than I felt. What was happening?

"I just got off the phone with your father," he said.

It was as if some monster had torn open my chest and scooped out my heart. I felt cavernous, drained of blood and organs. I was like a corpse in an autopsy, every little secret part of me exposed and displayed. Was I still breathing? It didn't feel like it. Did he really say "your father"?

"I don't understand," I said.

He nodded and was silent a moment, a moment that seemed like hours to me. "People say the world has grown so small. News in one corner can be picked up in another instantly, and with the Internet . . . well, it doesn't surprise me."

I shook my head. "What doesn't surprise you?"

"That your father out in California would have

someone mention to him that he saw your name on a social news blog and then describe your upcoming wedding."

"Is that what he told you?"

"Yes."

"What does he want? Why did he call you?"

"He wants to pay for your wedding," Mr. Dolan said. "Father of the bride and all that."

"But he's . . . he hasn't been my father. That's why I left home."

"He knows that. This is his way of making amends. I didn't say yes," he added quickly. "I told him I would be talking with you." He paused and then smiled. "Look, I'm a father. I know I haven't been a perfect father. I can't help but empathize and—"

"This is different. *He's* different."

"I know that's how you see it, how you have seen it, but time has passed. The reality of your being out of his life has settled in. He has obviously had the time to consider what has happened. He doesn't expect that you will reconcile overnight or even after weeks and months, maybe, but he would like to go more than half-way to make it up to you. He was actually pleading by the end of the call," Mr. Dolan added.

I looked up sharply. Daddy pleading? That would never happen. Why couldn't Mr. Dolan see through the subterfuge? I had thought he was smarter than most men. Daddy was manipulating him as easily as he could manipulate anyone. Now how did I look in Mr. Dolan's eyes? I was sitting before him, suddenly the bad one, the one who wouldn't forgive, recalcitrant, bitter and stubborn, maybe even spoiled. How could I be that way? What had happened to all the sensitivity I'd shown? I could hear those thoughts and see them coming at me. *How do I do this? How do I respond without saying too much?*

"Why don't you sleep on it?" Mr. Dolan said, seeing my reaction. "You're on your way toward making a whole new life for yourself. We're here for you, and we are powerful and formidable people," he added with pride. "You have nothing to worry about."

I nearly laughed aloud. It took all of my self-control not to do it. *You,* I thought, *powerful and formidable against my father?* It was so ridiculous a concept that I had to look down, close my eyes, and hold my breath.

"You won't go back to him. This is your home," Mr. Dolan continued, trying the reasonable approach. "You'll treat him like any other guest if that's what you want him to be."

I looked up quickly. "Guest? So, you're saying not only does he want to pay for the wedding but he also wants to attend?"

Mr. Dolan shrugged. "Look at it another way. He could have been totally uninterested, hated you, or tried to forget you, but that part of him that's good wants to see what every father surely wants to see, his daughter married and moving on to a life of her own. He wants to give away the bride. I know I'd be heartbroken if I wasn't at Julia's wedding to give her away. Think it over," he said again as he stood. "I have to go see Charley in the appliance center. Be back in a while. You can talk it over with anyone tonight. I'm sure Julia will be a good ear if you don't want to talk to Liam about it just yet."

He came around the desk. I stood up. He smiled at me and then hugged me. "Whatever you decide, I know it'll be right," he added, and started out.

I watched him leave the office and then sat hard on the chair again, stunned.

If anything, I felt trapped. It was worse than confronting Ava on some dark street and hearing her berate and threaten me. It wasn't Daddy's style to come at me violently. He would glide into Quincy, surfing on his wonderful, attractive smile, and charm everyone around him. I could just imagine him talking to Mrs. Winston. He would discuss her beloved Colonial history as if he had been there, because it was very likely he had.

"Oh, forgive him," they would all tell me. "He's a man. He has weaknesses, but it's wonderful that his love for you is too strong for him to ignore forever."

What would he do then? What did he want? Was this really his way of stopping my marriage and getting me back?

I felt drained of energy. Just the walk back to my desk exhausted me. I sat there staring at the computer and at the work I was doing. What was once so easy looked formidable. A strong part of me wanted me to get up and, as quickly and as quietly as I could, slip out of the building and do what I had done when I had left Buddy, hitch a ride out of there and continue my flight. It didn't matter where. Just keep going.

After an hour of moving through the paces without getting all that much done, I was actually on the verge of running off when Liam came into the office, practically bouncing with excitement.

"We got them!" he cried.

"Who?"

"Remember that band I wanted for the wedding? We played their CDs for you and you loved the way they mixed the old with the new. Remember?"

"Yes, Johnny and the Classics, but you found out they were previously booked."

"They were, sorta. Well, Dad made them an offer they couldn't refuse, and I don't mean like the Godfather. He's acting like money's no object when it comes to what we want. He just did it, and they accepted. They would have been crazy not to. He practically doubled their fee."

Maybe that was because he was expecting that I would agree to permitting my father to pay for the wedding. He had so much of it covered that he could afford to offer more for the band, I thought.

"Well? Aren't you pleased? I think he was doing it more for you than for me."

"Yes, of course. You just surprised me, that's all. And I was in the middle of something."

"Sure." He started to turn around and then stopped. "Oh, I decided to ask Clifford to be my best man. He agreed. Julia is very happy about it."

"That's nice, Liam."

"We've got to do what we can to help that romance along," he said, lowering his voice as if we were planning something secret.

"Okay," I said.

He looked at me for a long moment.

"What?"

"I just can't believe that in a matter of weeks now, you'll be mine. And I'll be yours, of course," he quickly added.

"I have trouble believing it, too," I said, maybe a little too seriously. His smile didn't fade, but it looked like something frozen on a computer monitor.

"Not too much trouble, I hope."

I shook my head.

He drew closer. "You look a little shaken up, Lorelei. Is something wrong?"

It was only a matter of time, maybe only a matter of hours, before he would find out anyway, I thought.

"A while ago, I learned that my father called your father to offer to pay for the wedding."

"What?"

"He wants to attend, too."

"You mean give away the bride?"

"Yes."

"Oh. And you're upset about it?"

"Yes."

"Well, whatever you want to do is all right with me, but—"

"But I'd look too unreasonable to everyone if I said no, right?"

"Most people don't know about your problems with him, and—"

"But they will, eventually."

He stood there quietly. I knew he was afraid to offer

advice either way and was ruminating on what words to choose. "What did you tell my dad?"

"I said I would think about it."

"So, do that," he said. "I repeat. Whatever you decide is all right with me."

I wanted to tell him that he didn't know my father. Whatever I decided wouldn't matter. He was coming here one way or another. There was, of course, the ever so slight chance that he was accepting my decision and wanted to pretend to be a normal father. Was it better to declare war and tell Mr. Dolan to say no, that I didn't want him, or was it better to take the chance? The third choice always remained: to run off again.

Liam came around the desk and knelt beside me. "I don't like to see you upset, even for a little while, Lorelei. What can I do?"

"Nothing. This is all on me, Liam."

"I don't understand how he could have been so indifferent to your feelings and now suddenly care so much."

What was my clever answer to this?

"As your father says, the reality of my being out of his life has finally sunken in, and then he found out about our wedding," I told him, practically parroting Mr. Dolan.

"Well, it's not a bad idea to start anew and give the wedding another layer of goodwill and happiness," he offered timidly.

I smiled and ran my hand softly through his hair. "I don't know what your mother was like, but I think you have more of your father in you than you can imagine."

"Maybe you do, too," he said.

That soft, intending-to-be-warm reply felt like a clap of thunder in my ears. I nodded.

"Maybe I do. Okay. I'll say yes," I said.

He smiled and rose slightly to kiss me. "We'll celebrate your father's resurrection Saturday night. See you later," he said and hurried off.

He was so full of energy and hope, while I sat there like someone on death row.

Somehow I managed to get through the remainder of the day. I told Mr. Dolan my decision, but I asked that he be the intermediary. I told him I wasn't ready to talk to my father. He said he understood and would handle it all. I shouldn't worry. Liam came by at the end of the day to take me home. He had made reservations at what was now our favorite little Italian restaurant. I really didn't feel like going out, but I knew he would be very upset and worried about me. More than ever, he wanted to do what he could to distract me and talk about happier things.

Before we left, Mr. Dolan came out to tell me that he had spoken to my father.

"He's pretty pleased with your reaction," he said. "I warned him that this was no five-and-dime wedding, but he didn't seem at all concerned about the expense. What does he really do?"

"That's not it, Mr. Dolan."

"Ken," he said. "It's after hours."

"That's not it, Ken. My father's inherited a great deal of money."

"And you always suspected that his new wife was after that, I bet."

I closed my eyes. It was getting too hard; the fiction was making me sick inside. Every time I told another lie, it was like swallowing a little more poison.

No, I imagined myself finally saying, *that's not it. You see, my father's been alive for centuries. I don't even know how long he's been alive. My sisters, who are also the mothers of his children, keep him alive by bringing him young, virile men, men whose lust for them has raised their blood and made it nourishing for him. I was destined to do the same before I ran away.*

Do you think I could still marry Liam?

My imaginary response nearly made me laugh insanely. There was a danger that I realized for the first time. I could go raving mad. Maybe that was what would happen in the end. I wouldn't escape even though I was physically away from him. I would go crazy and end up babbling things that no one would believe, until they put me in some clinic. That way, Daddy would be protected after all. They would all be protected. They would be so confident about it that they might even come visit me, which would set me screaming and get me into a restraining jacket and keep me on suicide watch in solitary.

"Yes," I finally said. "But my father is not some rich old man who's found an attractive new wife obviously after his money. He's a very handsome, charming man. In short, he's the whole package."

Ken Dolan nodded thoughtfully. "Well, I do look forward to meeting him. I hope I can help mend the rift between the two of you."

There was so much more I could say about that, but I turned to Liam instead.

"Ready?" he asked.

"Yes. Good night, Ken," I said.

He smiled, but he looked very thoughtful, too. I had planted some seeds.

Liam took my hand on the way out. I saw that he was very sensitive to my feelings and very concerned. He was so sweet and loving that I felt guilty about causing him any anxiety. Would this be the way it would be forever between us? Could I have this, something I had come to believe was impossible? Was it worth fighting hard for?

"I'm okay," I said. "Stop looking like someone who lost his pinkie finger."

"What?" he said, smiling.

It was something my father would tell me when I was much younger and something had bothered me. I would imagine my hand without a pinkie finger, and he would laugh and then lift me into his arms.

"That will never happen to you," he would say. "I will always protect you."

He always drove away any fears I might have.

Could I remember only the good things? Was that a surgery I could manage?

We drove off, talking now about things to do before the wedding and work that was already being started on the grounds of the Dolan estate. We didn't slow down until we made the turn and saw the police car in front of the Winston House.

19

We got out of Liam's car slowly.

"What's going on here?" Liam asked. "The last man wearing a uniform in this house was a member of the Continental Army."

I shook my head. I didn't even want to venture a guess.

When we entered, we heard voices in the living room and went directly there to find two police officers, one with a notepad open and the other apparently asking Mrs. Winston, Jim Lamb, Mr. Brady, and Mrs. McGruder questions. Mrs. Winston was in her colonial Windsor chair, and the others were seated on the settee. Everyone turned to us.

"What's happening?" Liam asked first.

"It's Collin Nickels," Mrs. Winston said. "This is the third day he's been missing. We thought it was time to inform the police. All of his things are still here, and he hadn't told us that he would be gone. He hasn't called. He paid for six weeks. Mrs. McGruder and I thought it was enough to be concerned."

She turned to the policemen.

"This is my great-nephew, Liam Dolan, and another of our guests, Lorelei Patio. Miss Patio is on the same wing of the house as Mr. Nickels and works for my nephew, Kenneth Dolan."

"Oh, Dolan Plumbing Supply," the policeman with the notepad said. From the look on his face, it was clear how impressive the Dolans were in Quincy.

The other patrolman turned to me.

"Have you had any conversations with him that would help us out?" he asked.

I shook my head. "I haven't seen him this past week at all."

"Collin is usually up for breakfast before anyone else stirs," Mrs. McGruder said. "And then quickly off to do his research, as if he's on some time clock."

"But you said he had taken your dinner plan," the policeman reminded her, and then looked at me. "What about the days before he was gone?"

"Lorelei has not been attending dinner here lately. She and Liam are planning their wedding with other members of the family," Mrs. Winston explained.

I looked at Jim Lamb, because he lowered his eyes quickly. Did he know something more, or was he just reacting to the mention of my upcoming marriage?

"I don't know why we are rushing to the conclusion that something terrible has happened to him," Martin Brady said. "He's old enough to go off on his own. Maybe he met some girl who's as crazy about his research as he is and they're going over parchment documents with a magnifying glass or something every night."

"I don't think this is something about which we can joke," Mrs. Winston said.

Mr. Brady withered in his chair but managed a weak "It's possible, isn't it?"

"Well, he's right about that," Jim said. "It is possible."

I turned to him. Yes, it was possible, I thought, but it was more than possible for a young man in this house to go missing, and not for any reason he could fathom.

"Don't you know anything that could help?" I asked him. Liam looked at me, obviously wondering why I was taking such an active interest.

"I knew most of the places he was going to visit in order to do his research, the library, the museums, some of the people he was speaking to," Jim said. "At Mrs. Winston's behest, I checked with every one of them. I even called the college and spoke with the professor who was overseeing his research. He hasn't heard from him during these past days. As a matter of fact, he hasn't heard from him for more than a week, and he usually checks in with some progress report weekly."

"When you spoke to Nickels, did he mention meeting a girl or someone who was interested in what he was doing?" the policeman with the notepad asked, glancing at Mr. Brady, who risked a smile.

"No, but he wasn't all that forthcoming with his personal life, so I can't tell you if he's met someone here or not. We haven't really developed any sort of friendship."

Everyone was quiet for a moment.

"We hesitate to contact his family, but in this situation . . ." the other police officer said.

"Of course you should contact his family," Mrs. Winston insisted. "Everyone who takes a room at my house knows they should have the decency to tell me when they are not going to be here for breakfast and dinner, if they've bought the meal plan. He has, and Mrs. McGruder prepares for the number of people we're having. We don't waste food, even if someone's paid for it," she told the policemen. They both nodded quickly like young grade-school boys in front of their stern teacher.

"Nothing like this has ever happened," Mrs. McGruder added. "We had that man, what was his name, Horner, who was drinking too much and passed out before dinner one night, remember? That's how we found out about him."

"And got rid of him the next day," Mrs. Winston added, pressing her lips into her mouth for stern emphasis.

"We'll start checking it out. If you should hear from him, any of you, or he returns . . ."

"Of course. We'll call you immediately," Mrs. Winston said. "I wouldn't want you to waste any more of your time on some philanderer."

The patrolman closed his notepad, and they both started out.

"Well, this is a bag of worms I don't need," Mrs. Winston muttered.

Liam looked at me and jerked his head toward the door. "I'll be by in an hour or so," he said.

"Okay."

He kissed me.

"Don't worry yourself so, Great-auntie Amelia," he told her. "It's nothing you can blame on yourself."

"People who board in my home are like my family," she replied sharply. "Of course I'd be concerned about their welfare."

He nodded, glanced at me, and hurried out, pausing in the doorway to put his hands over his ears. As she herself would say, Mrs. Winston would cotton to no indifference about the matter. I didn't laugh at Liam's antics. As soon as he left, I started for the stairway. I knew every moment I took to walk away that this was definitely no laughing matter.

This is Ava's doing, was the first thing I thought. I hadn't imagined her after all. She was there, and I wouldn't put it past her to have plucked poor Collin Nickels out of the herd, as she liked to refer to young men, just to show me that she was close and could do it. Maybe to show me that she could pluck Liam just as easily. I shuddered. Of course, this also confirmed for me that Daddy was probably nearby. This was her way of giving me a warning.

For a long while—too long—I just sat on my bed thinking and worrying. At times, when memories of threatening words, distorted raging faces, and my sisters' deliveries to my father returned, I trembled over what I had heard and seen. I had never thought about the families of any of those men and what they must have gone through once they were reported missing, just what Collin Nickels's family would soon be going through. Of course, they hadn't been men whom I, or even any of my sisters, would know much about. It had been easier not to care that way, I suppose, not that Ava had revealed any concern one way or another.

I was surprised at the knock on my door, surprised and grateful, because it snapped me out of my horrid reverie and made me realize how much time I had wasted ruminating. Liam would be there in a little more than a half hour. He was always on time, even now, especially now. It was as if he thought I wouldn't wait or would be angry enough to leave him after only ten minutes beyond our time to meet. It told me that his natural instincts were telling him that there was still something very tentative about me. I understood. He wouldn't think otherwise until he heard me pronounce those two words, "I do."

I opened the door to face Jim Lamb.

"Sorry to disturb you," he said. "I just wanted to tell you I wasn't completely forthcoming with the police just now."

"Why not?"

"I didn't want to involve you any more than you were just by being a fellow tenant."

"How could I be involved any more than that? I had much less to do with him than anyone else here had, especially you."

"Well, he did tell me some personal things."

"What? How did any of that concern me?" I was practically lunging at him. My aggressive questioning made him wince.

"He was infatuated with you," he said. "At times, he embarrassed me with his revelations, telling me how he fantasized about you. He even admitted to coming down the hallway very late at night and just standing here quietly, hoping to hear you move or sigh or something. It was . . . a little sick, I think. I told him so, and he stopped talking to me about you. I didn't say anything about it, because I can't see how it would relate to his disappearance, do you?"

I stared at him a moment. Of course I could see how it would relate. If Ava had confronted him, he would have seen the resemblances between Ava and myself, and she would have known enough to use my name to tempt and hook him. "Easy fish," she would call him.

"No," I told Jim in a calmer tone. "You're right. There was no need to mention that. It would just add something confusing."

"I'm sure he'll show up. He's a weird guy. Mrs. Winston doesn't appreciate how weird he is. I don't think it's beyond him to ignore what's proper etiquette as it relates to her and Mrs. McGruder."

"Probably so," I said.

He stood there searching for some other way to keep me talking.

"I don't mean to be rude, but I've got to get ready to go out, Jim. I'm sorry."

"Of course," he said, taking a step back. He didn't turn away. I had to close the door in his face.

When Liam came for me, he wanted to know more about Collin Nickels. He had given it more thought, especially because I had looked so disturbed to hear about him. I told him I hardly knew him at all.

"Except for one short conversation in the upstairs hallway, I barely exchanged another word with the man."

"You seemed really concerned about him," he said.

"I could see how disturbed your great-aunt Amelia was, that's all."

He nodded. For now, I got by with that, but there would surely be something else soon to make him wonder about me and my reactions.

Another week went by without any resolution to the mystery of the missing Collin Nickels. I learned that a police detective had come by while I was at work to go through Collin's things, and then eventually they had gathered everything and taken it down to the police station, hoping it would produce some lead. I hoped he hadn't written anything about me that would bring them back to question me further. Apparently, there was nothing. At breakfast daily, either Mrs. Winston or Mrs. McGruder would announce that another day had passed without any news.

"It's as if he literally disappeared," Mrs. Winston told me. "One day, he just evaporated. I didn't get to know him that well, but he had a real love for history. I enjoyed our little talks at breakfast and dinner."

"Oh, he'll turn up looking embarrassed about it all," Mr. Brady insisted. She gave him one of her disapproving glares, and he quickly returned to his breakfast.

Five days later, when I returned from work, Mrs. Winston and Mrs. McGruder greeted me in the hallway outside the dining room. They had apparently been waiting for my arrival. My first thought was that Collin Nickels's body had been found. I almost wished for that. No body of any man delivered to Daddy was ever found. If Collin's body was found, that would eliminate

Ava as a suspect. He had come to some other misfortune, which, whatever it was, wasn't as bad, I was sure. But they had something else on their minds.

"We both think you have made a very wise and very generous decision, Lorelei," Mrs. Winston began. The two of them wore identical smiles of approval.

"Decision? What decision?"

"To permit your father to do his fatherly duty and attend your wedding." She turned to draw my attention to a framed needlework on the hallway wall. It was a quote from Alexander Pope sewn in black thread on a milk-white background. She read it aloud. " 'To err is human; to forgive, divine.' "

I nodded. It was as I had thought it would be. Daddy would come gracefully into all of their lives, charming them so quickly and completely that they would wonder how things could have grown so bad between us in the first place. It would soon come to the point where if I ignored and avoided him or slighted him in any way, I would look like the bad one. Insidiously, he would thread his way into the lives of anyone who had grown close to me there, his friendship clearly a double-edged sword, for I knew that he could wipe any of them out of existence. Every relative's or friend's hand he shook, every woman's cheek he kissed, would be a marker indicating to whom or where he would return in his most vicious and volatile way. He would greet everyone but slide a smile toward me to remind me of his power.

"I'll do my best," I told them.

"It will all go well," Mrs. McGruder insisted, stepping forward to squeeze my hand gently.

"In the end, we all depend upon our families," Mrs. Winston added. "Blood is thicker than water."

She had no idea how true that was for my family. I nodded and went up to my room, moving now like someone waiting for the second shoe to drop, the lightning bolt to strike, and the earth to quake under my feet, sending me hurrying back into Daddy's arms and the life I had hoped to avoid. Practically every night, I reconsidered fleeing but always came to the same conclusion. If they could find me here, they could find me anywhere. It wasn't simply the announcement in the social news, for I had seen Ava before that appeared, and either someone from Daddy's clan or another living in the vicinity already had sent me a sharp, nearly deadly warning with the accident Jim and I were forced into having that night. Meeting the elderly man on the plane was no accident. I knew I was being shadowed, followed, and watched from the moment I had left Buddy and stepped into Moses's tractor-trailer, and in my heart of hearts, I knew I would always be on their radar.

In the days that followed, Mr. Dolan began to inform me when Daddy sent money to pay for things. They had apparently had a number of conversations about the arrangements. At just about every family gathering now, which included Mrs. Wakefield, Ken Dolan mentioned my father and his eagerness to see me whenever I would agree. I was always asked if I hadn't already spoken to him on the phone. I said no but added that it would be better for us to meet right before the wedding. A few days later, Mr. Dolan informed me that he was organizing the rehearsal dinner at one of

the fanciest restaurants in Quincy. It was planned for
the evening before our wedding. He had booked its
private room. Besides the family, there were some of his
business associates and their wives attending.

"People who watched Liam grow up," he told me.
"And some of the people who work at the company, like
Michael Thomas."

By now, he felt like an old friend to me, too. He was
always there in the morning to pick me up if Liam was
away and always there to volunteer to take me home if I
wanted a ride. He loved talking about his family, and I
loved listening.

"I wasn't sure if there was anyone you wanted to
invite," Mr. Dolan continued. "I mean, aside from your
father and his wife, you have no other guests on your
end, and—"

"No, no one," I said quickly. "I mean, I'm sure Mrs.
McGruder is invited to everything."

"Oh, absolutely. She and my aunt are attached at the
hip."

"They are," I said, smiling.

"Neither your father nor you have mentioned any
relatives. I know traveling to a wedding is always a burden, but . . ."

"No. There is no one I was close enough to whom I
would want at the wedding. My father knows that."

"Okay," he said, looking sad and concerned. "We'll
be the family you never had."

The subject was dropped, but then he finally asked
me about the disappearance of Collin Nickels. Mrs.
Winston was still talking about it.

"My aunt's obviously very disturbed. I looked into the police investigation myself, but there are no leads. Did you know him at all?"

"No," I said.

"As long as it isn't upsetting you, then," he added.

I assured him that it wasn't. I told him I felt sorry for the man's family, but I repeated that I didn't know him well enough to be emotionally involved.

"Right. Well, so much goes on that we will never understand."

"Yes, so much," I repeated, a little more emphatically than he expected.

We dropped that subject, too. Every day, however, I anticipated Ava's sudden appearance, with her confident smile. I searched every shadow, studied every woman who walked anywhere near me or near Liam and me when we were out. I was particularly nervous about it when Julia accompanied me to my wedding-dress fitting. I noticed something brighter in her eyes and a rosy flush in her cheeks when she came by to pick me up. She drove off with the impish smile of a cat that had swallowed a canary.

"What?" I asked.

She looked at me and widened her eyes. "You're obviously distracted this morning," she said. "Usually, you're more observant."

"What . . ." I gasped when I saw her engagement ring.

The look on my face made her laugh. She had to pull over to the side of the road, and we hugged.

"I really owe it to you," she said. "Ever since I took

your advice and let Clifford know about my feelings, he's been warmer and more loving."

"We have to celebrate this," I said.

"We will. We're all going to the Underground. Liam talked Clifford into it. It's time we all let our hair down a little," she added. "Anyway, it won't be long before we'll have another wedding on the estate."

"I'm really happy for you, Julia."

"Your coming here was truly a blessing for this family," she said. She had no idea why that made me feel so terrible. I forced a smile, but she knew me well enough by now to see through it. "What's wrong, Lorelei? Is it your father?"

"Yes."

"Well, don't be nervous about it. I'll be there for you. We'll all be. Even Clifford," she added with a bigger smile.

I had to relax. I had to overcome my fears, at least for the time being. What could happen next was something I tried desperately to avoid imagining. At some point, however, there would be no way to distract myself. The weight of concern would drag me down and make me the dark and unenthusiastic one in the room.

Julia hugged me again, and then we drove on.

"We'll worry about me later. Right now," she said, "we have to concentrate on your wedding. But just think how much I will learn from it. I'll avoid all your mistakes," she added, laughing.

"Yes," I said. "I'm the test pilot."

"You are, but you'll have a wonderful wedding and a great honeymoon, I'm sure."

Only if Daddy lets me, I thought, and couldn't imagine why he ever would. Julia couldn't stop talking, and I couldn't stop looking everywhere and at every person, waiting to see Ava or even Daddy standing off to the side watching me. I didn't see either of them, but that didn't bring any relief. I still had the feeling that I was being closely observed. I knew they would let me see them when they were ready. There was no catching either of them off-guard.

We had a great time at the dress fitting and then at lunch. Now that Julia was engaged, we had more in common. We were chattering away and laughing so much that I forgot all of my fears for the moment and luxuriated in the freedom and joy that the immediate future promised. Surely, I thought, when Daddy saw me, he would realize that it would be wrong to force me to come back. *Wrong or not,* another voice said, *he can't let you go in front of the others.* The danger was that they would think he was weak, and it wouldn't be only my sisters who would think it. There would be Mrs. Fennel and the others, the external family, as he once called them. When I was younger, I had been introduced to them as if they were uncles and aunts. Maybe they were, in a real sense. There was still so much I didn't know about Daddy's world, so much I was supposed to start learning.

Everything continued so smoothly that I began to wonder if it all might happen after all. Daddy had not appeared mysteriously in my room and told me to leave. He had put in the money for the wedding and apparently had good conversations with Mr. Dolan. Ava had not appeared at the front of the Winston House again. What was going on? They had done something to poor Collin Nickels, hadn't they? Was this just their way of tormenting me, hoping that I would throw up my hands and surrender? Were they hoping that I would choose to return without any further encouragement or threat?

Surely, my steadfastness and determination had given them second thoughts. Could Daddy have concluded that it made no sense now to pull me back into their world, that the best solution was to carry on the deception and let me go?

Should I pray?

Would the God who hadn't taken interest enough in all these centuries to stop Daddy and his kind suddenly care about my small soul?

The answers were finally revealed on Saturday night, when Julia, Clifford, and Liam came by to pick me up so the four of us could celebrate at the Underground. The joviality in the car resembled a New Year's Eve celebration. I welcomed it, thinking that yes, maybe this was the end of one story and the beginning of another. I'd be a different kind of Cinderella at midnight. Magically, I would stop being a princess in Daddy's kingdom and become an ordinary young woman in the world I longed to enjoy.

20

The four of us were more carefree and loose than we had ever been, together or separately. We were quickly the center of attention, especially out on the dance floor, sometimes moving together, exchanging partners, even dancing woman-to-woman and man-to-man. The music couldn't be too loud for Clifford right now. He was pretty buzzed very quickly, I thought, and I suspected that he and Julia might have begun celebrating before Liam had driven them to the Winston House to get me. They'd be sorry in the morning, I told myself. Alcohol didn't have anywhere near the effect on me that it had on them, but I was a good actress, mimicking and pretending that it did.

We took breaks to eat a little, drink a little more, toasting to our future and especially to the success of Liam's and my wedding. Just when I thought everyone had been sufficiently exhausted, they wanted to go back on the dance floor. To me, it seemed that Julia was finally letting go, doing what she always wanted and dreamed she would do, having a wild and carefree time with the man she loved. The more she got Clifford to do, the happier she was. It was as if it confirmed for her that they would have a good marriage after all.

It was going so well that I ignored any small alarms sounding inside me. After all, I wanted to drive back dark thoughts or worries as much as any of them and welcomed the way we infected one another with our excitement, our laughter, and our hugs and kisses. Only once did I pause to wonder if this was the way people had behaved right before the *Titanic* hit an iceberg. The glitter, the champagne, the wonderful food, and the music cloaked them in such joyous elation that they were oblivious to anything threatening and evil outside their warm embrace of deep joy.

And then I saw her, my own private iceberg.

She was suddenly there, dancing right beside us, drawing Liam's and Clifford's eyes to her with her ebullient sexuality, her ravishing beauty heightened in her electric eyes, her silky hair and bulging bosom drawing them deeper into her cleavage until they literally began to sway to her rhythm, not ours.

I screamed like someone who had stepped on a nail. It broke the spell. Both Clifford and Liam turned to me. I pretended to have twisted my ankle. The three of them surrounded me. Liam threw my right arm over his shoulders and, with his left around my waist, guided me hopping on one foot off the dance floor to our table. Swaying, unsteady himself, Clifford was down on his knees examining my ankle. I sat back, exaggerating the pain, gasping.

"She's probably strained a tendon," Clifford said. "Not too bad, no swelling or bruising around the joint.

I don't feel anything broken, but an X-ray can't hurt."

"You would suggest it," Julia said, trying to lighten the moment. "I think he gets a commission."

I looked past them onto the dance floor. She was gone.

"I feel so stupid. I'll be all right. I'll just put some ice on it, right, Julia?"

"I'll get some right now," Liam said, and rushed off to find a waiter.

In the meantime, Clifford put his cold vodka and soda glass against my ankle.

"I'm lucky I didn't pull or strain something out there, too," Julia said, reaching for my hand. "The last time I danced that way was . . ."

"The first time we were here."

"No, we weren't as wild as that. Were we?"

I nodded.

Clifford looked up at us, smiling stupidly. He still looked a bit wobbly, I thought.

"Get up, Clifford," Julia said, seeing the stupid grin on his face. "Wait for the ice. That's not going to do anything for her. It's not cold enough by now."

He shrugged, then stood up and almost collapsed in his chair. "I think I overdid it a bit," he muttered, closing his eyes and holding his hand over his heart.

Julia smiled at me as if we were conspirators who were succeeding. When more than ten minutes had passed, I sat up. Julia saw my concern and looked around the Underground.

"Where is he? How hard is it to get some ice?" Julia said.

She's going to take him, I thought. *God, no!*

I stood up. "Find him!" I cried. Clifford opened his eyes.

"What?"

"Find Liam!" I shouted at him. "Now!"

"Easy, Lorelei," Julia said. "What could happen to him? He's probably just—"

"No, forget the ice. I want to go. Now," I said firmly.

"Okay, okay. I'll go this way, Clifford. You go that way," she said, nodding.

My shouting and her orders sobered him quickly. He started in the direction Liam had gone. She looked back at me and then walked off, too, both of them disappearing into the thick cloud of revelers all around us.

"No worries. They're just having a little talk," I heard, and spun around. It sounded like Daddy standing right behind me, but there was no one there.

Moments later, I saw Liam rushing back to me. In his hands, he had ice wrapped in a cloth napkin. I felt the air trapped in my chest and throat escape and my body soften. Julia was heading back our way, too. She had seen him approaching the table.

"Sorry," he said, kneeling down. "No one was listening to me. They're a bit overwhelmed here, but some young woman heard me and was very persuasive. Otherwise, it might have taken another twenty minutes." He pressed the cold pack against my ankle. He looked up when Julia arrived. "Is this right?"

"That's good," she told him. "Where is Clifford?"

I looked back in the direction he had gone. "Find him, Julia. I want to leave."

"Right," she said, and hurried off.

"Sorry it took a while," Liam said. "But as I said . . ."

"Was it the same girl you saw on the dance floor?"

"What?"

"Both you and Clifford were hypnotized by that girl on the dance floor. Was it the same girl who helped you get the ice?"

He looked at me as if I had caught him cheating. "I think . . ."

"Here they are," I said, seeing Julia practically dragging Clifford back. "Take me home, Liam." I stood.

"You shouldn't put too much weight on that yet," Clifford advised.

"Lean on me," Liam said.

The four of us headed out, now looking like a defeated group of party soldiers, wounded, exhausted. Most people were too occupied to notice or care, however. When we reached the entrance, Liam told Julia to wait with me while he brought the car up front.

"No," I whispered to her. "Go with him."

"What?"

"Just go. Please," I said desperately. She gazed curiously at me and then shrugged.

"Clifford, stay with her," she said, and went after Liam.

"I knew this place would be dangerous," Clifford said, hoping to make me laugh.

"You have no idea," I said, so coldly serious that his smile unhinged and dropped away instantly.

I breathed relief when I saw Liam and Julia pull up to the entrance. Clifford helped me out and into the car.

"We decided you should come home with us, Lorelei," Liam said. "Julia can look after your ankle."

"I don't—"

"Don't argue. We've already called ahead and told Mrs. Wakefield to prepare the guest room next to my room," Julia said.

"You called her so late?"

"If we didn't, she'd be more upset," Liam said, laughing. "She's the captain of the ship when it comes to anything involving our house. I would have thought you saw that in the wedding planning. It's better that you come home with us."

"Okay," I said, seeing no way out, "but I'm not calling your great-aunt Amelia to tell her at this hour."

"She'll figure it out," Liam said.

"Just to be sure, I'll call her first thing in the morning," Julia added. "With that tenant of hers still missing and all . . ."

"That is so weird," Clifford said. He was quite sober now. "Not a clue."

"I've got it," Liam said. "He wasn't really from this century. He was from Great-auntie Amelia's favorite time in history, and he had to return."

Julia gave him a playful smack.

"Hey."

"It's not funny. Something bad obviously happened to him."

Liam nodded. "I know. I'm just . . . trying to stop Lorelei from worrying about things."

"Then you're forgiven," Julia said. She huddled up with Clifford in the back, and I looked into the rearview mirror to see if any other car had taken off after us.

Even though I saw none, there was no doubt in my mind now. Ava was right behind us and would be until she was satisfied. It had become personal with her, I thought. She was deadly dangerous when it wasn't, when she didn't care at all about her victims. What would she be like now?

It had already been decided, apparently, that Clifford would also stay the night. Those arrangements were made earlier, anticipating that he might not be in great condition to drive himself home. I felt guilty when we arrived, and I still had to pretend I had trouble putting weight on my ankle. On top of that, Mrs. Wakefield was waiting for us in her robe and looked very disapproving. Julia softened her by reminding her of a story she had once told about her own wild times when she was our age, even younger.

Liam practically carried me up the stairs to the guest room.

"Anything else I can do?" he asked Julia.

"No. Get Clifford settled in, look after yourself, and I'll take care of things here."

He kissed me good night and hurried off. Julia examined my ankle again and looked at me askance. The skepticism settled in the corners of her mouth when she smiled.

"It doesn't look bad, Lorelei, no swelling, no redness, nothing."

"I'm fine. Just very tired suddenly."

I could see the suspicion narrowing her eyelids. "What

really happened back there, Lorelei? You weren't just complaining about an ankle. I've gotten to know you better. Something was frightening you. I never saw you that intense."

If there was ever a moment when I would seriously consider telling Julia the truth, this was it. She had become more of a sister to me than any I had, and I believed her when she told me how much she cherished our friendship and love for each other. She was sincere in her hope that we would grow as family, share our problems, and rejoice in our successes and happiness. How could I go on lying and deceiving someone like her?

But what would happen if I did tell her the truth? Wouldn't she be terrified of me and frantically worried for her brother and father? Surely there would be no way we could go on together, and even if somehow she was able to handle the truth, believe in my effort to have a normal life and reject the world I had been in, how could she not forever wonder whether the genes within me would eventually overcome any resistance I had created? There would never be a wholly peaceful and pure moment between us again.

"You'll think so poorly of me if I tell you," I said.

"Never, Lorelei. Trust me," she said.

"I know exactly what you're going to say. You're going to blame it on my inexperienced, young imagination."

"I'm hardly a woman of great experience," she said. "You already know that. Stop worrying about it. What?"

I looked away, counted to five, and turned back to

her. "I saw the way Liam was looking at this very beautiful young woman dancing close to us. He was practically drooling over her, and we're on the threshold of our marriage."

She smiled. "He's only a man, Lorelei. We all want to idolize, even deify the one we fall in love with, ignoring his weaknesses and flaws and concentrating only on what is pleasing, but fantasies don't last. We make them into our own private movie stars. The same is true for the way men idolize their women. Supposedly, Rita Hayworth was heard to say about herself that they went to bed with Gilda, the ravishing beauty she played in the movie, but woke up with Rita Hayworth."

"You're right, of course. I should know better. I reacted like an immature, jealous teenager and . . ."

"Pretended you hurt your ankle?"

"Yes."

"I could tell. I've seen enough sprained ankles," she said, and patted mine. "Considering the reputation my brother had before he met you, I don't blame you for your overreaction at all."

She laughed.

"Actually, I think it was kind of funny. He deserved it. And by the way, thanks for not including Clifford when you mentioned the drooling. I wasn't as oblivious as I seemed out there. Whoever she was, she was like a magnet for male eyes."

I smiled at her. She bought it completely, I thought. It was partly true, anyway, this time. I was jealous of how Ava had commanded Liam's attention so easily and completely. I could live with this lie.

Julia yawned.

"I'll let you get to sleep. You can claim it got miraculously better by morning. There's a fresh nightgown in the closet and a brand-new toothbrush in the bathroom. We always treat our guests as if they were in a five-star hotel."

"It is like that. Better, in fact."

"You and Liam are going to live here for a while afterward, right?"

"Yes. We've talked about it. He wants to build a new house, but lately, your father's been adamant about us living here for the first few years, at least."

"I'm sure he hopes forever," she said. "He wouldn't want the property to go to anyone but family eventually, and it's certainly big enough for you two to have your privacy. Clifford and I could easily move in, too, and no one would get in anyone's way, especially with our busy schedules. We'll see," she said quickly. "Okay. Thanks for trusting me," she added, and gave me a hug and a kiss on the cheek. "Tomorrow we'll have another good laugh about it."

She started out, paused at the doorway, and turned to whisper, "I think I'll pay my radiologist a visit and make sure he's still able to read an X-ray."

In a moment, she was gone.

I fell back against the large pillow and just lay there looking up at the ceiling. How many more incidents like this would occur before Liam and I were married? Would I always succeed in saving him, saving us? What about the collateral damage? Who else would be hurt? Does it take more courage to stay or to flee? I was dizzy with worry. After a few more minutes of calming myself, I rose and found the nightgown Julia had mentioned. Then I prepared for bed.

All of the beds in the guest rooms were king-size, with soft-as-marshmallow oversized pillows and soft comforters. I was looking forward to getting some sleep. We'd all sleep late, I thought, but Mrs. Wakefield would have what Mrs. Winston would call a proper breakfast prepared, and I was sure we'd have a good time laughing at one another. This would be forgotten. I snuggled up in that optimism and closed my eyes.

I don't know how much time passed and how long I had been asleep, but when I first heard her, I thought it was merely a dream. I'd open my eyes wider and she'd pop like a bubble, but she didn't. Ava was standing there, gazing down at me with that confident and condescending smile on her face. She had followed us after all. I sat up slowly, my very bones chattering.

"Feeling safe in this castle?" she asked.

"I won't let you hurt anyone," I said, gathering my courage. "I'm not your baby sister anymore."

She widened her smile and nodded. "Think you're that tough now, huh?"

"Why can't you leave me alone? Is it because you wish you had done what I did and left?"

She laughed. "Hardly," she said. "Why would I ever want to leave Daddy and leave who and what we are? You think I envy you? What a joke. What's there to envy? Life here? Being stuck in some marriage with them as my family? How petty and small they are compared with us. They'll have their sicknesses and their pains, their constant struggles to be happy. Not a day will pass without them finding something over which to worry, whether it's their children or their spouses being faithful or the wrinkles in their faces. We soar above them. They are no more to us than chickens and fish are to them. And this is what you want to leave us for?"

"Yes," I said firmly.

She lost her smug smile. "Haven't you seen already that it's quite impossible? Didn't our little warnings ring bells in that thick, stupid skull of yours? Must we do more?"

"You do anything to hurt any of them and I'll . . ."

"You'll what, Lorelei? You fool. Once this family discovers who and what you are, you will come running back to us." She paused and smiled again. "Only Daddy might not take you back. Then where will you be?"

I threw the comforter off myself and got out of the bed so I could face her. Every muscle in my body tightened and hardened. I stepped toward her.

"I'm warning you," I said, keeping my eyes locked on hers. "You do anything to hurt me, and I will reveal everything about you."

"And Daddy?" she asked with a cold, confident smirk.

"And Daddy," I said, with a firmness that, like a wet washcloth, wiped the smirk off her face.

Her eyes widened, and she stepped back. It was the first time Ava had ever retreated from me.

"Do you think I would let you do that?" She raised her hands, her fingernails sharp and long like raccoon claws.

I didn't move. My body tightened more. She looked as if she would lunge at me, but I stood my ground, and then, before either of us could do anything more, Daddy stepped out from the shadowed corner of the bedroom. Ava looked almost as surprised as I was. She stepped farther back as he came forward. All of the resistance I had mounted in my body seeped out. No matter how hard I fought it, the sight of him turned me back into a little girl. I lowered my eyes, afraid of the power of his. I didn't look up until I felt his hand stroking my hair.

"Little Lorelei," he said. "My little Lorelei. I'm so sorry we never spoke before you started your flight that day."

He smiled down at me, that smile washing over me the way it always had, leaving me with a deep sense of calm and security. It was as if he could cut the whole world out, and there would be only the two of us.

"I could have reassured you. I don't want you to believe I could ever do you harm," he said, continuing to stroke my hair.

Ava looked even angrier, her jealousy overtaking her. I recalled how she was always envious of Daddy's small ways of showing affection for me, whether it was with a smile or a gentle caress. Because of that, I did believe that he loved me more than he loved her or any of his other daughters. This sort of sibling rivalry for Daddy's love didn't exist for them. It was only Ava who felt it with me, and Daddy knew. He knew, but he didn't chastise her in my presence, nor did he temper the way he favored me.

I felt the tears well up in my eyes. His words were

like the tentacles of an octopus wrapping around me and pulling me toward him. It was futile to resist. When he kissed me on the forehead, those tears broke free. All of those little-girl years were rushing back, our walks, my hand in his, his voice melodic, soothing as he wove together our history, the beautiful places he had been, and the things he had seen. How magical it had been and how special I had felt. He was everything, my daddy, my world.

"I'm sorry, Daddy," I said, sounding like a little girl again. "I couldn't stay and be what you wanted me to be."

"I know," he replied, surprising me. I saw that Ava was also surprised. "I knew there was something different about you. It happens once in a while over the course of a hundred years. I was hoping it wasn't so. My fault. My love for you was so great that I ignored what I knew and felt."

He shrugged. Ava came forward. She was shaking her head. She didn't want to hear this. I knew what she wanted. She wanted him to rage at me, to threaten and maybe even destroy me. The disappointment only hardened and angered her more. I could see that Daddy felt her fury growing. He turned to her and with a glance stopped her and sent her stepping back. Then he turned back to me. His smile was gone.

"I know I shouldn't have called upon others to help send you back to us. I knew you would resist. I can feel your resistance even now," he added.

"I'm sorry, Daddy. I can't help it," I said.

"No, you can't," he said, nodding. "You can't resist

what's stronger in you, just as Ava here can't resist what's stronger in her. The two of you are on the opposite sides of the same powerful force.

"But I just can't let you go and forget," he added.

What was he telling me? That because I was how I was, an anomaly, a freak to our kind, no better than a Renegade, he was here to destroy me? Was this the end? I glanced at Ava. She looked happier, more satisfied.

"You can understand that, can't you?" he asked.

I nodded.

"It's not easy for you, either, crossing from our world to this one."

"I'm not afraid of it," I said.

"Of course you're not," he replied. "You're my daughter, after all, are you not?"

I looked at him. How would it come? What would it be? A ravishing bite, a sweep of his powerful hand, or just the drawing out of all my breath and strength, leaving me folded in a heap at the foot of the bed? They'd find me like that in the morning, and some autopsy would conclude that I had suffered a heart attack.

Daddy saw the fear in my face. "I said I wouldn't harm you," he continued. Ava's smile disappeared. He took my hand into his and, for a few moments, just played with my fingers. "You always had the most beautiful hands of all my daughters. There were many different things about you. Some I cherished, but some I should have known would bring us to this moment."

If he wasn't going to harm me and he knew I was different, too different to be like any of his other daughters, what did he mean when he said he just couldn't let me go?

"You know that I've spoken to your future father-in-law a few times. He sounds like a very nice man, one who would be more of a father to you than a father-in-law. Ava here thinks your fiancé is quite handsome. She's drooling over the possibilities, aren't you, Ava?" he asked her. She smiled. "Possibilities she won't realize."

She stopped smiling again. She was on the same roller-coaster ride I was on, I thought, one moment hopeful and then another moment not. Our reasons for hope were very different, of course.

"And you know I've paid for this quite elaborate wedding that's being planned, and I've pleaded to give you away properly, as any other father would."

I nodded.

"By the way, how did you explain your flight and arrival in Quincy to these people?" he asked. "I'm sure you had a good explanation."

I told him what I had fabricated, and he looked at Ava and laughed.

"Terrific story. And you called my new wife Veronica, nicknamed Ronnie?"

"Stupid," Ava said.

"No, quite the contrary. It's so pedestrian that it's more credible. Good thinking, Lorelei."

Why was he giving me a compliment now?

He sighed. "Well, since you've done such a good job of it and I don't like wasting my time or my money . . ." he said. Now I was confused.

"What are you saying, Daddy?"

"You can go ahead and marry this man you love, enter this world you want, and live this life."

Ava looked more shocked than I had ever seen her, shocked and disappointed. "Daddy?" she said, stepping forward. He held up his hand, and she retreated again.

"I ask only one thing from you. Well, 'ask' isn't quite the word, I guess," he said. "I demand only one thing from you, and then you will be free of us, all of us. You will not be a threat to any other family, and there will never be a shadow for you ever to fear."

"What is it?" I asked, my breath so thin that my question seemed more like something I had thought and not spoken.

"If your first child is a girl, she will go with me," he said.

His words fell like thunder on my ears, like the pronouncements of some biblical prophet laying demands on the people who looked up to him, words so powerful and firm that they couldn't be erased or forgotten. They were words etched into the very souls of those who heard them.

Ava's smile returned.

My heart seemed to writhe in my chest as my blood froze. For a moment, I couldn't breathe.

"But how could I . . ."

"I'm making a great sacrifice in giving you up, Lorelei. You have to make one, too."

"But my daughter, a daughter created from my husband and me, surely couldn't be someone who would please you."

"She will in a different way," he said. "For many years, it will be like having you with me."

"But . . ."

"It's what I want," he said firmly. "Do you want the alternative?"

I shook my head.

He smiled. "Good. The daughter of my daughter will once again be close to me."

The very idea was so painful to me, but I was afraid to speak.

"You know that once you are impregnated by one of them, you will be one of them, and I don't mean figuratively or symbolically, Lorelei. You will lose all that you have as my daughter. You will suffer the same slings and arrows of misfortune that they suffer. You will, as Ava alluded to before, be full of silly, vain jealousies, grow old and sick in a second of time compared with us." He laughed. "Why, you'll need to go to a dentist."

"I don't care," I said.

His eyes brightened rather than darkening. "No, you don't. You're resilient. Ironically, you wouldn't be if you weren't a Patio, Lorelei, but you'd come back to us out of weakness and not willingly. I don't want that. Go forth, and cross over into their world," he said, like a bishop giving me a blessing.

He leaned toward me and brought his lips to mine. It was a kiss unlike any other he had given me. It was a kiss that sealed my fate. It was more like a royal stamp. I felt no warmth or love. He stroked my hair once more and then stepped back.

"Ava?" he said. "Leave on the feet of a kitten."

"Yes, Daddy," she said.

"Daddy?" I called. He turned. "That man, the guest in my rooming house, Collin Nickels."

"Yes, that was your sister's choice. Not the most nutritious," he said. "But she was trying to make a point. Perhaps a little too enthusiastically?"

Ava smirked. He nodded at the door.

They left like a whisper dying in the aftermath. I watched them go, the door barely closing behind them as they wove their way out through shadows into the darkness Daddy treasured.

And I stood there trapped between relief and great sadness, escaping the struggle between these two feelings only when I managed to fall asleep.

21

I didn't wake up until Julia touched my face and sat beside me on my bed.

"Sorry to wake you, but Mrs. Wakefield is pacing in the dining room. She'll wear a path in the rug if we're all not in there soon," she said.

I sat up, feeling a bit groggy. "What time is it?"

"Eleven thirty. We're going to call it brunch, not breakfast. The boys are showering. Clifford is moaning about his hangover and swearing he'll never do it again. He will," she said, laughing. She nodded at some clothes she had laid out for me over a chair. "I'm sure they'll all fit well enough," she said. "I'm also sure they'll look better on you. It's going to be a beautiful day. If you're up to it, we'll do some of that shopping we left for the last minute."

"Thanks. Yes, I'll be up to it." I scrubbed my face with my dry palms and ran my fingers through my hair. As I did so, I looked about the room as if I expected either Daddy or Ava still to be there.

"Are you all right?"

"I'm okay. I just had a night full of dreams. The sort

you can't remember or don't want to remember. You just have the heavy dark feeling."

"I've had plenty of those."

Not like these, I thought.

She stood up. "Take a good shower to wake up fully. That usually works for me. Oh, I called my great-aunt Amelia and explained that you had slept here. I stressed, in a guest room," she added. "She only would have asked. She's a Sagittarius, you know. She'll ask or say anything she wants."

"I think I know that by now," I muttered.

"I bet you do.

"Try to be down within a half hour. You don't want to be hit with one of Mrs. Wakefield's disapproving expressions this early. It could ruin your day. That woman could stop a charging bull with one of her glares."

I smiled. If she had seen one of Mrs. Fennel's disapproving expressions, she would think Mrs. Wakefield was a pushover. I rose quickly and did get downstairs in a little more than twenty minutes. The boys had just entered the dining room. Everyone was moaning and groaning, which seemed to please Mrs. Wakefield, who gave us a short lecture about how young people pay later on in life for how they abused their bodies.

"And you two in medicine should know that better than I do," she told Clifford and Julia, both smiling weakly. When she left, they looked at each other and laughed.

"If she only knew how poorly some doctors live, smoking, drinking, and keeping late hours. It's the old 'Do as I say, not as I do' thing," Julia said.

"Why do I feel like I'm five years old whenever I'm in that woman's presence?" Clifford asked.

"In her eyes, you probably are," Julia teased.

Everyone turned to me.

"Your ankle seems a lot better," Liam said.

I glanced at Julia, who covered her face with her right hand for a moment to hide her smile.

"Yes. The ice, I guess. Thank you, Liam."

"And don't forget my brilliant examination," Clifford followed. "I think I examined it. It's all a bit out of focus this morning."

"Well, here they are, the frolicking late-night revelers," Ken Dolan said, poking his head in the doorway. Our good mornings to him were more like grunts. "Do I detect a little too much of a good time was had by all?"

"I cannot tell a lie," Clifford said. "Julia made me do it."

She slapped him playfully.

"Well, lesson learned, and I'm sure to be forgotten in the future," Ken said. "What are your plans for the day besides recuperation?"

"Lorelei and I have some last-minute shopping to do for the wedding," Julia replied. "These two can nurse themselves, I'm sure."

"Absolutely not," Liam said. "We'll go along to be sure you two can navigate the department stores all right, right, Clifford?"

The look on Clifford's face confirmed that they wouldn't. We all laughed.

"I'm on my way to the office to catch up on some work for a few hours, and then Kelly and I are off to

Boston to see a show. Don't do anything else to irritate Mrs. Wakefield," he warned with a playful smile. He kissed Julia on the cheek, messed Liam's hair, winked at me, and left.

"Why is everyone so happy when they confront someone with headaches and squinting eyes in the morning?" Liam complained. "Especially fathers?"

"I think he's just happy about what he's doing. Sounds like he's going camping in Boston," Clifford quipped.

I looked at Julia and Liam to see how they were reacting to their father's more than budding romance. From what Liam and Julia had told me, he'd had fleeting affairs with women over the years but nothing that seemed to last as long as this one. They both liked Kelly Burnett very much. All three of them were now into relationships. Both Julia and Liam realized that, too. As soon as we heard Ken leave the house, Julia declared the Dolan mansion to be a "house of love."

"Don't tell Mrs. Wakefield," Clifford said. "She might not like that description. It sounds too New Orleans or something."

That brought more smiles and laughter. We were all revived. The joy and familial companionship I felt embracing all of us around that dining room table during our brunch held back the horrifying and dramatic meeting I'd had with Ava and Daddy the night before. For now, at least, I could put aside the deal with the devil that I had made and enjoy my new family.

Julia and I spent the remainder of the day together, and then Liam and Clifford met us for an early dinner.

We all agreed that it was best to make it an early night. We were returning to work in the morning. The whole time, I did feel a difference in the air. I no longer had a sense of being followed, watched. Shadows were just shadows.

Mrs. Winston and Mrs. McGruder were happy that Liam's and my wedding date was so close now. It helped take their minds off Collin Nickels's disappearance and stopped them from talking about historic kidnapping and murder cases in Quincy. Mrs. Winston was entertaining the prospect of a new tenant to take Collin's old room soon, but the mystery would haunt them both for a long time to come, I thought.

Daddy officially arrived on the day before the groom's dinner. I had suspected that he would choose to bring my real mother along to pretend to be his new wife, Veronica. She was as beautiful now as she was the first time I had seen her in that old orphanage. The first stop he made was the Winston House on the evening he arrived. He had called ahead to tell me he was coming so I could prepare Mrs. Winston and Mrs. McGruder.

"They're obviously a big influence on you," he said. "Maybe more than Mrs. Fennel was, so I can't wait to meet them."

I waited nervously in my room. When no one came up to tell me he had arrived, I grew curious and went downstairs. Halfway there, I heard laughter and Daddy's voice. He and my mother were in the living room with Mrs. Winston and Mrs. McGruder. They all turned my way when I appeared.

"Oh, hi, darling," Daddy said, rising. "I asked Mrs.

Winston to hold back on telling you we had arrived so we could get to know each other a little first. She offered us this special homemade elderberry wine. Delicious." He held his glass up. "It's the best I've had, and I've had more than my share."

I looked at the two elderly ladies. They were, as I had imagined they would be, charmed.

Daddy smiled, put down his glass, and held out his arms. "Let me give you a hug. You look like you're absolutely blossoming with radiance and love," he said. "I'm so happy for you. Both of us are," he added, and my mother stood up, too. "Thank you for letting us be a part of your wonderful event."

I saw that both Mrs. Winston and Mrs. McGruder were waiting for me to go to him. Slowly, I approached Daddy, who hugged and kissed me.

"I'm so sorry for any unhappiness I may have caused you," my mother offered. "I hope that you can find it in your heart to forgive me." She glanced at my father and added, "I'll never replace your real mother, but I'll always be there for you if you need me."

When she kissed me on the cheek, I saw the way both Mrs. Winston and Mrs. McGruder smiled. How quickly they had bought into it all, I thought, but from my short experience in this outside world, I realized that most people were eager to avoid any controversy, even if it meant compromising their ideals.

Anyway, what choice did I have? I felt as if I were in a straitjacket. There was nothing I could say or do to break out of this scene. It would be played repeatedly in many different ways over the next few days. Daddy would charm Ken Dolan and Kelly Burnett just as easily. He would win over Liam and Julia and Clifford, and my mother would dazzle every man she met at the dinner and the wedding. They were glamorous, the two of them glittering like celebrities and at home with everyone so quickly that anyone would think they were old friends or residents of Quincy. In fact, at the groom's dinner, Mr. Dolan asked Daddy to make a toast, and he did so, eloquently and with such emotion that he brought tears to the eyes of every father and mother at the affair. I had expected no less. I saw that he was enjoying all of it.

Because he was so handsome and energetic, winning people over with his poetic way of describing places he had been to and things he had seen, no one during those days believed for one moment that my father had been exploited by a younger, beautiful woman. He always looked fresh and debonair. In fact, most of the women at the dinner and the wedding wanted to talk to him, touch him, kiss his cheek, and get a little of his attention. Guest after guest told me how wonderful he was.

Most of our guests and friends didn't know the fabricated story I had told the Dolans, Mrs. Winston, and Mrs. McGruder, of course, so it was even easier for them to be won over, but those I had told thought I had made a generous and loving decision to forgive him and permit him to be part of my life again. If there ever was a little portal through which I could escape any of this, it was quickly closed. I had to smile. I had to hug and kiss. I had to put away the deal I had agreed to in the darkest cabinet in my mind and go forward as Daddy's little girl again, no matter how much I wanted not to do it.

Every smile Daddy directed at me, every kiss, and every loving touch only reinforced the power he held, not just over me but over everyone I cared for now. At any moment, he could change his mind and wreck not only my marriage and hope for a new life but also the lives of these people. Now that I knew he was close by, even when he wasn't with me, I felt his presence.

For most women, even in this age of frequent divorces, the day they make their marriage vows and bind themselves to another's life has to be the most significant and memorable day of their lives. Mrs. Winston told us that traditional marriage vows were traced back to the Book of Common Prayer in 1549. As a gift to her, Liam asked that we use those old words. I was to say, "I, Lorelei Patio, take thee, Liam Dolan, to be my lawful wedded husband, to have and to hold from this day forward, for better or for worse, for richer or poorer, in sickness and in health, to love and to cherish, till death us do part, according to God's holy ordinance; and thereto I plight thee my troth."

Daddy stood beside me after giving me away. I couldn't help but glance at him when I said "in sickness and in health." His eyes reminded me that those words had new and real meaning for me now. If he was telling me the truth about what would happen once I became pregnant with Liam's child, I was soon to expose myself to the same dangers and threats that Liam was exposed to. Repeating these marriage vows, therefore, was a much deeper commitment for me than it was for him, but I did not hesitate, nor did my voice weaken. There was no sign of any self-doubt. I was determined.

Daddy's smile during the ceremony was truly one of pride. He firmly believed that my strength came from him and that, ironically, I couldn't be doing this otherwise. Even my mother looked somewhat pleased. They were losing me, but they couldn't help looking and acting like proud parents. I rejoiced, knowing that somewhere off to the side, maybe behind a tree, Ava was fuming and eating her own insides out.

We had a most glorious day for our affair. It wasn't terribly hot, but it was warm, with a gentle sea breeze and a cobalt-blue sky. Even the birds seemed to be participating, drawn either by curiosity or the possibility of crumbs to come. Mrs. Winston told me that the reception we had planned with Mrs. Wakefield afterward was as close to a royal wedding reception in the colonies as any could be. She rattled off details about John Adams's wedding, as if she had been there. When Daddy told her just how accurate she was with certainty and then added details that she had forgotten, she was speechless for a moment.

"You surprise me, Mr. Patio," she said.

"Please. Call me Sergio."

"Your knowledge of our early history is so authentic. One might think you really were present at these events."

How he laughed, his eyes twinkling when he looked at me. *If she only knew,* he was saying with that impish smile. *If she only knew.*

I couldn't disagree with her about the wedding, not

that I had been to any. I had read about many and had seen videos of royal weddings. If there were any hors d'oeuvres or desserts left out of ours, no one would know it or miss it. The dinner for two hundred guests, including important politicians and government officials, was spectacular. There was the choice of lobster, filet mignon, free-range chicken, and fresh fish. Wine was poured as if it came from some endless fountain. We sat at the dais and oversaw it all just like royalty. Ken, I was sure to solidify my rapprochement with my father, asked him to make a toast right after Clifford, as best man, had made his.

All eyes were on my father when he stood. I had never seen him speak to an audience as large as this one. I looked at the guests and saw how attentive and already mesmerized they all were. No one moved; not a waiter or a busboy took a step or lifted a cup. Even the birds seemed to stop flying and instead were watching and listening.

"Lorelei," he said, turning to me, his glass of champagne in his hand, "there are two things a father tries to give his daughter. One is roots, and the other is wings. You have grown your wings strong and beautifully. After today, you will fly off, leave the nest, but you will always be loved and always have roots with our family. To Mr. and Mrs. Liam Dolan," he declared.

People were teary-eyed. Some actually were crying. In one voice, they all cried, "Hear, hear!" Daddy smiled at me. I could see it in his face. *There, I have done my part. Now remember to do yours.*

Liam and I kissed to the cheers of our guests, and the wedding reception really got under way.

The band Liam had wanted played well into the starry night. Mrs. Wakefield claimed she had never seen them twinkle so and reminded us that we were looking at the same night sky our forefathers saw. A few hundred years for us was nothing compared with the time it took that light to reach the earth. Liam and I did the traditional first dance, and then Daddy stepped in, and my mother danced with Liam.

"You're more beautiful than I had ever anticipated," Daddy told me. "You really are fulfilling your own destiny, Lorelei. It shows." I was about to thank him when he added, "Your daughter can't possibly be any less beautiful or wonderful."

I felt myself weaken, but he transferred his strength into me.

"Be brave," he whispered. "Remember, you are always potent, Lorelei. You don't have to wait, and I don't expect you will. The sooner you get pregnant, the easier it will be for you to have the future you want. Don't disappoint me," he added just as the song ended.

He kissed me on the cheek and held out my hand for Liam to take.

"Be good to her, Liam. She's very precious."

"I will, sir," he said.

My father smiled, nodded at my mother, and walked off the dance floor.

Later, we celebrated more with Julia and Clifford, who had decided that their wedding would be exactly a year from ours. They thought it would be fun to have the exact same day for an anniversary.

My most moving moment came when Ken Dolan asked me for a final dance as the evening was winding down.

"You are truly very, very beautiful, Lorelei," he began. "I must confess that when you came to me for the interview that first day, I was thinking ahead. Don't ask me why, but I looked at you and thought, This girl will win Liam's heart, but more important, she will turn him into a man. And you have," he said. "You have. Welcome to our family."

Was I crying? He was wiping away tears from my cheeks, tears I didn't know were there. Was I crying because of the wonderful things he was saying and the happiness I felt, or was I crying because deep in my heart, I believed that I had deceived them all and would most likely betray my husband very soon? I had agreed to do just that, hadn't I?

By the time the reception was drawing to a close, I felt drained. Liam also looked as if he was ready to give up. Daddy approached us with my mother to say his farewell.

"Enjoy your honeymoon," he told Liam. "I understand you were there when you were very little."

"Not old enough to really appreciate it," Liam said.

"Yes. I've been to Capri many times, and I agree with what you've been told about it. It's a magical place, for lovers especially."

"Thank you, sir," Liam said.

"Oh, please call me Dad," Daddy told him. He looked

at me and kissed me, stroked my hair, and whispered, "Little Lorelei, go forth and multiply."

We watched them walk away.

"Well," Liam said. "Now I know where you get so many of your great qualities. What a guy."

"Yes, what a guy," I parroted without feeling.

He was too foggy to notice. He tightened his grip on my hand and led me off. We were to be driven to Boston to fly out early in the morning. We'd sleep on the plane. All of our things were packed and ready. We said good-bye to everyone else. At the car, Julia hugged me.

"Make it good, marriage test pilot," she joked. "Sisters," she added.

"Yes, sisters," I said.

I was willing to trade all of those I had for her, but she had no idea what that meant.

Someday soon, I thought, *I will stop hoarding secrets. I live for that day.*

We got into the limousine and were driven away. I gazed out the window as we went down the long driveway and saw Ava standing near a fountain on the front lawn. She was caught in the moonlight. Her skin looked like gold, her eyes like bloodred rubies.

No matter what she says, I thought, *she is full of envy. She wishes in her heart that she were me, and that wish will haunt her for the rest of her very long life.* That thought comforted me. I was ready to cuddle up in Liam's arms and forget what waited in the darkness ahead.

In fact, I didn't think about any of it until we were in Capri. That was partly because of our journey. We did fall asleep on the plane. After that, we were constantly moving. There was a car waiting for us at the Naples airport. The driver took us and our luggage to the Molo Beverello port, where we boarded a hydrofoil. It was a magnificent cloudless day with the sea relatively calm. We sat outside on the deck and laughed at the spray created by the boat speeding through the water, welcoming the wet coolness on our cheeks. We waved to people on other boats and watched in awe as the isle of Capri seemed to rise before us, its magnificent palisades inviting us to the awe-inspiring views we were soon to enjoy. At the port, we were greeted by hotel bellhops who took our luggage. We spent a few minutes looking at the restaurants and shops located right there and then hired a convertible taxi to take us up the hill to the square. From there, we had to walk to our hotel, because there were no cars on the narrow, picturesque streets with restaurants and elegant shops on both sides.

Despite our travel fatigue, we were both too excited to think of resting. We wanted to go at everything like two little children set free in a candy store. Finally, we decided to catch our breath and paused at the Grand Hotel Quisisana, where we sat on the large patio and had two cappuccinos while we watched an endless stream of tourists speaking different languages parade by, everyone excited, happy, and curious. Most of the time, Liam held my hand as if he were afraid he was really in a dream that would end or that I would disappear.

"I can't believe we're really here," he said. "It seems like a storybook. I hope this never ends."

"It doesn't end, but it takes rests occasionally," I joked. He liked that and sealed it with a kiss. Somehow, holding and kissing each other in the middle of all this didn't seem odd. Anyone who saw us smiled, as if it was expected that everyone would hold hands and kiss there. Daddy was right, I thought. This was a magical place for lovers. Was he ever wrong?

After we settled in at our hotel, we went for a swim in the pool and then, finally, crawled into bed beside each other to consummate our marriage.

The first time you make love with the man you love has to be something extra special. Julia's warnings about building up your husband or him building you up so high that you can never truly be satisfied rang in my ears. But my lovemaking was much more involved and much more complicated than a traditional newly married woman's lovemaking. Of course, I recalled the first time I had been with Buddy, how my body had reacted, hardening to the point where he had noticed, and then how I suddenly was filled with an overwhelming hunger and passion that turned me into the aggressor. He joked about it afterward, but I knew I had crossed a line, stirring his curiosity. We were careful, of course. It was protected sex, but that didn't diminish the intensity of our lovemaking, or, more correctly, mine. I had practically ravished him.

I didn't want it to be like that with Liam. I called on all of my strength to hold back, to move slowly.

"You're so tense," he said. "Relax. I love you. I really love you, Lorelei."

Yes, you do, I thought. *And I really love you, but I could lose you so quickly.* All of this could become some distant memory in seconds. And he would never know why.

My hesitation might have looked like the hesitation of someone who wasn't confident in her sexuality or someone who wasn't experienced enough, but I knew it came from a different fear, the fear that I would become pregnant and that my child, a girl, would be taken from us. Liam would suffer so much. I would, too, but I would suffer without hope. He would pray that she would be found and be returned. I would still have to pretend, pray along with him, hope along with him, and, just like him, refuse to be disappointed or pessimistic, at least on the surface.

But what could I do now? Daddy knew more about me than I knew about myself, and he had told me that I was more fertile than any other young woman my age from the world Liam knew. He seemed confident that my first child would be a girl, the girl he demanded. I considered holding off on having children when Liam had brought it up. He wanted a family as quickly as possible. He believed that having our children young meant we would still be relatively young when they were our age, and we would enjoy them and our grand-children to come far more.

What reason could I offer for us to wait? Unlike other young couples, we did not have to worry about income, housing, providing for them in any way. I could easily have a nanny if I wanted. For that matter, Mrs. Wakefield could help for a while, at least. I wasn't pursuing a career, and I wasn't one of those narcissistic women who worried about losing their figures. Liam would never marry such a woman.

No, I had no choice, and rather than fight whatever

fate awaited, I decided in those first passionate moments to let myself go, to be the lover Liam wanted and the lover I wanted to be with him. Every day of our honeymoon, we made love the first thing in the morning and the last thing at night.

Even though Daddy had said good-bye, I couldn't help but think that he or one of his surrogates was there with us, watching. Maybe he thought I might back out of it all, my marriage, and therefore our agreement. One night, while we were making love, I saw what looked like Daddy silhouetted in the window. The curtains were drawn, but there was a full moon, and for those moments, I felt as if he were looking over our lovemaking, blessing it to result in what he wanted. The shadow left, but the feeling never did. I was just good at putting it aside.

There were days when we did nothing more than get up late, make love, have breakfast through room service, take our time getting dressed, and walk to the shopping areas. Almost anything I looked at twice was a purchase for Liam. Some days we had pizza and talked for hours at a restaurant, and some days we went to fancier restaurants.

One day, we hired a boat with a local man who took us to swim in the Blue Grotto, a sea cave on the coast of Capri. The sunlight shining through the seawater created a blue reflection that illuminated the cavern. It was fun swimming in it, and afterward, we were taken to a wonderful lunch on the side of the palisades. Our boat was too big, so a small boat had to come get us, a sea taxi run by a man who looked close to a hundred. He was delightful and as full of predictions as a gypsy fortune teller about our wonderful lives together. Everyone who met us seemed to know immediately that we were newlyweds.

The nights were the best, walking to a restaurant, stopping to talk to other people, going to art galleries, or just sitting on a bench holding hands and watching other couples. No one seemed as happy as we were. Liam told me a great deal about his boyhood, now being even more revealing about just how different he always felt, not having his mother.

"Mrs. Wakefield was as concerned and considerate as could be. I never doubted that she came to love us both, but . . ."

"She wasn't your mother. I know how that is."

"Yes. We have so much in common, and yet there is so much different about us. I think," he quickly added, "that the differences are good. Who wants to marry a clone?"

He didn't mind that I didn't talk very much about my own youth. I didn't want to keep inventing a life, but I certainly didn't want to talk about what mine was really like.

"Let's both just look to the future," I said. "Let's think only of who we are now and what we will have together."

He liked that. We talked again about building a house and having a family. Then he revealed a surprise, his father's wedding present to us.

"Dad's signed over a good portion of our property to me and given us the down payment to build our own home."

"I thought he wanted us to live in the mansion."

"He wants us to have something that's ours from the start. He came to that decision just before the wedding."

"And you didn't tell me?"

"I wanted it to be a surprise. We also talked about you still working for him. Until you are pregnant, that is. He's used to that. Remember, that's how you got the job . . . Michele Levy."

"Yes. That's fine with me. I enjoy the work and want to keep busy."

"Good. It's a family business, and you're part of it now, Lorelei. You're part of it all."

We made all sorts of pledges and predictions for ourselves that week. When it came time to leave, we felt as if we were stepping out of a fantasy storybook and re-entering the real world. We sat together at the rear of the hydrofoil, holding hands and watching Capri drift back and onto the shelf holding our most precious lifelong memories. Both of us were almost in tears.

When we returned to Quincy, Julia wanted to hear about every moment, demanding details. I did enjoy telling her, because it was like being there again. Although Liam and I were younger than Clifford and Julia, it was as if we had become the ones they should measure themselves and their love against. They even decided that they, too, would go to Capri for their honeymoon. It made me nervous to see how much of herself she was molding in my image. In fact, every loving thing she or Clifford, my father-in-law, and now my great-aunt Amelia said or did for us made me feel sicker and weaker inside. *This can't come to any good,* I feared. *There'll be a day when they will hate me.*

I lost myself in work to avoid thinking too much about any of it. Liam brought home some plans for our own home, and he, his father, and I began going over them. With dinners, social affairs, boating trips, and our work, the days and weeks passed quickly into months.

And then, one morning, I awoke, and even before the physical symptoms began, I realized that I was pregnant. As if somehow he knew it was coming, Daddy had called the day before to ask how everything was going. He had called me at work. My hand had trembled when I held the receiver.

"You're managing well, Lorelei," he had said, as though he had been watching me daily. I knew he didn't have to do that to know. I felt confident, however, that Ava wasn't spying on me anymore. She probably couldn't stand it.

We hadn't had a long conversation, but everything he said had stayed with me the remainder of the day and that night. When I had the realization in the morning, I could swear his face flashed before me. Two days later, I confided in Julia, and she recommended the doctor she thought was the best obstetrician, a woman, Dr. Steffen. Liam was elated, practically floating with joy. The first question I asked the doctor with Liam present was when we could know the baby's sex.

"Oh, we don't want to know that," he said. "Let's keep it a surprise."

Dr. Steffen laughed. "Most young couples want to know these days."

"We're different," he said firmly. "Right?"

I nodded and smiled, but in my heart, I hated the

thought of having this on my mind for so long. Besides, I didn't think Daddy would stand for it. The first time I went to see Dr. Steffen without Liam, I asked her again.

"I need to know," I told her. "My husband doesn't have to know. I know you can do a chorionic villus sampling, and a baby's sex can be determined as early as ten weeks. I'm into week twelve."

She widened her eyes. "Is there something in your family history you haven't told me, Lorelei, some chromosome abnormality? Because a CVS is usually done to determine if there have been inherited abnormalities. Are you afraid your child will have Down syndrome, for example?"

"No," I said quickly, but then I thought for a moment. Why couldn't our child have some abnormality? "Yes," I said. "I didn't want my husband to know about it."

"This is not something I like to keep from a prospective father. I must insist that he know and understand what we're doing. Won't you discuss it with him first, please?"

If I did, I'd have to lie again to the man I married, the man I loved. When will that end? Maybe never. And what would I do if we went ahead with the test and she told me it was a girl? I had been thinking and thinking about it, considering an abortion. But then what would that do? It would only anger Daddy, and he would take back his agreement, and it would devastate Liam. I could go on for weeks, months, and do what Liam wanted and not discover our baby's sex, but that would mean nights and days of anxiety.

No, I had made the agreement. It was better that I

knew in advance so I could find a way to prepare myself.

"Okay," I told my doctor. "I'll talk to my husband and bring him in when you do the testing and when you have the results."

So all of it came down to this, I thought when I left the doctor's office. From the moment I had decided to get up from the table in that restaurant and hitch a ride with Moses in that tractor-trailer until now, all that I had done to start a new life, my love affair and marriage to Liam, my finding a new family, all of it now depended on one of two words, "boy" or "girl." Somewhere not far away, Daddy was waiting to swoop in when it was time to do so and claim his prize. What would he do with her? How would he bring her up? Would he do all that he had done with me? And when she was old enough to understand, what would he do with her then?

Maybe he would find a way to use her the way he used his own daughters, at least until she had grown too old for it. Maybe she would become some sort of a servant, working beside Mrs. Fennel. Maybe Daddy would have a child with her to see what that child would be like. She would never know me or her father or any of this family. They'd probably tell her she was an orphan, too.

I left the doctor's office, and even though it was a bright, sunny day with cotton dab clouds scattered over a mellow blue sky, I felt as if I should have an umbrella. The rain would fall, only instead of drops of water, there would be drops of blood.

Epilogue

Instead of returning to work after my doctor visit, I called Liam and asked him to meet me at a coffee shop on the corner.

"Is something wrong?" he asked, his voice already starting to shake with anxiety.

"Just come. I need to talk to you," I said, and hung up.

He parked in front of the shop less than ten minutes later and hurried to my table on the patio.

"You want a coffee?"

"No, what's wrong?" he asked, and waved the waiter off.

"I have not been completely honest about my family," I began. It was odd, but whenever I lied about my family, created these fictions, I saw Daddy and Ava smiling. After all, I was confirming what they had predicted, the difficulty that I would always have after I left them.

"What do you mean?"

"I was afraid of scaring you off once I told you."

He sat back, smiling now. "There's nothing you can tell me, Lorelei, that would scare me off of you. Forget it. Just say it and get it over with. We've got things to do. It's a busy day."

I nearly smiled, too. *Why don't I tell him all of it?* I thought. Could any man's love for a woman be strong enough to withstand such truth?

"There have been some abnormalities on my mother's side."

"Abnormalities? Like what?"

"My mother had a younger sister with Down syndrome. She died about ten years ago. Supposedly, there were two cousins on her father's side who had similar problems."

He nodded, his face tightening as his eyes darkened. "I see."

"We have to go forward and have a CVS test done. Since there are some possible gender chromosome problems, we'll know the sex of our baby."

"Oh, that's not really something that would bother me. I just wanted to keep the surprise, but in this case, of course. When are you doing this?"

"I'd like to do it immediately, now. I'm far enough along."

"Okay." He reached for my hand. "We'll get through whatever it is, Lorelei, and I don't blame you one bit for keeping your secret. In fact, it tells me how much you love me, how much you wanted to be sure we would be together."

Oh, Liam, I thought, *you are a hopeless romantic after all. You have been so misjudged, but not by me. But what would you be like if you knew the truth and if you knew what bargain I had made with my father?* Looking into

Liam's trusting and loving eyes now made me despise my father more than I had thought possible. Look at the situation in which he had placed me. He had never really agreed to let me go. He had let me have this fling with a normal life, which would ironically bring me more pain than a long life with him and my sisters.

I returned to work with Liam, and two days later, he and I went into my doctor's office to have the diagnostic procedure. She removed some chorionic villus cells from my placenta at the point where it attached to the uterine wall. Using an ultrasound guide, she moved a thin catheter through my cervix to my placenta and, as she described it, gently suctioned the CV cells into a catheter.

"I'm putting a rush on it," she told us. "I'll call you as soon as I have the results."

Liam did his best to fill my every waking hour with something to distract me and to distract himself just as much, although he put on a good act pretending to be cool about it all. Every once in a while, he would repeat, "We'll deal with it, whatever it is, and it won't change us one bit."

We decided not to tell anyone else. I wouldn't tell Julia, and he wouldn't tell his father especially.

"It's our business now. Later, if we have to, we'll have a family meeting about it," he said. I knew he was thinking that if we had a genetically abnormal baby, we would seriously consider my aborting.

Sometimes during this waiting period, I almost wished that would be the result. What could Daddy do about that? It wasn't my fault. Perhaps Liam and I would adopt. In a way I would have found an avenue of escape, wouldn't I? Then I would feel terrible hoping for such a result. How selfish, I thought. I was certainly not considering Liam's feelings, and I didn't think I could survive the pity everyone would direct at me. I'd drown in it. In the end, it could very well destroy our marriage and send me back to my father and my sisters.

Maybe I wouldn't do that, either. Maybe I would swim out in the ocean on a moonlit night and tread water for a few minutes before lifting my hands toward the sky and sinking into the dark, cool grip of death below.

It was Dr. Steffen's receptionist who called me at the office to tell me that Liam and I should come to her office at four.

"Why didn't she call me herself?" I demanded, my voice trembling.

"She's delivering a baby."

"Well, are there results?"

"I'm sorry. You'll have to speak with the doctor," she replied.

I thanked her, and then, shaking as I stood, I went down to Liam's office. He was on the phone. He held up his hand while he finished his call quickly and then cradled the receiver, his face full of anticipation.

"Her secretary called. She's delivering a baby. She wants us there at four."

"Fine. Take it easy," he said, coming around his desk. "Don't read anything into anything yet. You want to go back to work, or do you want me—"

"No, no, I'll work. I don't want to think," I said.

Every once in a while, I would get up and go to the window to look out at the street. I had a very strong feeling that Daddy was out there, waiting to hear the news and as anxious about it as I was. I didn't see him, but that didn't mean anything. I felt him.

The hours seemed to drag. I hated the hands of the clock for being so slow. Fortunately, Ken was out on a job, so he didn't see how nervous I was. He would have been able to tell that something was seriously wrong. He could read me well by now.

At three thirty, Liam came for me. He tried to get me to talk, but I just shook my head. He held my hand as we walked out of the plant, and we drove in silence to the doctor's office.

She had a patient before us, and unfortunately, that ran past four o'clock. Finally, we were told to go in. Liam kept his arm around my waist as if he anticipated that I might faint.

Dr. Steffen stood up as soon as we entered and smiled.

"Everything is looking very good," she said. "There is nothing to worry us."

"Oh, thank God," Liam said.

"Do we have a girl or a boy?" I asked, barely above a whisper.

"You don't have to know. There are no gender issues."

"I want to know!" I said, so sharply that she lost her smile.

Liam loosened his grip around my waist. I glanced at him and saw the confusion. Then he smiled and nodded. "Yes, please, Dr. Steffen," he said.

"You're going to have a boy," she said.

I didn't know I was sinking until I felt Liam's arm around my waist again, only tightening this time. He guided me quickly to a chair.

Dr. Steffen came rushing over. "What is it, Lorelei?" she asked.

"I just . . . the anticipation . . ."

"Yes, yes, understandable. I'm sorry you had to wait, but I would have called you immediately if there was bad news," she said. "Just catch your breath. She'll be fine," she told Liam.

He looked concerned but also confused. "You were hoping for a girl. Is that it?" he asked.

I knew that if I didn't bring my hand to my mouth, I would burst into a mad laugh. I swallowed it back and shook my head.

"Maybe the next time," Dr. Steffen said.

"Sure," Liam said.

Dr. Steffen brought me some water and then insisted on checking my blood pressure. "Just take her home to rest," she told Liam.

"Will do. Thanks, Doc," he said. "Well," he said as we started out, "we have another good reason to celebrate. Why don't we go to the Spenser House? I feel like their rack of lamb."

"Maybe, after a little rest," I said.

"Sure."

We drove to the mansion, and he helped me into bed.

"I'll just head back to the office and finish up some things," he told me. "I'll let Mrs. Wakefield know that she should check up on you."

"No, no. I'll be fine, Liam."

"Okay," he said. He kissed me and left.

I was far more tired than I had imagined, and the moment I closed my eyes, I fell asleep. I think Mrs. Wakefield did stop by to check on me. I thought I opened my eyes for a moment and saw her standing there. Finally, I woke up. When I looked at the clock, I saw that it was nearly seven. Where was Liam? I rose, washed my face, and headed downstairs. Mrs. Wakefield was setting the table in the dining room.

"Oh, how are you, dear?" she asked.

"I'm okay. Where's Liam?"

"He called about a half hour ago to say he would be tied up until seven thirty. There's some sort of crisis on a job, and Mr. Dolan was unable to get there, so he went. He said to tell you that he'll take you to the Spenser House tomorrow night. I've got dinner organized. Nothing to worry about."

"Okay," I said.

It all sounded harmless enough. It wasn't the first time there was such an emergency since I started working at Dolan Plumbing Supply, and I was sure it wouldn't be the last, but I couldn't help being paranoid. Would I always be? Was that the lasting curse upon me for deserting my family, deserting Daddy?

I looked out the window and saw that it was becoming a night like the night I had imagined for my fatal escape into the ocean. The moon was full, the glow strong. I stepped out through the patio doors in the dining room and walked toward the front of the large house. From there, I could look off toward the tract of land Liam's father had given us. We'd have just as good a view. I imagined the house, my bedroom, and even saw myself standing there and looking out toward the ocean. *Won't I be very happy?*

I stood there dreaming about my future, raising my children, enjoying this family, all of us gathering in the mansion for holidays, Julia and Clifford having children of their own, Ken probably remarrying, all of the birthdays to come, anniversaries to celebrate. We'd have many good friends, too.

"It seems you have escaped," I heard, and I turned around quickly to see him not come out of the shadows as much as become shaped by them. The darkness, despite the strong glow of the full moon, seemed impregnable, his coat of armor and his shield. He stepped closer toward me until he was only inches away. Would he wipe me off the face of the earth in one motion? He had brought me here; he could take me away.

"You know," I said.

"Of course. I could see it in your face even if I didn't know, Lorelei. I must say, I am surprised. I didn't think Liam's genetic contribution would overpower yours, or should I say mine. Maybe if any of my daughters wanted it as much as you do, it would also turn out this way for them. I don't know. See? There are things I don't know."

"What will you do, Daddy?"

"Do? There's nothing more for me to do here, Lorelei.

I told you, warned you, that once you became pregnant with one of them, you would lose all of the protection you had. You're as vulnerable to all of the dangers and pain this world gives them. You made your choice. I'll miss you. I have missed you, but I have made you a promise, and I will keep it. Most likely, we'll never see each other again.

"I'm leaving with your sisters and Mrs. Fennel for Europe. It's our time to return to Hungary. We have family there. Don't worry. I'll speak with Ken Dolan and explain that my business is taking me away. I'll leave my return vague, and from time to time, I'll send you a letter or a postcard." He laughed. "Maybe even an e-mail. I really don't like e-mail. I like the penmanship of a letter, something that you can keep pressed between the pages of a book.

"They don't realize what they're losing with all of this technology, Lorelei. Speed and instant gratification are no substitute for the deep experiences and lasting joy that once was, that I still have. You'll feel that, too. I have a feeling you won't forget the things I taught you. I think you'll teach them to your children, especially your firstborn. I'm out of your life, but I'm not out of you."

Then he kissed me on the cheek, stroked my hair, and gazed down at me with those electric eyes that were so full of love.

"Will I really be safe now, Daddy? Will my family be safe? I mean, from the evil we feared?"

"Yes. You have left the world we live in," he said. "No one will sense you or notice you anymore. You can sleep in comfort. The truth is that you are no longer a threat to them. No Renegade, no other family, none of them."

I closed my eyes and opened them again with a wonderful sense of relief washing over me. He saw it and shook his head.

"You'll always be a mystery to me, Lorelei, but the truth is, I'm glad. If I didn't still find things mysterious, I would lose my own thirst for life. So, thank you," he said, laughing with his eyes.

He started away.

"Daddy!" I called.

He turned. "Yes?"

"Thank you," I said.

He nodded and then returned to the darkness that waited for him.

I didn't really see him leave, and sometimes, during the days, weeks, months, and years that followed, I felt as if he was still out there watching me, maybe waiting for me to return.

Everyone, even Daddy, could live in hope and dream of things that would never be.

Virginia Andrews
Into the Darkness

The spine-tingling new thriller from the bestselling author of *Flowers in the Attic*

For sixteen-year-old Amber Taylor, it's just another summer in the quiet rural village of Echo Lake, Oregon. Then the Matthews family arrives in the neighbourhood, bringing their seventeen-year-old son Brayden into Amber's life.

Amber – a shy and introspective girl – can't help being drawn to him, but Brayden remains elusive. He's outgoing, blunt, and unafraid of saying things that many would find outrageous. But that's normal for a seventeen-year-old boy, right?

The more Amber learns about him, and the more time she spends with him, the more she begins to notice strange, inexplicable things about Brayden; he seems to have an uncanny sixth sense, and Amber sometimes gets a sudden feeling of cold around him. But that's normal too . . . isn't it?

Though Amber's not the first girl to find herself confused by the beguiling emotions of young love, she'll discover that Brayden's mystery is more unfathomable than most.

Paperback ISBN 978-1-84983-786-6
Ebook ISBN 978-1-84983-787-3

**SIMON &
SCHUSTER**

IF YOU ENJOY GOOD BOOKS,
YOU'LL LOVE OUR GREAT OFFER
25% OFF THE RRP ON ALL
SIMON & SCHUSTER UK TITLES
WITH FREE POSTAGE AND PACKING (UK ONLY)

Simon & Schuster UK is one of the leading general book publishing
companies in the UK, publishing a wide and eclectic mix
of authors ranging across commercial fiction, literary fiction,
general non-fiction, illustrated and children's books.

For exclusive author interviews, features and competitions log onto:
www.simonandschuster.co.uk

*Titles also available in **eBook** format across all digital devices.*

How to buy your books

Credit and debit cards
Telephone Simon & Schuster Cash Sales at **Sparkle Direct** on **01326 569444**

Cheque
Send a cheque payable to *Simon & Schuster Bookshop* to:
Simon & Schuster Bookshop, PO Box 60, Helston, TR13 OTP

Email: sales@sparkledirect.co.uk
Website: www.sparkledirect.com

Prices and availability are subject to change without notice.